EXILE

I0619220

A Jade Ihara Adventure

Jade Ihara is caught in a centuries old power struggle between a slave cult who believes she might be the incarnation of the goddess of liberty, and a secret cabal with plans for world domination. Can she unravel the mystery of the Cult of Veritas and find their sacred relics before it's too late? David Wood and Sean Ellis deliver another action-packed thriller that will keep you on the edge of your seat! Fans of Indiana Jones, Tomb Raider, Rogue Angel, and Dane Maddock will love Exile!

Praise for David Wood and Sean Ellis

"I'll admit it. I am totally exhausted after finishing the latest Jade Ihara page-turner by David Wood and Sean Ellis. What an adventure! I kept asking myself how the co-authors came up with all this fantastic stuff. This is a great read that provides lots of action, and thoughtful insight as well, into strange realms that are sometimes best left unexplored." Paul Kemprecos, author of Cool Blue Tomb and The NUMA Files

"Dane and Bones.... Together they're unstoppable. Rip-roaring action from start to finish. Wit and humor throughout. Just one question - how soon until the next one? Because I can't wait."- Graham Brown, author of Shadows of the Midnight Sun

"Ellis and Wood are a partnership forged in the fires of Hell. Books don't burn hotter than this!"- Steven Savile, author of the Ogmios thrillers

Books by David Wood

The Dane Maddock Adventures
Dourado
Cibola
Quest
Icefall
Buccaneer
Atlantis
Ark
Xibalba
Loch
Solomon Key (forthcoming)

Dane Maddock Origins
Freedom
Hell Ship
Splashdown
Dead Ice
Liberty
Electra
Amber
Justice
Treasure of the Dead

Jake Crowley Adventures
Blood Codex
Anubis Key

Jade Ihara Adventures
Oracle
Changeling
Exile

Brock Stone Adventures
Arena of Souls
Track of the Beast (forthcoming)

EXILE

A JADE IHARA ADVENTURE

DAVID WOOD
SEAN ELLIS

Exile- A Jade Ihara Adventure

Copyright David Wood 2017
All rights reserved

Published by Adrenaline Press
www.adrenaline.press

Adrenaline Press is an imprint of Gryphonwood Press
www.gryphonwoodpress.com

Cover by Drazenka Kimpel
Edited by Melissa Bowersock

This book is a work of fiction. All persons, places, and
events are products of the authors' imaginations or are used
fictitiously.

ISBN-10: 1-940095-72-7
ISBN-13: 978-1-940095-72-1

PROLOGUE—GREAT AND TERRIBLE THINGS

THEN

Capua, Italia (Italy) 71 BCE

Despite being as thick as a hand span, the leather panels comprising the sides and peaked roof of the tent were not dense enough to completely muffle the wails of the wounded and dying. They were all going to die, but some would die sooner than others, and they would not go quietly it seemed. Yet there was another more ominous sound, a rhythmic thump, faintly hollow like a muted drum—*thwock*—that not only penetrated the walls of the tent, but vibrated up through the very earth itself.

Thwock. Thwock. Thwock.

It was the sound of axes striking tree boughs, and it had been going on for days, from the rising of the sun to its setting.

It would take a lot of trees to supply the wood for six thousand crosses but what a spectacle it would be.

There could be no quarter given. No mercy to the prisoners. No return to the houses they had abandoned. Even a death in the arena—the fate that would have awaited many of them even had they not chosen to rebel—was not permissible. Their bodies and blood would be a sign—a message that would stretch over a hundred miles, from Capua all the way to Rome. A message that history would never forget.

Know your place slave, or this will be your fate.

Hung upon a cross, eaten alive by crows, rotting in the sun, without an *obolus* for the boatman, never to reach Elysium but doomed to wander the earth as a shade.

It was brutal. Barbaric even, but necessary for the preservation of order in the world.

It was that willingness to embrace brutality that had enabled Marcus Licinius Crassus to win where others had failed, and not just on the field of battle. He was the wealthiest man in all of Rome, perhaps in all the world. One did not attain such lofty heights by being timid. He had taken his wealth, by the sword when necessary, but always through bold, and yes, sometimes brutal action.

When news of the slave uprising, and the defeat of Glaber and his Praetorian militia had reached Rome, Crassus had recognized what was at stake. And when the legions under Publicola and Clodianus had not merely failed to quash the uprising, but left the enemy forces poised to sweep into the Eternal City, Crassus had acted without hesitation, the only man in Rome to do so. This was partly to protect his own interests—he owned many slaves and if fires of revolt were not stamped out, they would spread—but also because he sensed an opportunity to increase his status in the Republic. With eight legions—40,000 trained soldiers to fight an equivalent number of former slaves and herdsman—he set out to surround the rebels and exterminate them utterly. Brutally.

When discipline began to break down in his own ranks, he had revived the ancient punishment for cowardice. Decimation—removal of the tenth.

In the cohorts where morale was perceived to be lowest, one man out of every ten, chosen by lottery, would suffer for the sins of all, regardless of whether he had personally committed any offense. The other nine would have to carry out the punishment, clubbing or stoning the man to death. More than a thousand legionaries had been executed in this way.

If Crassus did not hesitate to treat the men under his command so, his brutality against the conquered foe would have to be nothing short of exceptional.

And by Mars, it had worked.

His legions were more frightened of him than they were of the enemy, so when the forces met on the field near Petelia, it had not even been a contest. Six thousand enemy prisoners had been taken. At least as many had fled. The rest, including the infamous leader of the revolt, had died by the sword.

Perhaps if the survivors had known that their carcasses would adorn the roadside, Crassus mused, *they would have fought harder.*

Crassus did not enjoy brutality, but he did not shy away from it when it was called for. He just wished it wasn't such a noisy affair.

Thwock. Thwock.

He wiped a hand across his forehead, smearing the beads of perspiration into his short hair, and tried to shut out the noise so he could focus on the latest dispatch from Rome.

As he had feared, that whore's son Pompey had taken credit for *his* victory.

Crassus may have conquered the rebels, Pompey had told the Senate, *but I have extirpated the war entirely.*

He cursed and cast the missive onto the table. This was his own fault. Early in his campaign Crassus had experienced a moment of doubt. The rebels had been too well organized, their leader a master strategist, achieving one victory after another. There were whispers among the ranks that the man was favored by the gods. Crassus had put a stop to that kind of talk, but not before requesting additional legions. Following the savage defeat of two legions under the command of Mummius, Crassus' legate, the Senate had decided to honor the request by dispatching Pompey, who had just returned victorious from a long war in Hispania. But before those legions could arrive, Crassus had turned the tide and scored the decisive victory at Petelia, defeating the main force and more importantly, killing the rebel leader.

Pompey had arrived just in time to cut off an escaping force of deserters, cowards who had thrown down their weapons and fled the battle before it had even begun. And for that dubious victory, Pompey was calling himself the savior of Rome.

The man was ambitious and arrogant, the favorite of both the people and the Senate, destined many believed, to lead Rome, but he was not invincible. Crassus would take back the glory Pompey had so predictably stolen, remind the

Senate that it was he, not Pompey, who had struck down the rebel leader. He would line the Appian Way with a serpent of crucified rebel prisoners and at the head of that snake would hang the body of the fallen leader.

It was said that the Thracian had once fought with the Romans, first as a mercenary—as was the way of his people—and then as a soldier, before desertion had cost him his freedom. Why he had done so was only one of many mysteries that surrounded the man. He certainly had been no coward, demonstrating great prowess in the arena. He might easily have won back his freedom and lived a life of great acclaim, but instead he had chosen the path of pain. Perhaps he had been led to delusions of grandeur by the name given him by the master of the *ludus* at Capua. It was said his indomitable spirit had evoked memories of the fierce Thracian king of old, Spartokos.

But this man was no king, no hero. He was not even a man at all, but an animal—a slave who had forgotten his place. History would remember him, not as a great leader, but as an arrogant fool who had led others into ruin, and his story would end with his body hanging from a cross for every citizen and slave in Rome to see.

Favored by the gods no longer.

A rapping sound, louder and more immediate than the hewing of trees, distracted him from these musings. He raised his eyes to the entrance of his tent. "Come."

The covering panel drew back to reveal Gaius Junius, his lictor, and one other figure, a half-naked woman, her skin adorned with tattoos as was the way of the barbarians. Her face however was hidden behind a veil. Her hands were bound and there was a length of rope tied about her waist, which Junius held in his left hand. The latter strode forward, dragging the woman along, and stopped in front of the table where Crassus sat. He extended his right arm in a salute. "*Ave, Praetor.*"

As commander of an army in the field, Crassus rightfully held the rank of Praetor, but it was unlike Junius to be so formal. Ignoring the salutation, Crassus eyed the slave-prisoner disdainfully. "What do you want, Gaius?"

A strange, eager gleam appeared in the other man's eyes. "I've brought you something. A gift."

"A slave girl?" Crassus frowned. "You forget yourself, Gaius. I would not dream of withholding such simple pleasures from the men. Even to you, if that is what you desire, but why do you think I would sully myself in this way?"

Junius was unfazed by the rebuke. "You misapprehend, Praetor This is no mere slave girl. This is *his* woman."

Crassus did not need to ask to whom his aide was referring. "Spartacus." He spat the name like a curse. "Show me."

Junius ripped the veil away, revealing the woman's face. Crassus guessed that behind the dried mud and blood, her tear-streaked face would be considered pretty enough for plebian tastes, but he was not interested at all in what her body had to offer. He rose from his chair, and circled the table to stand before her. "Is it true? Were you his woman?"

The slave stared back at him, her mouth defiant, her eyes burning with hatred, but said nothing.

Crassus looked to Junius. "Are you certain it's her?"

"One of the other prisoners identified her, hoping for mercy. I… Questioned him at great length to get the truth of it. I believe it to be so." Junius paused a beat, then added. "I am not certain that she speaks the language of Rome."

Crassus nodded in understanding. Slaves taken from foreign lands were taught exactly as much of the civilized languages—Latin or Greek—as they needed to know to perform their duties. Over time, they picked up more, particularly if their masters saw fit to educate them, but there was great power in words and learning. Give a slave too much of either, and they would inevitably think themselves the equal of their masters.

"She is Thracian?"

"Of the Maedi."

The Maedi were a minor nomadic tribe of Thrace, situated north and east of Greece. The Thracians had their own barbaric language, and each tribe a distinctive dialect, but the men of Thrace had fought as mercenaries alongside the Greeks from before the time of Alexander the Great. If there was a common language between them, it would be Greek. Crassus tried again. "Are you the wife of the one they called Spartacus?"

She jerked her head at the sound of the name, but Crassus couldn't tell if the gesture signaled comprehension. He pressed on. "It is said that you are a Sybil. Is this true?"

The woman's lips parted, formed a word spoken too softly to be heard. "Sybil?"

"A prophetess. One who sees the future."

The woman looked down quickly.

Ah, yes. She understands.

"It is said," Crassus continued, "that you saw the death of your husband in a vision. Strangled by a snake."

"It was not a vision of death," she whispered. "That is not the way of the gift."

"What then did your vision portend?"

The woman now raised her eyes and spoke in a clear defiant voice. "That my husband was destined for great and terrible things."

"I would call that a prophecy of his death."

"You would," she replied, making it sound like an insult.

Crassus regarded her thoughtfully. The words of a Sybil... The power of one who saw the future, was not something to be taken lightly, or interpreted too hastily. Many a king had come to a disastrous end after twisting the words of an oracle to more closely align with the desires of his heart. Prophecy, a veiled glimpse of the future, was how the gods kept men humble.

He moved closer, bending down to look her in the eye. "Would you use your gift to advise me?"

"I will not beg for my life. Not from you."

Crassus did not relent. "Your fate is in the hands of the gods. Yours or mine, it matters not. I have decreed that no mercy be shown to any who partook in this uprising, and yet here you are before me. Tell me, prophetess. Do the gods wish your voice silenced?"

Silence was the only answer she gave.

Crassus straightened. "Would you like to see him? Your husband? His body, I mean? One last time before I hang him on a cross and let the crows peck out his eyes?"

The woman winced.

"Or…" Crassus paused allowing the hint of an alternative to hang in the air like a cloud passing in front of the sun. "Your people bury their dead in the ground, in the fashion of the Greeks, do they not?"

No reply.

"I confess," he went on. "I have never understood why anyone would want to preserve the physical *corpus*, much less leave it for maggots to feed upon. It is an anchor, binding the spirit to this world, preventing the dead from crossing the river."

He shrugged, made a dismissive gesture and turned away. "But perhaps it does not work that way. We know only what the gods choose to reveal. We are told that if the body is not cremated and properly interred, with offerings to the gods of the Underworld, the spirit will never reach the fields of Elysium, but will wander this earth as an unquiet shade. What a torment that would be. To see your beloved wife and children grow and wither and die and pass over, and never be reunited with them."

He paused again, letting this sink in for a moment, before returning his attention to the woman. "Do you wish to see him?" He got close again. "Not his empty vessel, but his spirit? Do you desire to be reunited with him in the Land of the Dead, at the end of your days?"

Still, she did not reply. Outside, the axes continued to fall.

Thwock. Thwock. Thwock.

"Serve me," he whispered. "Guide me with your vision, and in return, I will permit you to bury your husband in the way of your people."

Now her eyes came up to meet his. "You would do

this?"

Crassus did not need to reconsider his offer. Crucifying the dead Spartacus would not take back the glory Pompey had stolen. It would seem petty and self-aggrandizing. No, his fight with Pompey was not something that would be won or lost with a symbolic gesture. Their rivalry was a grand game that would play out over many years. He would need every advantage; Pompey was not a man to be underestimated.

"I swear it."

The Sybil's eyes narrowed, perhaps in suspicion, perhaps in contempt. It did not matter. Crassus knew that she had already chosen to serve him, and thus, to live.

NOW

Channelview, Texas

They descended on the target site like an invading army.

This was neither hyperbole, nor simile. The equipment being utilized and tactics employed were identical, and in some ways superior to those used by US military forces. Moreover, several of the men comprising the Special Response Team of the Houston field office of the Immigration and Customs Enforcement agency were military veterans with extensive combat experience, and had performed similar operations in Baghdad, Fallujah and Kandahar.

Regardless of the broader geographical context, the drill was the same: Conduct the operation in the dead of night, under cover of darkness when everyone, including the targets at the objective, were most likely to be asleep; establish a secure perimeter, which in this case involved blockading the roads leading into the trailer park situated in the grassy flat between Market Street and Interstate 10; and then, strike like lightning with overwhelming force and violence of action.

Shock and awe, thought Special Agent Jacob Purcell as

the armored black sport utility vehicle he was riding in skidded to a stop in front of a dilapidated mobile home. The black clad shock troops spilled out of the SUV, and Purcell spilled out along with them.

Hells yeah!

Purcell wasn't actually a member of the ICE-SRT, so he wouldn't be the first one through the door, but he damn sure wasn't going to wait in the car. This was his investigation, after all.

He was the lead HSI—Homeland Security Investigations division—agent on an interagency task force established to combat human trafficking—the buying and selling of human beings as property—and he took his job seriously. Human traffickers were the worst kind of scumbags—selling people, usually children, into slavery and prostitution, or harvesting their organs and tissue for sale on the black market. It was sick stuff. The worst, and it was happening all over, right under the noses of ordinary folk who had no idea.

Purcell knew he and his task force would never be able to win the war on human trafficking. Slavery—which was the less politically correct term—was as old as civilization. Maybe even older. It was inextricably woven into the fabric of the modern world, and nothing he could do would ever change that. Raiding a slave house here or there, or shutting down a smuggling route was like trying to soak up the ocean with a paper towel. No, winning the war wasn't the point. Winning the battles, enough of them to keep his career train on track, get noticed, maybe get his own FO, or better, a cushy appointment to DC—that was the point.

America was in a new age—the Age of Fear—and the Department of Homeland Security, on the front lines of a new kind of war, was the land of opportunity. While other federal agencies were being gutted by austerity measures and deregulation, the various departments of DHS—ICE, the Border Patrol, FEMA, the Coast Guard, and many others—were growing. DHS was the largest Cabinet level department in the US government unrelated to the military. Lots of opportunity for an ambitious player like Jacob Purcell. It didn't hurt that he now had friends in very high places thanks to sweeping changes in the power structure of the US government—changes that, not coincidentally, coincided with dawn of the new American Age of Fear.

Purcell followed the black-clad SRT operators swarming toward the target building. His service weapon—a SIG Sauer P320—was drawn and pointing skyward. His shoes crunched on the gravel as he jogged toward the trailer where the strike team was already stacking up beside the door, preparing to make a dynamic entry. To either side, the mobile home's aluminum siding bore the distinctive high-water stripe left over from the recent storm-related flooding.

God, what a shit hole, he thought as he fell into place behind them and waited for the fireworks to start.

And boy, oh boy, would there be fireworks.

With the trailer surrounded and every point of egress covered, the SRT leader gave the signal to execute. One man came forward with a Blackhawk Monoshock dynamic entry tool gripped in both hands. He drew back and then swung the thirty-two-pound battering ram forward, striking the trailer's front door right below the door knob.

The door buckled with the impact and the lock's strike plate was blasted away along with huge slivers of the doorframe, but the upper corner of the door only moved an inch or two, held in place by some kind of security chain which was evidently stronger than the door it was attached to.

This wrinkle did not greatly upset the SRT guys; things like that just happened sometimes. Rather than wail on the door with the ram, another officer stepped up, pointed the business end of his Mossberg 500 shotgun at the troublesome corner of the door, and pulled the trigger.

The top half of the door vanished in an eruption of smoke and noise.

The security chain had only delayed the team's entry by a second or two, but that was enough to disrupt the tempo of the raid, not to mention giving the perps inside time to prepare a potentially deadly response, so the team leader quickly tossed in a flash-bang.

Truth be told, they probably would have used the stun grenade anyway. What was the point of having tools like that in the toolbox if not to use them?

Fireworks!

When the flash-bang detonated inside the trailer, it was like putting a cherry-bomb in a mailbox. The metal siding bulged outward. All the windows—every single one of them, or so it seemed—exploded out in a shower of diamond-like fragments that briefly caught the lightning-bright flash of the detonation of the grenade's magnesium-impregnated core. Fortunately, there was just enough insulation in the trailer's walls to muffle the 170-decibel boom of the explosion, at least for Purcell and the rest of the SRT team outside. The poor saps inside would not be so lucky.

The team moved in, brandishing their weapons and shouting commands, which likely went completely unnoticed by the occupants of the trailer who were now deaf, blind, and probably crapping their pants. Purcell waited, holding his breath in anticipation. If all went according to plan, the SRT would sweep through the entire trailer, clearing every room and securing every living soul inside. But as the security chain on the front door so ably demonstrated, things rarely went according to plan. One scumbag with a gun getting off a lucky shot would be enough to turn a surgical strike into the OK Corral.

The team leader's voice crackled in Purcell's radio earpiece. "Clear and secure. Come on in."

Purcell kept his weapon drawn but kept the muzzle elevated as he moved inside the smoky interior of the trailer. It looked pretty much as he expected, just like countless other places he had raided as he worked his way up the ranks. There was very little in the way of functional furniture. Just ratty-looking twin-sized mattresses on the floor—eight of them—lined up in two rows in the living room, with barely enough room to walk between them. There were probably more beds in the trailer's bedrooms.

All of the mattresses were occupied by human figures, young women, most of them black or Hispanic-looking, all wearing soiled and tattered underclothes, all face down as the SRT operators methodically secured their hands with flexi-cuffs. Some of them were sobbing, but most just had a dazed, shell-shocked look, probably still feeling the effects of the flash-bang.

Purcell guessed these girls were mostly used as household servants. A few, not always the prettiest, ended up in the sex-trade. While the girls were technically victims not perps, Purcell knew from experience that they were, one and all, undocumented aliens. This group, according to the intel they had gathered, was mostly from Haiti and the Dominican Republic. Regardless of the circumstances under which they had been brought to America, they were in the country illegally, and so had to be detained for processing. It was also possible that one or more of them might be working with the slavers, but Purcell didn't think that very likely. Management had its perks, which usually meant a private bedroom.

He moved through into the dining room, past a beat-up old table that Goodwill probably would have rejected and a hodge-podge of chairs, and headed down the hallway, past an empty bathroom and into the bedroom at the end of the trailer. Sure enough, there were more mattresses here, and more girls getting zip-tied, but none of them looked like management material.

Purcell glanced over at the SRT leader. "This is everyone?"

The man nodded. "We checked all the closets. Even looked under the beds."

"Is that supposed to be funny?" Purcell asked, a little annoyed.

"I thought so."

Purcell snorted. It was kind of funny, but he was pissed off that they hadn't been able to identify a person in charge. He was here to find the zookeeper, not rescue the animals.

Modern slavery didn't require literal chains of bondage,

or even constant supervision. In most cases, the slaves were held in thrall with threats alone—sometimes threats of physical violence, but more often than not, with the threat of deportation. Since the girls—or sometimes guys—had no legal status, they couldn't find a place to live or even draw a legitimate paycheck, so in order to keep a roof overhead, they willingly inhabited squalid high-density residences like this trailer. Their fear of being sent back to whatever third-world hellhole they had been taken from was usually more than enough to keep them in line. But there was always someone in charge, someone paying the rent and utilities, buying the groceries—such as they were—and making sure that slaves got where they needed to go.

Not tonight though, he thought bitterly, turning away and stalking back down the hallway.

He would interview the girls in the morning, when a translator would be available. They might be able to provide a physical description of their minder. Maybe even recognize him or her from a mug shot. He would also lean on the owner of the trailer park. That would also probably be a dead end, but something might shake loose. There might even be some physical evidence in the trailer itself. A receipt from a grocery store or an ATM might lead to surveillance camera footage.

As he reached the dining room, Purcell had a nagging feeling that he'd just missed something important. He turned and walked back down the hall. This time, he didn't just stick his head in the bathroom, but went in and looked around. The lavatory was surprisingly clean, but otherwise seemed unremarkable. He opened the shower curtain, exposing the empty shower-bath combo, then turned around in a circle, taking in the room.

He shook his head and went back out into the hall. There was another door on his left just past the bathroom, opened to reveal the water heater closet, and then the bedroom at the end. There was, he knew, another bedroom at the opposite end of the trailer, but whatever was bugging him wasn't there.

It was here.

He went in the bedroom again, turned a slow circle, and then headed out again.

"It's here," he muttered.

"What's here?" asked the SRT leader.

Purcell ignored the question and instead began pacing off the length of the hallway. He went in the bathroom and mentally calculated its dimensions, adding it to the mental blueprint he was creating, then did the same with the water heater closet and the bedroom.

"It *is* here," he whispered, turning to the team leader and raising his finger to his lips to signal the man to keep silent.

"What?" the man mouthed.

Purcell faced the interior wall of the bedroom and began running his fingers along the cheap wood panel. "The hall is about four feet longer than it should be," he explained, still whispering. "They extended it to hide something. Maybe some kind of panic room."

The team leader's eyebrows shot up in surprise, and what might have been admiration. "The girls might know how to get in."

Purcell shook his head. "I got a better idea. Get me that ram."

There was an eager gleam in the other man's eyes as he hurried off to find the team's door breacher. While he was doing that, Purcell continued examining the walls, trying to figure out where best to strike. In the corner of the room, he felt the wood paneling give a little under his probing fingers. He looked up and down and spotted a screw head protruding from the wall, just above the baseboard. It wiggled a little at his touch, a sure sign that there was nothing structural on the other side.

With the SIG held at the ready, he reached down with his left hand and yanked on the screw.

From floor to ceiling, a three-foot wide section of paneling popped free, revealing a dimly lit space beyond. Leading with the pistol, Purcell stepped inside, pivoting to the left to look down the length of the narrow room.

Something moved… No, not something. Someone. A man—Caucasian, young but not too young, with a medium-build, dirty-blond hair and a wispy beard—was seated at a desk or table in front of an open laptop computer. He turned, looked right at Purcell, and then started reaching across the table….

Purcell aimed his weapon and fired.

The SIG's report was deafening in the small enclosure.

A mist of blood sprayed across the table.

The guy in the chair grunted and went rigid for a moment, then slumped onto the floor in a misshapen heap.

"Shit," Purcell muttered, suddenly feeling shaky from the adrenaline rush. He had not really intended to pull the trigger; it had been purely a reflexive action.

But the guy had been going for a gun, hadn't he?

It had definitely looked that way to Purcell, and the perception of danger was usually all it took to justify a shooting. The SRT guys would back him up, but just in case some bleeding-heart libtard on the review board decided to spin things a different direction, he decided it might be a good idea to secure the hypothetical weapon.

With his smoking pistol still trained on the dead guy, Purcell advanced into the room. He didn't immediately see a gun or anything else on the table aside from the computer. Fat red drops were streaking down the glowing screen. Through the spatter, a small dialogue box was visible.

Are you sure you want to permanently delete these files?

Purcell moved the cursor onto the "Cancel" button, and clicked once. The prompt disappeared, revealing a directory folder of files that had just narrowly escaped deletion.

"Nice try, asshole," he muttered.

Simply deleting the files would not have completely erased the data of course, and the guy must have known that, but the fact that he had been trying to destroy the evidence was enough to make Purcell think he'd probably found something significant.

Whether that would make up for wasting the guy remained to be seen.

He knelt beside the body, patting the fallen man down, still hoping to find a gun, or at the very least a knife. Anything to justify the shooting. The guy had definitely been reaching for something.

Hadn't he?

"Purcell?" The SRT team leader appeared in the room, his weapon at the high ready. "What the hell? Was that a shot?"

Purcell took a breath and stood up, pointing to the body at his feet. "Found this guy. He was going for a…"

He hesitated as he spotted something affixed to the side of the table. It was a small blue electrical box—such as might be used for a wall outlet or a single light switch—with a hinged cover. He flipped the cover up and saw an ordinary light switch. A thick, heavily insulated supply line emerged from the wall nearby and went into one end of the box, and a pair of wires—one black, one white—held together with strips of black electrical tape, extended from the other end. The latter disappeared under the table.

Purcell muttered, pulling the dead body out of the way so he could get a better look at the underside of the table. The wires from the switch ran down to disappear through a hole in the lid of a small gallon-sized plastic bucket on the floor.

His heart skipped a beat when he realized what it probably was.

"Bomb!" He backpedaled frantically. "There's a bomb here. Get everyone out."

The SRT leader didn't need to be told twice. He vanished from the opening, shouting for his men to evacuate. Purcell started after him, but the shock of the discovery was already giving way to a feeling of satisfaction. There would be no question about the shooting now. The official report would confirm that his quick reflexes had saved the entire SRT team, not to mention whatever evidence was on that laptop.

Purcell stopped as the significance of that finally hit home. The suspect had been ready to blow himself up to keep that computer from falling into the hands of law enforcement.

What could possibly be that important? He wondered.

His curiosity got the better of him. The answer was right there on the computer. He wouldn't even have to crack the log-in password.

The more he thought about it, the more he realized he needed to know what was on that computer. It might contain detailed information about a larger criminal organization. Time sensitive information. The dead guy had probably already warned his accomplices about the hit.

And the bomb wasn't going to just go off spontaneously. Not unless someone threw that switch. Evacuating the area was just a precaution, after all.

He turned and went back to the computer. He knew he wouldn't have much time, so he skimmed the directory, noting that the files were all spreadsheets. One contained a list of names, with accompanying biographical and physical data, as well as dates and addresses—the latter he guessed were the assigned workplaces for the illegals. Another file looked like a shipping schedule, with dates going back more than a year and extending three months into the future. One column in the list was labeled with the header "UNITS" and under it, in each row, was a number. 15, 25, 75.

He scrolled down to the next pending arrival, three days hence.

MV Mohebbi. Houston. 150.

One hundred and fifty units.

One hundred and fifty slaves.

That was good, but it wasn't enough. Purcell wanted more. The evacuation was proceeding apace but pretty soon the SRT leader would take a head count and realize Purcell was still inside. There wasn't time to go through every file, so he left the directory and opened the computer's email server.

Sure enough, an outgoing message had been sent just

minutes after the raid commenced. The content of the message was exactly what he expected, a frantic warning that law enforcement agents were on the premises. The recipient's email address was a meaningless and probably randomly generated string of letters and numbers, but it was a start.

He scrolled down the list, checking other recent messages. One subject line caught his eye.

The Chosen.

He clicked on the message and started reading.

After just a few lines, he realized his heart was pounding again. "Oh, my God."

He finished reading, went back and read it again, then took out his phone, scrolled through the contact list until he found a number he had never called before, that he had never even dreamed of calling.

Should he call it now?

Just as in the Department, there were protocols to be followed. Information flowed through the organization using proper channels, the chain of command. He was relatively new, and while he definitely wanted to distinguish himself, going over the head of his local chapter leader would bring the wrong kind of attention.

And yet the protocols were also clear about bypassing those channels in certain situations, scenarios involving... Well, the sort of thing he had just read.

It wasn't up to him to decide whether it was real or not; he had to follow the protocols.

He hit the send button and waited.

The message in the email was the stuff of conspiracy theory wet dreams, and yet if any of it was true, it was a bomb far more explosive than the improvised device under the table.

It might just blow up the whole world.

PART ONE—*SERVUS*

ONE

Unknown location

Jade Ihara woke up. Then she threw up.

Or maybe it was the other way around. Maybe it had been the uncontrollable heaving or the bitter taste of bile in her mouth, stinging her nose, choking her, that had pulled her up from the depths of unconsciousness. She couldn't say for sure, and anyway the exact sequence of events really didn't matter.

She felt miserable… No, this was worse than miserable. Her head throbbed, her gut churned with a mixture of intense hunger and profound queasiness. The smell of her own sick made her want to puke again, even though there was nothing left to void. It felt like the hangover from hell

No, it definitely *was* the hangover from hell.

Which was strange because she hadn't drunk that much….

The thought was like a piece of a jigsaw puzzle selected at random. By itself, it wasn't enough to form a more complete picture, and she couldn't immediately see how it connected to anything else, but she knew it was somehow important.

Wake up, Jade.

That was the problem. She was still half-asleep, her mind in a fog, and the pulsating pain shooting through her skull wasn't making it any easier to focus.

I didn't drink that much, she thought again. *But what did I drink?*

She recalled Yann insisting that she try one of the hotel's signature Passion Fruit Punch cocktails; lots of rum and fruit juice, kind of like a Hurricane cocktail.

She remembered that much but everything after the first few sips was a blur, and the simple act of trying to drill down into the memory, which was as unnaturally dark as the room around her, just exacerbated the nausea churning within her.

Breathe through it, she told herself, but the air was foul and stifling, and her deep inhalations only served to intensify the throbbing in her cranium.

She moaned, trying to muster the strength and determination to sit up, to leave her bed and throw open a window.

Bed...?

That was wrong. She wasn't in her hotel bed, but lying supine on a hard, flat surface, presumably the floor. She could feel the unyielding surface pressing into her tailbone and against the back of her head.

Didn't even make it to bed. That's it. I'm never drinking rum again.

But something about that explanation rang hollow.

Maybe she had gotten that drunk—unlikely, yes, but not completely impossible. Sugary drinks like the passion fruit punch cocktail could sneak up on a person. No, that wasn't what was wrong with this picture.

Why is it so dark in here?

True darkness was a rare thing. Outside light—whether from the sun in daytime or street lamps at night—had a way of creeping in around curtains and window blinds. Indoors, there was always an artificial light source somewhere; a clock on a coffee maker or an LED indicator on a television set in standby mode. Although power outages were just a fact of life in Haiti, as in all underdeveloped nations, the upscale hotel where she and Professor were staying had its own generator to ensure uninterrupted, round-the-clock electricity for guests. And even if that failed, there should have been some kind of light in the room and the fact that there was not, just as the rough surface under her was neither bed nor carpet, seemed to point toward one inarguable conclusion.

I'm not in my room.

So where the hell am I?

She knew the answers were not going to drop out of

the stale air and land on her head, so she tried again to will herself into motion.

She started to reach out, intending to plant her hands on the floor in order to lever herself to a seated position, but her arms, which were extended away from her torso in what felt like a lazy spread eagle, only moved a few inches before something arrested all movement, something rough and hard that dug into the skin of her wrists.

Something like handcuffs.

Adrenaline dumped into her bloodstream like an infusion of ice water. The hangover symptoms were gone in an instant, whisked away in the chemical rush, but she felt no relief. Only a deepening dread. She pulled again with the same results, and this time, the metallic clatter of the heavy chains attached to the manacles resonated through her like a death knell.

Chains!

Despite the total darkness enveloping her, Jade's vision was filled with flashes of red, like fireworks exploding all around her.

She struggled against the restraints, thrashing impotently for several seconds before finally bringing her panic under control.

"Get a grip, Jade," she muttered.

Easier said than done.

She took another deep breath which only served to confirm her earlier observation about the foul air.

"Hello!"

The echo was immediate, suggesting a relatively small but otherwise empty enclosed space.

"Professor? Anybody?"

No response.

She held her breath for a moment, straining to hear something, but the only sound was the steady—and too rapid—thump of her own heartbeat.

A dam broke within her. The pent-up panic joined now by rage reached critical mass and burst from her chest in a torrent of screamed obscenities. She shook her chains, straining against them until the pain of the manacles biting into her wrists was too great to bear.

The outburst lasted only a few seconds. That was all she could manage. She slumped on the floor, her body's energy reserves depleted. She was dehydrated. The air was thick with carbon dioxide and if she was right about being in a sealed room, she might very well be on the verge of passing out. Anger wasn't going to get her out of this. Just the opposite, she would need her wits to escape this trap, and those were going to get duller with each passing second.

Start from the beginning. How did I get here? Who did this?

She reached back into the dark memories of the night before....

No, that was another assumption. She had no idea how long ago that had been. Hours? Days?

I was at the hotel restaurant with Professor and Yann. Yann insisted I try the passion fruit punch.

Somebody roofied me.

Was it Yann?

She didn't want to believe that. Not only had Yann seemed like a genuinely nice guy, he had also passed Professor's rigorous vetting process without raising any red flags.

Yann Pierre was a Haitian of mixed descent. His mother was a school teacher whose lineage traced back to the African slaves whose revolt at the end of the 18th century had established the free nation of Haiti just two decades after the American Revolution. His father was a German architect who had lived in Haiti for the duration of a construction project. The two had not married—in fact, Yann's father had a wife and family waiting for him in Stuttgart, and had returned to them when his son was a barely formed embryo in Edoine Pierre's womb. To his credit, the man had sent money back to his former lover, just enough to ensure that Yann receive a full education. In Haiti, the poorest nation in the Western Hemisphere and number twenty on the list of poorest globally, a little bit went a long way, and a simple high school education was often enough to lift one out of poverty.

Pierre had taken full advantage of the boost, going on to earn a PhD in Ethnography from the prestigious Université d'État d'Haïti in Port au Prince, along with several lesser degrees in history and anthropology, and had subsequently taken a senior position at the Musée du Panthéon National Haïtien, or MUPANAH as the locals referred to it.

Not the kind of guy who would slip a girl a mickey, Jade thought, *but then again, who could tell with men?*

Still, it didn't make sense for Pierre to be the architect of her abduction. What could he possibly have to gain from imprisoning her?

Pierre had invited Jade to Port au Prince to consult on a recent archaeological discovery that promised to shed light on the seldom explored mystery of the origin of the Taino people—the native inhabitants of the Caribbean islands who had largely been wiped out by disease and violence shortly after the arrival of Christopher Columbus.

There were two prevailing theories about the Taino origin, if one did not count their traditional belief that they emerged from caves in a sacred mountain on the island Columbus had named Hispaniola. Both theories held that the Taino were descended from groups who had migrated from South America, but were divided between those who believed the Taino originated in the Amazon Basin and those who held that they had diffused from the Columbian Andes. Jade was no expert on the Taino, but she was well-versed in many other Meso-American cultures, and it was in this capacity that Yann Pierre had extended his invitation to her.

As if crushing poverty weren't bad enough, Haiti seemed to be a disaster magnet. The recent passage of Hurricane Irma—the most powerful Atlantic hurricane in recorded history—was just the latest in a long series of destructive events to visit the island. Besides being smack dab in the middle of hurricane alley, Haiti was also some of the most seismically active real estate in the Caribbean. A magnitude 7.0 earthquake had devastated Port au Prince in 2010, killing at least 92,000 people—unconfirmed estimates ranged as high as 320,000—and destroying a quarter of a million homes. Among the dead were a number of governmental and civic leaders, and aid workers including 85 members of the UN mission. The nation's already fragile infrastructure had been obliterated.

The relief effort had likewise been a disaster. In the years following, another 10,000 had died from cholera, inadvertently brought to the island by UN personnel from Nepal. Seven years later, hundreds of thousands were still homeless, living in squalid conditions in tent cities and refugee camps, while hundreds of millions of dollars raised for relief efforts had simply vanished. Yet, the slow process of demolishing and rebuilding the wrecked city had opened a few doors into the island's distant past, including the remains of what was believed to be an early Taino settlement.

The primitive tools and artifacts didn't have a lot of monetary value, even to collectors, but they did have a story to tell. Yann Pierre believed that some of the artifacts found at the site showed a distinctive Maya cultural influence, and he wanted Jade's expert opinion on the matter.

She and Professor had met Pierre at the museum in the afternoon to discuss the itinerary for the visit, and then again at the hotel restaurant for dinner. The following morning, they would have gone to the site, taken a few photographs *in situ*, and then Pierre's team would begin removing the artifacts for conservation. The discovery wasn't going to keep the bulldozers at bay for long, so time was a critical factor, but there was nothing particularly controversial about what he had asked her to do, and certainly nothing dangerous.

Nothing Professor couldn't handle. Or so she had told herself.

Pete "Professor" Chapman was a lot more than just her bodyguard. A former Navy SEAL, he had spent the last few years working with an elite task force code-named Myrmidons. Ostensibly organized as part of the Central Intelligence Agency, the Myrmidon's original mission was to root out and destroy a global criminal conspiracy collectively known as the Dominion.

In addition to grandiose dreams of world domination, the Dominion, a loose alliance of quasi-religious far-right racist organizations, had a tendency to fetishize historical artifacts and relics, especially those purported to have supernatural properties, which had placed Jade in their crosshairs on more than one occasion. The fact that she seemed to have a target painted on her back had prompted Tam Broderick, the leader of the Myrmidons, to send Professor to watch Jade's back on a semi-permanent basis. Jade didn't think Tam cared that much about her safety; it was more likely that her original intent had been to dangle Jade out in the open as bait, hoping to flush out Dominion.

Unfortunately, while Tam and her Myrmidons had been busy protecting America from external threats, the Dominion had found a legitimate way to achieve at least some of its goals. Against all odds and expectations, a populist outsider candidate had scored an upset victory in the recent U.S. presidential race. It was only later, following a failed attempt by a group of so-called "patriots" to sabotage a data farm in eastern Washington—and attempt thwarted by the Myrmidons—that the newly elected leader of the free world began to exhibit some alarming sympathies. His most flagrant action was the pardon of Texas millionaire—and Dominion leader—Roger Lavelle, who had been implicated in a plot to assassinate the president of Mexico, and the subsequent nomination of Lavelle's son Carl to the position of Secretary of Homeland Security. Now, the Dominion wasn't some shadow enemy scheming for the overthrow of the U.S. government—they *were* the government.

Now that they had achieved a sort of legitimacy, the Dominion appeared less intent on acquiring artifacts of religious or historical significance, so it seemed pretty unlikely that Jade would pop up on their radar again, but Professor was still around, not only watching Jade's back but assisting her with her field research. He was probably the smartest man she had ever known, at least as knowledgeable about pre-Columbian American history as she, to say nothing of his repository of knowledge on a variety of other subjects. The guy was a walking encyclopedia.

Truth be told, there were a lot of other reasons she liked having him around. They were friends. He genuinely cared for her, and she for him. They weren't romantically involved, but she could see it happening someday, and wondered if he felt the same.

She shook her head, trying to bring her attention back to the matter at hand.

If Professor wasn't also a hostage—she refused to entertain an even more dire possibility—then he would move heaven and earth to rescue her, but she wasn't about to sit here playing damsel in distress, waiting for him swoop in and save her.

She pulled against the manacles again, not frantically but in a methodical manner, testing them, trying to visualize how she was restrained. The chains rose from the cuffs to a point about four feet above her head and slightly behind her. Using her feet, she scooted herself toward that unseen location and promptly encountered a solid wall. There was enough slack in the chains now to allow her to place her hands palm-down on the rough floor and push herself to a sitting position with her back against the wall.

Something was protruding from the wall, right at head level, and after a moment of exploration, she realized that it was a metal ring, about two inches in diameter, affixed to the wall, through which the chain connecting her shackles had been threaded. She experimentally slid the chain back and forth through the ring, then turned her attention to the chain itself and to the cuffs around her wrist. The links were big and heavy, the kind used for securing gates or towing vehicles. They felt rough under her fingertips, rusty and pitted with corrosion, but still solid enough to withstand whatever she might throw at them.

She probed the cuffs around her wrists. Like the chains, they were thick and utilitarian. They were not precision machined like the handcuffs used by police officers, but were each fashioned from a single band of metal—iron, judging by the distinctive almost bloody smell in the air—bent into a circle barely large enough to wrap around her forearms, secured by the shank of a padlock that held the ends together. They felt like something from a medieval dungeon. The locks also felt like antiques, with bulky cylindrical lock bodies and oversized keyholes.

A glimmer of hope shone in the darkness. She was no expert on locks or picking them, but she knew that the older the lock, the simpler the mechanism inside. Had her captors used modern padlocks, easily enough obtained even in Haiti, she would have been sunk, but with these old relics, she just might have a chance.

But first she needed something to use as a pick, and she knew just the thing.

She patted herself down, verifying that she was still in the same clothes she had worn in her last memory. Only now did it occur to her to wonder if her captors had violated her during her unconsciousness. There was no evidence to suggest that had happened, but this brought only slight comfort. She was chained up in somebody's torture dungeon, so maybe that was still in the cards.

Not if I have anything to say about it.

She unbuttoned her shirt halfway and was just about to reach underneath when she felt a vibration shudder through the wall behind her. A torturous shrieking sound, like nails on a chalkboard, electrified the air around Jade, setting her teeth on edge.

And then her world was filled with fire.

TWO

Port au Prince, Haiti

Professor glanced down at the bright blue face of his Omega Seamaster wrist chronograph and noted the time; it was half-past nine p.m.

Jade had been missing for fourteen hours.

Scratch that, he amended silently. *I discovered she was missing fourteen hours ago. There's no telling how long she's really been gone.*

That thought, coupled with his own utter uselessness, filled him with white-hot rage.

Where is she?

He had awakened early, a deeply-ingrained habit held over from his Navy days, and gone to the hotel's fitness room for a forty-five-minute run on the treadmill. He would have preferred going outside, actually running instead of just pedaling the air on a moving belt and going nowhere. There was no better way to get to know a place than to lace up the running shoes and hit the pavement, but Port au Prince wasn't the most hospitable environment for aerobic exercise. The air quality alone was enough to give him pause. Exhaust from diesel power generators, and smoke from fires—both charcoal cooking fires and trash incinerators—combined to form a carcinogenic miasma, particularly in the early morning hours when automobile traffic was heaviest. Add in the threat of crime and the generally poor condition of the streets and sidewalks themselves, and Port au Prince became a place he wasn't particularly interested in getting to know better.

After the workout, he'd taken a leisurely shower and gotten dressed unhurriedly. They weren't supposed to meet Pierre until ten o'clock, and the museum was only a couple blocks away, so there was no reason to rush Jade. Finally, at around seven, he had decided it was time to give her a call.

As was the case in many developing countries, mobile

phone technology had leapfrogged communications in Haiti into the 21st Century, so despite the long string of disasters, or maybe because of them, Professor and Jade were able to get roaming access through a local provider.

For a few seconds, there was only silence and an occasional faint popping sound that might have been static, or just his imagination. Then he heard the electronic ringing sound.

It cycled twice and then there were more pops as the connection was made and Jade's voice sounded in his ear. "Hi, you've reached Jade's phone. I'm not—"

He ended the call with a faint growl of displeasure and then redialed. As the process repeated, he moved to the wall separating his lodging from hers—the rooms were adjacent but not adjoining—and cupped a hand to one ear, listening for Jade's ring tone.

"If she put it on silent..." he started to say, but then heard her ringtone sounding on the other side of the wallboard. He waited until it went to voice mail again, then hung up and tried a different tactic.

"Jade!" He pounded on the wall with his fist. "Wake your ass up!"

At some point, as he had escalated his efforts to rouse her, it had occurred to him that she might be hung over. Yann Pierre had started the dinner off with a round of the hotel's signature passion fruit punch cocktails. Professor had tasted his and found it sickeningly sweet—nothing but rum and fruit syrup—so after politely sipping at the first round, he had switched to mineral water, but Jade had downed at least three over the course of the night. Three drinks were enough to make driving a car a bad idea, but when he had walked Jade back to her room afterward, she had only seemed a little tipsy. She certainly hadn't been falling down drunk, but he knew that the combination of alcohol and sugary mixers could knock you on your ass if you didn't stay hydrated.

When pounding on the wall and then on the door to her room yielded no better results, he knew it was time to start worrying a little. He considered simply kicking the door in, and decided against it only because, deep down, he was hoping that he was just overreacting. Fifteen aggravating minutes later, when the front desk finally agreed to open the room for him, he regretted that decision.

Jade was not there.

After checking every corner of the room, the closet, the bathroom, even under the bed, he forced himself to stop and think.

Maybe she had gone for a workout or a swim.

He surveyed the room like a detective. Jade's mobile phone sat on the nightstand beside the bed. Next to it was her watch, a slightly smaller ladies' version of his Seamaster. The bed was made, though it looked a little rumpled, as if someone had lain on it without pulling back the blankets.

He checked the closet again, opening the small suitcase. Jade's clothes were neatly folded inside. He riffled through them, found a red bikini top, and then the matching bottom.

That eliminated the pool. He kept looking, and found a couple of oversized tee-shirts, but no athletic attire. Had she actually brought any along? He didn't think so, but then he realized something else was missing.

"Shoes."

He remembered her complaining about not having brought along any nice clothes for the dinner. This was a working trip after all, so all she had brought was her standard work uniform—cargo shorts, safari-style shirts with long sleeves that she almost always rolled-up, and her favorite hiking boots.

Had she already left? Without telling him?

He shook his head. She wouldn't do that. She knew better.

And yet, what other conclusion could he draw?

He had called the front desk again, asked if anyone had seen her leave or perhaps called a taxi for her. No one had. He called Yann Pierre, hoping against hope that she was sitting in his office at the museum—

Without her phone and her watch?

—but she wasn't there either. Pierre said he had not seen or spoken to her after their dinner together.

Something was very wrong.

He called the police.

The officer who took his call seemed unsurprised at the news that Jade was missing. Kidnappings were a problem in Haiti, especially for wealthy American tourists. He advised Professor to wait for the ransom demand to be made, and then to pay it and hope for the best.

He called the US Embassy, and received the same advice.

He wasn't prepared to sit around waiting around for something to happen, so he went back to the beginning.

Jade was missing.

Abducted?

That was the likeliest explanation.

When? That was harder to pin down. He had walked her to her room and bade her good night at around eleven o'clock the previous night, so obviously the kidnapping had occurred sometime during that eight-hour window. Her door had been locked and there was no sign of a struggle in the room, which meant that either she had opened the door for her abductors, or they had come with a key.

"Inside job," he murmured. "Has to be."

Someone working for the hotel had provided the kidnappers with a pass key. Probably the same someone who helped make sure that no one noticed their exit.

Or maybe they were still in the hotel. He recalled a recent incident where one of the people on the Myrmidons task force had been abducted from a high-rise office building in New Jersey. All efforts to track him had met with failure because his captors had not actually taken him out of the building, but merely relocated him to a vacant office on another floor of the same building.

He would have to question every hotel employee, search every room, turn over every rock... Whatever it took to find her.

And that was exactly what he did.

It was a big job for just one person with limited resources, so the first thing he did was call Yann Pierre again to advise him of the situation. The Haitian was predictably distraught, but echoed the same message Professor had heard over and over again: Kidnapping is a problem here.

Shit happens.

It was enough to make him want to scream, or slam his fists into the walls. Jade's safety was his primary mission, and he had failed her. But it was more than that. The half-Hawaiian half-Japanese archaeologist was more than just his assignment, more even than just a friend. She was important to him, in a way he wasn't quite ready to admit. Not to himself, and certainly not to her.

And now she was gone.

Professor clamped down on his emotional reaction and outlined his plan of action. Language, he explained, would be the biggest impediment. French was one of the official languages of Haiti, and Professor was fluent, but only the educated elites spoke it well. Most of the island's working-class inhabitants, which included all but a few of the hotel staff, spoke only the island's other official tongue: Haitian Creole, a unique language derived from French, but with multiple international and local influences.

Pierre had seemed reluctant to get involved, assuring him that the odds were good Jade would be returned unharmed—his actual words were *"mostly unharmed"*—if the ransom was paid, but Professor had rejected the attempted brush-off.

"Get over here," he growled. "Now." And then hung up.

To his credit, Pierre had shown up and done his part as both an interpreter and as "good cop" to Professor's surly, threatening "bad cop," smoothing ruffled feathers after Professor's harsh questions were answered.

Unfortunately, the answers were all the same. No one knew anything. Despite his increasing level of alarm, Professor was able to maintain the emotional detachment of a seasoned interrogator, and his instincts told him that they were all telling the truth.

After questioning everyone on the day-shift, he had carried out a systematic—and similarly futile—search of every square inch of the hotel. The hotel manager, recognizing his tenacity and perhaps fearing a lawsuit against the international corporation that owned the hotel, was particularly cooperative, even calling in everyone who had worked the previous night.

But none of it yielded a single lead as to Jade's whereabouts. And nobody had called with a ransom demand.

Fourteen hours.

"This isn't working," he snarled, more to himself than to Pierre. The Haitian, looking bleary-eyed from exhaustion, stared back at him, saying nothing.

"Somebody took her," Professor went on. "Who? Who is usually behind the kidnappings?"

Pierre spread his hands in a gesture of helplessness. "There are many desperate people in my country."

As far as Professor was concerned, that was no excuse for criminal behavior, but there was no denying the truth of the statement. He felt bad for the Haitian people, who seemed to have gotten a raw deal on every conceivable count. Misfortune seemed to be written into the islanders' collective DNA.

The African slaves who had won their freedom after a successful uprising against their French masters had nevertheless been obliged to make reparations to their former owners, a staggering sum of 150 million gold francs. It had taken the impoverished country 150 years to pay the debt, worth approximately $20 billion-with-a-B adjusted for inflation.

To make matters worse, in the early 20th century, Haiti had become a de facto colonial territory of the United States. In 1915, following the assassination of a pro-American president of Haiti, US President Woodrow Wilson had sent in the Marines, who had subsequently occupied the island for the next two decades, brutally enforcing martial law, even enslaving locals at gunpoint. Following the exit of the military in 1934, the US government continued to exert a heavy influence on Haitian politics, rarely to the benefit of the nation's citizens.

In 1957, Francois "Papa Doc" Duvalier took the reins of power. Although democratically elected, he quickly turned to terror and brutality to maintain control of the nation, declaring himself president-for-life. He disbanded the army after a failed coup attempt, and created a paramilitary organization known as the Cagoulards—the Hooded Men—to enforce his policies by publicly executing, or more often than not, simply disappearing anyone who spoke out against the government. The Haitians had another name for them—Tonton Macoutes. The name was an allusion to a folk tale about a cannibalistic bogeyman who would snatch wayward children in the dead of night, stuffing them in a sack for safekeeping until mealtime.

The end of the Duvalier dynasty in 1986 had brought no relief from turmoil. The years that followed were beset with political unrest—one coup after another—as well as compounding natural disasters, all of which left the citizens of what ought to have been an island paradise caught in the inescapable quicksand of poverty. Such conditions ensured only the worst of the worst survived and thrived.

"This wasn't a random street crime. Somebody targeted her. And somebody had the resources to get in here and get her out without anyone noticing. Desperate people don't have those resources. So who does?"

The Haitian pursed his lips together for a moment and for the first time that day, after asking countless hard-hitting questions, Professor sensed that the subject of his interrogation was holding back.

"Yann. Talk to me."

"If anyone would know…" He hesitated, lowered his gaze and his tone. "Baz."

"Baz?" Professor shook his head. The name meant nothing to him. "How can I contact him?"

"Baz is not a him. It is a Creole word that means 'base.' In many neighborhoods, there are men who have the real power. No business can be done, no food or fuel delivered unless they permit it. Everyone must pay a fee, and in exchange, receive protection and sometimes other services that the government can no longer provide. These men are the baz; the base of the neighborhood."

"So they're gangs?"

Pierre inclined his head. "In a word."

"And the kidnappings? That's their doing?"

"It is different in each neighborhood. For the most part, they aspire to be something better than mere criminals. But nothing happens without their permission, so if anyone would know what has happened to her…"

"Baz would know," Professor finished. "So who do we talk to? Who's the baz of this block?"

Pierre shook his head. "The baz are found in the poor neighborhoods, away from the city center and government control. The most powerful are in Martissant, a few miles from here. They control access to the highways leading from the port. However…" His voice became plaintive, almost a wail. "These are very dangerous men. If they are involved, they may kill Dr. Ihara if they feel threatened. Even if they are not directly involved, it is most unwise to attract their attention."

Professor ignored the admonition. He moved closer to Pierre until only a few inches separated them. "Give me a name."

Pierre's head drooped a little lower. "This is not my world," he said. "But it is said the most powerful baz is Cesar L'Enfant."

Cesar the child.

Without a moment's hesitation, Professor took out his mobile phone and placed a call. The party on the other end picked up on the first ring. Professor spoke first. "Tam, I need to know everything about a Haitian gangster named Cesar L'Enfant."

THREE

Unknown location

The light wasn't really that bright, but after God only knew how many hours of absolute darkness, it lanced through Jade's dilated pupils like the flash of an arc welder. She winced, looked away, squeezed her eyes shut, but the damage was already done. A green blob was now imprinted on her retinas like a photographic negative. It took her brain a second or two longer to process exactly what had been revealed by that flash.

Two figures, maybe more, stood about thirty feet away, at the end of a long room, more like a square tunnel really. The light came from their torches—actual flaming torches, just like the one used for the Olympics.

Keeping her head turned away, she blinked once—open and shut—then again, several more times. Tears were welling up, spilling from the corners, leaving cool trails down her cheeks, but the stinging was abating quickly. She could tell by the shifting shape and length of her own shadow that the torch bearers were advancing toward her.

"Who are you?" she shouted. Her voice was hoarse from screaming, her lungs raw from breathing the stale air, though she could already sense that it was fresher than it had been a moment before. "What do you want?"

When no answer was forthcoming, she narrowed her eyes until she was squinting through her eyelashes and half-turned to look at them. Even though the fire they carried was relatively cool, it was still too bright to look at directly. Instead, she looked low, at the feet of the torch bearers.

Bare feet.

As weird as that was, stranger still was the fact that, above the ankles, the shoeless figures seemed to be clad in long white garments, like the vestments of a priest. And there were a lot more than just two of them; half a dozen or more sets of feet, surrounded by swishing white robes, marched toward her. That was about all she could determine about them. Squeezing her eyes nearly shut, she risked a quick glance up. The glare immediately forced her to avert her gaze again, but not before she caught the full silhouette of the pair leading the procession. She couldn't make out much in the way of detail, but there was something eerily familiar about the pointy shape of their heads.

Crap, she thought. *Barefoot Klansmen.*

The idea was so ludicrous that, despite her terror, she almost burst out laughing. Why on earth would American white supremacists kidnap her in Haiti of all places?

Okay, so if it's not the KKK, who?

"Who are you?" she asked again, but to no better effect. The first two robed figures had already reached her, moving past to make room for the others. Now the torchlight was everywhere; she could feel the heat of the flames on her face.

"This is the one?"

The voice, a man's voice, made her jump. She instinctively knew that he was not speaking to her, and that just made her angry. "Hey! Asshole. Answer me. Who the hell are you?"

"Feisty," said another voice, also male but with just a hint of a southern twang. "I like her."

English, she realized. *Maybe they really are Klan?*

It made no sense, but what other possible explanation could there be?

She opened her mouth to shout another question but before she could utter a sound, one of the men bent down, his bulk eclipsing the torchlight, and shoved a rough hand into her mouth. She fought, more a reflexive action than anything else, but he easily overpowered her, shoving her head back against the wall. The impact dazed her for a second, and before she knew what was happening, his fingers were spreading her lips apart, baring her teeth and gums for inspection.

What the actual...?

The pressure vanished, the fingers moving away before she could even think to bite them. She swung her hands up, intending to strike the man or shove him away, but the chains snapped taut, holding her at bay.

"She's healthy enough," the first man remarked. "For whatever that's worth."

Jade's mouth felt hot and swollen, violated. The men were treating her like an animal, like livestock up for auction. Like a....

No. Not that.

She screamed—not in terror but in defiance, raw anger—until her throat closed up involuntarily. She strained against her chains, trying to unleash some kind of Hulk-like strength to rip the shackle from the wall so she could beat the men to death with them, but the metal refused to yield. As the echoes of her scream died away, so did whatever energy the breath of fresh air had restored to her. She collapsed in a puddle on the floor.

None of the men had moved. Ten seconds passed. Thirty. Finally, someone spoke. "Is everyone satisfied?"

The voice, low and gravelly, as if the person had chain-smoked for twenty years, was one Jade had not heard before. It might have been a woman's voice.

Several voices murmured, "Aye." There were no dissenters.

The gravelly voice came again, this time speaking words Jade could not comprehend. At least not right away. She caught one or two familiar words.

Latin?

As quickly as the invocation had begun, it was done. The speaker made a sharp flicking gesture with his—her?—hand and something cool, like raindrops, splashed in Jade's face, dampening the front of her shirt. Some of it got in her mouth and she spat it out reflexively. Whatever it was, it had no distinctive taste or smell; probably just plain water, but she wasn't going to take a chance. She blinked the offending liquid out of her eyes, and saw the procession making their way back from where they had come. As the torchlight illumed the furthest extent of the room, and the large double door opening that filled it, top to bottom and side to side, she realized she was not in a room.

Her prison was a shipping container.

The procession passed through the doors, and then the square of illumination cast by the torches narrowed as the double-doors began swinging shut. The narrow band of orange light became a thin line and then vanished altogether, plunging her into darkness.

"No!" Jade screamed again and shook her chains. "You can't leave me here!"

Her plea disappeared into the darkness and she could do nothing to hold back the tears.

She was a slave.

Or soon would be. There was no other way to assemble the facts before her. Someone had drugged her, put her here in a shipping container, which was probably on a boat already headed to... Where? Saudi Arabia? Japan? Maybe she would be headed back to America, and some sleazy underground brothel in Atlantic City or Miami. Maybe she wouldn't even know her ultimate destination. Maybe they would keep her like this, chained up and in the dark, or pump her so full of heroin that she didn't even care.

"No," she hissed through clenched teeth. "Not happening."

She sat up again and, moving by feel alone, reached inside her shirt and worked her fingers under the left cup of her bra.

"Assholes'd probably wet themselves if they could see me now," she muttered as she began pushing and manipulating the lacy fabric. It took a few minutes, but finally the garment yielded up what she was after: a thin curved piece of wire about eight inches long—the underwire from her bra.

She closed her eyes, even though it was impossible to tell the difference, and gripped the lock securing the manacle on her right hand with her left. Using her right forefinger as a guide, she threaded the wire into the keyhole and immediately began twisting and probing with it.

Aside from using a coat hanger to pop the privacy lock

on a bathroom door, Jade had never picked a lock before, but she knew that antique locks like the one on the cuffs were rudimentary at best. Modern locks employed small but precise mechanisms with several tiny pins, each of which had to be lifted to a precise height by the points on the corresponding key for the lock cylinder to turn, but older locks weren't quite so elaborate. Even so, it took a while—at least five minutes of experimental wiggling and twisting—before the wire in her cramped fingers moved the way she wanted it to. The makeshift pick rotated 180 degrees, and then, with a startlingly loud click, the lock body fell away from the hasp.

"Holy crap. I did it."

She almost dropped the wire in her eagerness to remove the lock from the manacles. Once it was clear of the bolt hole, the cuff sprang open and, with a shake of her hand, fell away, rebounding off her thighs to clatter on the floor of her prison.

She attacked the lock on the left manacle with the confidence of a veteran burglar, and three minutes later, the lock was open and the chains were off.

For a few seconds, all she could do was stare down at the darkness before her, visualizing the empty manacles on the floor, astonished at her success. She wasn't free yet, not by a long shot. Shipping container doors weren't designed to be opened from the inside and she hadn't a clue how she was going to overcome that obstacle—it would definitely take more than what she could pull out of her bra—but she was better off now than she had been five minutes earlier.

Keeping one hand against the wall for support, she rose to her feet, moving slowly, not trusting her legs to hold her up. Standing brought on another bout of queasiness. She knew this wasn't merely the result of stress or even exhaustion. She was badly dehydrated. Judging by her ravenous hunger, it had probably been at least twenty-four hours since her last meal—dinner with Professor and Yann at the hotel, her last memory of freedom—and unless her captors had given her an IV, that had also been the last time she'd taken in any fluids. Her legs felt weak and she feared she might pass out at any moment, but staying put wasn't going to bring relief, so she fought through the sensation and lurched forward. Maintaining contact with the wall, she staggered down the length of the shipping container. After a few steps, she put her other hand out in front of her so that she wouldn't slam face first into the door when she reached it.

The container seemed to go on forever. It was like being on a treadmill; her legs were definitely moving, but she didn't seem to be getting anywhere, and with nothing to use as a visual reference, there was no way to know if she actually was making progress. Maybe she really was on some kind of moving platform. Maybe this was some kind of human hamster wheel, a sick joke played on her by those bastards in white robes.

Her hand struck something, but it took a second or two for her addled brain to process the sensation, by which time the rest of her made contact. Fortunately, she wasn't moving fast enough to cause injury. Instead she simply rebounded off the barrier, arms windmilling as she toppled backward and landed hard on her backside.

The impact drove the wind from her lungs in whoosh, and sent a spear of pain up through her sacrum, but as she sat there on the floor of the shipping container, her mouth working like a fish as she tried to catch her breath, she realized that she could see again.

Not a lot. There wasn't really that much to see, but she could definitely make out a faintly glowing vertical stripe, bordered on either side by absolute black.

The door's open!

Jade couldn't believe her luck. Evidently her captors, trusting the manacles to keep her where she was, had not bothered to secure the doors from the outside. It might have even been an intentional action rather than an oversight; if she asphyxiated, they wouldn't be able to sell her at auction. Either way, the seemingly insurmountable problem of getting out of the shipping container had just been surmounted.

It occurred to her then that she had not thought much past that point. There were at least a dozen of the barefoot Klansmen—or whatever they were—out there, and just one of her. She had no idea where she was, and no one to turn to for help.

"So much for the easy part," she muttered, and then pushed the door open a little further and stepped through.

FOUR

Port au Prince, Haiti

Professor stared out the window of the beat-up taxi. He had seen bombed-out buildings in Afghanistan that looked more structurally sound than the graffiti-streaked ramshackle structure outside, but it was four walls and a roof, which was more than could be said for many of the other buildings they had passed during the ten-minute drive from the hotel. "That's the place?" he asked, without turning to look at Pierre.

He sensed the other man was nodding but it might have been his imagination. Either way, the lack of a response was answer enough.

Tam had put him in touch with a cultural attaché—the standard cover for CIA assets working out of US embassies—who had in turn given Professor the full rundown on Cesar L'Enfant. Cesar's base of operations was a nightclub in Martissant, a large and impoverished section of Port au Prince overlooking the bay. The building didn't look much like a nightclub. Professor guessed the term was meant as a euphemism, like "gentleman's club." There was no signage to indicate that it was a business establishment, no queue of young partiers waiting their turn to enter. The only human presence was three young men loitering near the door and smoking. Lookouts, he guessed.

He curled his hand around the molded plastic grip of a Magnum carrying case. The heavy-duty aluminum case was designed for transporting pistols, but its durability and size made it perfect for secure transport of other small items, such as the bundled stacks of ten and twenty dollar bills he had brought along. "All right. Showtime."

"This is a very bad idea," Pierre said, his Creole accent considerably thicker now. "These are very dangerous men."

"So am I." He said it without a hint of braggadocio, as if merely reminding himself of the fact.

Only a fool was truly without fear. Professor was well

aware of the dangers of what he intended, and knew that things could very easily and quickly go sideways, but his entire adult life had been an exercise in learning how to manage risk and harness the heightened sensory experience of fear. It had saved his life on many occasions, and he trusted it would do so this night as well. Yet, he also knew that Yann Pierre did not have his training or his experience. He needed the man to act as a translator, but if the Haitian could not get his fear under control, his presence might prove more a liability.

He turned to face Pierre. "I've got this. Why don't you head back to the hotel?"

Pierre shook his head miserably. "No. I will go with you."

Professor weighed the advantages and disadvantages, and decided to take Pierre at his word. "Just stick close to me, and you'll be fine."

As he got out, the three Haitians at the door stirred, their postures straightening to project strength. Menace.

The color of his skin, if nothing else, marked him as an outsider. A target, and a foolish one at that. Professor waited for Pierre to catch up before confidently striding forward. The trio remained where they were, like spiders waiting for the fly to blunder into their web. It was only when he stepped onto the porch, within easy reach of the men, that they began showing what he took for wariness. One of the men detached himself from the group and hastened through the door, presumably to apprise his compatriots inside of the situation unfolding outside. Professor held the gaze of the closer of the two remaining men and spoke in French.

"I need to speak to Cesar."

The young Haitian man stared back at him for several seconds, his face betraying nothing, then nodded at the case. *"Ki sa ki?"*

Professor didn't wait for a translation. "This?" He held it up. "This is for Cesar. It's a gift. Here, I'll show you."

He spun the case around, rotating it and placing it flat on his open left hand. The move was abrupt, startling the two men, but before they could do anything else, he worked the latch and popped open the lid, revealing its contents. As soon as he saw gleams of avarice in their eyes, he slammed the lid shut and thumbed the combination wheel.

The man's eyes came up to meet his stare. "*Remèt li bay m'.*"

Professor shook his head. "For Cesar."

The Haitian ignored him and made a grab for the case, but Professor deftly removed it from his reach, catching the man's outstretched arm by the wrist, and in one fluid motion, spun the man around and put him on his knees with his arm drawn up behind his back. The man let out a wail of pain and dismay. The other man lurched in place, unable to decide whether to come to his partner's aid or flee.

"For Cesar," Professor said again, and then released the man with a shove, propelling him toward the door.

By some curious coincidence, the door swung open at that moment and the man all but fell into the arms of the third young man who had chosen that moment to make his return. He was accompanied by another man, who appeared to be a few years older than the trio of lookouts. He was attired in a sweat-stained but otherwise serviceable linen suit which did not at all conceal the outline of a pistol in a shoulder holster under the jacket.

The newcomer regarded Professor with a cool gaze, then addressed him in clear French. "You have brought something for me?"

"It's for Cesar."

The man grinned and reached out a hand. "I am Cesar."

Professor shook his head. His CIA contact had given him a full description of the man who controlled the Montessant neighborhood, and this most definitely was not he. "No, you're not."

The man's grin did not falter, but the humor leached from the man's eyes. He glanced over at Pierre then looked back at Professor. "You give to me. I give it to Cesar. Maybe I let you walk away." He shrugged. "Or maybe I just take."

Professor surprised the man by holding the case out at arm's length, but when the man reached for it again, he did not let go. "There's five thousand dollars in here. But there's also five pounds of C-4. You know what that is, right?"

He took the man's widening eyes as an affirmative.

"Put in the wrong combination on the locks and—" Professor made a little explosion with his fingers. "So, there's two ways to do this. The easy way and the hard way. I'd prefer the easy way, where I open this and give the money to Cesar, but it's up to you. Or better yet, why don't you go ask Cesar what he wants you to do."

The man glowered at him for a moment, his eyes searching Professor's for any hint of duplicity or fear, but then he relented. "Come with me."

Pierre let out a nervous hiss but said nothing. Professor simply allowed the case to hang at his side and when the man turned and stepped through the door, he followed.

The interior of the building was dark, illuminated only by a couple of lanterns which hung from hooks on the walls. The air was a stifling perfume of body odor, animal musk and smoke—equal parts tobacco and charcoal. One corner was occupied by a makeshift stove, the source of the latter. As his eyes adjusted to the low light, Professor could see that the interior was a club of some sort, with a few mismatched tables and chairs, occupied by a handful of men who were smoking cigars and drinking from an equally motley collection of drinking vessels—repurposed Coke bottles, jars and tin cans.

Professor felt their scrutiny, but none of them moved. His guide took one of the lanterns and crossed the room to a doorway in the back wall. Professor, with Pierre still in tow, hastened to catch up. Beyond lay a hallway with more doorways, each one covered by a heavy blanket. The Haitian passed them all, continuing to the end of the hall and a narrow staircase leading down, presumably to the basement. The rickety wooden steps creaked ominously under the man's weight as he descended. Professor decided to wait for him to step off the flight before following.

The space at the bottom of the staircase was more of a dugout cave than an actual basement. The air was cooler but reeked of mildew, probably a result of perennial flooding from tropical storms. Floor to ceiling cabinets lined the walls, the wood warped and stained. The man in the linen suit approached one of the cabinets and threw open the door and then inexplicably rapped his knuckles on one of the empty shelves inside. The shelves immediately began to recede, swinging away, along with the back panel, to reveal a passage into another subterranean chamber.

As Professor stepped through, he realized that everything he had seen—and smelled—up to that point was merely camouflage. The hidden room wasn't just clean, it was immaculate, with painted concrete walls and only the faintest hint of mustiness. There were more shelves, but unlike those in the cabinets, these were in good repair and laden with crates and boxes. Linen Suit continued past all of these to another door—an actual door, not just a blanket—opened it, and went through.

The room on the other side of the door was large and open. The air was redolent with competing floral tones, but there were other smells as well—tobacco, incense, and something else—an unpleasant odor—that Professor couldn't quite identify. There was no furniture, but the walls were adorned with murals painted in the colorful folk-art style ubiquitous in the Caribbean, but depicting strange hybrid creatures. In the center of the room, an upright wooden beam rose from a larger pedestal to meet the rafters overhead. The beam was painted with vertical stripes of black and gray. Behind it, positioned against the wall in the back of the room, was a waist high stone altar, like a boulder that had been hollowed out in the middle. Lining the edges around the hollow were vases with bouquets of flowers, elaborately decorated jars, and a dozen or more burning candles, which provided the only light in the room. Carved into the floor in front of the altar was an elaborate picture of a cross atop a tombstone with coffins to either side of it.

Professor recognized many aspects of the décor as

components of Vodou. The figures painted on the walls were *loas*, spirit intercessors. The beam, called a *poteau-mitan*, symbolized the cosmic axis connecting sky to earth.

They were in an *ounfo*, essentially, a Vodou church, but there was something different about this one. It was underground, which was unusual as Vodou was a religion with deep ties to the natural world and growing things, especially trees. Many *ounfo* in fact, were situated outdoors. The *poteau-mitan* in most Vodou gathering places was painted to resemble a colorful rainbow, but this one was in grayscale—like a shadow-copy of a rainbow. And the picture on the floor, known as a *veve*, was a representation of Baron Samedi, the Vodou *loa* of death and resurrection.

There was one other unusual aspect of the place that had nothing to do with Vodou. Unlike the other rooms in the subterranean complex they had passed through, the *ounfo* was occupied.

The men—five of them in all—stood in a loose knot around the *poteau-mitan*. They wore faded blue jeans and tattered denim shirts and looked utterly unremarkable. They did not look at all surprised to see the new arrivals which told Professor that the site of this meeting had been chosen before Linen Suit ventured out to greet them. Professor scanned the faces, allowing his gaze to settle on the man in the center of the group. He was the oldest of them, a wizened man with short gray hair like a patch of steel wool framing his dark face. The man was leaning on a walking stick, ebony or some other black wood, capped with a large knob of white that was mostly hidden by his gnarled fingers. He looked like he might have been eighty years old, but if this was Cesar L'Enfant, as Professor believed, he wasn't a day over sixty-five.

It was the opinion of the Central Intelligence Agency that Cesar L'Enfant, the man in control of organized crime in the Montessant neighborhood, the Boss of the *baz*, had begun life as Cesar Dargent in 1951. Not long after, Hurricane Hazel had ravaged the island and thrown the always fragile republic into a crisis that saw no less than six different governments take power in less than a year's time. The last of those, led by Francois "Papa Doc" Duvalier, had endured, thanks in no small part to the brutality of his paramilitary secret police—the Tonton Macoute.

Around the time of his twentieth birthday, Cesar Dargent had earned the favor of the Macoutes' leader, Luckner Cambronne—called "the vampire of the Caribbean" because of his lucrative side endeavor, the international sale of blood plasma and cadavers—likely the bodies of political prisoners who disappeared by the thousands during the Duvalier regime. It was believed by some that tainted plasma from Cambronne's Hemo-Caribbean plasma center had brought the HIV/AIDS virus to North America. Whether or not this was true, there was little doubt that the unsanitary practices employed in the facility had contributed to Haiti's runaway AIDS epidemic.

Dargent—who may have earned his nickname "Cesar the Child" because of his relatively young age—had become one of Cambronne's most trusted lieutenants but had remained in Haiti after Cambronne's exile to Florida. With the eventual end of the Duvalier dynasty, Dargent, still a relatively young man in his early thirties, had gone underground, perhaps literally if this basement room was any indication, though it now seemed likely that he had spent much of that time growing his base of power, consolidating the street gangs into a small army of enforcers. Cesar's role was that of facilitator and protector for the lower tier criminals—everyone from drug smugglers to human traffickers—for which he received a tribute. Even legitimate businessmen were obliged to pay; it was simply the cost of doing business. The stories of what happened to those who refused to pay were almost certainly the stuff of urban myth, horror stories to ensure compliance.

In addition to raw brutality, the Macoutes had employed superstition as a weapon of mass control. Their common uniform—blue denim shirts, straw hats and sunglasses—had been carefully chosen to instill fear in the populace, fear of their namesake bogeyman. And many senior Macoutes had been practitioners of Vodou—Haitian voodoo.

That explained the décor.

Contrary to common belief, voodoo was not synonymous with black magic or devil worship. It was a religion, or more accurately, a belief system practiced by millions, and as valid as any other, at least as far as Professor was concerned.

Just as there were many different sects of Christianity, Islam or Buddhism, so too were there differences in the practices collectively known as voodoo. The rise of voodoo and similar Afro-American religions like Santeria and Obeah, had their genesis with the arrival of African slaves brought to work the plantations of the New World. Those slaves, in a desperate attempt to preserve their cultural identity, had continued worshipping spirits as their ancestors had, even as they were forced to convert to Christianity. The result was a new belief system with elements of both.

Despite lurid and sometimes bloody rituals, voodoo, like any other religion, also imposed moral obligations on worshippers. Christians had Satan and lesser demons; voodooists believed there were dark spirits—*petro loa*—who could take over the lives of those who sought to harm others. And just as with Satanism and black magic, Petro—dark voodoo—was more of a sensational ghost story than anything else. A cautionary tale designed to frighten worshipers away from immoral behavior. Many of the more universally recognized aspects of voodoo—the use of dolls to strike an enemy from a distance, the resurrection of the recently dead to serve as mindless slaves called "zombies" or "zombii"—were usually linked to Petro. Unfortunately, as was often the case with dualistic belief systems, some people were drawn inexorably to the dark side. In Haiti, that malevolent form of Vodou had become a weapon for the Tonton Macoute. Many of the senior members of the organization, including Dargent, were alleged to be *bokors*, priests of Petro, who not only used physical violence against any who resisted, but also magic, purportedly resurrecting their dead enemies and enslaving them as mindless zombies.

The old man regarded him with a vaguely indifferent stare. The whites of his eyes were the color of old ivory, probably the result of a lifetime spent in the tropical sun. When he spoke, his mouth barely moved. "You have gone to a great deal of trouble to see me." Cesar's voice was a treble monotone, gravelly, like that of an old woman. Professor was mildly surprised to hear English. "This will be a very costly visit for you, I think."

"Like I told your man," Professor replied, holding up the case. "I didn't come empty handed. Five thousand dollars. American dollars. It's yours. I just need to ask you a couple questions."

Cesar did not smile. "And if I don't answer your questions, you will just take it and walk away?"

Professor turned to Linen Suit and offered the case to him. The man shied away from it, turned to Cesar and jabbered in Creole. Professor just shrugged and placed the case on the concrete floor.

"I assume he was just telling you about the bomb in the case. It's true. If you try to force it open or put in the wrong combination, it will blow. The charge is big enough to bring this whole building down. It's just insurance. The money is yours whether or not you answer my questions. My gift to you. The explosives, too. I'm sure you can find a use for them."

He grinned and tipped a wink at Cesar. In truth, there were no explosives, though not for want of trying. Getting five thousand dollars had been simple enough, but procuring five pounds of C-4 would have taken time he didn't have. "Once Dr. Pierre and I are safely away, I'll call you with the combination."

He didn't pause to let this sink in, but pushed ahead. "My colleague... My friend Jade Ihara was abducted from her hotel room last night. I don't know who took her, but Yann tells me if it happens in Port au Prince, you know about it. I want her back. Unharmed. No questions asked. And I'm willing to pay for it. This…" He pointed to the case. "…was just to get me in the door. Name your price."

Cesar's yellow eyes narrowed into contemptuous slits. He took a step forward, and as he moved, his hand rotated on the knob of his walking stick, revealing it to be an extremely detailed carving of a human skull, but slightly smaller.

A child's skull, perhaps.

That's not a carving, Professor thought, and for the first time since entering Cesar L'Enfant's subterranean lair, felt a shiver of apprehension.

The old man raised his walking stick and thrust the skull end toward Professor. At the gesture, the four men surrounding him lurched forward as one, swarming around Professor.

They moved so suddenly, without any precursory warning, that he barely had time to react. He managed to curl his fingers around the handle of the aluminum case and draw it to his chest, but that was all. His plan—admittedly a desperate one—had been to play the bluff for all it was worth, with a threat to trigger the non-existent bomb by attempting to open the case, but the men caught his arms and pulled them out away from his body, immobilizing him.

He tried to pull free, but the lean, wiry Haitian men were prodigiously strong. They did not even seem to be exerting themselves. Their faces remained dull and expressionless, like sleepwalkers.

The chill he had been feeling spiked into a full-blown panic when he realized the significance of this.

"Zombies," he gasped. "Son of a bitch." He had a flash of memory—something his friends Maddock and Bones had said over drinks many years ago. They'd encountered what they'd called zombies in Haiti, but those had been different, hadn't they? Not the traditional Haitian zombies.

Despite being co-opted by Hollywood as the catch-all name for reanimated corpses, the term *zombie* actually had its roots in the folklore of Haitian Vodou. According to the legend, a *bokor* could revive the soulless bodies of the dead, enslaving them. Many anthropologists believed the story was a metaphor for literal slavery, but there was anecdotal evidence that the stories of voodoo zombies had a basis in fact.

The most noteworthy case involved a Haitian man called Clairvius Narcisse, who had died of a mysterious fever in 1962. His death had been recorded by two doctors, and his corpse positively identified by his sisters, Marie-Clare and Angelina, after which he had been buried. But eighteen year later, a man described by some accounts as "heavy-footed" and "vacant-eyed" had shambled up to Angelina in a village market and identified himself as her dead brother. He claimed that he had been raised from the dead by a *bokor*, made into a zombie and forced to work on a sugar plantation. American ethnobotanist Wade Davis, who had traveled to Haiti to investigate the story, hypothesized that Narcisse had been poisoned with an exotic toxin which simulated death, and that the subsequent trauma of being buried alive and waking up in a coffin left the victim in a highly suggestible state, which the *bokor* could maintain with regular doses of other narcotic substances. With higher brain function chemically suppressed, the zombie would not only be utterly without fear or compassion, but also possessed of almost limitless endurance and unbridled strength.

Just like the men who now held Professor.

He gritted his teeth against the pain from their crushing grip. "You won't get that case open," he gasped. "You'll just blow the money up, and yourself with it."

"Keep your money," Cesar said, his tone still flat but ominous and full of menace. "I'll bury it with you."

FIVE

Unknown location

Jade stepped out of the shipping container and into a narrow corridor formed by dozens more just like it. The containers were stacked three high, side-by-side with no gaps in between, to form opposing walls that stretched out in either direction as far as she could see, which admittedly wasn't all that far. Looking up, she could see just a narrow stripe of star-specked night sky peeking down into the man-made canyon.

She glanced at the other containers, wondering if any of them held human cargo.

She assumed that she was on a ship, but it was equally possible that the containers were in a shipyard, waiting to be loaded onto a vessel or onto some other mode of transport—a train or semi-hauler. The air, while considerably fresher than what she had been breathing in the container, remained warm and humid, and thick with the smell of sulfur and petroleum—industrial odors.

Alert to the possibility that her captors might return at any moment, or that the area might be patrolled or under video surveillance, she pushed the doors shut behind her and then, after mentally flipping a coin, turned right and started walking. She had only gone a few steps when the silence was disrupted by the strident whine of an engine turbine spinning up.

"Helicopter," she whispered. "Someone's leaving."

Jade had a pretty good idea who that someone was. Their inspection complete, her captors, the barefoot Klansmen, had no reason to hang around.

For a fleeting instant, she entertained the possibility of stowing away aboard the departing aircraft, perhaps secreting herself in a cargo hold, but she dismissed the idea as ill-conceived. She had no idea where the helicopter was situated, and even if she somehow managed to find it in the five minutes or so it would take for the engines to cycle up to operational speed, sneaking up on it was a lot easier said than done. If she was spotted, it would probably spell the end of her escape attempt; better to stay hidden, at least until she had a better idea of where she really was.

She hugged the wall as she made her way down the narrow corridor, ready to drop flat at the first sign of light.

Torches?

The thought bubbled up seemingly from nowhere.

Why torches? They've got a freaking helicopter, but they can't get their hands on a flashlight?

She dismissed the question. This was no time to get distracted by details.

The turbine noise increased in volume, echoing between the thirty-foot-high walls. She quickened her pace, almost to a run, and reached the end of the row a few seconds later.

Yep, she thought as she nearly tripped over a knee-high metal wall, the last thing between her and oblivion. *It's a ship.*

She knelt down, gripping the gunwale, and took a calming breath as she gazed out into the nothingness beyond. It was like looking out from the edge of the world. Where the ship ended, there was only the darkness of empty space. She kept staring into the void, searching for something familiar, and gradually realized that there was a faint glow off to her right—the ship's running lights. If this was a cargo ship, then those lights were probably mounted on an elevated superstructure rising above the stacked containers, situated in the aft part of the vessel—the back end. That meant the front of the ship—the bow—was to her left, which was also the direction the ship was traveling.

She raised her gaze to the sky, searching the stars until she found the Big Dipper. An imaginary line crossing the last two stars in the bowl helped her find Polaris, which was approximately at the two o'clock position, relative to where she thought the bow of the ship was located. That indicated a roughly north-northwest course. Assuming the vessel had left Port au Prince and stayed on that course, the most likely destination was the North American mainland. If they were on their way to Saudi Arabia or Japan by way of the Panama Canal, the North Star would have been on the other side of the ship. A more experienced navigator might have been able to determine a lot more, but that was the limit of her ability.

Professor would probably know exactly where we are, she thought, and then wondered what he was doing right now. *Does he even know I'm gone?*

She shook her head, trying to dismiss the self-piteous thoughts before they could take root and cling to her like creeper vines. She was tired and hungry and afraid, and her emotions were going to run away from her if she didn't get them under control.

Of course, Professor had noticed she was missing. Watching over her was his job after all….

Yeah, great job with that, Prof.

STOP IT!

She squeezed the gunwale, fighting the urge to scream it out loud, and tried to bring herself back to the moment. She had faith that Professor was looking for her, that he would move heaven and earth to find her, but she also knew that she alone bore the ultimate responsibility for saving herself. She took another deep breath and then turned her attention to figuring out exactly how she was going to do that.

The superstructure would house the ship's control room and the radio which she could use to call for help. There would probably also be a galley where she could get some food and water. Unfortunately, there would also be crewmen in those places, and she had to assume they were in cahoots with her captors; barefoot Klansmen coming and going by helicopter could hardly have done so without the permission of the boat's captain. Still, what choice did she have? It might be several days before the ship reached port; she couldn't last that long without water.

The noise of the helicopter, now a constant feverish roar which seemed to be coming from the same direction as the superstructure, abruptly changed, and Jade sensed the helicopter had just lifted off. She crouched down behind the gunwale, just in case the aircraft's flight path would put her in its view, and waited. A few seconds later, it swooped overhead, a dark dragon with two gleaming eyes, one green and one red. Then it was gone and silence returned. Except it wasn't completely quiet. She could hear the faint murmur of the ship's engines, vibrating through the deck plates, reminding her that, even though it didn't feel like she was moving, she was.

But going where?

She shook her head again, trying to stay focused on her first priority: Reaching the superstructure.

There was no wasted space on the cargo hauler. The shipping containers had been loaded tight against the gunwales, leaving almost no room for anyone to move past. It occurred to Jade that her captors had found a way; perhaps there was more room on the opposite side of the stacks, or another corridor between them, but rather than go looking for it and risk the chance of running into a roving sentry, she decided to take the most direct route.

The gunwale was a six-inch wide curb of welded steel, flaring out just a few degrees from where it met the deck, which left a slight gap—maybe another six inches—between it and the vertical wall of the shipping container.

Plenty of room, she thought.

She placed her right hand against the side of the shipping container, leaning her body into it, and then stepped up onto the short wall. Six inches really was plenty of room. She had walked on ledges a lot narrower than that. The real danger was not physical but psychological. The yawning void to her left seemed to exert its own gravitational pull, which she instinctively resisted by leaning into the container wall.

"Get a grip, Jade," she muttered, forcing herself to stand erect, maintaining only light contact with the wall of the shipping container. "You should be able to do this blindfolded."

A blindfold probably would have helped, but instead she focused her attention on a shifting point atop the gunwale, about ten feet out in front of her. That seemed to help, and before she knew it, she was fully committed to the endeavor.

The glow grew brighter as she progressed, and after a few minutes of shuffling along the top of the gunwale, she spotted a hard vertical line, dividing the ambient light from the running lights on the unseen superstructure from the shadow cast by the corner of the last shipping container, marking the end of her traverse. She made the final approach cautiously, once more leaning into the solid wall to her right. She peeked around the corner, revealing herself cautiously, by degrees, until she was certain that there was no one to see her.

As expected, a towering castle-like structure, easily five stories in height, rose above the deck. There were evenly spaced windows on its exterior, all of them dark except at the uppermost level which was lit up from within; the bridge, no doubt. The structure was crowned by an antenna mast, and barely visible from her vantage, the top of a lone smokestack poked up from behind it. There was an open area, about fifty feet long, spanning the width of the deck between the stacked containers and the superstructure, probably some kind of buffer zone to protect critical areas of the ship in the event of a cargo shift. Jade noticed several doors leading from the deck into the ship's interior, but her attention was drawn to the uncovered exterior staircase running up the starboard side of the superstructure and wreathed in darkness.

She remained where she was for several minutes, watching for some hint of activity. But for the lights and the steady hum of the engines, the vessel might have been mistaken for a drifting ghost ship. She had no idea how big a crew a ship like this required, but guessed most of the work would be done during the daylight hours. The night watch would be little more than a skeleton crew—just enough men to watch the radar screen and make sure all the lights on the control panel were green.

Hopefully.

Steeling herself against the risk of possible discovery, she edged past the corner and stepped down onto the open deck. Her movements were exaggerated, a parody of stealth, like the Scooby Doo gang trying to sneak past a dim-witted ersatz ghost.

I must look ridiculous, she thought, and forced herself to relax. If there was anyone around to see it, looking ridiculous would be the least of her worries.

With a determined but casual stride, she finished the crossing, ducking into the shadows beneath the steel frame of the staircase. She lingered there for a few more minutes, waiting for her hammering heart to settle down, and then cautiously mounted the stairs, rolling her feet with each step to minimize the noise. She did not even make it to the first mid-point landing before the wooziness started—or more accurately, returned with a vengeance. An ominous black haze closed in around her, but she clutched the rail and held on, taking deep breaths until the fainting spell passed. She started moving again, taking each step like she was free climbing a 5.10 ascent at Yosemite, moving each foot only when she was certain that she wasn't going to collapse from exhaustion or go tumbling back down the flight.

There was a door into the superstructure at the next landing. Through the small porthole at its center, she saw a dimly lit corridor. She checked to make sure it wasn't a fire exit with an alarm then eased the door open and slipped inside.

She stole down the hallway, pausing at each closed door she came to, wondering whether to risk having a look. One of those doors might open onto the galley, but then again, she might find herself walking into the captain's quarters. She decided not to take the chance, not until she had a better sense of the ship's layout.

Her patience was rewarded when, halfway down the hall, she found a framed emergency egress plan mounted on one wall. She scanned it and to her relief, discovered that she was standing right outside the crew's mess.

She turned the door handle, opened it a crack, and looked inside. The overhead fluorescent lights had been dimmed, casting a gray pall over the small dining area, but there was enough light for Jade to see that the room was unoccupied. She slipped inside and closed the door behind her.

The room was smaller than she expected, with just two large utilitarian tables, each surrounded by six metal frame chairs. One wall was mostly taken up with a counter, upon which sat a large coffee urn and various drink dispensers, along with napkins and condiments. Jade bypassed the counter, and went through the open doorway in one corner of the mess hall. The lights were out but there was enough spillover from the dining room for Jade to make out the stainless steel surfaces and appliances of an institutional kitchen—the ship's galley.

She located the dishwasher unit, and next to it, a sink with a long hose and sprayer nozzle attached to the spigot. After a little trial and error, she figured out how to divert the water from the sprayer to the spigot, and as water began flowing out, she cupped her hands under the stream and started to drink.

The tepid water had a faintly chemical flavor but Jade thought it was just about the best thing she had ever tasted. She gulped down several handfuls and almost instantly felt rejuvenated. And hungry. She splashed one more handful on her face, rubbing away the smell of her own puke, and started rummaging through the cupboards looking for something to eat.

The discovery of a shelf filled with single-serve cereal bowls was like finding buried treasure. She grabbed the closest one—Cheerios—tore back the foil lid and dumped the contents into her mouth.

She chewed tentatively at first, afraid that the sleeping ship might awaken at the noise of her crunching the toasted oat rings, but the need to actually ingest the food quickly overrode that concern. The dry cereal had the texture of a mouthful of packing peanuts, and a comparable taste, but chewing and swallowing it was a positively sublime experience. When the bowl was empty, she grabbed a second and downed it, too. When she was done, she returned to the sink and used the empty Styrofoam container as a cup to wash her meal down.

Satisfying the two most immediate priorities of survival left her feeling a little drowsy, so she splashed some more water on her face. She couldn't afford to let her guard down now. She debated whether to look for the ship's communication room or just find a place to hide out until the vessel reached port, and decided on the latter. Even if she somehow managed to find and use the radio, there was no telling how long it would take help to arrive, and once the crew realized what she had done, they wouldn't stop searching until they found her. If she hid out, there was a good chance they might not even realize she had escaped her chains.

She returned to the cereal cupboard and gathered an assortment, using the front of her shirt like a pouch. It might be several days before the ship reached its destination and she wasn't going to risk another trip to the galley. She doubted the cook would miss the cereal bowls, but even if he did, he would probably assume it was just one of the crew grabbing an after-hours snack.

Water was going to be a little more problematic though. She did another quick search of the kitchen, hoping to find something to use as a water vessel.

"There's cereal, so there has to be milk, right?" she murmured, and went looking for the refrigerator. Her logic was sound, but instead of one-gallon plastic jugs, the walk-in cooler yielded a stack of boxes, each containing five-gallon plastic bags designed for use with the countertop dispenser in the mess hall. The walk-in also held plastic Cambro containers and food grade five-gallon buckets, too bulky for her needs. There was also a one-gallon plastic pitcher, filled with salad dressing that she decided would be perfect, but rather than waste its contents and spend ten minutes rinsing out the flavor of buttermilk ranch, she decided to head back out the prep area to look for an empty one just like it. On her way out, she spotted a plastic tray filled with wrapped portions of cold cuts and sliced cheese, and helped herself to a few of each. Her stash was almost overfilling the makeshift food pouch, but the idea of something more substantial than Cheerios elevated her spirits. Since the meat and cheese wouldn't keep long, she decided to eat them as soon as she found her new hiding spot.

She pressed her free hand against the round interior push-release and was startled when the door flew open as if spring-loaded.

She was even more startled when she found herself face to face with a heavy-set dark-complected man wearing chef's whites.

For a moment, they just gaped at each other in surprise. Responses shuffled through Jade's mind like playing cards.

Oh hi, I'm the new deck hand. I don't think we've met yet....

I'm the captain's girlfriend. Don't tell anyone you saw me. I'm not supposed to leave his cabin....

I'm trying to find my tour group. Is this the Carnival Princess, or did I get on the wrong ship....

But before she could settle on one, she saw something change in the man's expression, and knew that he knew exactly who she was.

SIX

Port au Prince

Struggling accomplished nothing. The zombies dragged Professor forward until he was within easy reach of Cesar L'Enfant, then bore down on him, driving him to his knees and holding him in a kneeling position before the older man.

Even as he fought in vain to free himself, his rational brain was processing this turn of events which, regrettably, should not have come as a surprise. He had been warned, after all. Cesar was a *bokor*, an evil witch doctor who turned his enemies into zombies.

As if to confirm this suspicion, the old man began rotating his walking stick, twirling the skull around like a doorknob….

No, not twirling. Unscrewing.

The skull came away in Cesar's spidery fingers. The hollow skull had been turned into a receptacle filled with a white powdery substance.

Zombie powder.

During the course of his investigations into the strange case of Clairvius Narcisse, Wade Davis had obtained a sample of the substance which had purportedly caused the man's death-like state, leaving him vulnerable to the manipulations of his captor. The powder was a vile concoction made from the sort of things that would have sounded like something from a parody if not for the fact that the substance was all too real: Freshly-killed blue lizards; a dead toad wrapped in a dried sea worm; and most gruesome of all, the crushed skull of a deceased baby. But the real active ingredient came from the liver of the puffer fish which contained the powerful nerve poison tetrodotoxin, which in sufficient doses could paralyze the nervous system and induce a comatose state. Survival was possible of course, but not guaranteed.

Cesar jabbed the open vial toward his face. Professor clenched his eyes and mouth closed, turning away to avoid inhaling the substance, and tried again to wrestle free of the zombies' iron grip.

No good.

He stopped struggling and instead let his body fall slack in their grip. As he did, he curled his legs up, bringing his knees to his chest, and lashed out with both feet, driving his heels toward Cesar.

His feet struck nothing but air.

He opened his eyes, just enough to peek out. Cesar hadn't moved, but he had; the zombies had yanked him back, just far enough to keep him from making contact.

The *bokor*-gangster laughed, a dry rattling monotone.

"You don't want to do this," Professor said. "You have no idea what kind of hell will rain down on you if you kill me."

It was another bluff, as pathetic as his bogus suitcase bomb, and no more effective.

"When you are my zombie," Cesar cackled, "you will open your suitcase for me and give me all your money. Then maybe I keep you here, like one of these. Or sell you."

Perversely, the threat gave Professor a measure of hope. If the zombie powder was a narcotic cocktail, then he might just have a chance, even if Cesar managed to dose him. If Narcisse's experiences were any indication, then not only was it possible to survive the physical effects, but also to overcome the mental programming and narcotic dependency.

As a SEAL, Professor had gone through military SERE school—Survival, Escape, Resistance and Evasion—a brutal course that included physical and psychological tortures—sleep deprivation, waterboarding, sensory bombardment. SERE school didn't pull any punches because its purpose was to prepare soldiers for the possibility of being captured by an enemy who wouldn't pull any punches either. Professor was reasonably certain that, if he could survive the initial physical shock of tetrodotoxin poisoning, there was a very good chance he could withstand whatever trauma followed, maintain his grip on sanity, and then, when Cesar's guard was down, he would turn the tables. Maybe give him a taste of his own medicine.

But first, there was something he had to know. "Is that what you did to Jade? Did you make her a zombie?"

Once more, Cesar did not deign to answer. Instead, he spoke to his zombies. "Hold his head."

A pair of unseen hands clamped onto either side of Professor's skull, squeezing him so tight he could feel his eyes bulging out. Cesar moved in close again. "Open his mouth."

This time, there was nothing Professor could do to resist. The hands holding his head shifted, one sliding under his jaw, the other bracing against the back of his cranium, and then his jaws were forced apart. The grinning ancient face of Cesar L'Enfant loomed before him, and then the skull came into view, lowering toward his open mouth. Closer....

"Stop!"

The shout came from behind him. It was Yann Pierre.

In his distress, Professor had almost forgotten about Pierre. He had assumed that the Haitian historian had also been restrained by Cesar's zombies, or maybe held at gunpoint by the man in the linen suit, and that he too would be subject to the same brutal treatment. Hearing the man's protest sent a twinge of guilt through Professor. He had dragged the young man into this, heedless of the warnings, and now he would bear the responsibility for whatever befell them both.

And yet, to his complete amazement, Cesar hesitated, and then drew back.

"Release him," Pierre said. There was a quaver in his voice, but he sounded a lot calmer than Professor felt.

Cesar stared past his intended victim, eyes narrowing with contempt. "You brought this man here. What did you think would happen?"

"He doesn't understand."

What the hell? Professor felt like his brain had just slammed into a pothole. Zombies and black magic-wielding gangsters—that was something he could wrap his head around, but he genuinely had no idea what was going on now.

Cesar's face screwed up, like a child refusing to eat his vegetables. "Then you should have explained it to him."

"Release him," Pierre repeated. "Accept the money he has brought you and let us go."

The *bokor* spat a curse and then turned away, jamming the skull back onto the end of his walking stick. The zombie let go of Professor's head. The grip on his arms relaxed somewhat, permitting him to stand, and then those hands fell away, too. The zombies shuffled toward their master, forming a defensive ring around him, but Professor had already lost interest in the witch doctor.

He whirled to face Pierre. The young Haitian stood near the exit, arms crossed over his chest. There were no zombies near him, and the man in the linen suit was nowhere to be seen.

"Yann? You're in on this?"

Pierre refused to meet his eyes. "You don't understand. I told you not to come here."

"Are you…?" He trailed off, trying to figure out what question to ask. "Did you kidnap Jade? Do you know where she is?"

Without even realizing what he was doing, Professor crossed the distance to Pierre, grabbed his shirt front, thrust him backward, slamming him against the wall. Pierre's breath was driven from his lungs in a fine aerosol spray of saliva.

Professor shouted into his face. "What did you do? Where is she?"

Pierre coughed, gasping for air. Professor just tightened his grip and slammed the other man against the wall again. He half-expected Cesar's zombies to tear him off the treacherous historian, and that lent an urgency to his demands. "Where is she?"

"Gone," Pierre managed to croak after another tooth-loosening impact. "Won't… Find…"

Professor closed one hand around Pierre's neck, fingers digging in. If the zombies tried to pull him away, he would take a piece of Yann Pierre's throat with him.

But the zombies did not intervene.

After a few seconds of this, Pierre's eyes shifted, looking past Professor. "Tell… Him…"

From the other side of the room, Cesar L'Enfant let out a weary sigh. "Your woman is aboard the *Mohebbi*. It left Port au Prince early this morning."

Professor was still struggling to process everything. "Aboard? She's on a ship? Jade's on a ship? Where's it headed?"

"America." The old man shrugged when he said it, as if that were the limit of his knowledge.

Professor turned back to Pierre, wanting to squeeze the life out of the man. But he did not. There were still a lot of questions that needed answers, and Pierre couldn't talk if he was dead. "Why?"

Pierre managed to gasp out just one word. "Chosen."

Chosen? What the hell does that mean?

But before he could ask, Professor sensed movement behind him. Cesar's zombies were stirring, growing restive. The *bokor* himself was leaning on his walking stick, regarding Professor with an increasingly baleful glare.

"Leave this place," he said in that same ominous, flat monotone. "Leave Haiti. Do not return. Next time, I will not be so merciful."

Cesar held all the cards. Whatever his arrangement with Yann Pierre, it seemed like an uneasy alliance at best, and the gangster looked like he might be getting ready to cut his losses and simply kill both of them.

Professor let go of Pierre's throat and took a step back, turning to face Cesar. He pointed a finger at the old man, defiant. "If anything happens to Jade, so help me God, I *will* come back."

With that empty threat delivered, he reached down and snagged the handle of the case full of money, then spun on his heel and ran from the room like all the zombies on the

island were chasing him.
Maybe they were.

SEVEN

M/V Mohebbi

Jade reacted without thinking, flinging the contents of her makeshift food pouch at the man whose bulk filled the doorway of the walk-in cooler. His response was similarly reflexive; he threw up his arms to ward off the barrage. As he swatted the lightweight cereal containers away, Jade ducked under his swinging arms, squeezed past him, and kept going.

The snack had restored some of her vital energy, enough that she didn't feel like she was going to pass out as she dashed through the galley and out into the mess hall. Yet, even as she poured on the speed, zigzagging around the tables, a wave of despair crashed over her.

She was on a ship at sea. Where was she supposed to go now?

Now that they knew she had escaped her chains, the crew would turn the ship upside down to find her.

She wondered if she ought to double back, try to overpower the man, maybe knock him out or even kill him. That would buy her some time. Time to maneuver. Time to think. But that was a stupid idea. The man was twice... three times her size, and she wasn't exactly at peak physical condition. No, the only alternative to surrender was to keep moving.

She burst through the door into the dark corridor beyond, and then wheeled toward the exit to the staircase; backtracking felt like a safer choice than blundering through the towering superstructure. As she neared the end of the hall, a shout chased after her. The cook, or whatever he was, was yelling for her to stop, or maybe he was trying to sound the alarm. She didn't stop, but hit the door without slowing and burst out onto the metal landing.

With one hand sliding along the rail, just in case she lost her footing, she started down, taking quick little steps, and in a matter of seconds was standing on the main deck. It was exactly as she had last seen it—spacious, empty, quiet—but she knew this was only an illusion, the calm before the storm. She stood there, in the shadow of the superstructure, weighing her next decision. The most logical course of action was to play hide-and-seek, but should she try to lose herself in the stacks of shipping containers, or conceal herself within the body of the ship?

A sudden harsh ringing sound—like a school bell or an old-fashioned telephone—tore the quiet calm asunder.

Even in the 21st century, ships continued to use bells to sound the watch and, if necessary, raise alarm. The bell rang in short bursts interspersed with a single longer interval that echoed off the container stacks, filling the air with noise. There was a pattern to it, a specific message that the crew would recognize instantly.

And here comes the storm, she thought.

She sprinted across the open deck, heading for the narrow ledge she had earlier walked, once more choosing the familiar over the unknown. Just as she reached the corner, and before she could muster up the nerve to step up onto the gunwale, the world around her was suddenly filled with blinding light. Searchlights, the kind that might be used to search for sailors lost overboard, flashed on, but instead of scanning the dark water to either side of the ship, the beams splashed across the deck and began sweeping across the cargo stacks.

She froze. It was primal reaction, an evolutionary holdover, albeit one that sometimes did the trick. The eye was drawn to movement, so if she did not move... Well, that was the next best thing to being invisible, right?

Evidently, it was not. As a spotlight fell upon her motionless form, it stopped moving, then intensified as more lights joined it. She could hear shouting now, multiple voices overlapping into an incomprehensible burr that was mostly drowned out by the unceasing clamor of the bell. Since it was obvious that staying motionless wasn't working, she turned her gaze back toward the base of the superstructure to see a group of crewmen spilling from the main door, headed her way.

She took the step forward, rising onto the six-inch-wide gunwale. As soon as she did, she experienced a moment of disorientation and panic. The brief exposure to the spotlight had left her night blind. Everything beyond the line of shadow cast by the corner of the container was a few shades darker than she remembered, barely distinguishable. Worse, it was all backward now. When she had done this before, the cargo containers had formed a solid wall on her right side, something to lean against when she felt she might be losing her balance. Now, there was only empty space to her right. The wall was to her left, her non-dominant side and even though it was only mildly disconcerting, it was a distraction she didn't need. Gritting her teeth, she leaned her weight against her outstretched left hand, and started moving.

The lights could not reach her here, but while the alarm was partially muted the shouts were growing louder. She glanced back again, which was probably a bad idea, and saw the silhouetted heads of several crewmen peering around the corner of the container. They were holding back, perhaps wary of following her.

Or maybe they're just keeping an eye on me while their buddies take the long way around.

She brought her gaze forward again and started moving, shuffling her feet without lifting them, practically dragging her body along the upright surface to her left.

One step at a time, she told herself. *Just keep moving.*

Her eyes were slowly readjusting to the darkness, and after a minute of sliding along, she spotted another vertical line—the far corner, her destination—and quickened her pace. Ten yards became ten feet, five feet, five more short steps, one more, and then she was down, dropping back to the deck in the narrow canyon between the stacks of shipping containers.

For just a second, she felt a mordant impulse to run back to her former prison, the place where she had awakened to this nightmare... Snap on her chains and pretend nothing had happened.

A glance in that direction told her that ship had already sailed. A gaggle of crewmen, wielding flashlights and probably an improvised weapon or two, were charging down the aisle toward her.

She turned back to the edge of the ship, this time heading toward the row of containers on her left, closer to the bow end of the ship, and stepped onto the gunwale once more. The experience was no different but she knew that this time, she was advancing into unfamiliar territory. What would she find as she moved toward the front of the ship? A place to hide? A dead end? More crewmen ready to pummel her into submission and return her to her chains?

Never, she thought. *I'll die before I let them chain me again.*

It was an offhand thought. Throwaway bravado, except as soon as it popped into her head, she knew she really meant it.

She could feel the yawning emptiness to her right, beckoning her like the song of a siren, seducing her to ruination.

Are women immune to the songs of sirens? She wondered absently. She supposed the gender of the sailor didn't really make much of a difference. *I'll bet Professor would know.*

Professor.

She shook her head, trying to focus on the problem of staying alive. If they left her no choice, she would jump. She might even survive the impact with the water, though if that didn't kill her, and she wasn't sucked into the ship's propellers and cut up into fish bait, she would probably drift on the sea until she either died of thirst or became a snack for Mr. Jaws.

But then again, maybe she wouldn't have to jump. Maybe she would find a lifeboat, or a place to hide.

I really would like to see Professor again, she thought, and then decided, *No, I am going to see him again.*

She started moving, more surefooted now, taking full steps, one foot in front of the other, rather than shuffling as she had before. She could just barely make out the sharp line of the gunwale, slicing forward ahead of her before disappearing into the gloom. Further out, miles ahead it seemed, she could see twinkling lights, too bright to be stars; another ship she guessed. It had to be miles away, but the simple fact of its presence filled her with hope.

I'm not alone out here, wherever here is.

She just had to keep going, stay alive, stay one step ahead of her captors. Emboldened, she quickened her step. The wall of containers beside her seemed to go on forever, easily twice the distance of the stacks that had stood between her and the bridge castle. After traversing the distance of a football field, her journey ended, but not as she had expected. Instead of continuing past the cargo area to open deck, the gunwale abruptly rose, sweeping up at least ten feet, maybe more. The upraised bow was designed to prevent the ship from becoming swamped when driving head-on into high seas, but for Jade, it was a dead end. She would never be able to shinny up the nearly vertical rise, and the gap between the containers and the inside wall was too narrow for her to slip through.

Or was it?

She checked the distance again. The containers had been loaded in flush against the bottom edge of the raised barrier, but the gunwale flared out, just a little, as it rose from the deck. That distance was only about six inches near the bottom, but the width continued to increase as it went up—almost eighteen inches at the level of Jade's head.

I can get through that, she thought, and promptly insinuated herself into the gap.

She immediately discovered the difference between what was physically possible and what was practical. The space was indeed wide enough to accommodate her, but not wide enough to allow much of a range of motion. She could only move sideways, squirming forward a few inches at a time. She had to twist her legs awkwardly at the knees, splaying her feet out in opposite directions like a ballerina preparing to perform a *plie*. Her feet kept getting jammed into the tight angle at the bottom of the artificial crevasse, and the only way to get them free and keep moving forward was to brace herself up, pressing her palms against the shipping container wall in front of her and her backside against the gunwale behind.

Every inch was a struggle. Desperation was an effective lubricant, but the ordeal was taking its toll. Her will to survive and a couple bowls of Cheerios could only take her so far.

Fortunately, she didn't have that far to go. After only about ten feet of the hellish crevasse traverse, she reached the end of the last row of containers. With a final push, she burst free, tumbling forward onto the foredeck. On hands and knees, she looked up and took stock of her surroundings.

An enormous mast dominated the foredeck. It was at least as high as the aft superstructure, and hung with lights and various antennae. Lined up to either side of it were several small, intermittently spaced freestanding structures that looked remarkably like aluminum garden sheds. To her right, the head-high starboard gunwale continued forward a few yards before curving inward, toward the center of the ship and disappearing from her view behind the sheds.

Jade was still trying to figure out what to do next when a pair of flashlight-waving crewmen emerged from behind the cargo stacks. As their lights played across the deck, moving inexorably toward her, she started forward hoping to reach the relative concealment of the sheds before they spotted her. A shout signaled her failure.

She cut back toward the starboard gunwale, following its curve toward the bow. From the corner of her eye, she could see the two men diverging, one giving chase, the other presumably heading toward the port gunwale in order to come around from the other direction. She was almost out of moves. More crewmen would be arriving soon, and then that would be the end of her bid for freedom. Even the ultimate escape of leaping from the ship and taking her chances in the water below was denied her; there was no way to climb the high steel wall. No ladders or handholds.

Rather than let herself be caught between the two crewmen like a baseball player stuck in the hotbox between first base and second, she pivoted across the open foredeck, heading toward the mast. She had chosen it as an intermediate destination simply because it was there, but as she neared it, a plan—a desperate one—began to form.

There was a ladder on the mast, welded steel rungs enclosed in a cylindrical safety cage above the eight-foot mark. Jade barely stopped herself in time to avoid colliding with the mast, then stepped onto the lowest rung and hauled herself off the deck, but when the top of her head was level with the bottom of the cage, she reached back and grabbed it instead. She took a couple more steps up the ladder while curling her body around the metal cage and pulling herself up its exterior, using widely spaced crosspieces of the frame as rungs.

Something brushed against her right foot. She glanced down and saw that one of the crewman had snagged her boot. She kicked, trying to shake him loose, but he held on, tenacious, and then started pulling her toward him. Her fingers, which were curled around the flat strap assembly of the cage, immediately registered the increase load. If she didn't let go, the edges would cut her fingers off at the knuckles.

But she was not about to surrender.

She slipped her left foot off of the rung and raked it down the inside of her right ankle. Her boot sole crushed the crewman's fingers and he let go with an audible cry. Her body swung away from the mast to dangle from the outside of the cage. Despite the pain shooting through her hands, she heaved herself up, trying to get her feet out of the man's reach and onto the bottom of the safety cage.

The second crewman appeared below her as well. He started up the ladder staying within the confines of the cage. He did not stop to engage her, but scurried past, intent on reaching the top before her. Jade however had no intention of climbing that high. As soon as she got both her feet on the frame, she let go with her left hand and allowed her body to swing away from the cage.

Six feet away and just a couple feet below her was a utility shed. Fixing her gaze on it, she flexed her knees and then launched herself away from the mast, turning in mid-air to land on her feet atop the shed's roof. The aluminum popped and buckled with the sudden addition of her weight, and for a terrifying instant, she thought she had overestimated its structural integrity. It held together however. She steadied herself there, but only for a moment, fixing her gaze on the roof of the next shed in line, and the one beyond it, and then she started running again.

When she reached the edge of the shed, she leaped across the narrow gap to the next one, and kept going; jumping from roof to roof, building up momentum for one final leap across the deck to the elevated starboard gunwale. She easily cleared the distance to the flared wall and flung her hands over its top a millisecond before the rest of her slammed into it.

The broadside impact hurt like hell, but she had been expecting it and didn't let it slow her down. Instead, she pulled herself up, planting the soles of her boots flat against the metal wall—a technique rock climbers called "smearing"—for an additional boost. She gained a foot on her first try, enough to hook her left elbow over the top. Another push, and she was able to fold her torso over the wall. She twisted sideways, got her right leg up and over the gunwale, and sat up astride it, half of her aboard the ship, half out, dangling above the void.

A breeze tickled her face. It wasn't actual wind, but rather the still air that she, and the ship beneath her, were disturbing with their passage. Until that moment, she hadn't given much thought to the fact that the ship was constantly, relentlessly moving forward.

How fast? Twenty knots? That seemed about right.

She sat there, staring out at the twinkling lights on the horizon, vaguely aware of the crewmen gathering below, clamoring for her to come down. She was going to come down eventually, she couldn't stay where she was forever.

But would she choose the relative safety of chains or the uncertainty of a plunge into the deep?

"The Devil or the deep blue sea?" she murmured.

No contest. She had grown up with the latter; it was part of her, and she of it. The Devil—the chains—was a less certain fate. True, while there was life, there was hope, but if she surrendered to them now, it would be a defeat from which she might never recover.

She planted her palms flat atop the gunwale, and pushed up to a crouch, as if preparing to ride the nose of the world's biggest surfboard. Then, slowly, smoothly, she stood up.

The wind pushed against her, nudging her back toward the foredeck, as if to say *you really don't want to do this*. The men below fell into a shocked silence, perhaps fearful of accidentally cajoling her into taking that final fateful step.

You don't want me doing that, do you, she thought. *Can't sell what you don't have.*

She took a deep breath, leaning into the wind just a little, and stared out into the night. The ship's lights sparkled off the water in the distance, but the area surrounding the hull remained cloaked in shadow. How far down was it? A hundred feet?

Okay. This is kind of scary.

The cracks fracturing her resolve were small, but structural. If she didn't jump now, she knew she never would.

She took another breath, held it, and closed her eyes.

Just one more step....

That was when she heard the helicopters in the distance.

Jade's curiosity got the better of her, and contrary to conventional wisdom, probably saved her. She opened her eyes and saw that the distant twinkling lights were definitely not stars, and not even all that distant anymore, but drawing closer with each passing second.

There were three of them, and Jade didn't think they were the same kind of helicopter as the one that had taken off from the ship earlier. The roar of their jet turbines fought for supremacy with the rapid-fire thump-thump of the rotors. These aircraft sounded more powerful than that first one, the difference between a mid-sized sedan and a monster truck. Searchlights lanced out from formation, transfixing her with in their beams. She wasn't at all surprised when an electronically amplified voice boomed from the heavens.

"This is the United States Coast Guard. Heave to and prepare to be boarded."

EIGHT

It didn't exactly feel like a rescue.

Jade was trying to be patient about it. She knew the Coast Guardsmen had protocols and procedures to follow, but her initial sense of relief at their arrival was fading fast.

Several of them had fast-roped down from the helicopters and immediately taken the crewmen harassing Jade into custody. In their dark tactical combat attire, armed with M4 assault carbines, they looked more like Navy SEALs than Coasties—but she knew the Coast Guard's mission encompassed law-enforcement as well as maritime rescue. Once the crew were secured with flexi-cuffs, the Coast Guard commandos had helped her down from the gunwale, and then promptly zip-tied her as well.

Her efforts to explain that she was a hostage, an unwilling abductee, seemed to fall on deaf ears. She was left there on the foredeck, surrounded by the men who had just chased her all over the ship, while the takeover of the ship continued.

Protocols, she told herself. They had to follow their SOP—standard operating procedures—which meant first securing the entire scene, treating everyone as a potentially hostile suspect. At least she was safe, and there was light at end of the tunnel. Eventually it would get sorted out and she would be released. Free.

But why was it taking so long? Wasn't it obvious that she was the victim here?

She could hear the sounds of activity. Helicopters touched down at various points on the ship behind or possibly on top of the cargo stacked on the deck, and then took off again just as quickly, leaving the vicinity, probably headed back to shore. After a time—it seemed like at least an hour—someone activated one of the ship's boom cranes and began moving shipping containers around. Clearly, the Coast Guard were looking for something, and it occurred to Jade that the interdiction might not have anything to do with her at all.

That would explain why they were treating her like a suspect. She supposed she should thank her lucky stars that they just happened to show up when they did, but right now, she just wanted a chance to tell her story to whomever was in charge.

After another hour or so, the Coast Guardsmen started herding the prisoners—Jade included—down toward the bridge castle. There was a narrow aisle between the cargo stacks, running down the center of the ship. Jade had suspected as much, but still felt a little dismayed by the fact that she had taken the much more difficult route along the gunwale, not once but twice.

Oh well, live and learn.

The deck in front of the superstructure was already crowded with people. In addition to the Coast Guard personnel—many of whom were dressed in the more traditional dark blue work uniform instead of commando gear—there were at least a hundred people, maybe even two hundred, seated on the deck in groups. The split between male and female looked about even, though maybe there were a few more women than men. All appeared to be of African descent—Jade assumed they were Haitians. All were young, early twenties, teenagers perhaps, and a few were preadolescent children. And all of them looked like they'd just stumbled out of hell itself.

Jade knew the feeling, and knew exactly what she was looking at.

Slaves.

Human trafficking was the preferred term since it encompassed other forms of exploitation, but it all came down to the same thing. People depriving other people of their humanity, treating them like animals, like property.

It was much more of a problem in places where poverty was endemic, places like Haiti. Children were often sold into servitude to pay for the debts of their parents, sent to work in the houses of the wealthy or on sugarcane plantations. Many however were sent off to foreign destinations to be used for labor or even forced into prostitution. Removing a person from their homeland, severing all ties with family and culture, had always been the slavers' preferred method of breaking a person, stripping away their will to resist.

That's what they were going to do to me, too, she thought, feeling a pang of empathy.

The Coast Guard people were moving among the freed slaves, handing out bottled water and conducting cursory medical examinations. Jade and the other restrained crewmen were lined up against a bulkhead and ordered to sit down and keep quiet. Jade wanted to ask for some water, but got the distinct impression that, as long as the Coasties thought she was with the crew, she would get only their scorn.

Fair enough, she thought. *But when can I make my damn phone call?*

She sensed she would get her chance to explain when a pair of men wearing blue windbreakers and ball caps emblazoned with white letters that read, "POLICE—IMMIGRATIONS AND CUSTOMS ENFORCEMENT" began pulling individual crewmen away from the group, ushering them into the superstructure, presumably for interrogation.

"Hey! Take me. I want to confess everything." She figured that would get her to the guy in charge a lot faster than protesting her innocence.

The men exchanged a glance and then one of them shrugged. "Why not?" He came over and grabbed her biceps, pulling her to her feet. "Move it, sweet cheeks."

Jade resisted the urge to put her knee in the man's crotch, and did as instructed, following the other prisoners into the bridge castle.

She was brought to another familiar spot—the mess hall—which had been transformed into an interrogation room, with more ICE agents interviewing members of the crew, most of whom seemed to be loudly denying any knowledge of the ship's human cargo. Jade knew better, and grinned at the thought of incriminating them all.

The two agents sat her down at a table opposite another agent. The guy had a shaved head and Novocain dull expression—kind of like a smaller, uglier Vin Diesel. He studied her for a moment, his gaze a vaguely contemptuous leer, then said, "Speak English?"

"Depends on who I'm talking to," she replied, and then regretted it. This guy didn't look like he had much of a sense humor and she needed him on her side.

The man's lip curled into something that was more sneer than smile. "That a fact?"

She felt things were already starting to go off the rails, so she quickly added. "Yes. I'm an American. I was kidnapped from Port au Prince. My name is Jade Ihara."

"Sounds like a Jap name. Thought you said you were American?"

"I am. I was born in Hawaii."

"Oh." The man drew the word out until it dripped with sarcasm. "I suppose you can show me your birth certificate, too."

"Really?" Jade snapped, but then brought herself back under control. "My passport is probably still in Port au Prince. I told you. I was kidnapped. From my hotel. I can prove who I am if you'll just let me make a phone call."

"Kidnapped." The man rubbed his chin thoughtfully. "That happens sometimes." He tilted his head to the side and gave her another of his creepy appraising looks. It was almost as bad as when her captors had looked at her teeth. "You good with nails?"

"Excuse me?"

"Nails. Mani-pedi. Asian chicks are usually pretty good with that stuff. Maybe that's why they grabbed you. Maybe they were planning to sell you to a nail salon. Which ain't that bad I suppose. Better than the old rub-and-tug, right?"

Jade worked her jaw sideways and bit down until the urge to scream at the man subsided. "They drugged me," she said, speaking slowly, enunciating every word. "They took me from my hotel and chained me in a shipping container. I got free and was trying to escape. The crew is in on it. They were chasing me when you got here. But there are these other guys, the barefoot Klansmen. They're the ones running the show, I think. They left by helicopter before you guys got here."

The agent nodded, slowly, condescendingly, and then made a show of writing something in his notebook. "Barefoot. Klansmen. That's Klan with a K, right? Not like Scottish Highland clans?"

"It's just what I call them. They were wearing robes and pointy hats. And they had torches. Actual torches, like in the movies. It reminded me of the KKK guys."

"Pointy hats," he said. "And they were barefoot?"

"Yes. They came in and poked and prodded me." She shuddered at the memory. "Look I'm not making this up. I can show you where they kept me. I'll show you the chains."

She met his gaze, imploring him to help with her eyes, and was surprised to see that his expression had changed. Less boorish, more serious. He stood up abruptly, unclipping a folding knife from his belt as he walked around to her side of the table. The knife flicked open in his hand. He lifted her up, urgently but not as roughly as she expected. She felt something sliding against the skin of her wrist, and then felt a sudden release as the plastic cuffs were cut away.

She rubbed her wrists, noting for the first time since her escape from the manacles the deep abrasions they had left behind. "That's more like it," she murmured.

"Show me." He made an open-handed gesture, indicating that she should take the lead.

Jade considered asking him to let her use the restroom and maybe get something more to eat. She really wanted to get to a phone, to call Professor and let him know that she was still alive. But there was no telling how long the agent's change of mood would last. She decided to tough it out. Maybe once he saw the chains—the wrist manacles and the old antique locks—he'd treat her differently.

Either way, what was ten more minutes? She could handle it.

As she headed for the door, she looked over her shoulder at him. "I didn't catch your name."

A frown flickered across his face. "Special Agent Purcell."

"Nice to meet you Special Agent Purcell. I'm Jade."

"You already told me that."

He sounded impatient, so she stopped trying. She backtracked down to the main deck and then headed for the center aisle. Everything looked different now, partly because some of the containers had been moved, probably to get access to the containers where the ship's human cargo had been imprisoned, but mostly because for the first time, she was moving about as a free woman.

She turned down the first row she came to, heading toward the starboard side of the ship. If she was where she thought she was, her former prison was about halfway down on the right, and unless someone else had come along after her escape and closed it, the door would still be unlatched.

It was.

"There." She pointed at a pair of red doors, all that was visible of the container's exterior. One of the doors was slightly ajar. "That's the one."

Purcell took a small flashlight from his pocket and shone it at the door, moving it up and down as if checking for booby traps. He nodded to Jade. "Open it."

"There's nothing else in there," she said, unsure why he wanted her to go first, but then shrugged and did as directed, pulling the half-open door toward her.

The interior of the container was strangely unfamiliar. She had spent uncounted hours here, left it only a short while ago, and yet standing in the opening, she had no memory of the place. Then Purcell's light swept down its empty length and illumed a dark serpentine mass on the floor, rising up one wall like a creeper vine, and she remembered everything.

She shuddered, the earlier queasy feeling returning with a vengeance.

"Those are the chains?" asked Purcell.

Jade nodded.

He motioned for her to go in, and despite the fact that every fiber of her being was urging her to run away, she complied, but only after pushing the door all the way open so that there was no chance of accidentally getting shut inside.

Purcell walked beside her, matching her pace until they were standing over the chains.

She had barely gotten a look at them during her imprisonment. Just a brief glimpse of the manacles, during the torch-lit inspection, and that through eyes that were stinging from exposure to light after so many hours in total darkness. Now she could see what she had only felt earlier.

The chains were covered in rust and looked old. Some of the links looked almost rusted through. She was surprised they had held up to her thrashing.

Purcell knelt down and picked something off the floor, one of the padlocks. Like the chains and manacles, it too was heavily oxidized.

"This thing looks vintage," Purcell murmured, turning the lock over in his hand.

"Yeah," Jade remembered how she had successfully picked it. It had almost been too easy. Of course, without that little strip of wire from her bra, she wouldn't have been able to do much of anything.

"They go to all the trouble of kidnapping you out of your hotel. Getting you here to this boat. And then use these shitty old antiques to hold you? Does that make sense to you?"

Jade didn't like the agent's tone at all. "About as much sense as running around barefoot wearing pointy hats and carrying torches. I didn't make this up."

"And they never said anything about why they did it?"

Jade searched her memory, shuddering again. "They said I was healthy. And then they... They took a vote. I don't know what it was about, but it was unanimous. Then they threw some water in my face and said something. Latin, I think it was."

"Latin," said Purcell, nodding. "Like on this?"

He held up the lock and then tossed it to her. The unexpectedness of the action surprised her, and instead of trying to catch it, she jolted and stepped out of the way. The lock hit the floor with a heavy clank that echoed in the hollow emptiness.

"What the hell did you do that for?" Jade snapped. "You scared the crap out of me!"

Purcell just stared back, coldly. "Look at it."

Shaking her head in annoyance, she bent down to retrieve the fallen padlock. Even before she touched it, she could see what had prompted his question. There was something engraved on the back of the lock body.

SERVVS.

Jade read, or rather spelled it out, one letter at a time. "If this is supposed to be Latin—Classical Latin—then one of the Vs would actually be a U. Servus? I think that means 'slave.'"

She looked up to see what he thought of her translation. Her blood went cold when she realized that he was now pointing his gun at her.

"You're kidding, right?" Jade couldn't actually think of a better response, but whether the question was directed at Purcell or whatever entity was in charge of her fate, she couldn't say.

There was no trace of humor in Purcell's eyes however. His cruel unsmiling lips were pursed so tightly, his mouth seemed to disappear, barely opening when he finally spoke. All he said was, "It will look better if you attack me."

"Attack you?" Jade said, but even before the words were out, she realized the deeper meaning of his words. *Attack me, so I can kill you and make it look like self-defense.*

She realized something else, too. He was going to kill her no matter what she did.

So, she obliged him.

His mouth opened again, perhaps to goad her or maybe even apologize, but before he could utter a syllable, she was moving. She dropped straight down, out of his direct line of fire, and in the same motion, hurled the lock at his face.

The gun discharged, the report absolutely deafening. She could feel heat on her face, something like the spatter of cooking grease, and her nostrils were filled with a sulfurous odor. But the bullet didn't hit her, at least she didn't think so. She had heard stories about people being so pumped up on adrenaline that they could perform seemingly superhuman feats, even after sustaining a mortal injury. She was definitely feeling an endorphin rush, but was pretty sure she would have felt something—a bump or a stinging sensation—if she had been shot.

She didn't linger to see if her throw struck its target, but pivoted and took off running for the exit. Halfway there, a premonition of danger prompted her to duck her head, and right on cue, a bullet sizzled through the air next to her, slamming into the half-open door.

Then she was outside again, her second escape from the container, only this time the hunter was already on her trail. As she sprinted down the artificial canyon between the rows, the same route she had followed the first time, some part of her was grappling with Purcell's unprovoked attack. The guy was a douchebag, sure, but why was he trying to kill her? She had been careful to avoid pissing him off. Mostly. She definitely hadn't said or done anything to earn a bullet. So what was his deal?

The answer was obvious. *He's one of them.*

There were probably some logical flaws with that conclusion, but parsing it would take more brain power than she could spare at the moment. Maybe when—if—she got herself out of this mess.

There was another report behind her, and the corduroy zipping sound of a bullet creasing the air right beside her. The familiar gunwale loomed ahead; fifteen feet, ten… She had to slow down or risk going right over the side and into oblivion, but slowing down would give him time to put her in his sights, so she swerved to the left, and then cut back to the right, using the turns to bleed off some of her momentum like a skier cutting across the face of a steep downhill slope. She was nearly running parallel to the half wall when she reached it, and with a light hop, she bounded onto it, leaning into the container wall as she ran toward the stern of the ship.

Jade had not worked out exactly what she would do when she reached it. Purcell probably wasn't acting alone. It would be his word against hers. If the Coasties and ICE agents didn't shoot her outright, they would lock her up, isolate her. Purcell would no doubt make sure she never got a chance to have her day in court. She would meet with a fatal accident or conveniently commit suicide.

So what did that leave her?

She knew the answer; she just wasn't ready to admit it.

Ten yards along the gunwale, she was.

Another report split the air. The round pinged off the container beside her, throwing a spray of hot metal sparks at her. She glanced back, even though she knew it was a mistake, and saw Purcell, leaning carefully over the gunwale, steadying his pistol with both hands, taking his time to make sure the next shot found its mark.

Jade entertained a fleeting notion of spinning around and charging toward him. Professor was always saying, "Run away from a knife, but run toward a gun." Of course, the reasoning behind that old chestnut was that you couldn't outrun a bullet, so you might as well do something desperate. Maybe the craziness of the kamikaze rush would leave him too paralyzed to pull the trigger.

Probably not, though. He was going to pull the trigger, and he wasn't going to miss. Not unless she did the truly unthinkable.

It would probably kill her, but then again, maybe it wouldn't. Either way though, she was going to take the power of life and death away from him, and into her own hands.

She turned her body parallel to the ship, her back to the water below, placed her palms flat against the container wall, and pushed.

PART TWO: EXILE

NINE

The helicopter—a Sikorsky MH-60T "Jayhawk" painted with the distinctive orange and white color scheme of the United States Coast Guard—touched down on the ad hoc helipad established atop the stacked shipping containers on the mid-deck of the Liberian-flagged cargo hauler *M/V Mohebbi*. Unlike the other helicopters that had been coming and going with some regularity since the interdiction on the high seas several hours earlier, this aircraft was based out of Miami, rather than Houston—which was both the ultimate destination for the freighter and the jumping off point for the intercept operation. There was one other significant difference—the Jayhawk carried only a single passenger.

As soon as the bird's wheels bumped against the shipping container, that passenger hopped out. With one hand firmly holding his brown Explorer fedora in place, he hastened out from under the spinning rotor disc, and moved to the taped border of the helipad where a pair of Coast Guardsmen and a man with a shaved head wearing the ubiquitous blue windbreaker of a federal law enforcement agent were waiting to greet him. The latter had a ragged-looking gash on his forehead, held shut with butterfly sutures, and made no effort to disguise his annoyance. Handshakes were exchanged—the bare minimum of cordiality—but the roar of the idling Jayhawk made conversation impossible. The noise abruptly increased in pitch and intensity, and with a blast of air nearly strong enough to knock a grown man off his feet, the helicopter rose once more and moved off in the direction of the sun which was just breaking over the horizon.

In the relative quiet that followed, the man in the blue windbreaker spoke. "You're Chapman?"

Professor nodded. "And you must be Special Agent Purcell."

Purcell just frowned. "I don't know what arrangement you made with the Coast Guard, Mr. Chapman, but this is my crime scene. Unless you've got some credentials that say otherwise, you're not authorized to be here. You can either call that bird back, or you can ride back on one of the cutters, but you're getting off this ship, one way or another."

Professor ignored the rant. "My colleague, Jade Ihara, was kidnapped in Port au Prince. She's here, on this ship. And I'm not going anywhere until I find her."

"She's not here."

Professor squared off, facing Purcell, hands on hips in a classic confrontational posture. Purcell was bigger than he and probably accustomed to using his size to intimidate others—suspects and subordinates alike. Professor was not intimidated in the slightest. "Yes. She is."

"No. She isn't," Purcell shot back. "She jumped."

Professor took an unconscious step backward. He felt like someone had just let the air out him. His fists slid away from his hips. His arms hung limp at his sides like spaghetti noodles. "Jumped?"

"Right after she assaulted me. I doubt she made it, but the Coast Guard have a couple cutters running lanes in the area, looking for the body. Whatever the sharks don't eat."

Professor was having difficulty hearing the Homeland Security agent, and even more trouble believing what he was hearing. "Assaulted you? There must be some kind of mistake."

Purcell jabbed a finger at the wound on his forehead. "You're right. This is it. Maybe you didn't know this Ihara chick as well as you thought."

"Jade wouldn't just attack you. There must be some kind—" He stopped himself. "Start from the beginning. Tell me everything."

The agent glanced at the Coast Guard officers with a look that said, *Can you believe the nerve of this guy?* Then he faced Professor again. "I'm sorry, but just who the hell are you? Really? The Coast Guard wouldn't fly you all the way out here if you were just a concerned party."

"I can't get into the particulars, but let's just say we have the same employer."

Purcell rolled his eyes, a touch too dramatically. "Ah, you're a spook. That's frigging outstanding. And Ihara? Her, too?"

"I can't get into the—"

"Of course, you can't. Well, unless you can give me something on the record, as far as I'm concerned, you're a tourist and you're in my way."

"Fine. I'll call your boss." Professor snapped, reaching into a pocket for his satellite enabled smart phone. His initial shock was giving way to numbness. Denial. Jade couldn't be dead, not after everything he had done to find her. None of this made any sense. She wouldn't have attacked a federal agent, not without some kind of....

The memory of Cesar L'Enfant and his zombie protectors came to him, unbidden. What if the *bokor* had dosed Jade with zombie dust before putting her on the ship? That might explain her erratic behavior.

Purcell's grating voice pulled him back to the moment. "All right. You don't have to do that."

Professor looked back at him, his finger poised to make a call to Tam Broderick.

Purcell gestured to a ladder, the top of which protruded from the side of the container. "Follow me. I'll break it down for you."

After descending to the main deck, Purcell led the way through the maze of corridors between the stacked containers. As they walked, he reviewed the events leading up to the seizure of the *Mohebbi*. "A few days ago, we raided a trailer in the Houston area where several victims of human exploitation were being housed."

"Human exploitation. You mean 'slaves.'"

"I mean 'slaves,'" Purcell confirmed, matter-of-factly. "Some of the evidence we recovered indicated that this ship would be transporting a hundred and fifty *units*."

"So that's why you were already here, even before I put in the call to intercept the ship. Was Jade with the others? Was she one of those units?"

"No, she wasn't. We found her on the foredeck. It

looked like she was being chased by the crew."

"She escaped?" *That's my girl,* he added silently.

Purcell cleared his throat. "We found something else in that trailer." He took out his own smart phone and after tapping the touch screen a few times, passed it to Professor. The device displayed a screen capture of an email message.

To: All
From: Undisclosed
Subject: The Chosen

Professor's heart skipped a beat. Yann Pierre had offered that one word—Chosen—as his explanation for luring Jade to Haiti and arranging her abduction.

The rest of the message was brief, but cryptic.

A potential candidate has been identified and will shortly undergo the Servus Trial. If the Goddess wills, she will escape the Chains of Slavery, demonstrating that she is worthy to enter the temple and retrieve the sacred relics of our covenant.

Pray that she does.

The time is near, brothers and sisters. Gird yourselves for battle.

Professor read the message twice before handing the phone back. With an effort, he kept his face an emotionless mask. "I think your human traffickers are religious fanatics."

"Heh, yeah. Something like that."

"*Servus* is Latin for 'slave,'" Professor went on. "But there are a lot of goddesses. Any idea which one they're talking about?"

"We're looking into it, but clearly this Chosen One is going to lead this cult in some kind of violent action. Maybe a terror attack."

"What does this have to do with Jade?"

Purcell gestured ahead to an open container, and then went inside. As he strode down the length of the container, he produced a MiniMaglite and directed its beam to the only thing in the otherwise empty chamber—a length of chain with manacles and padlocks at either end, threaded through an iron shackle mounted to the wall. He handed one of the locks to Professor and then shone his light on the back, illuming the letters carved into it.

"Servus," Professor muttered. "So?"

"Your colleague admitted to having escaped from these chains. Right before she tried to kill me. With this." He shook the lock for emphasis. "Face it. Jade Ihara was this Chosen One. I don't know, maybe they brainwashed her or something. Got inside her head, like Patty Hearst. Or maybe she was always a part of it. People keep secrets. I don't know, but she definitely went over to the dark side."

Professor didn't know what to say, so he just stared at the other man.

Jade had *not* gone over to the dark side. He refused to believe it, just as he refused to accept that she was really dead. And really, what proof was there for either? Just Purcell's word.

Okay, Chapman. Think. Focus. What do you really know?

Assuming Jade had actually attacked Purcell, what had provoked her? Maybe she was disoriented from her captivity, or had mistaken the brute for one of her captors. Maybe Purcell was dirty. Maybe *he* had tried to assault *her*.

He could definitely believe that, but how to prove it?

He stared back at the agent, looking for any hint of culpability or deception. Purcell endured his stare for a moment, then blinked and looked away. "Satisfied? We're done here."

Professor remained motionless.

Assuming Jade had really jumped over the side, was it possible she might still be alive?

He had reviewed and memorized the technical specifications of the *Mohebbi* on the flight from Port au Prince to Miami. The ship was a small feeder-type cargo vessel, rated for 420 TEU—twenty-foot equivalent units, a common but imprecise measurement of cargo space— capable of carrying about 5,000 tons of deadweight cargo. Its draft—the measurement from keel to waterline when fully loaded—was twenty-eight feet. The main deck was roughly double that distance, which meant Jade would have fallen about sixty feet—roughly the height of a six-story building before hitting the water.

That was an absolutely survivable fall; professional cliff divers jumped anywhere from sixty to eighty-five feet. The record was close to one hundred fifty feet. But it was one thing to make a clean dive into familiar water. Quite another to jump off a moving cargo ship in the dead of night. And even the professionals sometimes hit the water the wrong way and broke their necks or got knocked unconscious, and drowned.

But Purcell said they hadn't found a body. If Jade had died on impact, her body would have floated to the surface, at least long enough for the Coast Guard to pull her out of the sea.

Assumption: She's alive.

"Purcell!"

The federal agent stopped, turned to look at him.

"Can you get me out to one of those search cutters?"

Purcell regarded him for several seconds before offering a grim smile. "I think I can arrange that." He paused a beat, and then added. "Hey, I hope you find her. I really do."

After another helicopter ride out to one of the Coast Guard patrol ships searching the area where Jade had gone overboard, Professor placed a call to Tam Broderick. Protecting Jade was his primary mission and Tam was his boss, so he was obligated to make contact and report his failure, but that wasn't his primary motivation.

After bringing her up to date and explaining his intention to join the search, he broached the real reason for his call. "This Special Agent Purcell is a real piece of work. He insists that Jade attacked him, and I'm wondering if maybe he didn't give her a good reason to. Can you look into him? Check his disciplinary record. Any complaints against him? Sexual assault, or anything like that."

Tam was silent for a long time, so long that Professor thought maybe the call had gotten lost in the ether. "Pete, you need to be very careful."

The admonition caught him off guard. Tam Broderick rarely advised caution. "Excuse me?"

"In case you hadn't noticed, we're in a brave new world," Tam said. "I think you know what I'm talking about. Our situation is... Evolving."

"You're being cryptic, Tam. You're never cryptic."

"When we launched the Myrmidons, we had one mission: take down the Dominion. We knew it would be a long fight. We were ready for that. But somehow, even though we managed to win most of the battles, we lost the war."

"That's nonsense."

"It's not. The Dominion couldn't achieve their goals with outright violence, so instead they used fear. Right-wing extremism, racism and xenophobia. That's our new normal, and it's everywhere. Even in the government. I don't want to suggest that our boss is a Dominion sleeper, but he's definitely sympathetic to their goals."

Professor didn't need to ask what "new boss" Tam was referring to. "I get that, Tam. And I know you're on the razor's edge with this. But all I care about is finding out what happened to Jade, and Purcell isn't giving me the whole story."

"Purcell is DHS."

"So?"

"The Department of Homeland Security is now the most powerful civilian agency in the government—with nearly absolute power on American soil. And Carl Lavelle, the Secretary of DHS, is the son of a known Dominion leader. If he wanted to, the President could reassign the Myrmidons to DHS by executive order, and there wouldn't be a thing I could do stop him or Lavelle from wiping us out of existence with the stroke of a pen. I'm not ready to poke that hornet's nest. We're the last line of defense, Pete. And right now, we need to keep a very low profile."

"Well, what am I supposed to do? Pretend this didn't happen? Purcell is lying."

"If you're right, then it's that much more important for *you* to keep a low profile." Tam allowed that to sink in before continuing. "First things first. Jade needs you. And she's the only one who can answer your questions. Find her."

Tam did not qualify the statement by adding, *If she's still alive.* It would have served no purpose.

"Stay close to the investigation if you can," she went on. "Find out more about this goddess cult, or whatever it is. Your contact in Haiti…"

"Yann Pierre."

"Maybe he's involved. Maybe this has something to do with voodoo."

Professor shook his head. "That's unlikely. Vodou practitioners wouldn't use the word 'goddess.'"

"Regardless, these people kidnapped Jade for a reason. And if that email you read is correct, they may be preparing for some kind of attack. Stopping fanatics from killing innocent people is still our primary mission."

"Understood." But he couldn't help thinking about the first part of the message. *If the goddess wills, she will escape the Chains of Slavery, demonstrating that she is worthy to enter the temple and retrieve the sacred relics of our covenant.*

Jade *had* escaped those chains. He just hoped that the goddess, whoever she was, still had plans for her Chosen.

TEN

The leap from the deck of the container ship had been a physical shock to the system, but Jade had not sustained any serious injury, which on balance, meant the experience had not been nearly as bad as she had anticipated. Indeed, she had not expected to survive, so when she hit the water and felt the pain shooting through her entire body, the air driven from her lungs, the sudden pressure of descending twenty feet of water in a fraction of a second squeezing her head like a vise, some part of her recognized that these sensations were proof that she was still alive.

Despite the circumstances, her decision to jump had not been a purely suicidal gesture. She knew, in principle at least, how to survive a high fall, though just how high this one would be, she really didn't know. She had kept her body vertical, toes pointing down, feet pressed together to form a sort of arrowhead to pierce the water. Arms tucked in, hands covering her crotch, butt muscles clenched and pressing together—a necessary precaution, but one that did not absolutely preclude getting a salt water enema. At the moment of contact with the water, she was supposed to throw her arms and legs out wide to keep from sinking too deep, but the impact left her too stunned to perform the braking maneuver, and so she shot like a torpedo into the dark depths.

After desperately clawing her way back to the surface—another ordeal that she had not completely believed she would survive—she bobbed back to the dark surface of the tepid water, and saw the imposing vertical wall of the freighter beside her.

She could see it moving, and felt the eddies of water rolling off the hull as it drove relentlessly forward. If she did not get clear, those eddies would pull her into the ship's screws, so gritting her teeth against the pain, she rolled over in the water and started swimming as hard and fast as she could.

It wasn't until she was surfing the vessel's wake that she realized there were other ships in the water.

At first, all she could see were lights bobbing above the surface. Intuitively grasping that these were the running lights of other vessels—probably Coast Guard cutters supporting the interdiction of the slave ship—she began swimming toward them. She didn't know whether the Coasties would save her or shoot her, or if they would save her just to let Purcell shoot her later on, but knew that if she couldn't get aboard one of those vessels, she would have a very long swim ahead of her. The only problem was that the cutters were matching the freighter's speed—probably somewhere in the neighborhood of fifteen knots—which meant that even if she managed to get close to one of them, she was as likely to be run over as she was to be rescued from the water.

Still, it was something to do.

Then it seemed as if Lady Luck had decided to throw her a bone. The Coast Guard flotilla slowed and began moving back and forth across the wake of the cargo hauler.

In retrospect, it was not such a remarkable development. They were looking for her. Purcell, or someone else aboard the freighter, had alerted them to Jade's desperate plunge. And once more, she found herself caught between uncertain fates. Let herself be rescued by men who might try to kill her, or stay in the water and hope for some other salvation? When searchlights began sweeping the water nearby, she made her decision almost without thinking, ducking her head beneath the surface and diving deep before the light could find her.

Underwater, she could hear the steady thrum of engines, screws churning the water and growing louder as one of the cutters headed her way. She did not think they had spotted her; the light continued to sweep across the surface, a bright spot moving above her like the disk of the full moon in an overcast sky, but moving well away from where she was swimming.

Cautiously, she returned to the surface, grabbed a

breath, and then ducked under again. That brief look however confirmed that the cutter would pass within a few yards of her.

Maybe?

She dove deep, waiting until the ship was practically right on top of her, and then kicked back to the surface, one hand extended until she felt the hard hull moving under her fingertips. She broke the surface, hidden she hoped, from the line of sight of any lookouts, and began searching desperately for something to hold onto as the ship continued past. The hull was smooth and slick, but she felt something, a hole—a scupper for draining the deck—and jammed her hand into it.

The water rushed past her, the drag tugging at her, trying to pull her back into the sea. She wondered if the crew would feel a change in the way the boat was moving through water, and knew she couldn't linger where she was. She kicked hard, propelling herself a foot or two higher in the water, stretched her other arm out as far as she could, and caught the edge of the deck with her fingertips. Another kick lofted her high enough to catch the edge with both hands, after which she was just able to slip the toes of one foot into the scupper, giving her three more or less secure points of contact, all of them above the water.

She stayed like that for almost a minute, waiting for someone to appear above her, to either pull her aboard or kick her back into the water, but that did not happen. Tentatively, she stepped up and pulled herself high enough to get a look at the aft deck.

There was no sign of anyone. The crew, she surmised, were all at their duty stations, or perhaps in the bow of the cutter, searching the waves for her.

A guardrail encircled the aft deck, more of a fantail, really. There was a small boom crane mounted to the deck, and suspended from it, a few feet off the deck, was a medium-sized rigid-hulled inflatable boat. A flight of stairs led up to the main deck, but from her vantage, that was about all Jade could discern. Using the guardrail like ladder rungs, she climbed up and over, dropping lightly onto the deck, then stole quickly over to the small launch, which swayed back and forth as the cutter plowed through the cargo hauler's wake. She immediately crawled under the hanging boat and stretched herself out flat, like a child taking refuge under a mattress. It wasn't an ideal hiding place, but for the moment, it was better than treading water in the middle of the ocean. She was sore and exhausted, mentally and physically.

I'll just rest here for a few minutes, she told herself.

The blast of a ship's horn roused her, and when she opened her eyes, gradually remembering where she was and how she had come to be there, she saw that the sky was lightening with the approach of dawn. She could not fathom the miracle that had allowed her to remain undiscovered while she slept, but was grateful for it. She actually felt refreshed. And famished.

The cutter was moving parallel to a shoreline. She could see low green hills, dotted with houses and other man-made structures. Ships—civilian ships, large and small—were passing by on their port side, presumably making their way out of a harbor. She rolled her head over to get a look at the starboard side, and saw the imposing black hull of the cargo freighter, only fifty yards away. She also saw boots.

Two crewmen were standing at the starboard rail, engaged in conversation. She couldn't make out what they were saying, but judging by the lack of urgency in their voices, she guessed it was idle chitchat.

Although she couldn't see where the cutter was going, she assumed that it was nearing shore. Jade knew that if she waited until the cutter was tied up at dock, the chances of being spotted by the vessel's crew increased dramatically. Getting off the ship now, slipping over the side and back into the water to swim to shore would also be risky, but she determined to take the chance if the opportunity arose. She stayed where she was, motionless, waiting for the two Coasties to finish their smoke break, and got ready to make her move.

As she lay there, she realized that the sky was getting darker not lighter. At first, she thought they might be sailing into a storm, but no, conditions looked clear. When streaks of orange and purple began to appear in that small sliver of sky that she could see, Jade realized her error. She wasn't witnessing the twilight at the break of dawn but rather the approach of dusk.

She had slept through an entire day.

The realization was overwhelming but she pushed it from her mind. All that mattered was what happened next. She had to get off the Coast Guard vessel, slip into the water and swim for shore.

And then what?

She had no idea where she was, no money, nobody she could trust. She couldn't go to the police. With no way to back up her story, they would have to alert Purcell, and that would be the end of that. Maybe if she could find a pay phone, she could make a collect call to Professor or Tam, but even that seemed like a monumental undertaking.

One thing at a time, she told herself.

The ship's horn sounded again, and Jade could feel it decelerating, maneuvering. The sky continued to darken as both the cutter and the big cargo vessel made their final approach to port. The two crewmen on the deck seemed to have no intention of leaving, so Jade stayed put.

More crewmen came and went from the aft deck, performing last minute tasks in preparation for putting ashore. Thankfully, none of these tasks involved looking under the launch, and Jade remained unnoticed. Finally, more than an hour after the engines went quiet, the deck cleared and stayed that way. Jade counted to a hundred, just to be sure, then squirmed out from under the launch. After a quick look around to confirm that no one was there to observe her, she crawled to the port rail, lowered herself over the side and dropped into the soup-warm oily water.

She swam underwater until she was well clear of the cutter and surfaced near the motionless hull of the cargo vessel, then continued down its length and around the stern.

Behind the enormous vessel lay the harbor, a sprawling ugly industrial extrusion, clinging to the shore like a spreading fungus. A forest of creosote-coated wooden pilings supported the pier to which the freighter was moored, and after a quick check to make sure nobody was around to see her, Jade swam toward them.

She found a low boat dock with a long ramp connecting it to the main pier. Still wary of being discovered, she pulled herself up onto it, and then started up the ramp staying low and moving slow, willing herself to blend in with the shadows of descending night. As she neared the top of the ramp, she heard voices—one voice in particular—and froze.

It was the man who had tried to kill her, Special Agent Purcell.

Although she couldn't make out everything that was being said, it sounded to her like an argument. Purcell was shouting, clearly trying to overwhelm the other person with threats. The other voice was harder to hear, but judging by Purcell's increasingly exasperated tone, the second party was not the least bit intimidated. Curious, Jade dropped flat and crawled the rest of the way up the ramp, raising her head just high enough to see what was happening.

She immediately spotted the federal agent, about twenty yards away, hands on his hips, towering over his adversary, who turned out to be a stout-looking woman, a little older than middle-aged, wearing a rather frumpy beige tunic dress. The woman was half-turned away so Jade couldn't get a good look at her face. Her posture was defiant, but when she spoke, her voice was still too soft for Jade to make out any words.

The shouting match was only a small part of the bustle of activity on the pier. Behind the argumentative pair, a line of people—the liberated human cargo—were being ushered off the ship by Coast Guardsmen and ICE agents in their ubiquitous blue windbreakers. The freed victims were led down a gangplank to the enormous parking-lot-sized loading dock, where they were immediately put aboard a line of waiting buses.

The woman kept repeatedly gesturing toward the refugees as she spoke. Although her voice was still inaudible, there was no mistaking her concern, and Jade wondered just what her part was in the unfolding drama. She didn't look like someone with any kind of official status. A reporter, maybe? Someone from Amnesty International, or a similar human rights group?

Whoever she was, she was no friend of Purcell, which meant she might be just the ally Jade needed.

"Call whoever you want," Purcell snarled as he took a menacing step forward. "Just stay out of my way."

The woman stood her ground. Purcell uttered—or rather spluttered—a flood of invective then threw his hands up and stalked away to join a group of agents standing in front of the buses.

The woman remained where she was, glaring at the retreating figure, but after a few seconds, she reached into a pocket and took out a pack of cigarettes. She tapped one out and lit it with a disposable lighter. Jade could now see that the woman's hands were shaking a little with pent-up emotion, but as she took a deep drag on the cigarette, she seemed to calm down a little. She lingered there, her left arm horizontal across her torso, left hand supporting the right elbow at just the right height to keep the cigarette in her right hand at lip level, while she intently watched the stream of refugees as they were loaded onto the buses. She barely moved at all, except to occasionally flick the ashes away.

Jade decided to take a chance. In a stage whisper, she hissed, "Hey!" several times until the woman's head cocked to the side and she started to turn around.

"Don't look," Jade urged. "Just act normal. Don't do anything to attract attention."

The woman raised a hand to her mouth and turned her head as if coughing. Her eyes swept the area where Jade was hiding. Jade raised her hand and gave a little wave.

"Who are you?" the woman asked, still feigning a cough.

"I was on that ship," Jade said. "I escaped. Went into the water. Can you help me?"

The woman took another long pull on the cigarette, then slowly turned and ambled to the edge of the dock until she was standing right above Jade. She did not look down, but gazed out into distance, to all appearances, relishing her nicotine fix. "The folks coming off that ship are mostly Haitians and Dominicans. You don't sound like y'all are from the islands."

Jade felt a twist of apprehension in her gut. She could see how this was going to play out. She would explain how she had been kidnapped, and the woman would ask why she didn't just go over to those nice federal agents and ask them for help. It would only devolve from there. The woman might believe her story about Purcell trying to kill her, but if she didn't….

Jade wasn't going to risk it. "I'm sorry, this was a mistake. I have to go."

"Now just hold your horses there, darlin'." The woman's voice had a note of urgency that was at odds with the slow Southern drawl. "You say you escaped? Like they was holding you against your will?"

Jade nodded.

"I came here tonight to help people who need help, so if you need help, then I'm here for you. I just need to know right up front what kind of shit I'll be stepping in. The one kind I can't abide is bullshit, so if you're into something illegal, you best tell it like it is right now, and let me decide whether I want to walk across the pasture."

Jade almost laughed despite herself. It was hard to take the woman seriously. She was a walking talking contradiction, with her round, rosy-cheeked matronly face, puffing away on a cigarette, and the thickly accented speech effortlessly shifting between homily and profanity, and yet there was something about the woman that engendered trust. And Jade really didn't have anyone else to turn to.

"It's a really long story," Jade said. "I haven't done anything illegal but I can't go to the cops. Not these cops, anyway. So, will you help me?"

"All right, darlin', I'll do what I can for you right now, but y'all are gonna tell me that story before the night is done, agreed?" She didn't wait for an answer. "What's your name, darlin'?"

"Jade. Jade Ihara."

"That's a lovely name, Jade. I look forward to getting to know you better. I'm Diane Lindsey. Now, I'm guessing you'd just as soon avoid having to saunter past those fine federal law enforcement agents."

"That obvious?"

"Here's what you're gonna have to do. About a half a mile down the channel, there's a little private marina with a store and a boat ramp. Think you can swim that far?"

Jade groaned. "If I have to."

"You come up that boat ramp, and stay hidden until I get there. I'll distract the fella in the store while you slip around to the parking lot. I'm driving a silver Ford Taurus. I'll leave it unlocked. When you find it, just honk the horn couple times, and I'll come out. That sound good to you?"

"Other than the part where I have to swim half-a-mile, it sounds perfect."

"All right then, Jade. See you down the road." Diane flicked her fingers and sent her cigarette butt sailing over Jade and out over the water where it vanished with a faint hiss. Then, she too was gone.

ELEVEN

Diane was as good as her word. When Jade crawled out of the water, she could hear the woman's voice issuing from the little convenience store at the marina's edge, haranguing the clerk about some minor dereliction. Her volume level was so exaggerated that Jade had difficulty believing it was the same woman who had quietly defied Special Agent Purcell. The distraction served its purpose though, allowing Jade to move unnoticed to the parking lot where Diane's Ford waited. Because she was soaking wet, Jade didn't get in the car, but simply reached in and gave the horn two quick beeps. A few seconds later, Diane emerged from the store holding a plastic grocery bag.

"I thought maybe you could use a little snack," she said, passing the bag to Jade. It contained a half-liter bottle of Coca-Cola, a bag of potato chips and a packet of peanuts. "Hope you're not allergic to anything in there."

"I'm not. Thanks."

Diane gave Jade a quick head-to-toe appraisal, then reached in the back seat and produced a folded blanket. "Here. You can sit on this while you dry out. I'm not worried about the upholstery or anything, but it'll be more comfortable."

Jade tried to thank the woman again, but was overcome with emotion. After two days of hell and privation, the thought of someone looking out for her was almost too much to bear.

Diane just smiled. "I know, darlin'. Get in. Unless you've got a better idea, I know a place where we can get you a proper meal and a hot shower. When you feel up to it, you can tell me what happened to you."

The interior of the car smelled like stale cigarettes, which did no favors to Jade's appetite. Nevertheless, she forced herself to eat the potato chips, washing them down with Coke that was already lukewarm, while Diane navigated through a semi-rural industrial margin around the port, and onto Interstate 10, heading west. Jade had already guessed that she was in one of the Gulf Coast states, but road signs and billboards helped her narrow it down a little.

"Texas," she murmured.

Diane glanced over. "That's right, darlin'. Specifically, the Greater Houston metropolitan area. You didn't know?"

Jade shook her head. "I went to bed in my hotel in Port au Prince a couple nights ago and woke up on that ship. Chained up in a shipping container."

"You mentioned that," Diane said. "Chained up? That's unusual. Most of the folks who get sucked into this go along willingly. At first, anyway."

"What do you mean, 'willingly'? Why would anyone do that?"

"Chasing a better life. Someone promises them a job, a fresh start, a piece of the American dream. Hell, a lot of 'em pay their way. And then when they get here, they find out they were lied to, and now they're caught. No visa, no money. They can't go to the authorities because they'll get deported. Or worse. So they go along with it." She shrugged. "No need for actual chains."

"Well, that's not what happened to me."

"No?"

"No. I'm already an American citizen, and I already have a job. I'm an archaeologist."

"Is that a fact?" Diane sounded almost amused.

"It is." Jade looked over at the other woman, trying to decide whether to take offense. "What were you doing there tonight? At the dock, I mean. You know a lot about this, yeah? You a reporter?"

Diane smiled. "No. Well, I blog about it sometimes, so I guess nowadays, that makes me a journalist. But no, I'm more of a victims' advocate."

"That would have been my second guess."

"I work for an organization dedicated to helping people take control of their lives. One area of special concern is human trafficking. Sadly, it doesn't get nearly the attention it deserves. People don't want to know about it, because if they know and don't do something, they're partly to blame for it. Ignorance is bliss, as they say."

Jade frowned at the implicit accusation, but Diane had already moved on.

"Once in a while though, something makes the news. Like the feds taking over that ship. It's all about image these days. Spin. Never mind that it's just one tentacle of the beast." She looked over at Jade. "Sorry, darlin', I get worked up about this stuff.

"Anyways, what usually happens after something like this is that the feds get a great photo op, while the poor folks who get *liberated*—you will note my ironic use of the word—end up in a processing center, and eventually get sent back to wherever they came from to do it all over again. That's where I come in. My organization provides humanitarian support and legal aid, such as we can."

"But Purcell wouldn't let you help them?"

Diane glanced over again. "Special Agent Jacob Purcell of the Homeland Security Investigations department. I take it you've made his acquaintance?"

Jade was still hesitant to tell the whole story, so she said simply, "Yeah. He's a dick."

A broad smile broke over Diane's face. "On that we can certainly agree. He likes to play at being the hero. The white knight, slaying dragons, but he doesn't give a damn about the people he's supposedly saving. Tonight, he was especially…dickish. Shut me out completely. Called me a 'liberal,' and other words I won't repeat in polite company."

Diane laughed and for a few minutes, said nothing, focusing instead on the drive as the freeway took them deeper into urban Houston. Finally, after exiting onto Interstate 69, continuing west, she picked up the thread of conversation again. "Earlier, you said you needed my help," she prompted.

Jade nodded. "You've already helped a lot. I don't have any money. I mean, I've got money in my bank account, but without my wallet—my cards and ID—I'm kind of stuck."

"Is there someone you want to call? Family? A

husband or a boyfriend?"

Jade grimaced, guiltily. There was one person in particular that she wanted to call, and would have asked Diane for a phone already if not for one little problem. "This is going to sound terrible but… I don't know their numbers. All that information was on my phone."

"That's what we call a 'first world problem,'" Diane said, laughing again. "Don't fret. Honestly, I don't even know my own phone number. How about email? Would that work?"

Jade felt a glimmer of hope. "That would be perfect. If I can remember my Gmail password."

Diane signaled and took the next exit, leaving the freeway and entering the quiet surface streets. Judging by the density of small office buildings and business signs, Jade guessed they were in a commercial area, but there were a few houses and apartment buildings and she guessed one of these would be Diane's residence. She was a little surprised then when Diane pulled into the mostly empty parking lot of a business complex and stopped the car in front of one of the buildings.

"Here we are." Diane shut off the engine and got out, heading immediately to the entrance of the closest suite.

Jade hurried to catch up, and as Diane unlocked the door, Jade studied the logo emblazoned on the glass door, a silhouette of a tower on a promontory, with a beam of light shining out from its top. Stylized letters above the image read: "Lighthouse Worldwide."

"Lighthouse," Jade said. "Is that the name of your organization?"

"It is." Diane gave her a sidelong glance. "Heard of us?"

Jade shrugged. "I'm not sure. Sounds kind of familiar."

"Well, it's not exactly the most unique name, but we think it's appropriate. We help people who are trying to find their way out of a sea of troubles, just like a beacon on the hill." She smiled and swung the door open. "That's what it says in the brochures, anyway. This is our headquarters, but as the second part of the name suggests, we are everywhere."

Beyond the door was a dimly lit lobby. The lighthouse logo adorned the back wall behind the reception desk and there were framed posters on the walls of the sitting area, each one featuring young, good-looking people in happy, active poses. The legend beneath one read: "Find your way out of the darkness." The others had similar exhortations.

Jade felt suddenly wary, ill at ease, but she tried to project a calm, merely curious demeanor. "So are you... um, affiliated with a church?"

"Nothing like that, darlin'." Diane headed into the corridor at the back of the lobby. "We don't attach any kind of commitment to the services we provide." She looked back and winked. "But we do charge for them of course."

"Uh... I told you I don't have any—"

Diane laughed. "I didn't mean *you*. Most of our operating revenue comes from our life-coaching seminars. Lots of people nowadays have money to burn, but they're not happy and they don't know why. We show them why and show them how to find real meaning in their lives. In return, they give us some of that money which wasn't really doing anything for 'em anyway, and we use it to help people who have real problems and not much money."

She led Jade through a large conference room with tables and chairs, and into another room lined with empty cots. "Here you go. There's a bathroom with a shower down the hall. The cupboard over there has towels, blankets, pillows. I'll see if I can find you something to wear and then maybe rustle up some take out."

"This is some kind of shelter, yeah?"

"Not exactly. Some of our intensive seminars last several days, and since it's critical to avoid outside distractions, we keep the participants sequestered." Diane smiled again. "But for you, tonight, it can certainly be that. Why don't you get cleaned up and comfortable, and then maybe after we've had a bite, we can get you to a computer so you can reach out to your family and let them know you're alive and well."

"Thanks, so much," Jade replied, managing a smile. Diane seemed nice enough, genuine even, and Jade was grateful, but despite the allure of a hot shower, a hot meal and chance to make contact with Professor, there was something off about Lighthouse Worldwide. She wasn't going to be "comfortable" until she was back in her own world.

The shower did help though. She stood under the spray for what felt like an hour—probably closer to fifteen minutes— letting the hot water sluice away the grimy residue of her underwater excursions. Her wrists were still raw where the manacles had dug into her skin and stung a little, but she scrubbed the abrasions vigorously nevertheless. Finally, when the water began to cool a little, she shut it off and got out.

The bathroom was an institutional affair, like the locker room at a school or gym, with toilet stalls and a sink at one end, and four shower stalls and a dressing room at the other. Jade had left two towels on the wooden bench in the changing area, and her clothes in a heap on the floor beside it. Diane had evidently come in at some point, taking away the soiled clothes, and left behind a gray fleece sweatshirt, matching sweatpants, and a pair of flip-flops. Jade wasn't surprised to see the Lighthouse logo on the shirt.

"Just 'cause I'm wearing your shirt, doesn't mean I'm joining the cult," she muttered, shaking her head.

"It ain't a prerequisite, darlin'."

Jade whirled in surprise, scooping up one of the towels in a reflexive attempt to cover her nakedness. Diane was standing at the entrance to the changing room, leaning against the wall and smiling lopsidedly.

"Sorry," Jade said. "Didn't see you there."

"I guess you didn't. Don't mind me, none. Hope everything fits. I put your clothes in the washing machine, but I'm not sure it'll do any good. They're in pretty bad shape, as you can imagine."

"Thanks." Jade carefully wrapped the towel around her. Diane just stood there, watching her like a chaperone or a warden.

Exactly like a warden, Jade thought.

She wasn't ordinarily shy. Growing up in Hawaii, she'd changed out of her bikini on the side of the road dozens of times, not caring who was around to observe, but this was different. She hadn't been given any say in the matter.

That's it, she thought. *I'm outta here.*

"I'll be right out," she said, trying to sound sweet and innocent, and not the least bit creeped out. "I promise not to sneak out the windows."

"Oh, I ain't worried, darlin'. They don't open."

Despite her best efforts, Jade's eyes went wide in alarm, but then Diane laughed. "I'm just foolin'. Seriously, there aren't any windows in here, but if you want to leave, I'll call you a cab."

Jade laughed along to hide her unease, and then turned away, trying to ignore the woman's continued presence as she pulled on the sweatpants under the towel, and then donned the sweatshirt over it, removing it only when she was completely covered. She wound the towel around her damp hair like a turban.

"All done," she chirped as she turned to Diane again.

But the woman was already gone.

Guess she finally got the hint.

She slipped on the sandals and headed back to the room with the cots, expecting to find Diane already camped out, but there was no sign of her there, or in the conference room. Curious despite herself, Jade started back toward the lobby, but on her way down the hall passed an open door to an office, where she found Diane seated at a desk, partially hidden behind a flat screen computer monitor.

"There you are," Diane said, as if the awkward scene in the changing room had not just happened. "I ordered some take out. Tex-Mex. Hope that's okay." She tapped a few more keys on her computer, then rose and gestured for Jade to take her place. "Here you go. All yours."

Jade was surprised and a little wary. Her remark about "joining the cult" wasn't entirely in jest. Lighthouse Worldwide had a sort of cult-vibe going on. Not tennis-shoes and mass-suicide though; more like a multi-level-marketing scheme. Jade wasn't entirely comfortable about using Diane's computer to log into her email account.

"Well," Diane said, not waiting for Jade to sit. "While you take care of your business, I'm going to have a cigarette." She raised her hands as if trying to ward off an accusation. "I know, I know. It's bad for me. I should quit. My doctor tells me all the time. Truth is, we're all in chains of some kind." She held up the cigarette pack. "It takes real strength to break free."

"I thought that's what you did here," Jade said. "Helped people take control of their lives."

Diane tapped a finger to her nose and winked, then turned and exited without another word.

"Friggin' weird," Jade muttered, shaking her head. She settled into the chair behind the computer and debated what to do next.

Maybe she was just being paranoid. What was the worst that could happen? Could Diane, or someone else working for Lighthouse, use her email password to steal her identity? And if they tried it, so what? After being abducted and chained up in a shipping container, having someone hack her bank account didn't seem nearly as terrifying. And she wasn't exactly helpless. She knew people who could put Lighthouse Worldwide out of business permanently if they tried anything like that.

She nodded, feeling better about her position, and scooted closer to the keyboard. A few keystrokes later, and she was composing an email message to Professor, mumbling the words as she typed them.

Hey, I'm alive! You won't believe what happened to me. Well, maybe you will. Somebody shanghaied me out of my room. You probably figured that part out, but I woke up on a ship. Chained up in a shipping container. Can you believe that?

She stopped, and deleted the last line.

Things got really weird then. There were these guys in robes and pointy hats, speaking Latin and checking my teeth like I was a prize horse or something. I managed to get away, and then the Coast Guard seized the ship. I thought that would be the end of it, but then this ICE agent named Purcell tried to shoot me. Long story short, I got away. Now I'm stuck in Houston.

She stopped again, wondering whether to mention Diane Lindsey and Lighthouse Worldwide. She decided it could wait. If everything was on the level, there would be no need.

I don't have my passport or any ID, so I'm kind of stranded, but I'm alive, and mostly okay. And I really miss you. Come and get me, and then let's go after the bastards who did this. Sound good to you? See you soon. Love, Jade.

She backspaced, but then changed her mind and typed it in again.

Love, Jade.

Professor wouldn't read too much into it, so why not say it?

Before she could lose her nerve, she hit send, and then blew out the breath she didn't even realize she had been holding.

How long would it take him to answer? A few minutes? Hours? She couldn't recall ever seeing him check his email, but he had to of course. It was the 21st Century, after all. She clicked on the inbox, hoping to see a reply.

Nothing.

She drummed her fingers on the desktop. "This sucks," she muttered, staring at the screen and hitting the inbox button again.

The hotel in Port au Prince had full Internet access, but would Professor be there? Was he even still in Haiti?

"I can call the hotel," she realized, and then thought about Yann Pierre. Surely, Professor would have enlisted his help in finding her. She scrolled down the list of messages, looking for the original email Pierre had sent. His phone number was in it. She would call him and he would be able to connect her with Professor....

She stopped, overcome by a sudden feeling of dread, like a premonition of danger.

No, not a premonition. A memory.

Dinner with Yann and Professor. Yann insisting she try the passion fruit punch cocktails. The rum had left her feeling a little tipsy, but not falling down drunk. Dinner over, Professor had walked her back to her room. Another awkward good night, with her wanting to ask him in, but afraid he might say no…

A knock at the door.

Not Professor.

Yann Pierre.

And then chains.

She shuddered. Pierre had done this to her. Drugged her. Kidnapped her. Sold her into slavery.

She had to tell Professor, had to let him know.

But why had Pierre done it? Whatever else he was, Yann Pierre was a respected scholar. What possible motive could he have had for the betrayal?

As she pondered this, she began to wonder at her other assumptions. The barefoot Klansmen. Torches and Latin. The chains… What was all that about?

She opened a search engine and typed in the words "servus" and "chains." There were a few relevant answers, confirming that *servus* was Latin for "slave" and that some slaves in ancient times were kept in chains. She tried adding the word "torches"—nothing noteworthy there—and then typed in "pointy hat."

One of the first hits took her to an article about the Ku Klux Klan, which made her feel a little better about leaping to that particular conclusion. She scrolled down the list and saw another article that discussed the history of conical hats as a symbol of witches. The excerpt mentioned Phrygian caps, and when she clicked on that, she was taken to the Wikipedia entry.

She read the first paragraph, and then sat back in the chair as if physically stunned.

"You okay, darlin'?"

Jade looked up and found Diane in the doorway, a

plastic grocery sack full of food containers in one hand. "Uh, yeah. I… Uh, just read something really strange."

Diane set the bag down and began removing the contents, arranging the Styrofoam boxes like items on a serving line. "Do tell."

"Well, I think I've got a lead on the people that kidnapped me."

Diane looked up, one eyebrow raised.

"Maybe 'lead' isn't the right word, but it's a clue." She scooted close again. "When I was on the ship, there were these people who came in. They were wearing white robes and these pointy hats, and carrying torches. And they were barefoot. They poked and prodded me like a piece of meat, and then said something in Latin. And later, when I got free, I found the word 'servus' written on the chains. That's Latin for 'slave.'

"So I Googled those terms and found this. Listen: 'The Phrygian cap is a soft conical cap with the top pulled forward, associated in antiquity with several peoples in Eastern Europe and Anatolia, including Phrygia, Dacia, and the Balkans. In early modern Europe it came to signify *freedom*—" She stressed the word. "—and the pursuit of liberty through a confusion with the *pileus*, the felt cap of emancipated *slaves* of ancient Rome."

Diane stared at her, unblinking.

"Don't you see? The pointy hats I saw. They were these… *pileuses*…. *pileums*. I don't know how you'd say the plural. But somehow that's important."

Diane's eyebrows were drawn together in a frown. "Important how?"

"I think it was some kind of ritual." Another memory came to her and she snapped her fingers. "One of the…whatever they were… chanted some kind of Latin incantation and then sprinkled me with water. Like a ritual cleansing."

She cleared the search engine entry bar and began entering a new query. "They kidnapped me for some kind of religious ritual. I'm sure of it. And if I can figure out exactly what it all means, I'll know who they were."

"Libertas," Diane said, her voice soft, almost a whisper. Just as it had been on the dock.

Jade looked up. "What's that mean?"

"Libertas was the Roman goddess of Liberty."

"Okay. How do you spell that?" She didn't wait for an answer but took her best guess, typing the word in, but as she hit the 'enter' key, something inside her clicked. She looked up, her heart beginning to pound, as if her body already knew something her head was only just beginning to figure out. "How did you know that?"

Diane Lindsey took a deep breath and let it out slowly. When she spoke, her exaggerated drawl was gone. "I wasn't entirely honest with you earlier. Tonight, at the dock, I wasn't there to help those people. I was there for you, Jade."

"How did you know I would be there?" She already knew the answer. "Are you one of them Diane? One of the people who took me?"

Diane took another breath. "Let me explain…."

TWELVE

Jade's heart was pounding so hard, she thought she could feel her chest beating against the loose fabric of the sweatshirt. She looked around at the desktop, searching for something that might work as a weapon.

There was a coffee mug—with the Lighthouse logo, of course—filled with pens and pencils. She could use one of the latter as a stabbing weapon, and the cup itself as a crude bludgeon. Not exactly ideal, but it would get the job done.

She grabbed the cup with her left hand, snatched a pencil out with her right, gripping it overhand like a dagger, and jumped to her feet in a defensive stance.

Diane was a lot older, out of shape, a smoker. Jade felt certain she would prevail if it came to a fight.

But what if she's already called for backup?

"I wasn't kidding earlier," Diane said, "You are free to walk out of here and do as you please. But I pray to the goddess that you will at least hear me out first."

Jade wondered if the woman was stalling, maybe trying to keep her here until the reinforcements arrived. She wanted nothing more than to leave, knew she might not get another chance, and yet some part of her needed to understand why everything had happened.

She shook the pencil at Diane. "If you're trying to jerk me around…"

Diane shook her head. "Jade, you don't understand. You're the Chosen. You proved that when you passed the Servus Trial. If I had any doubt, you proved it to me when you figured out who we were. The blessing of the goddess is upon you."

"What the hell is that supposed to mean? Chosen for what? Human sacrifice?"

"Chosen to lead." Another breath. "Don't suppose you'd care to let me finish this outside. I could really use another smoke."

"No," Jade answered, flatly. Her initial panic was giving

way to pure rage. *The nerve of this woman....* "That was you on the ship, wasn't it? You sprinkled water on me."

"I anointed you as Chosen." Diane sighed. "You have to believe me, Jade. I was opposed to subjecting you to the Servus Trial without your consent, but it was necessary."

"You're talking about the chains."

"Yes. Libertas is the embodiment of freedom. One who is born free has no need of her blessing. Only a slave can know what it truly means to be liberated."

"Bullshit."

Diane returned a wan smile. "It is the truth, though. It is the fundamental doctrine of our faith. Every one of us— those who worship the goddess, and we are many—have escaped slavery."

"Slavery," Jade scoffed. "Being addicted to nicotine isn't slavery."

Something flashed in Diane's eyes. Anger? Hurt? "I wasn't referring to that." She waved a dismissive hand. "I told you I would explain everything. Here goes.

"I heard what you said earlier, about this being a cult. You're not wrong, though the word no longer means what it once did. Two thousand years ago, the word simply referred to the worship of a particular god or goddess. The Cult of Libertas welcomed all freed slaves, those who had been granted the *pileus*, as a symbol of manumission, as well as those who escaped, though of course the latter remained fugitives and worshipped in secret. But all prayed to the goddess that their freedom might never be taken away. While Christianity supplanted the gods of antiquity, it did not bring an end to slavery, and so the Cult of Libertas endured."

"Is this the short version?" Jade snapped.

Diane inclined her head. "My apologies. I only wish for you to know that this is not some modern aberration. We are an ancient religion, older than Christianity, devoted to the cause of freedom and liberty. She was the goddess of the gens Junia, and of Marcus Junius Brutus the Younger, who led the uprising against the Julian dictator—"

"Julian dictator. You mean Julius Caesar. And Brutus as in '*et tu, Brute*?'"

"He has been maligned as an assassin, and yet what he really did was strike a blow to liberate Rome from an illegitimate oppressive ruler."

Jade raised her hands. "Enough. Get to the point."

"This is the point, Jade. Servilia, the mother of Brutus and mother-in-law of Cassius, was Chosen, just as you are."

"Oh, wonderful. Thanks, but no thanks. I'm an archaeologist, not an assassin."

Diane shook her head. "Being Chosen simply means that you may enter the temple of the goddess to bring forth the sacred relics. They were entrusted to Servilia when the temple to Libertas was demolished in 48 B.C.E."

"Get somebody else." Jade pointed the pencil at her. "Why don't you do it?"

"Because, I don't know where it is." She sighed. "After Brutus was defeated, the sacred relics were returned to Servilia, but what she did with them is not known, at least not to any of us. You were Chosen *because* you are an archaeologist. You find things that have been lost."

"If you wanted to hire me to look for it, you should have just sent me an email. Ancient Rome isn't really my field, but I might have said yes. Now? No way. Not a chance in hell."

Diane pursed her lips together. "As I said, I favored a more honest approach, but the final decision was not mine. The fact is, you passed the test, escaped the chains. The goddess favors you, and I believe she wants you to find her temple."

"Oh, well." Jade said with a disingenuous shrug. "Better luck next time."

There wasn't going to be a next time, though. Not if she had anything to say about it. She would burn this place down. Once she made contact with Professor, they would come back with a SWAT team and shut down Lighthouse Worldwide and the Cult of Libertas, permanently.

"Jade," Diane pleaded. "Why do you think I do this?

Human trafficking. Slavery. It's real. Human beings treated like property. We can do something about it. *You* can do something about it."

Jade gritted her teeth, and pushed past the woman, doing her best to shut out the emotional appeal. Those were real problems, but the solution wasn't going to be found in some ancient temple.

Diane wasn't giving up. She followed Jade down the hall. "Why do you do it, Jade? Archaeology. It's not for the money. I can tell you don't care about that. It's the mystery, isn't it? I'm giving you a chance to solve a mystery like nothing else in the world."

That one hit a little closer to the mark, Jade thought, mentally putting her fingers in her ears. *La-la-la-la. Not listening.*

But the seed had already sprouted. She stopped, curious despite herself. "What mystery? What are these sacred relics, anyway?"

"There are two items. One is a scroll, a Sibylline oracle. Are you familiar with the term?"

"I know a little about oracles."

"The Sibylline scrolls were oracular books. Sort of like a book of horoscopes, containing prophetic passages that only a priest could properly interpret. There were many such books in ancient Rome, but the scroll in the temple of the goddess was different. It was written by the wife of the greatest warrior to ever follow the path of the goddess. He was a slave, a gladiator who took his freedom at the tip of a sword, and led one of the greatest slave revolts in history.

"The chest containing his skeletal remains is the second sacred item. His true name has been forgotten. We know him as Spartacus."

"Okay, I've heard of him," Jade admitted, grudgingly. "I seem to recall that his story didn't exactly have a happy ending."

"There's a saying, maybe you've heard it. 'Better to die on your feet, than live on your knees.' In death, Spartacus gained immortality. He became a symbol of slaves breaking the chains of captivity, destroying their masters. In 1791, when Toussaint Louverture led the slaves of Haiti in a successful revolt, establishing the first black republic in history, he earned the nickname 'Black Spartacus.'"

Jade wondered if it was a coincidence that the Cult of Libertas had chosen to lure her to the homeland of Black Spartacus in order to abduct her. Probably not.

"How would finding his bones help you?" she asked.

"As a symbol of our struggle. The publicity surrounding such a discovery would burn away the apathy of the masses, forcing them to confront the reality."

"Reality?"

"That all of us have been lifted up on the bent backs of slaves. Human exploitation pervades every part of our world. Our clothes are stitched together in third world sweatshops. The phones and computers that keep the world moving forward are assembled by workers who are paid mere pennies a day. The food we eat is cultivated and harvested by slaves. Do you like chocolate? Seventy percent of the world's cacao supply is harvested by millions of child laborers in Africa. Most people don't want to think about the suffering that goes into their candy bars, but the discovery of the sacred relics in the temple will force them to acknowledge it. And then maybe they will do something about it."

"Thanks for ruining chocolate for me," Jade muttered.

Try as she might though, she couldn't sustain her unbridled anger. She was still pissed off, but on some level she could sympathize. She had seen human exploitation with her own eyes, and had witnessed the grinding poverty that forced people into a life of bondage. She doubted finding Spartacus' bones would make a dent in that problem, but she couldn't deny being intrigued by the prospect of looking for them.

She sighed. "I'm not saying I'll do it… But if I did, where would I even start looking?"

"The last known location of the temple was in Rome. On Palatine Hill. But that temple was demolished and never rebuilt. We have always assumed that Servilia kept them."

"That's all you've got?"

Diane gave a helpless shrug. "If finding them was a simple matter, we wouldn't need you."

"Don't flatter me. I'm not in the mood."

"Sorry, darlin'."

Jade pointed the pencil at her. "Watch it."

Diane nodded, chastened. "We can get you to Rome, provide whatever logistical support you might need. Worldwide isn't just a clever name. We'll have to get you some new duds first. Can't have you jet-setting in pajamas."

"I haven't said 'yes,' yet," Jade warned, but then lowered the pencil. "Okay. Let's say 'maybe.' One thing. That ICE agent, Purcell. Is he one of you?"

Diane's forehead creased. "No. Why?"

"When he questioned me on the ship, I told him what had happened, how I had been kidnapped and chained up. When I showed him the chains, he tried to kill me. I thought maybe that was another one of your tests."

For the first time since their initial encounter on the dock, Diane looked truly astonished. "I'm sorry, but I have no idea why he would have done that. But Jade, if he tried to kill you *because* you are the Chosen, then you aren't safe. He may already know of the connection between Lighthouse and Libertas. You must leave for Rome. Immediately."

As he turned off the Beltway Frontage road and pulled his car into the secure parking lot of the three-story glass and concrete building that housed the Houston field offices of the U.S. Department of the Treasury and the Department of Homeland Security, some twenty miles away from the local headquarters of Lighthouse Worldwide, Special Agent Jacob Purcell was thinking about Jade Ihara.

Her plunge over the side of the *Mohebbi* and his failure to find her body or bring back proof that she was really dead were the only blemishes on an otherwise perfect operation. A ship and crew seized, a hundred-and-fifty *units* liberated and on their way to the processing facility. On any other day, that would have been a satisfying accomplishment, something to be proud of. But today, it felt like the golden ticket had slipped through his fingers.

If he had succeeded in taking out the cult's so-called Chosen, nipping the uprising in the bud, it might not have meant much for his career in law enforcement, but his standing in the organization would have been greatly improved. He would almost certainly have advanced a couple degrees in rank, perhaps even be given an invitation to join the governing council.

Career successes could only take him so far, but earning status within Dominion could take him all the way to the top.

Still, he had not been expecting to find the Chosen One on the *Mohebbi*. It had been a fluke, and the fact that he had acted decisively would certainly count in his favor, wouldn't it?

Then why haven't I made the phone call, yet? But he knew the answer. Failure was failure.

It had been easy to procrastinate while surrounded by fellow agents and Coast Guardsmen aboard the ship, but now that he was back on solid ground and alone, he knew he had to report what had happened.

He took out the phone, and located the number—the same number he had called just a week ago when he had stumbled on that fateful email.

The Chosen.

Although he had not grasped its full significance at the time, he had recognized that is was important. The Dominion leadership had filled in some of the blanks, though their knowledge of the Cult of Libertas was also limited.

They were an ancient religious society with ties to the modern world and a dangerous tendency to foment rebellion and instability. Like most revolutionary and terrorist groups, they found fertile ground among the poor and disenfranchised, offering them a violent outlet for their frustrations, which was always easier than simply telling them to take responsibility for their own actions, stop whining and get a job. But the meaning of the Chosen emails was clear; the Cult was getting ready to launch a major offensive, and they had chosen an archaeologist named Jade Ihara to carry their banner

Jade's boyfriend, Chapman, was almost certainly a Company man. Probably not part of the cult, though anything was possible. He might try to stir things up, call for an investigation into Purcell's claim that Jade had attacked him, but that probably wouldn't amount to anything. CIA operatives had nearly wiped out an earlier version of the Dominion, but the pendulum had swung the other way, and now it was the Agency that lived in the shadow of existential fear. If Chapman or his handlers tried to raise a stink, the leadership would simply crush them.

Purcell shook his head, trying to order his thoughts before making the call. He couldn't afford to leave out a single detail.

The phone vibrated in his hand, surprising him. He turned it to display the caller ID—not one of his contacts, but he recognized the number as one of the department extensions. "Saved by the buzz," he muttered, and thumbed the green button to accept the call. "This is SA Purcell."

"Special Agent Purcell, it's Duarte from Sci-Tech."

Purcell nodded. He remembered Duarte. A white guy with a spic name. What was that about?

"Sure. What's up?"

"I've been working data retrieval on that laptop you recovered last week. Well, it just got a new email. Looks like it might be in code or something."

"Code?"

"Yeah, it's the same code as one I found in the deleted file. I don't think whoever sent it realizes that the guy this computer belonged to got burned."

Purcell frowned when he realized that Duarte was talking about the Chosen email. Acting on instructions from the Dominion leadership, Purcell had deleted it and emptied the trash basket, but evidently this techno geek had brought it back. "Well, what's it say?"

"It's short. The subject line is 'The Chosen.' The message reads: 'The candidate has returned from the Servus Trial. The blessing of the goddess is upon her. Her quest to find the sacred relics begins. Be ready. The time draws near!' Sounds like some kind of Lord of the Rings shit, doesn't it?"

Purcell sat up a little straighter. "When was this sent?"

"Just now. Five minutes ago, max."

"Son of a bitch. She's still alive."

"What?"

Purcell shook his head. "Nothing. Give me a second." He lowered the phone and stared straight ahead without really seeing anything.

Jade Ihara had survived. That was the only explanation. She had probably made it back onto the ship and gone into hiding until the ship made port. That was the only possible explanation for the timing of this email.

And if Jade was still alive, that meant he had been given another chance to end her and the Cult of Libertas, permanently.

But how to find her?

He raised the phone again. "Duarte, you still there?"

"Yes, sir."

"Are you getting anywhere with your backtrace on those emails?"

"No. That's probably a dead-end. They're using proxies to cover their tracks. The fact that this account is still active and on the send-list is just pure dumb luck."

"Dead end," Purcell muttered. "Okay, we'll have to try something different. The suspect mentioned in that email may try to make contact with her known associates. We'll need to establish surveillance on them."

"Wait, you mean you understand what that email means?"

"Don't worry about that. Just start the surveillance. The suspect is Jade Ihara. Can't be too many people in the world with a name like that. First known associate is Pete Chapman. I have a contact number for him; that should give you a place to start."

"Uh, sir, I'm going to need a warrant to initiate electronic surveillance measures."

"I'll take care of the warrant. You just get me the taps."

There was a long pause. "I'll get things ready," Duarte finally said, guardedly.

Purcell hung up, but remained seated in his car, still gazing through the windshield, looking at nothing. He felt like he was putting all his eggs in a basket with a great big hole in the bottom. If Chapman really was CIA, his digital presence would have additional safeguards that Duarte might not be able to subvert, and doing so might even raise some red flags within the Department.

He couldn't afford to wait and see. Immediate action was called for.

He returned his attention to the phone, dialed a number and explained what he needed to the person on the other end of the call. There was a brief pause as the call was rerouted through a satellite network and then the click of a reconnection and a cautious greeting.

"Hello?"

"Mr. Chapman. It's Jacob Purcell. I wanted to let you know that I'm going to recommend suspending the search effort."

"Why?"

"Because Jade Ihara is still alive. We just got confirmation that she's here in Houston. Thought you might like to know."

THIRTEEN

Rome, Italy

If Diane Lindsey's lifestyle was any indication, the devotees of Libertas did not live lives of conspicuous consumption, but they definitely had resources. There was a Gulfstream V jet waiting on the tarmac at an airport west of Houston, and within minutes of their arrival, the plane was in the air and on its way to Rome.

Diane had remained in Texas, citing a need to maintain the illusion of business as usual. "I don't know if Purcell has figured it out yet, but if I just up and vanish, he's bound to sit up and take note. But don't you worry none. I'll make sure there's someone at the other end to help you do what needs doin'."

"But I don't have my passport," Jade protested. "I don't even have a toothbrush."

"We'll take care of everything, darlin'. You just concentrate on finding the temple."

It seemed a preferable alternative to a bullet, so she had boarded the plane and allowed the world to take her where it would.

Twelve hours and nearly 6,000 miles later, Jade still wasn't entirely sure she wanted to join Diane's crusade to find the bones of Spartacus and rid the world of human trafficking, but getting out of Houston, beyond the reach of the murderous Special Agent Purcell, seemed like a good idea, and it was nice to be traveling in style for a change. The plush reclining chairs on the jet were, she did not doubt, a lot more comfortable than the canvas cot Diane had originally offered, and definitely a step up from the deck of the Coast Guard cutter. There was gourmet fare in the galley, a fully-stocked bar, and a top-notch entertainment system. The only thing missing was a wi-fi connected computer; she was eager to reconnect with Professor and bring him fully up to date.

Because of the time difference, it was early afternoon

when the Gulfstream touched down, once more at a small airport outside the city. Jade was still attired in sweats and flip-flops, but she was, for the first time in days, well-rested and physically refreshed.

As she deplaned in a private hangar, well away from the eyes of any customs officials, a buxom young woman stepped forward to greet her. The newcomer was pretty, but not in a fake fashion-model way. Curvy and ripe, her long chestnut brown hair was held away from her face by a pair of designer sunglasses, perched atop her head to create the impression of cat's ears. She was bedecked in a bright floral-pattern jumper that hugged her body, accentuating her femininity as she swayed across the tarmac. Jade was conspicuously aware of her own dismal attire. As the woman drew close, she threw her hand up in a carefree wave and shouted, *"Buongiorno! Benvenuto in Roma!"*

Jade was already predisposed to dislike the woman, but the display of cheerfulness was like rubbing lemon juice in a paper cut. "Sorry. I don't... *No hablo...* Or *parlez*—"

The woman laughed. "Don't worry. I only use Italian to welcome you, but I speak English." She took another step closer and opened her arms, inviting Jade into her embrace. "I'm Giachetta Ruffino, but you must call me Gia."

Without waiting for Jade to move, Gia enfolded her, crushing Jade against her ample bosom, and pressed her cheek to Jade's, making kissing sounds.

"Now, come. I will take you to my villa."

"I'm going to need some clothes."

"Si, si, I have clothes. At my villa."

Jade gave Gia an appraising look. "I'm not sure your stuff will fit me."

Gia laughed. "I have food, too. You stay with me long enough, and maybe they will fit, no?" She put her hands to either side of her breasts and plumped them suggestively, then laughed again. "I kid. Diane gave me your measurements. If you don't like, maybe we go shopping later."

"Right."

"Come," Gia said, still cheerful but now with a slightly imperious manner.

Helpless to do otherwise, Jade followed the other woman through the hangar and out the exit to a parking lot where a little red convertible waited, the top already down. Jade noted the round logo on the grill—a red cross next to a snake, and the words "Alfa Romeo" on the circle surrounding the image.

Definitely an upgrade from Diane's old Taurus, Jade thought, but felt even more conspicuous in her sweats.

Gia slid in behind the wheel and started the engine, which roared to life as if the car were eager to be in motion. Jade sensed that if she did not hurry, she would be left behind. She dropped into the passenger's seat and before she could even get her seat belt on, Gia reversed out of the parking space and launched the convertible from the lot like a fighter jet off the deck of an aircraft carrier.

As they cruised down the paved road, Jade took in the lush green countryside, which was dotted with surprisingly few structures, most elegant white houses with red tile roofs. She had been to Rome before, and this looked nothing like what she remembered. "Where are we?" She had to shout to be heard over the roar of the engine and the rush of air passing by.

Gia laughed. "Castello—Castel Gandalfo, on the shore of Lago Albano."

"I thought we were in Rome."

"Si, Roma is there." She made a casual gesture that didn't indicate any direction in particular. "Twenty kilometers. We go later to look for the temple."

She reached over and patted Jade's knee. "This is very exciting. We make history, no?"

Jade returned a noncommittal smile as she filed the information away. Twenty kilometers; about twelve miles.

Five minutes and just as many turns later, Gia steered the little convertible through the gate of a fenced-in compound, and stopped under the portico of a palatial residence. The villa was beautiful, fronted with marble columns, fountains, and elaborately sculpted topiaries, but Jade was feeling increasingly uneasy. She was completely reliant on Gia for everything, and she was starting to suspect that had been the plan all along.

Gia ushered her inside and gave her the grand tour before showing her to an extravagantly appointed bedroom, more a suite really, with a full bath and a dressing area which adjoined a walk-in closet, the latter filled with a variety of outfits ranging from Jade's preferred work uniform—cargo shorts and cotton safari shirts—to slinky cocktail dresses. There was a freestanding vanity with a variety of cosmetics and grooming utensils, and drawers containing a similarly comprehensive array of undergarments. "When can I get started looking for the temple?"

Gia looked over at her with a smile that seemed refreshingly sincere. "As soon as you like."

Jade nodded. "Might as well jump in. I'll need a computer with Internet access."

Gia nodded but seemed a little less enthusiastic about the request. "*Si, si*. The computer is in the library, just down the hall to your right. Everything you need. We have an extensive database of historical information. We have been looking for the temple for many years."

Jade resisted the impulse to probe Gia further on the subject. She wasn't sure how she was going to find something that had so eluded the highly-motivated members of the Cult of Libertas, but right now, her priority was getting to a computer so she could check her email and let Professor know where she was.

When the other woman was gone, Jade wasted no time shedding her tired sweats and, after freshening up, got dressed. On an impulse, she decided to eschew her customary attire, and instead selected a bright floral sundress and a pair of comfortable canvas flats.

The library was about what she expected—full of leather-bound collectible books, framed maps, landscapes, and not a single work of popular fiction anywhere to be found. She was just getting settled in at the computer desk when Gia arrived, bearing a tray with a pitcher of ice water, glasses, and a plate of finger sandwiches.

"You need anything, you just ask."

Jade nodded. "Thanks. Nothing right now."

She moved the mouse to wake the computer up, and was pleased to see that there was no login screen. She opened an Internet browser and directed it to her Gmail account. The screen went blank and stayed that way for a while, prompting Jade to check to verify that she actually had a connection. Gia fussed about in the background but then seemed to get the hint, and exited quietly, just as the page finally loaded. Jade immediately checked her inbox.

Nothing from Professor.

Disappointment hit her like a wave, rocking her back in her chair. The words on the screen went blurry, and when she blinked to bring them back into focus, she felt tears streaking down her cheeks.

Nothing?

Then a horrible thought crossed her mind.

What if Professor had never received her email.

She had sent it from Diane Lindsey's computer *before* learning of the woman's affiliation and true agenda. And from that moment forward—indeed, from the moment she had asked for and accepted Diane's help, she had been completely under the control of the woman or her agents. Even now, she had no way of knowing if Gia or someone else from the Cult of Libertas was monitoring her computer usage, intercepting all attempts to make contact with Professor or anyone else.

She was trapped here. With no money or identification, a foreigner who didn't even speak the language. If she went to the Italian police or to the US Embassy, there was a very real possibility that Special Agent Purcell, or whomever he was really working for, would learn of her whereabouts and make another attempt on her life.

It seemed as if Diane and her cult had covered every contingency, but as long as they believed Jade was unaware of their deception, she had the slim advantage of surprise on her side.

But how to use it?

She wiped away the film of tears, and pulled herself closer to the keyboard. While she didn't yet have a plan, she knew that she had to give the appearance of cooperation, not to mention complete ignorance of what was really going on, and that meant looking for the Temple of Libertas and the sacred relics it supposedly contained. If, by some stroke of luck, she succeeded, she would have even more leverage to use against them.

"Okay, let's start with Spartacus," she said aloud, as much for the benefit of any listening ears as to shift her focus. She typed the gladiator's name into the search bar, and immersed herself in research.

She knew the bare bones of the story; the gladiator who led an ultimately unsuccessful slave revolt. His demise, as imagined by filmmaker Stanley Kubrick in the eponymous 1960 motion picture—crucified on the roadside with his fellow rebels, all shouting the refrain "I am Spartacus" in a show of solidarity—had added to his legend, though as Jade soon learned, nothing like that scene had actually transpired. According to historical sources, Spartacus—the name given to a Thracian fighter accused of desertion from the Roman ranks and subsequently consigned to the arena—had been mortally wounded in battle, his body never identified.

That would make the job of finding his remains next to impossible, Jade thought, but then remembered that she wasn't looking for Spartacus per se, but rather for the Temple of Libertas.

If the Cult of Libertas predated the rebellion of Spartacus, then it wasn't too hard to imagine the devotees of the goddess stealing the remains of the fallen warrior off the battlefield and enshrining them as a symbol of their cause. It wouldn't even have to have been the real Spartacus; any old corpse would have sufficed. Such was the true power of symbols.

Diane had told her that the original temple to Libertas had been demolished in 48 B.C.E. more than twenty years after the end of the Third Servile War and the death of Spartacus. That, she decided, would be her starting point.

She typed "Libertas" into the search bar and skimmed the results.

Like many Roman gods, Libertas had been repurposed from the Greek pantheon—specifically the lesser-known goddess Eleutheria, who some believed was an aspect of Artemis. Curiously, Libertas had not been conceived as a deity for slaves, but rather as a general symbol of freedom from oppression—specifically the oppression of the tyrannical Tarquin kings, whose overthrow had ushered in the period of the Roman Republic at the end of the Sixth Century B.C.E. Two thousand-plus years later, a similar goddess-like figure, called "Columbia" would become an early symbol of the American Republic.

As testimony to the importance of Libertas, the census records of the Republic had been kept in her temple on Aventine Hill for nearly two hundred years. A newer temple, on Palatine Hill, had been erected in 57 B.C.E, but it had lasted only ten years before a dispute over the ownership of the temple site had led to its destruction. That, Jade knew, was the temple Diane had spoken of, the temple where Servilia of the influential Junii family had worshipped.

Jade was a little surprised to learn that the Roman Senate had voted to build a shrine to Libertas to honor Julius Caesar, just two years before Brutus of the Junii would lead the conspiracy to assassinate him. Politics could be fickle like that; today's liberator could very easily become tomorrow's tyrant. No shrine had ever been constructed, but a statue of the goddess had been set up in the Forum.

"The Forum," she murmured. "Where's that?"

A couple clicks later and she was looking at a satellite image of stone pavements and crumbling ruins dating back two and half millennia, situated in the very heart of metropolitan Rome. Just to the right of the old temple complex, a distinctive oval-shaped structure stared up at her like a huge lidless eye, and Jade's lips curled up a little as a plan began to take shape.

She closed the browser window and studied the icons on the desktop, looking for the database Gia had spoken of. One tile bore the distinctive logo of Lighthouse Worldwide, and clicking on it took her to the intranet for that organization, and presumably, the Cult of Libertas.

It was clear from even a cursory glance that the contents of the site were not meant for public consumption. Indeed, without log-in credentials, Jade's explorations were confined to ahandful of documents relating to the search for the temple and the sacred relics, along with some historical information about the Cult and its various incarnations throughout the ages. Jade got the impression that the information had been curated specifically for her, and although she only had a passing interest in any of it now, she read it carefully to further reinforce the façade of cooperation.

The information relating to the temple was similar to what she had discovered elsewhere, but there was more background on the so-called sacred relics.

According to an unnamed historical source, following the decisive final battle in the Third Servile War, Marcus Licinius Crassus, the wealthy and ambitious leader of the Roman legionary force, had removed the body of Spartacus from the field of battle. This contradicted Jade's earlier research which indicated that Spartacus' remains had never been identified. The account further revealed that the Thracian wife of Spartacus, who was known to be a prophetess, had been captured by Crassus and re-enslaved as his personal oracle or Sybil. As a surety to guarantee that she would not use her gifts to manipulate him into ruin, Crassus had promised to give the rebel gladiator a proper burial to ensure that the couple might someday be reunited in the afterlife. Unlike the Romans, who practiced cremation, the Thracians buried their dead, so Crassus had the body of Spartacus placed in an unmarked crypt on his property. In the years that followed, the Sybil prepared an oracular book for Crassus, which he used evidently to great effect, forging a historic triumvirate with his rival Pompey the Great and his good friend and ally, Julius Caesar. When the woman eventually died—no cause of death was indicated, but given her age, the circumstances were suspicious—Crassus buried her with her husband.

Not long after, Crassus set out to the wealthy province of Syria, where he was to serve as governor. The book, along with the bones of Spartacus and his wife, came into the possession of Julius Caesar, who in turn gave them to his mistress, Servilia of the Junii. Recognizing their symbolic power, Servilia placed the relics within the temple of Libertas on Palatine Hill. Meanwhile, Crassus, without his Sibylline book to guide him, came to his end in Syria, dying in a failed bid to conquer the Parthian Empire.

The death of Crassus not only collapsed the triumvirate, which ultimately paved the way for Julius Caesar's rise as dictator, but also directly resulted in the destruction of the Temple of Libertas, which had been built on property seized from the exiled former consul, Cicero. The land had been consecrated in a political maneuver to prevent Cicero from reclaiming it when his exile ended, but after Crassus' death and the disastrous campaign in Syria, Cicero made a successful bid to have the consecration reversed, after which the temple was razed. It was assumed that Servilia thereafter kept the relics at her home, the same house where the conspiracy to assassinate her lover Julius Caesar was hatched. It was no coincidence that Brutus and Cassius named themselves "*Liberatores*"—the Liberators.

It was generally believed that the relics accompanied Brutus during the Liberators' Civil War, fought against the combined armies of Caesar's heir Octavian—who would eventually be named Augustus Caesar—and Mark Antony. Despite some initial successes, Brutus was eventually defeated, choosing to end his own life rather than face capture. His ashes, and presumably everything else he had carried with him, including the sacred relics, were returned to Servilia.

The trail seemed to end there, though the Cult's researchers had come up with several potential lines of research.

The first hypothesis held that Servilia had remained guardian of the relics until her death sometime after 42 B.C.E. The historical record was silent on the matter of her death, but it did indicate that, following the death of her son, Servilia retired to the home of a wealthy equestrian banker and publisher named Titus Pomponius Atticus where she lived out the remainder of her days. Inasmuch as the second triumvirate, which eventually launched the Roman Empire, seemed to have little use for a goddess of liberty, it was reasonable to assume that the temple treasures might have been interred with Servilia's ashes, though exactly where was a question the Cult's researchers had not been able to answer.

The second hypothesis posited that the relics might not have been returned with Brutus' ashes after all, but had been kept by Mark Antony, who might have sought guidance from the Sibylline book in anticipation of a future confrontation with Octavian. That confrontation did occur some ten years later when Octavian, seeking to eliminate his political rivals, declared war on Antony and his lover, Cleopatra, Queen of Egypt. After his defeat at the Battle of Actium, Antony committed suicide, dying in Cleopatra's arms. Cleopatra was permitted to bury Antony, and when she eventually succeeded in taking her own life, shortly thereafter, her remains were interred with him. The exact location of the tomb, somewhere near Alexandria, Egypt, was unknown, but it was not unreasonable to believe that Cleopatra might have concealed the sacred relics of Libertas inside, or even in another location.

These speculations were merely the starting point for multiple tangents. Maybe the relics had been claimed— either from Servilia's mausoleum, Antony's tomb, or elsewhere—by someone else, maybe a faction of the cult, unknown to history, or perhaps an enemy intent on eradicating the symbol of freedom.

All that was really known for certain was that the cult had not died with the Liberators, but had endured, and ultimately, transformed the world with the establishment of the American Republic, followed shortly thereafter by the French Revolution, both of which utilized icons of Libertas—the Americans named her 'Columbia', and the French, 'Marianne'—as symbols of freedom and the republic. It was even possible that those latter-day devotees of the goddess had possessed the sacred relics, drawing both inspiration and guidance from them.

Despite her determination to escape the cult's clutches at the earliest opportunity, Jade felt the inexorable attraction of a mystery. Once she was free and reunited with Professor, perhaps she would accept this challenge, but if she did, it would be on her own terms.

Satisfied that she had put in a decent amount of library time, Jade pushed away from the computer, stretched to work out the kinks from sitting too long, and went looking for Gia.

"I've done all I can here," she said when she found the woman lounging poolside, reading from her tablet computer. "Time to put boots on the ground."

"Boots?" Gia made a sour face and glanced down at Jade's feet.

"It's just a figure of speech. I need to see some of the places I've been reading about. Let's start with the Forum."

Gia shook her head. "You will find nothing there, I think. The Forum is where everybody looks for history."

"I didn't say we'd find it there," Jade countered. "I just said that's where I want to start. This is my process. Do you want me to find the lost temple or not?"

Gia's face scrunched up in a dismayed frown. "Is late. We should wait until morning."

"It's not late." Jade reflexively checked her wrist, but her watch wasn't there. She looked to the sky and found the sun, low in the western sky but still well above the horizon. "What time is it, anyway?"

"*Le diciannove.* You would say seven o'clock in the afternoon. Soon, everything will be closed."

Jade curled her hands into fists like an eager child

preparing to throw a tantrum. "Seven isn't late. Isn't Rome the city that never sleeps?"

"That is New York City," Gia grumbled. "Roma *is la città eterna.*"

"Come on, Gia. I spent all day cooped up. I want to get out. See the city. Soak up some of that Eternal City vibe. What's the point of being free, if you can't enjoy it, right?"

Jade could tell she had chosen the right argument. Gia's frown remained but she let out an exasperated sigh. "*Bene.* We go."

FOURTEEN

Gia's little Alfa Romeo Spider was more like a time machine than a car, as it flew down the narrow highway at what felt like the speed of light, through a historical mosaic pieced together over the course of nearly three millennia.

Jade was glad to have something to distract her from the actual journey. Italy was living up to its reputation as a nation of racecar drivers, and Gia was clearly intent on taking the checkered flag. She wove in and out of traffic, cursing liberally at the drivers of cars who got in her way, and then laughing as she whipped the little convertible around them like they were standing still. For Jade, the initial thrill of the wild ride soon transformed into existential dread, and then simple exhaustion.

The sense of moving through living history only intensified as they left the countryside behind and drove into the heart of the city. Everything looked like it belonged in a museum: fountains, columns and arches, statues, and churches everywhere. The Flavian Amphitheatre, known to most simply as the Colosseum, gradually came into view, rising like a small planet from the horizon. A few seconds later, it was right in front of them, a massive structure of stacked arches, broken in places, but still a monumental architectural accomplishment. And then, it was behind them.

Jade couldn't help but flash a tiny grin, remembering that her sort-of friend Bones Bonebrake had once found himself trapped in a secret passage within the confines of the historic structure. In typical Bones fashion, he'd busted a hole in the wall and fled, much to the surprise and chagrin of the nearby tourists. She wondered if the hole was still there. In some ways, the man was the worst sort of treasure hunter. Her smile faded. Thoughts of Bones brought with them memories she'd prefer to forget.

With what seemed like great reluctance, Gia slowed and turned off the main thoroughfare, negotiating a maze of side streets until they were turned completely around, heading toward the Colosseum again.

"The Forum is just over there," Gia said, nodding her head to the left. "But we may be too late. It closes an hour before sunset."

"Can't hurt to try."

Gia's frown suggested that in fact it might, but nevertheless steered to an available parking spot, shut off the engine, and then dropped the key into a small purse— Dolce & Gabanna, Jade noticed, and not a knock-off.

Jade got out and turned a slow circle, as if taking in the grandeur of the place, though in reality she was looking to see if anyone had followed them. She did not think Gia would risk taking her out in public without having backup ready in case she tried to slip away. There were quite a few people—mostly tourists by the look of them—making their way up and down the sidewalks, many of them heading toward waiting tour buses parked to either side of the long tree-lined avenue, but she also saw a pair of uniformed men standing together at the nearby intersection, idly watching the flow of pedestrian traffic.

She assumed they were policemen. They wore dark blue polo shirts with red shield patches on the shoulder, and blue-gray trousers with red piping, but the belts with holstered pistols and sundry equipment pouches were the giveaway. She supposed they could have been private security guards or even park rangers. Regardless, she intended to give them a wide berth.

Gia pointed up the street and started walking. "We'll need to hurry if we want to get in before they close. The good news is, the ticket is good for two days so we can come back tomorrow if you need another look."

Jade fell into step beside her. "That's a good idea. I might need to spend a lot of time here."

"You think the sacred relics might be here?" Gia asked, clearly skeptical. "Buried for all this time?"

"Who knows? Archaeology requires patience."

They maneuvered against the stream of tourists leaving

the complex and turned onto a cobblestone street that led through the massive Arch of Constantine, built to commemorate the victory of Constantine at the Battle of Milvian Bridge against the forces of Emperor Maxentius. The outcome of that battle had changed more than just the leadership of the Roman Empire. According to historians of the day, shortly before the fight, Constantine claimed to have received a vision of a cross in the sky and a promise that by converting to Christianity, he would be victorious. He was, and so began the Christianization of Europe, though in fact there were no Christian symbols on the towering triple-arch.

To the left, behind a tall fence, was a complex of half-demolished buildings rising up the side of a low hill. The distinctive arches and curved walls marked them as being of ancient Roman design. Jade could just make out the Arch of Titus, at the entrance to the Forum. Though not quite as large as Constantine's arch, the Arch of Titus, marked another victory that had fundamentally shaped the modern world. Built to commemorate the siege and destruction of Jerusalem in the 1st century C.E. the arch showed a procession of triumphant Romans carrying off the spoils of the Holy Temple, including the Golden Menorah—an enormous six-branched lampstand. The destruction of Jerusalem had begun the Jewish diaspora, and despite the formation of the State of Israel in modern times, the only holy building on the Temple Mount was a Muslim mosque.

In the other direction, beyond the arch was a large open grassy area, where the foundations of long forgotten structures were still visible, and just past that stood the Colosseum.

Despite the circumstances, Jade felt a mild thrill of excitement at the thought of sharing the same physical space, albeit separated by more than two thousand years, as men who had truly shaped the course of history. Julius Caesar, Mark Antony, Augustus Caesar, and dozens more throughout the ages—all of them had walked here.

She was no stranger to walking in historic places, but

because her field of expertise focused primarily on pre-Columbian Meso-America, most of the people who had walked in ancient places like Tenochtitlan, Teotihuacan, and Macchu Pichu, had passed from the earth without leaving a mark. Even the most famous—men like Moctezuma and Atahualpa—were not exactly household names, and their brief moment on the stage of history had mostly vanished like a pebble thrown into the ocean. The great cultures they had presided over were gone, their societies all but wiped out by foreign conquerors and the diseases they had brought. The descendants of the Maya, Aztec and Inca were still extant, but the words and deeds of their rulers were almost completely unknown, while the men who had ruled the world of their day from Palatine Hill had left an indelible mark.

She stopped and made another slow turn, to all appearances just one more tourist gawking at the ancient wonders. She immediately caught a glimpse of the two policemen, about fifty yards back, casually making their way up the sidewalk. Closer, but conspicuously moving in the same direction as Gia and herself—and against the flow of traffic—was a young couple. They were holding hands, and as Jade's gaze settled on them, they turned toward each other and laughed as if sharing a joke.

Gotcha, Jade thought, turning away again. She smiled at Gia and then took a quick step sideways, right into the path of a stocky middle-aged man wearing a broad brimmed straw hat and a loud Hawaiian shirt.

From the corner of her eye, she could see Gia stiffening in alarm. Jade glanced back quickly and saw the young couple start forward, then stop uncertainly, clearly caught flat-footed by Jade's unexpected action. Further back, the policemen were reacting as well, quickening their step as if they had just witnessed a crime.

So, they're in on it, too.

Once again, the cultists had covered all their bases. If Jade tried to run, or better yet, appealed to these police officers for help, they would be able to regain control of her without drawing undue attention from onlookers.

Nothing to see here, folks. Police business. Move along.

The man in the loud shirt stopped short, surprised and a little irritated. He shifted direction, trying to go around her, but Jade reached out with both hands as if intending to embrace the man. "Hey! Long ways from home, yeah?"

This stopped the man. It also stopped Gia and the other cultists. Jade could just see them in her peripheral vision, moving up alongside her, ready to pounce, but not wanting to make a scene.

The man blinked at her for a moment, clearly searching his memory, and then offered a wan but hopeful smile. He clearly didn't remember her, but he wasn't about to admit it. "Hi… You."

"It's Jack, right?"

"Ummm… No. Uh, Bill, actually."

Jade made a pouty face. "Are you sure?" Then she laughed. "Crazy, huh. Hey, I left my phone back at the hotel and I don't want to leave here without getting a selfie. Can you snap me?"

Bill blinked again, still struggling to process this random encounter. He was obviously not a man who frequently found himself accosted by attractive women on the street. After a quick look around, perhaps to make sure that he wasn't about to become the unwitting star of a viral internet prank, he grinned at his good fortune. "Sure thing."

He dug out his phone—a weary-looking iPhone 4— and began thumbing the touchscreen, which was spider-webbed with fractures, to bring up the camera function. As he did, Jade took another quick glance around, marking the location of the hand-holding couple and the ersatz cops. The former had continued up the path a little ways and were looking at each other with moon eyes, gamely attempting to maintain the illusion that they were just young lovers out for a stroll. The cops weren't even trying. They had split up, positioning themselves behind her, about ten yards apart, forming a triangle with her at the top. Gia was a few steps away, glaring at her, but nobody else seemed to have any interest in her.

"Ready," Bill announced, holding the camera up.

Jade turned so the Colosseum was at her back. "Make sure you get a wide shot. I want everyone to know where I really am."

"You betcha. Okay, smile and say 'sex.'"

Jade grimaced and, in a flat voice said, "Cheese."

"Heh. Okay. Got it."

"Great. Can you text it to me?"

Bill was suddenly nonplussed. "I... Uh, don't know if I have your number."

Jade smacked a hand to her forehead. "Duh. Of course." She reached out. "Here. Let me."

Bill smiled, knowing that he was mere seconds from having Jade's digits. Jade attached the photo to a text message that read, "Meet me here!" and sent it to herself.

She might not have remembered Professor's number, or anyone else's for that matter, but she did know her own. Her plan—at least this part of it—hinged on the likelihood that Professor would be monitoring her phone in hopes of tracking her down or making contact with the kidnappers, but just in case, she took the added measure of logging into her seldom used Facebook account, posting the picture with the same message and tagging her location.

When she was done, she logged out and handed the phone back to Bill. "Perfect. Hey, we should grab a drink somewhere and catch up."

Suddenly an arm enfolded her like a tentacle. "Jade, *bella*, have you forgotten? We have things to do. So busy." The honey dripping from Gia's voice could not disguise the underlying tone of menace. She waved one hand at the hapless Bill, and chirped, "*Ciao*." Then, she steered Jade away, back in the direction from which they had come, and without letting her fake smile drop, hissed through clenched teeth, "That was not a good thing to do."

Jade set her jaw. "Wouldn't be a very good Chosen One if I couldn't tell when I'm still in chains, yeah?" She paused a beat, then added, "Or know how to break them."

As soon as she said it, she stomped down on Gia's left foot, grinding her heel onto the pointed toes of the woman's expensive leather shoes. In the same motion, she dropped down into a crouch, slipping out of Gia's restraining one-armed hug, ripping the woman's purse away in the process. As soon as she was free, she launched herself to the side, hopping over the low rail that separated the paved walk from the grassy area.

She immediately took off running, sprinting across the open area, hopping over the low stone footings and dashing past meandering tourists who gaped in disbelief, uncertain what to make of the woman in the floral dress doing parkour on the ruins of the old Forum. Jade sensed that the bogus cops were probably giving chase, maybe the love-struck couple too, but she didn't look back. She was running all out, and either she would outdistance them or she wouldn't; there was nothing to be gained, and everything to be lost by taking her eyes off her destination. That actually didn't pose much of a problem since her destination—the Colosseum—pretty much filled the world ahead of her.

As she neared the ring of arched entrances, she veered to the right, running along the outer perimeter of the massive amphitheater. Each archway was blocked by a fence of tightly-spaced steel poles, easily twice as high as Jade was tall, but she could see through to the shadowy interior where the last wave of tourists were roaming about. She sprinted until the burning in her lungs forced her to slow—maybe two hundred yards, which got her maybe a quarter of the way around—but forced herself to keep moving at a fast jog.

Another fifty yards brought her around to the east flank of the Colosseum. To her left, a low hill disappeared behind a high retaining wall, and just above it, she could see buildings. Though she couldn't see it, Jade knew the main boulevard Gia had driven in on was just up there. A stairway provided pedestrian access from the Colosseum walk up to the street level, while directly in front of her, the path jogged to the left around the original perimeter wall, only half of which still stood, extending out another fifty feet or so along the north half of the structure.

Jade now risked a quick look back. If the phony cops were chasing her—and she had to believe they were—they were eclipsed from view by the curve of the Colosseum. She briefly considered abandoning her original plan and trying for the stairs, but rejected the idea as it would almost certainly reveal her to the pursuing cultists. Instead, she made the slight adjustment to get around the exterior wall, and kept going, pouring on another burst of speed, albeit a short-lived one. It was not exhaustion that slowed her however, but opportunity.

After passing a couple arches that were completely bricked in, she came to another that was gated-off. The plaster façade covering the cut travertine that formed the arches was pocked with enormous holes—holes big enough to serve as handholds, which was exactly what she planned to use them for. She scrambled onto the façade, using the fence and the divots in the wall like a ladder until she was high enough to crest the steel rods and slip beneath the arch. Once over, she gripped a pole with either hand, braced the arches of her feet against them, and then slid down.

The whole process took less than ten seconds.

As soon as her feet hit the paving stones, she whirled and started down the entrance tunnel. Situated on the eastern side as it was, the tunnel was shrouded in gloom, with just a couple patches of indirect daylight filtering through to show her the way. There were no tourists here, no one on the inside to witness her trespass, and as soon as she was away from the arch, she ducked down to watch and see if anyone would follow. Across the way, something caught her eye—a spot where the wall had recently been patched. To the average observer it would have probably gone unnoticed, but to her trained eye it stuck out like a sore thumb. *Good old Bones.*

Her antics had not gone unobserved. A handful of tourists idling on the walk had witnessed her illicit entry, and yet as was all too often the case in such situations, after a moment of incredulity, most simply went back to what they were doing. It didn't concern them and there was probably a simple mundane explanation.

A few seconds later, the two-policeman pounded past the entrance, their heads bobbing as they surveyed the crowd. They were so intently focused on looking for her that they ignored the furtive glances and even a couple shouts from the crowd urging them to turn their attention to the archway, and after a moment, they were gone from her view.

Jade sagged back against the walls, panting to catch her breath. She hoped her message would reach Professor, and that he would understand it, but it would be at least another twelve hours before he could reach her. She would have to find better place to hide, though from what she'd seen of the Colosseum in documentaries, that wouldn't be a problem.

She took a moment to check the contents of the little purse she had pilfered from Gia. Aside from the Alfa Romeo key, there was a travel-sized makeup kit, a lipstick— probably the same deep red shade Gia had been wearing— and a slim wallet that contained a few euro bills in various denominations. There were no credit cards or identifying documents, and no phone. It was almost as if Gia had planned ahead for the possibility that Jade might try to snatch her purse and make a run for it.

The money might come in handy, though she was hesitant to emerge from hiding. She doubted the rest of it would do her any good, but nevertheless jury-rigged a repair on the broken strap and slung the purse over one shoulder.

As she moved deeper into the gloom, it occurred to her that she was once more on the run, hunted and friendless. Despite having traveled to the other side of the world, she was basically no better off than she had been twenty-four hours earlier.

FIFTEEN

Professor saw Jade's photo half an hour after it posted thanks to a head's up from Tam, who despite having her own crises, had managed to divert some of the Myrmidons' resources to the search.

"Rome?" He muttered, double-checking the metadata to make sure the picture really had been sent from where it appeared to have been shot. "She was supposed to be in Houston."

Houston was where he had spent the previous night and all of the day so far, waiting and hoping for Jade to either make contact with him, or pop up on Purcell's radar.

"Why Rome?" It was a rhetorical question; only Jade would be able to answer. "How did she get there?"

"Can't help you with that," Tam answered. "She didn't clear customs anywhere in the Eurozone. She must be getting help from someone. Maybe she's working with that cult you heard about?"

"More likely, she's still their captive. Don't you see? This photo was a cry for help. They're keeping her under wraps."

"She doesn't exactly looked 'wrapped' to me," Tam replied.

"'Meet me here.' That's for me, Tam. You need to get me there. ASAP."

Tam equivocated for about a minute, but then agreed to make the arrangements, which was why, fourteen hours later, he was standing in almost exactly the same place Jade had been standing when she'd been photographed.

During that interval, he had learned a little more about the picture. It had been taken with an iPhone that belonged to a William Craig of Muncie, Indiana, who was presently vacationing in Rome as part of a group tour.

After a quick background check on the man, which yielded nothing of interest, Professor called the phone and, after identifying himself as Special Agent Purcell from DHS, questioned Craig about the circumstances of the photo.

"I already told the cops everything I know about it," Craig protested. "This chick just came up to me out of the blue like she knew me and asked me to take her picture. Then, before I knew what was happening, she took off running with a couple of cops on her tail. Never saw her again. Too bad, too. I was in the mood for some spicy Chinese food, if you know what I mean."

"Be glad you didn't get a taste of that," Professor had said, suppressing the urge to tell the man what he really thought of the comment. "We don't call her the Black Widow Killer for nothing."

Craig gulped nervously and Professor hung up on him.

He had a pretty good idea of why Jade had done what she had. It seemed evident that she had slipped the leash of her captors and had reached out to him in the only way she knew how. He was troubled by Craig's mention of 'cops,' and checked again to see if Jade—or anyone matching her general description—had been picked up. Not only was the response negative, but there was no mention of either city police or Carabinieri officers being involved in an incident near the Colosseum.

Which meant the officers who had questioned Craig and chased after Jade had not been real policemen at all, or at least had not been acting in an official capacity. But had they managed to catch her?

"Meet me here," he muttered as he stared at the building. "Okay, Jade where are you?"

She probably hadn't meant for him to literally meet her on that exact spot. In fact, he favored a broader interpretation of the message. *Meet me here, at the Colosseum.* But that was a little like saying "meet me at Wrigley Field on opening day." The interior of the Colosseum covered an area of six acres, and at any given time during daylight hours, there might be hundreds if not thousands of people visiting it. And Jade's message had given only a place, not a time.

His flight, which had departed Houston in late afternoon, had delivered him to Rome shortly before sunrise, whereupon he had come directly here by taxi. It was still early morning, the sun not even visible above the trees in the foreground. The Colosseum and Forum would not be open for visitors for another hour, but there was already a line of people waiting to go in as soon as the gates rose. Professor scanned the faces, looking for Jade, but it was like playing Where's Waldo.

Maybe she would have better luck finding him.

He got in the ticket queue and waited his turn. As he stood there, half-listening to the conversations of his fellow linemates and chuckling at some of the more preposterous bits of trivia he overheard, he studied the crowd from beneath the brim of his fedora. He was looking for Jade but also looking for anyone who looked like they might also be looking for her; anyone who seemed just a little too devoted to people-watching, or who looked like they were trying too hard to look like wide-eyed tourists. The policemen who had questioned Bill Craig had no doubt seen the text message, and it was reasonable to assume that they were staking out the place, and probably not in uniform.

There was also a very real chance that they were looking for *him*. They certainly knew about his friendship with Jade, and Yann Pierre would have reported in on what had happened in Haiti. It wouldn't take a genius to figure out that Jade's message was intended for him.

The line finally began moving, the first visitors of the day making their way into the nearly two-thousand-year-old entertainment venue. He shuffled along with the others into the outer arcade, where he purchased his entry ticket and passed through the metal detector at the security checkpoint.

He wandered along, to all appearances taking in the sights, eavesdropping on tour guides as they described the construction of the Colosseum and the bloody gladiatorial games that had taken place in its arena. He knew much of this already, but the stops gave him an excuse to remain in one place and look around. He moved down to the edge of the arena and looked out across the forest of stone walls and pillars that had once formed the sub-floor of the arena—the hypogeum—where gladiators and animals awaited their rendezvous with destiny. The original wooden floor was gone, exposing the underground chambers to view.

The shadowy maze was exactly the kind of place where an archaeologist like Jade would have felt right at home. Access to the hypogeum was limited to authorized tour groups, so if he wanted to check it out, he would either need to call one of the tour companies, or sneak in.

Sneaking would probably be easier, he decided. The tours were typically booked solid several weeks in advance.

He lingered at the edge of the arena a little longer, figuring that if Jade was hiding down there, she would see him and come find him, then started back up to the main balcony. He wasn't leaving though. He would keep doing this—wandering back and forth, peeking into the shadows, even venturing into off-limits areas—until he found her.

Just as he was about to turn the corner onto the upper level, he glimpsed movement in his peripheral vision. Someone was moving toward him—practically charging—from behind and to the right. He spun, ready to meet the charge, but was half a second too late. He felt his assailant's arms close around his middle, squeezing him hard enough to force the air from his lungs.

It took his SEAL-trained reflexes just two-tenths of a second to react, to read the situation and decide the appropriate response.

He threw his arms around the shorter figure and hugged her back almost as fiercely.

"Jade," he whispered with the last of his breath. "Thank God."

"You got my message," she said into his chest. He could feel her shaking, crying.

"I did."

"They kidnapped me," she said, the words coming out in little gasps. "Yann. He's part of the cult—"

"Shhhh," Professor whispered, giving her another gentle squeeze. He had a million questions, and knew she probably did too, but now that she had revealed herself to him, they had to get moving. As gently as he could, he pulled her loose and held her at arm's length. She was wearing the same dress as in the picture, looking just a little more rumpled, but otherwise seemed no worse for wear considering her ordeal. "Let's get out of here. You can tell me everything when you're safe."

"They won't try anything now that you're here," Jade said, her confident smile strangely complementing her glistening eyes.

"I hope you're right," he said, taking her hand and turning her around to head back down toward the exit.

They only made it as far as the main level before those hopes were dashed.

Jade stiffened as the four figures—three men and a woman, all dressed in military-style black uniforms, replete with bulky tactical vests, and topped with dark berets—seemed to materialize in front of them. Her joy at being reunited with Professor evaporated faster than the tears that streaked her cheeks. "Cops. Crap! They're working with the cult!"

She started to turn away, but two things stopped her: Professor's hand on her arm, and the fact that two more policeman—or whatever they were—had appeared behind them, blocking that avenue of escape.

"Carabinieri," muttered Professor. "Maybe this isn't what it looks like."

"Wanna bet?" Jade said, eyeing the uniformed men warily as they closed in, forming a circle around the two of them. The six Carabinieri officers were not alone. Behind them, several more—some of them dressed in the same paramilitary fashion, others wearing a more traditional police uniform with sky blue shirt and peaked cap—were quietly ushering the other visitors from the area. Then she spotted someone else approaching them, someone not in uniform, but familiar nonetheless.

Jade's heart became a jackhammer in her chest. She reflexively tried to pull away from Professor, even though there was nowhere to go.

"Purcell?" Professor said, sounding genuinely surprised. "What are you doing here? Did you follow me?"

Special Agent Jacob Purcell continued forward, stopping at the edge of the surrounding circle. "Let's not make a scene, Chapman."

"I think it's too late for that," Professor shot back. "You're way out of line here. Not to mention out of your jurisdiction." He abruptly turned his gaze to one of the beret-wearing Carabinieri officers, and barked something in rapid-fire Italian.

A surprised look came over the other man's face, and Purcell's forehead creased in dismay. Jade had no idea what Professor had just said, but it seemed pretty clear that he had just pulled rank on Purcell.

The Italian officer replied in the same tongue, a question, Jade surmised, which Professor answered quickly and authoritatively. He then tilted his head toward Jade. "I told him Purcell is running a rogue op and convinced him to kick this up the chain of command. We'll have to go along with them, but we'll get this all sorted out."

"He tried to kill me," Jade hissed.

"I know. We'll get that sorted out, too."

"You *know*? And you still let him follow you here?"

"I didn't *let* him do anything," Professor gave an exasperated sigh. "Just trust me. I'm not going to—"

His assurance was interrupted by a series of loud staccato pops, like a string of firecrackers, or….

Before Jade could reach the obvious conclusion, Professor yanked her arm down, pulling her to a prone position beside him, even as the circle of people around them broke apart, the individual Carabinieri reacting to the sound of incoming gun fire. One of them, Jade noticed, was writhing on the ground in obvious pain.

More shots followed, but now they were coming from different places, different guns, the reports overlapping. The Carabinieri were answering the attack, returning fire. All around them, the stone pavement was erupting in little explosions of dust.

"What…? Who…?"

Professor raised his head then popped to his feet, dragging Jade along with him. She stumbled behind him, trying to get her feet under her, succeeding just as he pulled her down again behind the relative cover of an arch that had once held up a section of the seating area reserved for lesser aristocrats.

After another volley of fire was exchanged, Professor poked his head around the corner for a second, then drew back. "Looks like one or two of the Carabinieri switched sides," he said. "Or maybe they were ringers. But that wasn't Purcell trying to kill you."

"Guess not," Jade said, knowing exactly who was behind the attack. "And I don't think they're trying to kill me."

Professor turned and fixed her with a look that was almost accusatory. "You mean because you're their Chosen?"

"You know about that?" She recoiled a little from the intensity of his expression. "I'm not with them. They kidnapped me. Who do you think I just escaped from?"

He frowned but then nodded. "I know. I believe you." His tone however suggested that his trust was not without some reservation.

Jade pulled back even further and then stood up, her hands on her hips. "You know what? Screw you. I was doing just fine without your help."

"Jade, wait—"

Jade had no intention of waiting. She didn't really want to ditch Professor, but she wasn't going to wait for him to save her, or worse, allow him to unwittingly deliver her into Purcell's hands for summary execution. She spun around and darted out into the open, right through the midst of the embattled Carabinieri.

Although it might have seemed like a hysterical reaction, Jade knew exactly what she was doing. She had spent much of the previous night wandering the Colosseum, dodging night watchmen and familiarizing herself with its many passages, and she had mapped out an escape route, just in case the cultists found her before Professor. She just needed to reach the edge of the arena, and the shortest path to that destination required her to run the gauntlet.

Jade was pretty sure the cultists wouldn't shoot her. She was the Chosen, after all; they needed her alive. She didn't think the Carabinieri would shoot her either, not intentionally anyway. Some part of her actually hoped both sides would stop shooting altogether, just to avoid accidentally hitting her, but even if they didn't, it was a risk she was willing to take to avoid being taken captive again.

But as she raced past the uniformed officers who were hiding behind arches and pillars, she realized there was a variable she had not accounted for.

Purcell.

He was now armed with a pistol—not the SIG he had aimed at her in the shipping container, but a Beretta, the same kind of gun the Carabinieri officers were using. He had probably taken it off the man who had been injured in the initial attack. And he was looking right at her.

She had been counting on the fact that he wouldn't try to murder her in front of witnesses, but with lead flying from every direction, he could simply claim that she stepped in front of a bullet. She could tell by the look in his eyes that he was thinking exactly the same thing.

Crap!

She saw him shift the barrel in her direction, and then forced herself to look away. If she kept moving, zigging and zagging, he might miss. He might even think twice about pulling the trigger. Or, he would have to shoot her in the back. Since there was nothing she could do to stop him, she just lowered her head and poured on the speed, sprinting toward the chest-high metal rail that separated visitors from the open pit at the center of the amphitheater.

In ancient times, the entire area had been covered by the wooden floor of the arena, and a layer of sand—the word arena in fact derived from the Latin word for 'sand'—

to soak up uncountable gallons of blood from hundreds of thousands of gladiators and criminals sentenced to be executed, along with millions of animals, killed for sport.

The sand was gone, along with the floor, but evidently the arena was still hungry for blood—her blood.

She winced with each report, expecting to feel a bullet slam into her. Maybe she wouldn't feel anything at all, but simply wink out of existence like a snuffed-out candle flame. But then she reached the rail, and just as she had mentally rehearsed, she planted one hand atop it and vaulted over.

As she touched down on the uneven surface atop the outermost wall of the hypogeum, she spied a lone figure giving chase, just a few steps behind her, and realized why no bullets had found her. It was Professor, his fist wrapped around the grip of a Beretta. Behind him, she could see Purcell sprawled out and unmoving on the stone floor.

She allowed herself a quick smile. "Believe me now?"

Professor ignored the comment, slowing at the last instant and using the rail to arrest his momentum. "Move it!"

Figuring that was as close to an apology as she was going to get under the circumstances, she turned and dropped flat, then lowered herself down into the shadows of the hypogeum. The irregularly weathered stone was a perfect climbing surface, though she only descended a few feet before pushing off the wall and dropping the rest of the way down. Professor landed beside her a moment later, and she took off running.

The hypogeum was relatively small—an area about half the size of a football field—but the broken walls and pillars that filled that space posed a formidable maze which Jade had explored extensively during the night, marking her escape route with discreet little red arrows. Gia's lipstick had come in handy for something after all.

With Professor right behind her, she navigated the labyrinth, reaching a flight of modern stairs that ascended to the main level on the east side of the structure, not far from where she had entered. As she raced toward the huge arch at the entrance, she could see the retaining wall and the staircase leading up to street level. A twelve-foot-high iron fence, each vertical picket ending in a brutal-looking point, barred their way. Beyond it, lay a small courtyard, a buffer zone that encompassed several of the arched entrances, surrounded by a second fence—this one with pointed pickets turned outward at a forty-five-degree angle to discourage intruders.

Jade, who had mentally rehearsed her escape countless times during the night, ran up to the first barrier and without a moment's hesitation, began climbing, using the fence and the pock-marked arch to which it was attached like the rungs of a ladder.

The points at the top of the pickets were more a psychological measure than a practical one. Ignoring the perceived threat of impalement, Jade swung her body up and over, and then slid down, using the pickets like a fire pole. As she landed, she realized that Professor was staring out at her from the inside, a look of incredulity on his face.

"Coming?"

Professor shook his head and mounted the fence, beginning his own ascent.

Jade spun away, heading for the second fence. Beyond it, scores of early morning visitors were milling about. More than a few gaped in astonishment at her as she scrambled up and over the iron uprights with the alacrity of a gecko and dropped down into their midst.

Ignoring the voices of outrage, and not a few awed compliments—presumably from adrenaline junkies—she turned to check on Professor's progress. He had just crested the top of the inner fence, and eschewing caution, leaped away from it, landing in a controlled shoulder roll— probably something he had learned to do as a SEAL. He bounded back to his feet, and in three giant strides, reached the outer fence. He scaled it effortlessly and landed beside her.

"Now what?"

Jade was bent over, hands on her knees, panting to

catch her breath after running the obstacle course, but after one more deep inhale, she straightened. "This way."

Jade turned toward the steps, realizing only then that the crowd of astonished onlookers was now blocking their escape route. She tried weaving through the crowd but it seemed that every time she found a gap, it closed before she could slip through.

Suddenly, the report of a pistol cracked in the air behind her. A wave of dread crashed over her as she threw herself flat on the paving stones, along with almost everyone else around her. She had really hoped that running the obstacle course through the hypogeum would give her enough of a lead on the pursuit. When she glanced back however, she saw Professor still standing, holding the Beretta in one upraised hand.

"Everybody stay down," he shouted, then glanced at Jade and added, "Except you."

Jade didn't need further urging. She sprang to her feet and resumed her dash to the stairs, hopping over the prostrated forms of tourists who would definitely have stories to tell about their vacation.

The congestion cleared as she reached the steps, bounding up them two at a time until she reached the street level, where cars and buses were whizzing by, the drivers utterly unaware of the drama that had played out just a short distance away. Jade had not worked out the details of her escape route much past this point, but it was obvious that they would never make it across the busy street. That left two choices: left, or right.

To the left, the road dipped down and curved around the Colosseum. Jade recalled passing that way with Gia the day before. That journey had ended with them circling back around to the other side of Palatine Hill, to the west of the Forum complex.

I wonder…?

It was a crazy thought, too much to hope for, but the seed was already planted and taking root.

She reached back and grabbed Professor's hand. The

pistol was gone now, probably tucked in his belt and covered with his shirttail. "This way!" she said, steering him to the right.

A dense stand of trees hid them from the stunned onlookers below, but as they moved out into the open, Jade could see and hear panic moving through the crowd, spreading like a contagion. She quickened her pace to a brisk but hopefully inconspicuous jog and continued in a clockwise direction around the south end of the Colosseum. Below, the human stampede had begun, a slow wave flowing away from the amphitheater. The leading edge was spilling through the Arch of Constantine, clogging the main approach. The sidewalk ahead was already filling up with pedestrians who had climbed the hill and hopped over the low guardrails in their rush to escape the nameless horror that had descended upon the historic monument.

"Hurry!" Jade said, veering onto the street. One car after another flew past, none slowing or even swerving to avoid her. The noise of honking horns joined the general tumult, but Jade ignored it all, running down the hill, and toward the stampede.

"You do have a plan, right?" Professor shouted from behind her. His tone was urgent but steady. "Or are you trusting chaos theory to save us?"

Jade felt a twinge of irritation, partly at the question but mostly at the fact that Professor wasn't even breathing heavily. She felt like her lungs were on fire.

"Yes," she said. "Plan. How 'bout…" *Gasp.* "You trust me for a change."

She didn't waste breath trying to explain, but reached into her reserves for one last burst of speed.

At the bottom of the hill, the road straightened and continued south. To either side, an unbroken line of parked tour buses stretched to the limit of vision.

"Almost there," she rasped, more for her own benefit than Professor's. He probably hadn't even heard.

As the end of the mad dash drew close, doubts began to bubble up, supplanting the hope that had spurred her into action.

What were you thinking? There's no way it's still there.

What had seemed at least faintly plausible at the beginning now seemed like pure foolishness. A waste of time and energy.

Maybe we can duck onto one of these buses, she thought, and was about to suggest this to Professor when she spotted it, right where she had last seen it, twelve hours earlier. She skidded to a stop.

"What?" Professor asked, stopping beside her, his flared nostrils the only indication that he had exerted himself at all.

She nodded to the bright red Alfa Romeo Spider convertible parked beside them, and held up a key. "This is my ride."

SIXTEEN

As Jade reached for the door handle, Professor's hand shot out, catching her by the wrist. "Whoa there, Speed Racer. Give me the key. I've got this."

She yanked her hand free. "Excuse me?"

"Jade, I'm a better driver than you. You know it's true."

"The hell I do," she shot back, reaching for the door handle again.

"Do you know the way to the airport?"

That stopped her. She knew she was just being obstinate; in truth, she wasn't all that confident in her ability to drive in Roman traffic.

"Fine." She slapped the key into his open palm and circled around to the other side, to slide into the passenger seat. Professor was already seated beside her, his long legs pressed up against the bottom of the steering wheel. He adjusted both the column and the low-slung seat for max legroom, which still didn't look very comfortable to Jade, and then worked the ignition.

The seat belt chime was as loud as an anti-theft alarm, but that sound was drowned out by the throaty roar of the engine starting. Professor revved the motor a couple times as he studied the console, searching for the gearshift lever and the brake release, and then with only a quick look to make sure that the coast was clear, cranked the wheel and punched the accelerator.

The Spider burst out of the parking space like a rocket, and almost immediately, the sound of a honking horn and screeching tires filled the air. Jade looked in the side mirror and saw a van in the lane behind them, surrounded by a blue haze of smoke. Professor never looked back, but kept accelerating, working his way through gears as they shot down the straightaway, all the while hooting like a kid on a roller coaster.

Holy crap. Jade thought, sinking lower in her seat and

squeezing her eyes shut. *And I thought Gia was a crazy driver.*

She felt something on her lap and opened her eyes to find Professor shoving his fedora at her. "Hold this for me," he shouted.

She took it, gripping the brim of the hat with both hands to keep it from being sucked out by the rush of air moving through the open interior.

"We should be at the airport in about twenty minutes," he went on. "Maybe a little sooner if our luck holds and the traffic is light."

"I'd rather get there alive," Jade retorted.

Professor laughed. "You're safe now."

As if to contradict him, at that exact moment, the distinctive two-tone high-low wail of sirens became audible, growing louder as a convoy of black cars, outfitted with flashing lights, approached from the opposite direction— Carabinieri officers responding to the pandemonium at the Colosseum. Professor eased off the accelerator as they passed, but only a little, and Jade held her breath, half-expecting one of the vehicles to swerve in front of them, cutting off their escape, exhaling only when the last of the sedans blew past and the noise of the sirens began to fade.

She glanced in the mirror again, watching as the last of the police cars disappeared around the bend in the road. The Colosseum was already gone, hidden from view by the trees that lined the road. The van that had almost hit them when they'd pulled out however was still behind them, and impossible though it seemed, was closing on them.

That was when Jade realized the jet turbine roar of the Alfa Romeo's engine had gone quiet.

"Crap," Professor muttered. "It just died."

He worked the gear shift, putting the car in neutral and allowing it to coast as he tried the ignition again.

Nothing happened.

"I think we just got Lojacked." He wrestled the steering wheel to the right, coasting the stricken vehicle to the curb. The front end narrowly missed a young man who had just dismounted from a pumpkin-orange Vespa. As the car stopped moving, Professor turned to her, his tone that of a weary parent no longer surprised by anything his wayward child might do. "Jade, did we just steal this car?"

She flushed, embarrassed not so much at the accusation as she was at her own naivete. The cultists had played her. They had left the car parked there, knowing that Jade had stolen Gia's keys, watching and waiting, just in case she tried to take it. They had probably been watching it the whole time. A trap, and she had fallen right in. "Well… kinda."

"That would fall under the category of useful things to tell me ahead of time."

Her earlier irritation with him rose back to the surface. "I thought it was kind of obvious that I didn't have my very own Italian convertible. Just what the hell do you think I've been doing the last three days? Bopping around the world on vacation?"

"I don't know. You're here. You had the key. What was I supposed to think?"

"God, with friends like you…" She shoved his fedora at his chest, then grabbed the key from the ignition.

"Jade, wait—"

She was done waiting. She grabbed the top of the windshield and pulled herself up, stepping over the still closed passenger door to land beside the young man who was cursing at her—in German, no less—as he struggled, unnecessarily, to roll his scooter away from the now motionless car.

Another friggin' tourist, she thought, and held up the key, waving it in front of him. "Hey. Trade ya?"

The Teutonic tirade ceased instantly, the dangling key clearly transcending the language barrier. The kid's eyes went wide and then a smile broke across his face as he began nodding vigorously.

She tossed the key to him, and in the same motion, grabbed the handlebars of the scooter. Behind her, Professor was climbing across the interior of the Alfa Romeo in order to exit on the sheltered side of the vehicle.

"Jade. Just hang on a sec."

She ignored him, straddling the scooter, which was ridiculously easy since, unlike a motorcycle or even a bicycle, there was nothing between the padded seat and the steering column except a flat platform just a few inches off the ground. A quick glance at the column revealed a dearth of actual controls, but it had squeeze hand brakes like a bike and the right handgrip twisted back and forth like the throttle on a motorcycle.

So how do you turn it on?

She spotted a key protruding from the column, a few inches below the panel and gave it a twist. There was a faint whirring sound, like a small pump motor and the fuel indicator flashed on, but nothing else happened.

Great. Now I'm going to have to ask the German kid how this thing works. Maybe I should have thought this through a little better.

She glanced over and saw the Vespa's former operator already behind the wheel, trying to figure out why the sports car wouldn't start.

Where's Prof…?

Something bumped against her from behind and the scooter rocked a little as additional weight settled onto its tires. Professor had just climbed on behind her. Before she knew what was happening, he had reached around from either side to grip the handlebars, closing his hands over hers.

"Hey…" Her protest died as she glimpsed the van—the same van that had almost hit them—screeching to a stop alongside the derelict Alfa Romeo. All of its doors opened simultaneously, disgorging at least half a dozen people. Jade recognized the young lovers and one of the policemen who had chased her the previous afternoon, though he was no longer wearing his uniform.

Probably wasn't a real cop, Jade thought.

Gia was there too, hobbling toward the sidewalk, wincing each time she put her left foot down.

Good. I hope it's broken.

"Hang on!" Professor shouted. He stomped his left

foot down on the kickstarter and the scooter's little motor sputtered to life.

Kickstarter! Jade mentally smacked herself in the forehead. *Duh.*

She felt pressure on her hand as Professor rotated the throttle forward and the Vespa shot ahead, bumping up onto the sidewalk. Jade yelped a little as the scooter wobbled, and stuck her feet out, letting them drag along the pavement to maintain balance.

One of the cultists made a grab for them, but Professor let go with his left hand and swatted the man away. Then they were out of reach, zipping along the sidewalk parallel to a fence that enclosed a vast field, that looked like a dry lake bed or canal, as wide as a football field and at least a quarter of a mile long, studded with crumbling ruins.

"Pull your feet in," Professor shouted in her ear.

She complied, albeit with trepidation and reluctance, but after a few seconds, began to trust that the forward motion would sustain their balance. *Just like riding a bike,* she thought.

Professor continued along the fence line, turning left around the end of the long field, and after weaving through a gaggle of pedestrians, only some of whom appeared willing to get out of the way, managed to steer the Vespa onto the street, which fortunately was a one-way street running in the direction they were headed.

Professor rotated Jade's hand—and the throttle control grip she was holding—forward, and the scooter shot ahead. The speedometer ticked past fifty kilometers per hour... sixty... seventy. Jade didn't need to do a metric conversion to know they were probably pushing the envelope of safety. It was definitely a lot faster than any bicycle she'd ever ridden, and she felt a lot more exposed than on any motorcycle she had ever ridden.

"Huh," Professor remarked in her ear. "You know what that is over there?"

She assumed he was referring to the vast field off to

their left. It looked like a flood drainage area. "No," she shouted, the rush of air passing by stealing her breath away.

"Circus Maximus. They used to race chariots there, like in *Ben-Hur*."

"That's a movie, yeah?"

"Whoops. Hold on."

Jade returned her attention forward and saw an intersection looming ahead. A traffic signal mounted to a pole on the left sidewalk, so inconspicuous as to be nearly invisible, showed red, and the cars directly ahead of them were slowing.

"Let go," Professor said, and then without waiting for her to comply, deftly plucked her hands off the grips, one at a time, and moved them to the inside of the handlebars, replacing them with his own. Jade immediately felt the scooter decelerating, gradually at first as he relaxed the throttle and then more dramatically as he squeezed the brake levers, bringing them to a complete stop. The Vespa shook gently at idle.

"You mean to tell me you've never seen *Ben-Hur*?" Professor went on. "Charlton Heston. Epic sea battles. Chariot races. Political intrigue and homoerotic undertones. The Crucifixion. None of that rings a bell?"

Jade shrugged. "Some of us played outside as kids."

"I suppose next you'll tell me that you've never seen *Roman Holiday*."

"After today, I'm not sure I want to."

"One of the best scenes in it was filmed just up there. *Bocca della Verite*."

Before Jade could ask which movie he was talking about, he yelled. "Hang on!" and then, despite the fact that the light was still red, he released the brakes and twisted the throttle.

The Vespa did not exactly leap forward, but it did lurch with enough of a jolt that Jade was thrown back into Professor. She reflexively gripped the handlebars and felt them moving as Professor steered hard to the right, swerving around a waiting sedan and threading the scooter between the two parallel rows of cars waiting at the light. As they raced toward the intersection, Jade saw the reason for Professor's precipitous action. To their left, racing down the cross street at the northwest end of the Circus Maximus like a bright red Jade-seeking-missile was Gia's Alfa Romeo.

Jade didn't dare hope that it was just the German kid wanting his scooter back.

As they reached the intersection, Professor cranked the handlebars to the right, turning them onto the narrow side street. It took Jade about a second to realize that all the cars entering the intersection from that direction were coming right toward them. It was a one-way street and they were going the wrong way.

The street erupted into a cacophony of horns honking and brakes squealing, with Jade supplying backing vocals in the form of a single protracted obscenity that never quite reached its final consonant. Professor jerked the handlebars back and forth, swerving around oncoming cars, fighting his way through the opposing traffic like a salmon thrashing up a waterfall, and somehow managed to avoid getting them both killed.

After about a hundred yards, they came to a narrow alley that sloped away to the left, toward yet another old arch—this one smaller and in considerably worse shape than either of the arches at the Forum. Jade let her screamed curse fade unfinished and held on tight to the handle bars as Professor turned toward it and away from certain death.

The alley wended through what looked like the grounds of an old church, though in Rome it was hard to tell, and finally emptied into a parking area surrounded by centuries-old stone buildings. Professor had slowed down a little as they traversed the alley, but when they reached the parking lot, he opened throttle up again, building up momentum as they shot toward a main thoroughfare directly ahead. As they neared it, Jade spied the red convertible a couple blocks away to their left, but moving up fast. Professor must have seen it too, for he whipped the Vespa to the right, joining the flow of traffic, and pushed the throttle wide open.

The traffic was moving fast, and for a few seconds, Jade thought they were going to get run off the road, but as they picked up speed, the cars and buses became obstacles in their path. Professor's solution was to imitate the other motorcycles and scooters that simply drove down the center of the road.

In the side mirror mounted to the handlebars, Jade could see the red sports car weaving in and out of traffic behind them, closing the gap. On the dashboard, the speedometer display ticked past sixty... Seventy... Eighty kilometers per hour. They were moving at highway speeds up a city street, and the scary part was that the other motorcycles going the same direction were passing them by, sometimes veering into the opposing lane in order avoid the mortal sin of using the brakes.

She closed her eyes for a second, but decided that not seeing was even scarier. "I hate this place!"

Rome's historic appeal was definitely wearing thin, even for Jade. They passed temples and churches and ruins. The road curved to the right, rising gently up a hill before descending into a busy plaza that looked familiar, like something from a travel poster. To the right rose an enormous white structure—all columns and sweeping staircases—with fountains and statues of horses and angels. It reminded Jade a little of the Lincoln Memorial in Washington D.C. only two or three times bigger. To the left, more churches—or maybe just one really big church with elaborate decorative domes—and of course, more ruins. There appeared to be an extensive ongoing archaeological dig right in the middle of the plaza.

Jade checked the mirror again. Gia, in the Alfa Romeo, was just cresting the hill, still a hundred yards back. The traffic had slowed her down, but only a little. The wide-open plaza would give the woman plenty of room to maneuver.

Jade felt Professor tense, his arms going rigid as the applied the brakes, a rare profanity escaping his lips. She raised her eyes and saw the reason for his reaction. A white van—the same van that had chased them earlier—was rolling into the plaza from the opposite direction. In the instant that she saw it, the vehicle swerved toward them, as if the driver were challenging them to a game of chicken.

SEVENTEEN

Jade stared at the vehicle, incredulous. "How'd they know we'd be here?"

"It's their city," Professor growled "There were only so many places we could have gone."

"All roads lead to us, is that it?"

He cut hard to the left, across the lanes of oncoming traffic, toward a large open excavation—a square about fifty yards across, barricaded with K-rails and temporary fences—near the church, and then said, "I'm sure your friend in the convertible is keeping them updated."

"She's not my friend," Jade snapped.

Professor ignored her, turning again so they were traveling with traffic, opposite the direction they had been going. Behind them, the driver of the van was honking and forcing his way across the plaza toward them. Gia had overshot, but was in the process of turning around to rejoin the chase.

"Damn it," Professor growled. "Has this thing got a horn? Find the horn. It should be on the left side."

"Why?" she asked as she started searching with her fingers.

"Because I'd rather not have to shoot in the air again."

As that moment, they passed the southwest corner of the dig site and Professor turned into the narrow street that ran between it and the church. The way ahead was choked with pedestrians and waiting taxis, all of whom were in their way.

Jade's fingers found a button next to the left handgrip. She pushed it and was rewarded with an almost comical "beep." She held it down and began waving her free hand. "Move it people. *Scusi! Scusi!*"

The crowd parted. Grudgingly, but it parted. Professor coaxed the scooter forward, dodging the people who refused to get out of the way, but as they emerged on the far side of the excavation, Gia's convertible skidded into view, cutting off their access to the main street. Professor turned the opposite direction, toward a towering freestanding column of white marble at least a hundred feet high, topped with a statue of copper or bronze if the green patina was any indication. The column occupied the north end of what appeared to be a park devoted to the excavated ruins of another structure or possibly several structures presumably associated with the column. At a distance, the column's exterior looked rough and irregular, like many of the other artifacts of Roman antiquity Jade had seen but as they drew closer to it, she realized that what she had mistaken for irregularity was actually decorative sculpture. The exterior of the entire column was covered in bas relief images, arranged in a single long strip that spiraled around it like the grooves in the barrel of a rifle.

Jade kept beeping the horn as Professor steered through the narrow gap between the fenced border of the park and the front of the church. There was no way Gia or the cultists would be able to follow, and from what Jade could tell, they would have to go back the other way several hundred yards to get around the park.

Professor kept going straight, down a narrow street lined with parked cars and crowded with pedestrians, and as she looked down its length, Jade saw the reason why there were no moving cars. About fifty yards down, the pavement between the buildings became a flight of rising stairs.

"Dead end!" Jade shouted.

"Nope!" retorted Professor. "Grab the throttle. Keep us moving."

"What?"

Without answering, Professor hopped off the back of the moving scooter, sprinting alongside it as the stairs loomed closer. He grabbed the handlebars with his left hand, the back of the seat with his right, and kept running beside Jade, like a dutiful father trying to teach his daughter how to ride a bike. Jade, unable to comprehend what he was doing, unconsciously let the throttle slip back to the 'neutral' position.

"Keep it going," Professor admonished. "We're gonna climb the stairs!"

"That's not possible."

"Trust me!"

Gritting her teeth, Jade nudged the throttle and the Vespa began accelerating again. Professor was shouting in Italian, warning people to get out of the way. The stairs were right in front of her. She braced herself, anticipating the sudden violent stop when the front tire crunched into the first step.

But it didn't, at least not the way she thought it would. In the instant before the collision, Jade felt the front end of the scooter rise. Just a little. Just enough that when the spinning wheel hit the corner, it rolled up and onto the step, and then onto the next one and the next after that. Suddenly, the scooter was tilted up at a forty-five-degree angle and it was all she could do to hang on and not fall off backward.

"Give it some gas," Professor grunted, still beside her, although they were barely moving now. He was half-dragging the scooter up the steps, but he was rapidly losing momentum. Jade eased the throttle forward again, and felt the scooter take off, bumping violently up the steps.

The punishment was brutal but brief. Thirty bone-shaking steps later, the front of the Vespa dipped down onto pavement, and after a few more bumps, the scooter was on flat pavement once more. Then, to Jade's complete astonishment, Professor steered the scooter back onto the sidewalk and squeezed the brakes, bringing the Vespa to a complete stop. Then, he reached down and switched off the key.

"Come on. We'll hoof it from here."

"What? Why?" Jade planted her feet on the sidewalk, but held onto the handlebars possessively.

"We're too conspicuous on that thing."

"What do you mean? Half the people in the city are using them."

"Yeah, but have you noticed they're all wearing

helmets?"

Jade had not noticed. "I was kinda busy with the whole running for my life thing."

"My guess is, they take helmet laws pretty seriously. So unless you want the police chasing us too…" He offered his hand. "Coming?"

She frowned but relented, swiveling off the seat and taking his hand. "I wish you'd realized that before making me ride up those stairs."

"I didn't want your friends to see—"

Jade yanked her hand away. "They aren't my friends. I wish you'd stop saying that."

His expression softened. "Sorry. It's just an expression."

"It's a sucky one."

"Fair enough." He gestured to the sidewalk. "We should get moving. I'll give Tam a call. See if there's a safe house where we can crash."

"I just want to get out of here. Didn't you say something about the airport?"

"Yeah, about that." He grimaced. "I'm betting that Purcell is going to be watching the airport. Probably all the other routes in or out of the country. And those whackos…the cult? Seems like they're everywhere, too."

Jade sagged in disappointment. "Fantastic. So we're stuck here?"

"I'll figure something out." He reached out and took her hand again and gave it a squeeze. "Jade. I'm sorry."

"It's fine. I'm just sick of not having any control over my life."

He shook his head. "No, I mean I'm sorry I let this happen."

His sincerity brought her emotions back to the surface. How was she supposed to respond to that?

Damn right, you're sorry. You had one job. Or maybe, *I don't need you looking out for me. I can take care of myself. I was doing just fine before you showed up.*

There were a lot of things she wanted to say, but none

of them felt quite right, so instead she simply turned to him, rose up on her tiptoes and kissed his cheek. "Apology accepted. Just don't let it happen again."

Five minutes or so after ditching the Vespa, Professor flagged down a taxi, and ten minutes after that, they were in a CIA safe house in a quiet neighborhood to the east of the city. Jade retreated to the bathroom to clean up, while Professor began making travel arrangements. A car would pick them up later in the day and take them to a private airport where a chartered plane would be waiting, but there remained the question of what their next destination would be.

After a shower and a meal—which a ravenous Jade practically inhaled—she felt ready to talk. It took a while for Jade to get her story out. Remembering was like reliving the experiences all over again—the shock of waking up in chains; the humiliation of being poked and prodded by the cultists; the terror of being chased over the side of the ship by the treacherous Special Agent Purcell; and perhaps worst of all, the realization that, despite the appearance of being free, she was still ensnared by the Cult of Libertas.

Professor listened, asked only a few questions—mostly during her recollection of the historical information regarding the disposition of the sacred relics—and offered what comfort he could when Jade's raw emotions threatened to overtake her, which took the form of keeping her wine glass topped off, and an occasional reassuring hug. The best thing he did for her though was laugh out loud when she described how she had stomped on Gia's foot.

"I've heard about this Lighthouse group," Professor said when she had finished the tale up to the point of their reunion at the Colosseum. "They present as a self-improvement service, but the high-pressure techniques they use in their seminars are your basic light version of cult-programming. I'm not surprised they're a front for an actual cult." He steepled his fingers together in a fair approximation of Mr. Spock. "Libertas. I'll have to do some digging on that one. Maybe bring Avery in on this."

Avery Halsey was a history professor and the Myrmidons' lead researcher. If anyone could uncover the secret history of the Cult of Libertas, it would be her.

"This Lindsey woman," he went on. "Did she give you any sense of what their endgame is? Why they want these sacred relics?"

"She said they would be a symbol to help rally support against human trafficking." The explanation had made a sort of sense to her when Diane had given it, but when weighed against the extraordinary measures the cult had taken to capture and contain her, it no longer rang true. "I don't know. She was probably lying to me about that, too."

"Purcell had an intercepted email message, presumably sent out to cult members, about the Chosen undergoing something called 'the Servus Trial.' I think that was a reference to you escaping from those chains. A test, but also a sort of initiation."

"Diane told me only a slave can know what it means to be liberated." She shivered at the memory.

Professor nodded. "When you showed him those chains, he realized that you were their Chosen."

"And that's when he tried to kill me."

"Which tells us two things. First, Diane didn't give you the whole story about what's expected of the Chosen. Second, Purcell knows a lot more about this than we do. Which begs the question, where did he get his information?" He accordioned his steepled fingers, back and forth. "He might be Dominion."

"Those assholes?"

"Tam thinks they may have infiltrated the Department of Homeland Security and other top-level government agencies. They might know a lot more about this cult than we do. The email talked about getting ready for battle. That might not be figurative language. Maybe the Cult of Libertas is planning to overthrow the government." He gave her a sideways glance. "Maybe you're supposed to be the next Spartacus."

"I've already told Diane I wasn't interested."

"Hmm. For Purcell to be so worried about this that he would try to kill you on sight, there must be more to these relics than just symbolic power. I wonder. Maybe what they're really after is the oracular book. Maybe they think it will guide them to victory."

"If they think that, then they obviously didn't pay attention in history class."

"What do you mean?"

"Well, think about it. Spartacus' wife was the Sybil who wrote the book. His uprising failed. Crassus had the book, but he was defeated. After that, it was the Liberatores— Brutus and Cassius. They failed. If it ended up with Mark Antony—and that's where I'd bet my money—he failed, too. Everyone who looked to the oracle for guidance eventually lost." She gave a bitter laugh. "Maybe the best thing to do would be to let them actually have it. Solve all our problems."

"You know, I think you might be on to something."

She grinned. "Does that mean I'm now the brains of this operation?"

He lowered his hands and sat up straighter. "Spartacus was a Thracian. He didn't worship Libertas or any other Roman gods or goddesses, and he wasn't fighting to put an end to slavery in the Roman Republic. He was just winging it. For a while, things went well, but realistically, there was no way the Romans would have let him upset their order."

"Their order," Jade murmured, thinking back to something else Diane had told her. *All of us have been lifted up on the bent backs of slaves.*

That was what the Dominion was fighting to preserve. It was why Purcell had tried to kill her.

"But the interesting thing about the Thracians," Professor continued, "is that their funerary customs included burying the living wife with her deceased husband."

"Great." Jade rolled her eyes. "I'll bet they had different rules if the wife died first."

"You might not like it, but it was important to them.

Crassus may have thought he was doing Spartacus' wife a favor by promising to give her husband a proper burial, but by keeping her alive, he was denying her the most important part of their funerary tradition."

Jade thought she saw what he was leading up to. "So she tricked him by giving him a book of prophecies that would backfire."

"Why not? Maybe she set it up in such a way that the person consulting the oracle would have success at first, and then a big failure. A sucker's game."

"So like I said, let 'em have it. Maybe they'll take the Dominion down with them."

Professor offered a patient smile. "Well, this is all conjecture. What we do know for a fact is that when people decide it's time for a religious crusade—no matter the religion—a lot of innocent people will suffer. That's reason enough to stop this from happening."

Jade slumped. "I suppose you're right."

"And now that you've slipped their leash, they'll probably just find a new Chosen One."

"So the only way to really stop this uprising is to find those relics first and take them out of play."

"Even that may not be enough, but it's a start." He tapped his fingertips together again. "Any ideas where they might be?"

Jade sat back in her chair. "Based on the research the cult already did, my vote is that it they ended up with Mark Antony and Cleopatra in Egypt."

"Hmm. That's plausible enough." His fingers steepled again. "I think we're missing something here."

"Like what?"

"They brought you here. To Rome. Why? And don't tell me it's because they seriously believe there's a lost temple to Libertas here somewhere. This feels orchestrated. Choreographed. They were leading you along. Revealing information to you when they were ready, and only what they wanted you to know."

"Another test?"

"Possibly. All we can say for sure is that there's more to this cult than what they've revealed to you. For all we know, this business about Spartacus and the Sibylline book might be a ruse."

"Well, that clears everything up."

He smiled. "Maybe what we need to do is borrow a page from their playbook."

She blinked at him. "Wait, you mean kidnap one of them?"

"Technically, it's only kidnapping if you demand a ransom. What we're going to do is just called 'abduction,' though I think the Agency prefers the term 'extraordinary rendition.'"

Jade checked her moral compass and decided she really didn't have a problem with it. "Maybe it will make them appreciate freedom a little more. So who are we gonna grab? Gia? I'm not sure I could lead you back to her villa, but I'll give it a shot."

Professor shook her head. "I've got someone else in mind. Someone who I suspect will only be too willing to help us."

PART THREE: CHOSEN

EIGHTEEN

Houston, Texas

Diane Lindsey took a long drag from her cigarette, then dropped it on the asphalt of the parking lot and heeled it out before exhaling the smoke into the humid air. She debated firing up another—her nerves were practically begging her to do so—but decided to head back into her motel room to see if there was any more news.

She knew there would not be, or rather that if there were, none of it would be good, but at least the simple act of going inside and checking her email would keep her from actually chain-smoking, and therefore give her the illusion of self-control. It probably wouldn't make much of a difference. Nicotine was about the only thing that helped her cope with the stress even though eventually it would be the death of her.

Maybe that would be better, she thought glumly. *Then I wouldn't have to see it all fall apart.*

She understood now why Brutus and Mark Anthony and so many others in ancient times had chosen to end their lives rather than live, even briefly, with their failures. If she died now, she could at least breathe her last clinging to the slim hope that things might turn out as planned after all. If she lived through the next few days, she would witness even that flickering candle of optimism utterly snuffed out forever.

The last news out of Rome was all bad. Gia Ruffino and several other members of the Italian chapter of the cult had been taken into custody following Jade's escape and the disastrously high-profile attempt to recapture her at the Colosseum. There was little doubt in Diane's mind that the authorities would follow the trail of clues to Lighthouse Worldwide, to her as one of the senior directors, and perhaps even to the Cult of Libertas.

Nothing left now but to fall on her sword.

She knew she was probably being overly dramatic.

The cult would endure. Its ideals would endure. This wasn't even a defeat; merely a setback. A delay. So what if Jade Ihara had decided to go off script? Her role in the plan was important, there was no denying that, but it could still go forward without her active participation. And even if Lighthouse was finished, there was no evidence linking the cult or its followers to what would happen next. The plan could still succeed, but only if Diane gave the order to execute the masterstroke, and soon, before the window of opportunity closed.

The problem was that Jade knew too much about the Cult of Libertas, and so there was a chance—actually, a very good chance—that Jade would recognize what was really happening, and who was behind it. She might already have gone to the authorities, in which case the plan was well and truly ruined.

In order for the plan to move forward, Jade Ihara had to die. It was as simple as that. And if the plan came to fruition, the woman would go out with a bang!

"But where is she?" Diane muttered.

The muggy afternoon air gave her no answer, but as she reached into her purse for the key card to unlock her room door, she felt her phone vibrating.

She had debated destroying the mobile device. Even though the account was anonymous and the dedicated network it utilized heavily encrypted, with the Italian chapter possibly compromised, there was a chance that it could lead the authorities straight to her. But it was the only thing tethering her to the cult, and regardless of whether it would prove to be a lifeline or the rope that would hang her, she could not bear to sever it.

She hit the 'accept' button without even a glance at the caller ID display; the spoofed number would reveal nothing about the person on the other end. "Hello?"

"She is here."

Something like an electric current jolted through Diane. She didn't have to ask who it was; there was no mistaking that voice.

She staggered back a step, turned and headed back outside. Now she definitely needed another smoke.

With one trembling hand, she shook a cigarette from the pack, put it between her lips and struck the flint wheel on her lighter. Only when she had taken another deep drag did she respond. "What's she doing back there?"

"I do not know. And evidently, you do not either."

"Can you get her for me?"

The caller made a harsh sound that might have been laughter. "You misunderstand. This was a courtesy. I was merely curious about the purpose of her visit here. I have my own plans for her. I am not asking your permission and I certainly am not here to do your bidding."

"Of course not." Diane was quick to answer, but made sure to infuse a little of her Texas drawl into her response. "Y'all will have to forgive me if I gave that impression. I simply meant that I'd like to make an offer on her."

There was a moment of silence on the line, long enough that Diane had to check to make sure the call was still live.

Finally, there was a sigh on the line. "Perhaps I didn't make myself clear. When I said I have plans—"

"Oh, I understood you just fine, sugar. You go on and do whatever you like to her. I'll take whatever's left."

Another pause and then another harsh chuckle. "And they call me a devil."

Diane laughed. "Well, I never called you that. When can I take delivery?"

"Forty-eight hours. If she survives."

"I don't need her alive. I just need *her*. I'll contact you as soon as I make arrangements for transportation." She ended the call, eschewing the customary formality of saying goodbye. Forty-eight hours was plenty of time to get the wheels of the plan moving again, but she was eager to begin making the arrangements. It wouldn't be the perfectly choreographed dance that she had intended, but it was going to happen.

"Thank the goddess," she murmured, stubbing out the

cigarette. "And bless your heart, Jade Ihara."

But as she began making phone calls, one question kept nagging at her subconscious.

Why did she go back to Haiti?

NINETEEN

Port au Prince, Haiti

Yann Pierre's gaze rested on the computer screen, which displayed field notes from the archaeological dig at the recently uncovered Taino settlement west of Port au Prince, but his thoughts were miles away. He knew it was important to maintain the illusion of normalcy, particularly now, with the end in sight, but try as he might, he could not find it in himself to care about a distant past that had nothing to do with him, or a people who had left virtually no permanent mark upon the world. History—real history—was about to be made; he could think of nothing else.

What would the world look like in a month? A year? Ten years? As a historian, he understood that events were subject to inertia. Sometimes sweeping changes happened overnight, a king or president felled by a single bullet, a government swept out of power in one decisive action, but institutions—entrenched ideas that arose from the collective DNA of human society—were much harder to overturn. Indeed, servants of the goddess had been fighting to end slavery for centuries, millennia even, and yet it persisted.

He checked the clock on the wall, saw that it was nearly five o'clock in the evening. The museum would be closed soon. His normal custom was to stay until six or later, but as his work often took him into the field, no one would think it unusual for him to leave the office early.

He doubted anyone was even paying attention.

His role in the selection of the candidate was done, his part in the great unfolding drama concluded. Perhaps there would be more for him to do in the new society that would follow—indeed, he hoped that would prove to be the case—but for the moment, he was merely a spectator.

"Enough," he muttered, pushing away from his desk. He rose, donned his suit jacket, and headed out into the museum.

Despite his earlier frustration, as he moved through the

galleries and exhibits, displaying the history of the island nation—he felt a little of what had drawn him to his profession. It was not however in the rooms dedicated to the earliest inhabitants, the Arawak and Taino people, but rather the relics and murals devoted to the early days of the Haitian republic and the men who had built it from less than nothing. They were his heroes. Jean-Jacques Dessalines, the general who led resistance forces at the Battle of Crête-à-Pierrot, and went on to become the first ruler of independent Haiti. His successor, Henri Christophe. And of course, François-Dominique Toussaint Louverture, the father of Haiti who defied Napoleon Bonaparte and set in motion the revolt that would free Haiti from its colonial masters. Former slaves, one and all. Blessed by the goddess of freedom.

Just like him.

And yet, each one of them had failed the fundamental test of faith, squandering the blessing of liberty, enslaving their fellow men, sometimes more brutally than even the Europeans. Dessalines had named himself Emperor Jacques I, and had used military force to enforce a plantation labor system that was little different than slavery. Christophe, who named himself King Henry I had continued the forced labor practices, known as *corvee*, until he was overthrown by a coup, committing suicide rather than surrendering. Even Louverture, the great hero of the Republic, had fallen victim to the hypocrisy of power. The wealth and status that had eventually elevated him to a position of authority had come from the success of his own plantation, worked by more than a dozen slaves.

All of them had come to ruin. Louverture had been arrested by Napoleon, imprisoned in Fort-de-Joux, a remote castle in the Jura mountains of France, where he eventually succumbed to tuberculosis. He had not lived to see a free Haiti.

There was a memorial to Louverture at the entrance to the museum, which owing to its design resembled a crypt, albeit a magnificent one. Originally intended to serve as a

pantheon—a mausoleum to honor Haiti's national heroes—
the museum was a circular structure, partially buried after
construction, with earth rising on all sides to form an
artificial hill. Visitors could either descend into the museum,
or ascend up one of the broad staircases located to either
side of the entrance corridor to the rooftop, which was itself
a celebrated monument, with a reflecting pool and several
large sculptures—truncated cones were meant to resemble
the thatched roofs of native huts. Contrary to popular belief,
the memorial urn at the entrance did not actually contain
Louverture's remains, but only a symbolic shovelful of dirt
from Fort-de-Joux where he had likely been interred in an
unmarked grave.

Pierre stopped in front of the memorial, as he often
did, to pay his respects. *Will we use the gift of the goddess more
wisely than you?* He wondered silently.

A voice intruded on his reverie. "Is it true they called
him 'the Black Spartacus'?"

It was a female voice, speaking English. Familiar
somehow.

He turned, ready to answer, but when he beheld the
face of the woman, he nearly fell back into the niche
containing the memorial. "Jade!"

"Hello again, Yann," Jade said. She was smiling, but
there was no humor or warmth in her eyes.

Pierre looked past her to the glass doors, mentally
planning his escape route, but before he could move,
another familiar figure stepped in front of him blocking his
path. It was Pete Chapman, the man Jade had called
Professor.

Jade spoke again. "I've got some questions for you,
Yann."

"I... I don't—"

"Why don't we discuss this in your office?" Professor
said. "Unless you'd prefer we do this in a cell at Gitmo. I'm
good either way."

Jade was a little disappointed that Pierre chose the

first option. After everything she had gone through, all of it the result of the Haitian's treachery, a little enhanced interrogation didn't sound like such a bad thing. She had entertained herself with the notion during their long flight from Rome, though truthfully, she wasn't really interested in torturing Pierre. Nevertheless, in the relative privacy of his office in the back of the museum, she let him know, without any ambiguity, that she was pissed as hell.

Although he was not openly defiant, refusing to meet her gaze, Pierre offered no apologies. "It was necessary. You are the Chosen. I pray that one day you will understand. Only one who has known the chains of servitude and imprisonment can receive the blessings of the goddess."

"Maybe you should give it a try," she retorted. "Tell me if you still feel the same way."

His head ducked even lower. "I have known it," he said, his voice barely a whisper. "I was *restavek*."

Jade glanced over at Professor for an explanation.

"It's a local practice," he explained in a quiet voice. "Poor parents who can't provide will basically send their children to work as domestic servants for wealthier families. In exchange, they're supposed to get food, a place to live, an education."

Jade looked at Pierre, feeling an unexpected pang of sympathy for her abductor. "Your mom sold you?"

"It doesn't quite work like that," Professor amended quickly. "It's more like voluntarily putting your kid in foster care."

Pierre spat out a bitter laugh. "It is nothing like that."

Jade was incredulous. "This is illegal, right?"

Professor shook his head. "Not really, but it's tolerated. I've read that about a quarter of Haitian children are *restavek*." He caught Pierre's gaze. "There's nothing about that in your CV."

"Do you think I would have this position if the truth were known? My father was a foreign contractor, but he never sent my mother a single *centime*. She felt she had no choice but to make me *restavek*."

Jade sensed there was a lot more to the story, and that it was a source of profound pain for the man. "Then how can you, of all people, be part of this? You drugged me. Kidnapped me…" She shot a glance at Professor and then corrected herself. "You abducted me and put me in chains on that container ship. What would have happened to me if I hadn't gotten free?"

"You would have been released, but…" He shook his head. "I knew that you would get free. You are the Chosen. The blessing of the goddess is upon you, but that blessing must be earned through fighting for your own freedom."

"So you did me a favor by kidnapping me?"

"We gave you the opportunity to gain your blessing and become who you were meant to be—the Chosen. You will usher in a new age. A world without slaves."

Jade ground her teeth together in frustration. "Yann, you're a smart guy. You know that's not how the world works."

"I know it in my head. But in my heart, I also believe that sometimes, miracles can happen."

"Let's talk about those miracles," Professor broke in. "What exactly is it that Jade is supposed to do for you?"

"Just as it was in ancient Rome, only those who are Chosen of the goddess may enter the temple."

"Or else what?"

Pierre blinked, uncomprehending. "I don't understand?"

"What's the penalty if someone other than the Chosen goes in?"

"You misunderstand. It is not a question of permission. The temple will not open to anyone else."

Jade exchanged a look with Professor. "Are we talking some sort of magical biometric lock?" he asked.

Pierre gave a helpless shrug. "This has not been explained to me. I only know what the priestess told me."

"The priestess? Would that be Diane Lindsey?"

Another shrug. "I do not know her name."

"So Jade is supposed to go into this temple and… Do

what exactly?"

"Retrieve the sacred relics of Libertas: The remains of Spartacus the Liberator; and the Sibylline book."

"And then?"

Pierre shook his head. "The priestess determines the will of the goddess, but I would surmise that the relics will be used to inspire all those who are now enslaved, and all who value freedom and liberty to fight, literally if necessary, to end slavery once and for all."

Jade sensed that Pierre was telling the truth, at least in so far as Diane Lindsey had revealed it to him. So far, everything he was saying agreed with what Diane and Gia had said, and if that was indeed their true agenda, it was in principle at least, something Jade could agree with.

"End it how?" Professor pressed. "With violence?"

"If necessary." Pierre cocked his head to the side. "Do you not think it a cause worth fighting for?"

"Of course, I do. The bloodiest war in American history was fought over the issue of slavery."

"And still it persists, even in your country."

"Illegally," Jade said. "No sane person would condone slavery. Not here or anywhere."

Pierre shook his head with a sad expression. "They condone it with their willful ignorance."

Jade frowned and crossed her arms over her chest. "Look, I had this conversation once before already. I get it. Slavery or human exploitation or whatever you want to call it is bad. It needs to stop. You won't get an argument from me about that. But you're not going to change it with some old bones and prophecies."

"But isn't it at least worth trying?"

"Maybe. I don't know." She sighed. "So I'm just supposed to find the temple and get the relics, and then my part of it is done, right?"

Pierre's forehead creased with a frown. "I don't understand. Find the temple? Did not the priestess tell you its location?"

"No. Why? Does she know where it is?"

"I assumed that she would."

Professor cut in. "Do you know where it is?"

"Not precisely, but I cannot imagine that the priestess would be unaware of the exact location of the temple."

Jade turned to Professor. "They were screwing with me. Probably thought if I could follow the trail of bread crumbs and find it myself, I'd be more invested in their cause. A freaking mind game. If they wanted my help, they should have just asked nicely. I hate mind games."

"Maybe it's another test for the Chosen," suggested Professor. "A discovery ritual."

"I hate those, too." She shook her head. "All right, where is it? Approximately."

Pierre pursed his lips. "There have been many temples to Libertas throughout the ages. Any place will serve, so long as it has been consecrated. To the best of my knowledge, the last time the relics were sealed away was at the end of Napoleon's reign."

Jade blinked. "Napoleon? The short French guy?"

Professor laughed. "He wasn't actually—"

"Shhh." Jade kept her gaze on Pierre. "Napoleon lived in the late 18th Century, right? The research notes I saw indicated that the relics disappeared from ancient Rome in the 1st Century B.C.E. Almost two thousand years before Napoleon."

"No, this makes sense," Professor said. "You mentioned that the relics might have ended up with Mark Antony and Cleopatra in Egypt. In 1798 Napoleon led a campaign in Egypt. In addition to fighting British and Egyptian forces, he conducted the first scientific survey of the region. That was basically the genesis of Egyptology. He also helped himself to quite a few artifacts, including the Rosetta Stone. Maybe he found…" He trailed off for a second and then snapped his fingers. "The Oraculum!"

Jade spread her palms in a *whatever* gesture, prompting him to continue.

"In 1839, a book was published that purported to be the oracular book used by Napoleon to guide his campaigns.

The story goes that after his defeat at the Battle of Leipzig, Napoleon left behind his Cabinet of Curiosities which was captured by a Prussian officer. The cabinet was a sort of trophy chest and in it—again, so the story goes—was a book, translated from a scroll Napoleon had discovered in a royal tomb during his campaigns in Egypt.

"The published book, *called Napoleon's Oraculum*, or sometimes his *Book of Fate* or his dreambook, contains a system for fortune telling using a sort of pseudorandom number generator and a series of pre-asked questions. Stuff like, 'Will I live to an old age?' or 'Will my lover be true in my absence?' or 'Will I make my fortune gambling?' Real critical stuff for planning an invasion of Russia. It's basically an early version of a Magic 8-Ball, and about as reliable. Needless to say, the provenance of the book is pretty suspicious. I'm not aware of anyone who takes it seriously, but there may be a kernel of truth in the story. Napoleon was known to be a very superstitious man, and he might very well have possessed an oracular scroll, taken from a tomb in Egypt."

"The Sibylline book," Jade murmured.

"He could have consulted it in his military campaigns."

"For all the good it did him."

Professor nodded. "Sounds familiar, right? Initial success, followed by a catastrophic failure. Just like everybody else who consulted the Sibylline book. I think you're right about it being a double-edged sword."

"Like many others before him," said Pierre, "Napoleon followed his ambitions and lost favor with the goddess. However, I do not believe he acquired the sacred relics in the manner you have described."

He straightened in his chair, no longer a captive being subjected to an interrogation, but a true believer, pontificating on a subject he held dear. "Where there is human exploitation—whether it is outright slavery or simply authoritarian oppression—the goddess will find followers. The Romans understood this. Even under the rule of the harshest dictators, the goddess was always honored. The form of Christianity that became the religion of Rome, and subsequently the world, was a syncretism of Judaic beliefs and the worship of the old gods. Libertas, the goddess of freedom, became an aspect of the Virgin Mary in the form of Our Lady of Perpetual Succor."

"You're saying the sacred relics weren't lost after all? The Church has them?"

Pierre shook his head. "Not exactly. Although veneration of the goddess was folded into Christianity, there have always been priests and priestesses who preserve the unadulterated faith, protecting the location of the temple and, as the need arises, selecting a Chosen to enter the temple so that the sacred relics might be used to advance the cause of freedom and liberty. This has happened many times in the last two millennia, but the most noteworthy instance was the American Revolution and the subsequent establishment of a democratic republic that now leads the free world."

"Libertas was involved in the American Revolution? You're kidding, right?"

"Many of your Founding Fathers were priests of the cult: Benjamin Franklin; Thomas Jefferson; John Hancock; George Washington."

Professor interjected. "Those men were all deists. Secularists. Jefferson was probably an atheist."

"I do not profess to know what was in their hearts, but I believe that for men such as Franklin and Jefferson, the appeal of the cult was its humanist philosophy. They did not worship the goddess so much as the idea of the goddess and what she represented. In this, they are not so different than we who worship today."

"You've said repeatedly that only those who have been enslaved can truly know the blessing of your goddess. I'll grant that the Founding Fathers felt oppressed and subjugated by the Crown, but I would hardly call them slaves. Most of them owned slaves. That sounds pretty hypocritical to me."

"The goddess does not judge the master, but blesses

the slave who seeks liberty." Pierre's explanation sounded canned, rehearsed, as if he was not particularly comfortable with the rationale. "And not all who worship the goddess have known the oppression of slavery but they may revere the goddess of freedom and liberty all the same. The Junia gens—the family of Servilia and Brutus—were wealthy patricians. Servilia herself lived at the whim of her husbands and lovers but suffered no other real oppression. That is the reason for the Servus Trial. A symbolic enslavement from which the candidate must escape through her own ingenuity."

"So which one of the Founding Fathers let himself get locked up in a shipping container?" asked Jade, making no effort to hide her sarcasm.

"None. In those days, the Chosen was an actual former slave, originally from West Africa. When she was just seven years old, she was brought to Massachusetts colony aboard a ship named *The Phillis*, sold to a prosperous merchant named John Wheatley, who named her for the ship that had brought her across the ocean."

"Phillis Wheatley was the Chosen?" said Professor. Without being prompted, he looked over at Jade and explained. "Phillis Wheatley was a renowned poet. The first female African-American poet to be published."

Jade rolled her eyes. "Why am I not surprised you know that?"

"The Wheatley family was very progressive for their time. They felt it was their Christian obligation to educate Phillis, and when she showed real talent as a poet, they found a publisher for her. They even emancipated her."

"The goddess called to her and blessed her with freedom," Pierre interjected. "She used her intellect and talent to figuratively break the chains of her slavery.

"'*Celestial choir! Enthron'd in realms of light. Columbia's scenes of glorious toils I write.*'"

From the change in his timbre and cadence, Jade sensed that he was quoting one of Phillis Wheatley's poems.

"'While freedom's cause her anxious breast alarms,
She flashes dreadful in refulgent arms.
See mother earth her offspring's fate bemoan,
And nations gaze at scenes before unknown!
See the bright beams of heaven's revolving light
Involved in sorrows and the veil of night!'"

Professor confirmed Jade's hunch. "That's from the poem 'To His Excellency General Washington, written in 1775. It was the first time where Columbia—that's what they originally wanted to call the independent nation... That was the first time it was personified as a goddess."

Jade leaned close to him and whispered, "What's 'refulgent'?"

"It's just a fancy word for 'shining'."

Pierre nodded enthusiastically and resumed his recitation:

"'Proceed, great chief, with virtue on thy side,
Thy ev'ry action let the Goddess guide.
A crown, a mansion, and a throne that shine,
With gold unfading, Washington! Be thine.'"

He paused, his beatific smile softening. "Washington and the others recognized that the goddess was speaking through her and in February of 1776, he invited her to visit him at Cambridge, which she did. They met briefly, the visit lasted only about an hour, and no official record of it exists, but not long thereafter, the writing of the Declaration of Independence—the fundamental doctrine of modern liberty—commenced, while General Washington fought the war, guided by the goddess."

Jade saw where he was going. "So this Phillis went into the temple and gave George Washington the sacred relics, which he used to beat the British."

"Washington didn't really beat the British, so much as outlast them," Professor countered. "But I'll grant you, it's an interesting coincidence."

"If the meeting between Wheatley and Washington only lasted an hour," Jade said, "that places the temple in Cambridge. How did it get from Rome to Massachusetts?"

Professor answered before Pierre could. "The Founding Fathers were all Freemasons. That's the connection, isn't it?"

Pierre nodded. "The cult sustained itself on the fringes of the Church during the early years of Christianity, but during the Enlightenment, it found renewed purpose among those who were drawn to the equality and equanimity of the Masonic Lodges. How the sacred relics came to be in the Americas, or for that matter, how they moved through the preceding centuries, I cannot say, but what happened from 1776 onward is established within the lore of the cult.

"After the colonies won independence, the relics were taken to France. As you are doubtless aware, many in French society supported America's revolution. For some, this was a cynical decision—France and England were enemies—but many were dedicated to the goddess, whom they named 'Marianne.' The goddess, adorned with the *pileus*—the cap of freedom—became the symbol of the new French Republic, under the leadership of the priest Maximillien Robespierre, assisted by his Chosen—the prophetess Catherine Théot."

"Robespierre," said Professor. "Another leader in your cult brought to ruin on the advice of your goddess and her sacred relics. Tell me again why you're looking for them?"

"I am not a priest, nor can I know the thoughts of the goddess, but you and I both know that Robespierre had many enemies."

"Okay, so after Robespierre, Napoleon steps onto the stage. No doubt Josephine was his Chosen." Professor paused abruptly as if struck by a revelation. "But I've forgotten something. The Haitian Revolution under the leadership of the Black Spartacus."

Pierre's eyes narrowed, a hint of bitterness entering his voice. "The sacred relics never came to Haiti. Although Robespierre openly denounced slavery in all French territories, and Toussaint Louverture, as a former slave was certainly a worthy candidate, Robespierre refused to support a slave uprising, both publicly and with the sacred relics of Libertas in his trust. Perhaps that is why Robespierre lost the favor of the goddess. I cannot say.

"Nor did the Americans give support. President Thomas Jefferson, the author of the Declaration of Independence and the words 'all men are created equal and endowed with the inalienable right of Liberty,' feared that an act of true liberation—a slave revolt—would embolden American slaves to rise up against their masters, and so instead of supporting the cause of freedom, the Americans threw their support to the French colonists."

There was a long uncomfortable silence which Pierre finally broke with a heavy sigh. "But your first assumption was correct. Napoleon took possession of the sacred relics and for a time, was the most powerful man in the world."

"And afterward?" Jade prompted. "What happened to the relics? Where did they go?"

"Back to France, I presume. As I said, the priestess knows the location of the temple. We know that, for the last two hundred years, the blessing of the goddess—democracy, civil rights, an end to dictators and despots—has transformed the world. The hand of the goddess can be seen in this ideological shift. And yet, human exploitation continues, hidden in the shadows, carried on by wealthy, powerful men who have no respect for the law or humanity."

Jade threw a knowing glance to Professor and mouthed the word, "Dominion."

Professor nodded.

"They seek a return to the time of empires and serfdom. A world where they own everything and everyone. And if they are not stopped, if we the oppressed do not rise up and stop them, they will succeed." Pierre fixed her with an imploring stare. "That is why you have been Chosen, Jade."

Jade frowned. "Yann, I'm not going to be a figurehead

in your crusade. And as much as I want to sympathize with you, I can't agree with your methods or your beliefs. You imprisoned me. Lied to me. Diane is probably lying to all of you, using you so she can get more power. This cult of yours isn't offering freedom or liberty. It's just another form of slavery."

She rose and turned to Professor. "Let's get out of here."

"But—"

She silenced him with a hard look. "We're done here."

Professor spread his hands in a show of surrender. "You're the boss, boss."

"Jade, please," Pierre pleaded, but Jade strode for the door, refusing to meet his gaze.

She heard Professor's parting shot as she stepped into the hallway. "Stay away from her. All of you."

He caught up to her a few seconds later. "Jade, I understand what you're feeling, but I don't think this is just going to go away. We need a plan. And I think he knows more than he just told us."

"I'll puke if I have to listen to any more of that crap about freedom and liberty," Jade said without breaking her stride. "And besides, I've *got* a plan."

"Oh? I can't wait to hear this."

Jade took a quick look around to make sure that no one was there to overhear. The dimly lit halls of the museum were empty and Pierre did not appear to be following them but she remained wary. Dropping her voice to a low whisper, she said, "Like I told you in Rome. I'm going to get the sacred relics before anyone else, and take them out of play. Give them to a museum. Or maybe just destroy them. Once the relics are out of the temple, the cult won't need me anymore. And Purcell won't have a reason to kill me."

"That won't be the end of it. The cult will still want their revolution."

"And the Dominion will still want to rule the world. Right now, I don't see a better answer than letting them slug it out. Maybe the rest of the world will wake up and demand something that actually works for everyone for a change."

"A lot of innocent people might get hurt."

"Innocent people are suffering right now. Revolution sucks, but so does the status quo. But if you've got a better answer, I'm all ears."

He frowned but was silent for a moment. "That still leaves us with the problem of finding the temple. Even if everything Yann told us is true, it doesn't exactly narrow it down."

She glanced around again. The memorial to Toussaint Louverture lay just ahead, and the exit just beyond it. They still appeared to be alone, but Jade definitely didn't want anyone overhearing what she was about to say. She took Professor's hand and as she drew him onward, she whispered. "I already know where the temple is."

"You do?"

She flashed a triumphant grin. "It's not very often that I get to be the smart one. Is this how you feel all the time?"

"Just tell me."

As they passed through the doors and started up the short flight of stairs to street level she continued, "You really don't know? It's so obvious. France. The Freemasons. Libertas. It was right there in that poem. Think about it for a second. You'll figure it out."

Professor stopped in his tracks. For a moment, Jade thought he was reacting to her hints—it really was obvious, after all—but then she saw that he was staring straight ahead at a pair of men—dark-skinned, probably locals—standing on the sidewalk, about twenty yards ahead of them. The larger of the two was tall but lean. The sleeves of his soiled denim shirt had been cut away to reveal ropey muscles that twisted like snakes under his skin. He wore a dull expression, staring straight ahead but seemingly looking at nothing. That was not the case however with his companion. Although the diminutive old man with short steel-gray hair was leaning on a walking stick and hunched over so that he appeared even smaller, his eyes were focused like lasers on Professor.

"I warned you not to return," the old man said. "Did you think I would not know? My eyes are everywhere."

His voice was high-pitched but oddly flat and atonal; the dispassionate drone of a sociopath. It was a voice, Jade now realized, that she had heard before, on the night of her abduction.

"Cesar," Professor whispered.

Even without fully comprehending who the man was or what was happening, Jade knew they were in trouble. She glanced around, looking for help or an escape route. Even though the museum was closed, she felt sure there would be at least a few tourists wandering the slope or idling on the rooftop, but all she saw were more disheveled figures in tattered jeans and denim shirts shambling toward them, blocking every path of egress.

They reminded her of zombies. Not Romero's walking dead, but the voodoo variety like they supposedly had in Haiti….

"Oh, crap," she muttered. "They are zombies."

"Jade," Professor said, his voice calm but urgent. "Run."

"Like hell." She balled her fists and shifted her feet to a fighting stance. "I'm not leaving you."

"Damn it, Jade. You need to—"

"Now," the old man droned, "you will answer for your insults."

He raised his walking stick—which Jade now saw was tipped with an amazingly realistic carving of a small skull—and the zombies lurched forward, moving toward Jade and Professor with predatory swiftness. Before she knew what was happening, the zombies were on them. One of them seized her from behind, wrapped a powerful arm around her middle, lifted her off the ground. She opened her mouth to scream for help, but a hand clamped over her face, stifling the cry, suffocating her. From the corner of her eye, she saw Professor struggling in vain against three zombies, but then something was pulled over her head and she saw nothing.

TWENTY

After a short journey in a vehicle—judging by the flat deck beneath her, Jade guessed it was a truck or panel van— she was roughly removed and half-carried, half-dragged inside a structure—another supposition based on the change in noise level. She sensed a descent—a flight of stairs, perhaps—and not long after that, her captors came to a sudden and complete stop. The hood covering her head prevented her from seeing where they were going, but the sounds that had reached her ears through the heavy cloth sack during the drive suggested they were still in the city.

She had given up on demanding an explanation from her captors. The zombies seemed completely immune to her harangues. Aside from a few grunts, they made no noise at all.

Some side effect of having your soulless body brought back from the dead, she guessed.

She was a little surprised that she did not feel terrified. She was worried, even a little scared, but it was not a paralyzing fright. Rather, what she felt was more of a heightened awareness, the alertness of a combat soldier, pinned down by the enemy but ready to seize the initiative if an opportunity to turn the tables arose.

And Professor was with her. Between the two of them, they would find a way out of this mess. She was confident of that.

The hood was yanked away, along with a few strands of hair.

"Ow!" She winced, squinting against the brightness of the light that now bathed her face, though in fact, the light—which issued from a couple dozen candles, grouped together on a table or some kind of votive altar—wasn't really all that bright. After a moment or two, her eyes adjusted and, blinking away the tears, she took in her immediate surroundings.

She was indoors, though it was hard to tell. There were

no windows and no doors that she could immediately see. In fact, the room was mostly empty. The most noteworthy feature was a single support pillar in the center of the room, painted with black and white stripes. The walls, at least what she could see of them, were more colorful, with lurid murals, human figures and semi-human monsters that seemed to move and dance in the flickering candle light. She could now see the altar with the candles a little better, a large stone block, hollowed out in the middle. In the candle light, it looked like there was something moving in the hollow space. It might have been a trick of light and shadow, but Jade got the impression of something slithering there.

She was no expert, but she knew voodoo when she saw it.

Which meant the old guy with the creepy walking stick standing beside the altar was some kind of voodoo witch doctor.

The zombies were there, too. Two of them held her suspended between them. A glance behind her revealed Professor, his face hidden beneath a hood, likewise held up by a pair of zombies.

She wondered, absently, what had become of his fedora. It was probably still on the sidewalk outside the museum, if it had not already become the property of a local wandering by.

I guess I'll have to buy him another one, she thought. *Once we get out of here.*

She brought her gaze back to the old man. "He called you Cesar. Is that right?"

The old man rocked back and forth on his heels, regarding her with his yellow eyes, but gave no answer.

"I recognized your voice," Jade went on. "You were there when they put me in that shipping container. Are you part of the cult?"

This evoked a reaction, albeit a subtle one. The man's lips parted, baring his teeth in what looked like a smile, or maybe a grimace. "They are fools. But fools who pay me very well." His nostrils flared contemptuously. "I see their chains did not hold you for long."

"Haven't you heard? I'm the Chosen."

Cesar made a strange braying sound. It took Jade a moment to realize he was laughing. "Yes. Maybe they will pay to get you back. This time, I think, they will find you somewhat more..." He flicked his gaze to one of the zombies holding her and nodded his chin toward the man. "Compliant."

He then looked past her. "Bring him forward."

The zombies holding Professor advanced until their prisoner was in front of the altar, almost face to face with Cesar. One of them removed the hood.

Professor blinked at the sudden light, but recovered quickly, looking around until he found Jade. He nodded to her, a gesture she took to be one of reassurance, then brought his gaze to Cesar. "You have to let her go."

"Hey," Jade cried out. "I'm not going anywhere without you."

"Shut up, Jade," Professor said with uncharacteristic harshness. His gaze remained fixed on Cesar. "Your beef is with me. She's no part of this. Do what you want with me, but don't hurt her. The cult won't pay you a red cent if you turn her into a zombie."

Jade swallowed nervously. *Turn me into what?*

Cesar stared back, impassive. "Is it possible that you still do not understand me? I do not care about their money. Money is how one man controls another man. Owns him. Makes him into that." He gestured with the skull walking stick to one of the zombies. "They will know, just as you now know, that I do not serve any man."

He lowered the walking stick in a quick, slashing gesture. The zombies forced Professor to his knees. One of them grasped ahold of his head with both hands, tilting it back so his face was looking up at Cesar, who was turning the skull at the end of the walking stick, rotating it, unscrewing it.

"Cesar, you don't have to do this."

Something in Professor's tone broke Jade's resolve. He

was pleading with Cesar, begging for the voodoo priest to spare Jade, even at the cost of his own life.

Okay, now I'm a little scared.

Cesar inverted the skull as it came free of the stick, but not before a puff of white powder escaped from the container hidden inside it. Jade could see the dust falling, swirling in the candlelight.

Cesar extended his arm out, holding the upside-down skull above Professor's face. "If Baron Samedi wills it, you will pass into the Underworld. But if he refuses, you will return as my *zombi*."

"Stop it," Jade shrieked. "I'll do whatever you want, but don't hurt him."

Cesar gave no indication that he had heard her, but something got his attention. He drew the skull back and turned his gaze to the rear of the room. Jade followed his line of sight and realized that someone was trying to force his way past the zombies guarding the door.

It was Yann Pierre.

"Cesar!" he gasped. "Are you mad? Taking them in public? Did you think no one would see you?"

"This does not concern you, boy."

"It most certainly does. You have to release them now. Unharmed."

Cesar made a flicking gesture with his decapitated stick, signaling the zombies to let him enter. Pierre hurried into the room, but stopped in front of Jade. "I am so sorry this has happened. I promise, I will take care of this."

"That is a promise you will be unable to keep," Cesar said, the droning of his voice growing tight with irritation. "You should leave now, boy. Or perhaps you would rather join them?"

Undaunted by the threat, Pierre whirled to confront Cesar. "You do not want the servants of the goddess as your enemies, Cesar."

Cesar seemed to find this notion amusing. "Do you speak for your priestess?"

The question seemed to surprise Pierre. His forehead

wrinkled in a frown of concentration. "You know our plans for this one. She is the Chosen. The harbinger of a new age."

"So?"

"So?" Pierre sputtered in exasperation. "You can't turn the Chosen of the goddess into a zombie."

"That's right," Jade said, feeling vaguely foolish at trying to argue her way out of the situation. "I'm the Chosen of Libertas. Goddess of *freedom*." She emphasized the last word.

"She has already passed your test. When she is *zombi*, your priestess may command her to do as she will. I am doing her a favor."

"That's absurd," Pierre shot back. "The goddess stands for freedom. Your zombies… That's the worst kind of slavery. It's an abomination."

Cesar brayed with laughter again. Jade thought he sounded a little like a smoke alarm. "I think your priestess does not share that point of view."

"Dealing with you was a necessary evil. It was required for the Servus Trial, but I assure you, we will not make that mistake again."

"You are a very naïve young man," Cesar said, wagging his head in mock dismay.

"Don't you get it Yann?" Professor said. "Your cult has been working with him all along. They're the other end of his human trafficking pipeline. He supplies the bodies, and the cult finds the buyers."

Pierre's frown deepened. "No. That's absurd. We're trying to put a stop to human exploitation."

"If that was true, Yann," said Jade, "Do you really think they would be working with Cesar at all?"

Cesar laughed again. "You've blinded yourself to the reality of your own beliefs, boy. Your goddess cannot exist in a world without slavery. Free men do not pray for liberation."

"It's true," Jade added. "Diane lied to you. She doesn't want an end to human trafficking because that would mean the end of your cult. And her power."

"I doubt her motives are that Machiavellian," Professor added. "She's probably just in it for the money."

"But…" Pierre seemed to stagger under the weight of this revelation. He looked at Jade again. "You *are* the Chosen. This is your destiny."

"Destiny?" Jade scoffed. "By your own admission, the leaders of your cult have used the relics to gain political power, but did any of them end slavery? Julius Caesar and Mark Antony. Washington and Jefferson. Robespierre. Napoleon. None of them even tried, and do you know why? Because Libertas needs slaves the way the Church needs sinners. Whatever Diane has planned, I promise you, it won't put an end to human exploitation. It will probably just make it even worse."

Pierre was blinking furiously, looking from side to side as he processed the accusations, struggling to find some fatal flaw in Jade's logic.

"Yann," Professor said, an added note of urgency. "You can make this right. Take Jade and get out—"

His exhortation was cut off when a swiping blow from Cesar's stick caught the side of his head.

"Enough," the old man said. "None of you will leave here. False hope will only cause you to despair. Better you should pray to whatever god or goddess you worship before you go to meet Baron Samedi."

Then, he held the skull out over Professor's upturned face, and then turned it over.

TWENTY-ONE

"No!" Jade screamed as a clump of white powder fell from the skull and hit Professor square in the face.

A puff of dust, as fine as flour, arose from the point of impact, momentarily obscuring his face, but Jade could see him moving, shaking his head as if in the grip of a seizure. The dust settled quickly, revealing his face, scrunched up to prevent even a single mote of the substance from getting into his mouth, nose or eyes. The powder however clung to his skin like a death mask.

Cesar rotated the skull again so that no more of the powder escaped, and then turned his attention to Jade. "Now you will join him. Bring her forward."

"Let. Go. Of. Me." Jade struggled again to get free of her captors, but the zombies' grip was as unyielding as stone. They dragged her forward until she was in front of the altar. One zombie held her shoulders, immobilizing her arms. He forced her to kneel, while a second turned her face up to Cesar.

Beside her, Professor coughed, blowing out another cloud of the white powder. "Hold your breath," he gasped. "Don't get it in your eyes."

Cesar gave an atonal chuckle. "It would be better for you to breathe in deeply," he advised. "Less… painful."

He held the skull out over her face and began rotating it.

"Cesar!" Pierre shouted. "I can't let you do this."

With her head held in the vise-like grip of a zombie, Jade didn't see exactly what happened next, but the pressure on her shoulders abruptly disappeared. The zombie had let go of her. She surmised that Pierre had done something precipitous, perhaps made a move to physically restrain or assault Cesar, and the zombie, seeing that as the more immediate priority, had moved to intercept.

Cesar glanced away, momentarily distracted by whatever was going on behind Jade. The half-turned skull seemed to float above her, mere inches from her face, the empty eye sockets appearing to look at her sidelong.

She shot her hands out, catching the skull and the hand that held it. Her first thought was to push the vile thing away from her, but as soon as she had ahold of it, she knew doing that would merely postpone the inevitable.

She felt Cesar reacting, saw his attention return to her. He tried to pull free of her grip, a reflex action. Jade fought his first attempt, but when he tried again, with more vigor, she stopped fighting him, and instead shoved the skull away with all her strength, adding his power to her own. The skull shot upward and smashed into Cesar's face, shattering in an eruption of white powder.

Cesar staggered back and let out a hideous shriek as he got a taste of his own medicine.

Remembering Professor's warning, Jade immediately closed her eyes and mouth, exhaling through her nose to hopefully blow out any of the dust that might have gotten into her nostrils.

And then the hands gripping her head fell away. The second zombie had let go of her.

She was free.

Without opening her eyes, she backpedaled away. When she had put some distance between herself and the noxious cloud around Cesar, she rubbed her hand across her face, hoping to brush away any particles that might have settled there. Then she risked opening her eyes, though only wide enough to squint through her eyelashes.

Strangely, the light in the room had gone dim, as if her act of resistance had blown out some of the candles. She could barely make out anything in fact, just silhouettes and shadows, moving in front of the altar in a chaotic and eerily quiet dance.

Then, a cry of unimaginable agony tore through the stillness. Not Cesar this time, but Yann Pierre. Jade turned in the direction of the sound, but all she could make out was a squirming mass of darkness, wriggling and pulsating like some kind of Lovecraftian monstrosity. The zombies—at least three, maybe more—were clustered around Pierre, arms rising and falling with pummeling blows. Then the scream was silenced and the only sound she could hear was the thudding of fists on flesh and the crunch of bones breaking. They were beating him to death, tearing him apart.

"Jade?" Professor's voice was a hoarse whisper behind her. She half-turned and began crawling toward him. She realized that the light was growing brighter again, as if someone were systematically relighting the candles, but she did not look away from the kneeling figure before her.

Professor's face, coated in the white powder, was starkly visible in the flickering orange light.

"I'm here," she whispered. She reached him, reached out and took his hand. "I'm here."

Suddenly the light flared more brightly than a hundred candle flames. She turned to it, involuntarily, and saw the silhouette of a man, outlined against the orange flames that were rising from the altar behind him. By his diminutive size, Jade knew it could only be Cesar, but the wail that issued from his lips was an inhuman sound. He twisted in place, writhing in agony. For a moment Jade thought it must be the effect of the powder—Cesar had surely received a massive dose of the substance, whatever it was—but then she realized that the flames were not coming from behind Cesar. They were coming from him.

After recoiling from Jade's attack, he had fallen into the candles burning on the altar, saturating his denim clothing in melted wax. Most of them had been snuffed out in the fall, but one or two had stayed lit, and had ignited Cesar's clothing.

In a matter of seconds the voodoo witch doctor was fully engulfed, his cries silenced again as the flames burned the oxygen from his lungs. He remained upright for a moment or two, a living creature made of fire, and then staggered forward toward Jade and Professor.

That jolted Jade into action. She launched herself onto Professor, shoving him sideways, getting them both out of the burning man's path.

If Cesar saw them, he gave no indication. He simply kept going, lurching toward the wooden pillar in the center of the room. The zombies looked up from their grisly task in almost perfect unison, and then, in what appeared to be a display of primal terror, fled to the corners of the room. Cesar crashed into the pillar a moment later and then sank to his knees, but the flames of his immolation clung to the painted wood and began rising up the vertical surface to lick at the cross-beams overhead.

Jade got to her feet and pulled Professor along. "Come on. We have to go."

"Cesar?" he said, a little breathlessly.

"He's toast."

"Good." A pause, then, "You'll have to lead me out of here. I can't see very well."

The heat radiating from the blazing pillar was intense, but she stayed as close to it as she could, trusting it to keep the zombies back, at least long enough for them to reach the exit. Beyond that point, she had no idea what they would find.

One crisis at a time, she told herself.

They reached the door, passed through it into another room, this one illuminated by a lantern hanging from a hook protruding from the far wall near another door. Absent any other choices, Jade started toward the latter, pulling Professor along, but before they had gotten halfway, a man wearing a sweat-stained suit stepped out, an alarmed look on his face. His gaze locked onto Jade and he shouted something in Creole.

Beside her, Professor stiffened defensively, but then answered the challenge in French, pointing behind them. Jade recognize a couple of the words he used. "*Un fue… Aider Cesar.*"

Fire. Help Cesar.

The man looked past them to the orange glow emanating from the room they had exited and the smoke billowing out, and then he was moving, running. Jade tensed, preparing for a physical attack, but the man hurried past them, plunging headlong into the burning room.

Jade let out her breath in a sigh. "He fell for it."

"Good," Professor said. "But he won't be fooled for long. We have to hurry."

He started forward, pulling Jade along. He kept one hand outstretched before him, groping his way forward, but even though he obviously couldn't see where he was going he moved infallibly toward the far door. Jade had to quicken her pace to keep up.

Beyond the door was a musty storeroom, possibly a cellar, which appeared to be unoccupied, though it was hard to tell in the gloom.

"There's some stairs coming up," Professor whispered, still moving briskly. "At the top, there's going to be a hallway with a bunch of curtained-off rooms. We're going to go down it and hook a left. We'll have to go straight through Cesar's night club. There might be more of his men waiting there. Not zombies. Just regular hoodlums. We're going to just move through like we own the place. No stopping. Maybe we'll catch them off guard. If you think someone's going to try to stop us, just squeeze my hand and I'll try bluffing like I did before. If we have to fight... Well, do what comes naturally and remember the moves I've taught you. There might be a couple more outside. Just blow past and keep going. Run if you have to. Got it?"

"Umm, how do you know all this?"

"I've been here before. When I was trying to find you."

"Ah. Well that explains how you got to be on a first name basis with big bad voodoo daddy."

Professor said nothing more, but instead focused on the challenge of shuffling blindly up the rickety steps. At the top, as promised, Jade saw a long unlit hallway with blankets hung to cover entrances to side rooms.

"All clear," she whispered.

They moved forward at a fast walk, turning into a large room that smelled of stale smoke and body odor. Evidently, Professor had been somewhat disingenuous in calling it a "night club." Fortunately, there were only a couple men occupying tables in the dimly lit room. Jade spotted the door and hurried toward it, watching the men in her peripheral vision but not looking directly at them. She thought she saw one of the men start to rise, but then they were at the door, bursting out into the open.

The sky was darkening with the approach of dusk, but the city was still alive with cars and trucks, and people moving about on their various errands, oblivious to the horror that had transpired practically under their feet. Jade, still holding Professor's hand, did not look to see if there were any of Cesar's men standing watch as gatekeepers, but made a beeline for the edge of the street and the flow of pedestrian traffic.

"Which way?"

"Doesn't matter." Professor's voice was strained.

Jade glanced over and saw his face contorted into a grimace of agony. His eyes were still squeezed shut, but tiny blisters appeared to be breaking out on his forehead, weeping fluid that left trails through the coating of white dust that still clung to his skin. "Just pick one and keep moving. Get us a taxi if you can."

She had only taken a few steps when she spotted a minibus, garishly painted in a Caribbean color scheme—red, green and gold—along with an airbrushed mural of a Haitian sunset. "Will a Camionette work?"

Port au Prince did not have a regular municipal transit service, but the Camionettes—brightly painted vans or trucks which were often stuffed with passengers and blasting upbeat *kompa* dance music—offered a similar service and were a cheaper alternative to taxis, but like regular buses, followed a predetermined route.

"Are we being followed?" He seemed to groan the words.

Jade glanced back but saw no indication of pursuit. "I don't think so."

He slowed to a more normal walking pace, but shook his head. "We need a taxi to take us directly to the embassy."

"The embassy? Don't you think you should get to a

hospital?"

"They can take care of that at the embassy. Two birds with one stone."

Jade resumed scanning the street. The taxis they had ridden in on previous occasions were newer model vehicles, painted bright yellow with distinctive markings, but all she saw here were old beaters with missing fenders, belching blue smoke.

Professor groaned again. "Jade, stop a minute. I need to talk to you."

Something about his tone, and the effort required for him to speak the words, sent a chill through Jade. "Can't it wait?"

"No. I need to tell you this now. Just in case."

"Just in case what?" Her voice edged up an octave.

"Did you get any of that powder on you?"

"I don't know. I don't think so."

"The powder contains tetrodotoxin," Professor went on, pausing to catch his breath after every few words. "The stuff in pufferfish. You remember *fugu*?"

Jade did. When she and Professor had done some work in Japan for the Myrmidons, a sushi vendor had offered her *sashimi* made from the pufferfish, which they called *fugu*. It was a potentially lethal delicacy since the fish's liver contained a deadly neurotoxin. Great care was needed when preparing the dish to avoid contaminating the meat and poisoning the customer, though from what she had observed, the risk was a large part of its appeal.

"There was something else in it, too. A blistering agent. Probably a tertiary transmission vector. If inhalation and ingestion don't work, the toxin can enter the bloodstream through skin contact. I got some of it in my eyes. Burns like a mother."

Jade swallowed down the emotion rising in her throat. "I'll find some water. Rinse it out?"

"That might help, but right now you need to just listen. You'll need to tell the doctor this so he'll know how to treat it. I'll probably start to experience symptoms in about twenty minutes, give or take, depending on how much of it I was exposed to. The longer it takes, the better my chances of surviving it."

"Don't talk like that. Of course, you're going to survive it. We'll get you the antidote."

"There isn't an antidote, but it is survivable as long as you can keep me breathing. The reason *bokors* use tetrodotoxin in their zombie powder is because the paralysis and coma is so total that it is easily mistaken for death, but it is survivable. That's why you have to listen to me. You have to remember."

She swallowed again, her mouth suddenly feeling very dry. "Okay."

"Death usually results from respiratory failure. The toxin causes total paralysis. It will initially present with numbness, loss of coordination and mental faculty. I may not even be aware of it happening, so you need to watch me. If I go down…" He wobbled a little, as if standing on the deck of a storm-tossed ship. "Uh, oh. Looks like … Math… Wrong… Keep breath—"

And then he toppled over, crashing onto the sidewalk beside her.

Maybe it was his advance warning, or the adrenaline that was still coursing through her bloodstream from their escape, but Jade did not freeze or panic. She felt a knife-like stab of grief in her heart, but her body reacted with near-autonomous efficiency.

She immediately dropped to her knees beside him, rolled him over onto his back. She didn't check for a pulse, that would have been a waste of time. Instead, she placed a hand on his chest, looking for the telltale rise and fall. It wasn't there.

Professor had stopped breathing.

Muscle memory took over. The techniques of cardiopulmonary resuscitation and rescue breathing had been drilled into her during countless lifeguard courses taken during her childhood in Hawaii, and despite the intervening years since her last certification, her subconscious knew exactly what to do. She took hold of his head, tilting it back and repositioning his jaw to clear his airway. It was only when she lowered her face to his, intending to breathe into his lungs, that her conscious brain started waving red flags.

His face was covered in the toxic powder. If she touched him with her mouth, the poison might transfer to her, and then they might both die.

But if she didn't, he would definitely die.

She tugged up a corner of his shirt and wiped away as much of the offending substance as she could. In the failing light, she could see beads of blood appearing on his forehead and around his eyes where the blistering agent had burned through his skin.

Pushing aside her concerns about accidental exposure, she pinched his nose shut, drew in a deep breath and then put her mouth to his.

She could feel the breath go into him without resistance.

After repeating the process a second time, she raised her head, only now aware that a crowd had gathered around her, watching in astonished silence. "Get help!" she cried out. "Call an ambulance. A doctor. Hurry."

She didn't wait to see if anyone heeded her plea, but returned her attention to Professor, gave him two more breaths before finally checking to see if he had a pulse. It took her several seconds to feel the rhythmic, and unusually rapid, beat of his heart.

"Get help," she cried out again, and then lowered her mouth to his.

Keep me breathing, he had told her.

That was the only thing in the world that mattered to her now.

PART FOUR: LIBERATOR

TWENTY-TWO

In the hours—or perhaps days—that followed, Pete Chapman, known to his friends as Professor, came to intimately understand how the *bokors* of the form of Vodou known as *petro*, were able to use naturally occurring chemicals to transform an otherwise healthy individual into something that resembled a soulless reanimated corpse.

It was not a neurological effect, or rather it was but only indirectly. It was also very different from what he remembered of the zombii experiments Maddock and Bones had foiled years ago. There was some kind of stimulant mixed into the powder, along with a powerful hallucinogenic compound, but nothing that actually caused permanent harm to the brain as a physical organ.

The effect on his psyche however was something else altogether.

He was experiencing the chemical equivalent of a medical condition known as locked-in syndrome, unable to move or speak, but completely conscious. In fact, the stimulant prevented his body and brain from entering into a state of sleep, which compounded with the mortal terror of what his body was going through, left him in a perpetual state of high anxiety. He lost all sense of time, and with the added effect of the hallucinogen, was plunged into a nightmare that seemed to go on forever.

He could well imagine how a typical Haitian, steeped in the superstitions of Vodou and already predisposed to believe in the powers of the *bokor*, might not only interpret the experience as a journey into Hell, but actually be so traumatized as to lapse into a permanent dissociative fugue state.

His eyes wouldn't open, but the hallucinogen supplied vivid images—swirls of light and darkness locked in an apocalyptic battle for his soul. There were voices, too. Some real, others imagined, all distorted and ghastly. He could feel himself being moved, probed, violated. Something was rammed down his throat, and later, he could feel something that felt like a red-hot poker snaking up his urethra.

And yet, these physical sensations gradually helped him return from the torment of the abyss.

A breathing tube, he thought. *I've been intubated and ventilated.*

The urinary catheter would be necessary to monitor the level of the toxin in his urine and therefore in his bloodstream. There was no cure for tetrodotoxin poisoning but the body could excrete the toxin if the patient was kept alive.

Good girl, Jade. You told them.

That thought triggered another cascade of anxiety.

Jade.

I've let her down again.

The spiral into this particular black hole was harder to escape, if only because deep down, he knew it was true.

He had misjudged the threat posed by Cesar, and it had nearly cost both of them dearly. That he was still alive and receiving medical treatment was evidence that she had gotten clear of Cesar's neighborhood, but that did not mean she was safe from possible retaliations from the deceased gangster's lieutenants. And of course, there was the ongoing threat from both the Cult of Libertas and Purcell, whom he assumed was acting on behalf of the Dominion.

Trapped in his body as he was, there was nothing he could do to protect her. Jade was on her own.

She's done pretty good on her own this far, he thought, but this brought him no comfort. Indeed, he was beginning to realize that Jade didn't need him anymore. She didn't need a protector or a bodyguard, and without that, what reason was there for him to be in her life?

He churned over this for a brief eternity, and despite his best efforts to cajole himself—*suck it up and drive on, sailor*—or to simply think about something else—he tried counting prime numbers, reciting the Declaration of Independence, replaying in his head the entirety of the rock-opera *Tommy* by The Who, which seemed appropriate given his condition—but his anxiety about Jade kept returning at every unguarded moment.

Eventually though, the hallucinations became less vivid and then stopped altogether. The voices normalized into the banter of doctors and nurses, speaking French, remarking on the state of his recovery. Their words gave him hope; he was going to live after all.

But one voice remained conspicuously absent.

Jade? Are you there?

He could not articulate the question. He longed to hear her voice, feel her hand in his with a reassuring squeeze, but if she was there, she remained silent, out of reach.

More time passed and then a new voice reached into the prison of his mind. "Pete? Can you hear me?"

It wasn't Jade, but the voice was female and familiar, and speaking English. He tried to answer, but was immediately reminded of the plastic tube inserted in his windpipe.

"Don't try to speak," the woman said. "You've got a breathing tube in."

The fact that his reaction had been observed strongly suggested that the paralysis was finally wearing off. He searched his memories, trying to put a face and a name to the voice, then he remembered.

It was Kasey Kim. The young woman, a first-generation native California girl from a Korean family, was one of Tam's operations officers at the Myrmidons.

Where's Jade? He longed to ask the question.

"The docs want to keep you on the vent a little longer, but it sounds like you're almost out of the woods."

He tried to make a thumbs-up gesture. Kasey's soft laughter told him that he had at least partially succeeded.

"Trust me," she went on. "I know how you feel."

He did not doubt that. A few months earlier, Kasey had been seriously injured during an operation in the south of France, and was still awaiting medical clearance for active duty, which was probably why Tam had sent her to check up on him.

"You got some nasty burns from whatever that substance was, but no permanent damage. The only reason you can't see me right now is because they've got bandages over your eyes, but those will probably come off once the breathing tube is out."

He signaled comprehension again.

"Pete, Do you know where Jade is?"

The question hit him like a physical blow. He jolted, as if waking from a dream.

"Easy," Kasey said. He felt her hand on his arm. "I'll take that as a 'no.' The docs say that she came in with you. Some good Samaritans gave you both a ride in the back of a pickup. She was doing CPR the whole time. They say she saved your life. But once they got you checked in and tubed, she slipped away. I thought maybe that was something you told her to do."

He shook his head, or tried to.

Kasey's reply was characteristically understated. "Damn."

Professor's mind raced down dark paths. Had one of Cesar's men grabbed her from the hospital? The *bokor* had intimated that his spies were everywhere, but if they had that kind of access, they would have finished him off as well. He dismissed that possibility. He similarly rejected the likelihood of another abduction by the Cult of Libertas. Jade had been extraordinarily canny in avoiding them.

The more he thought about it, the more he knew that was exactly what she was doing. Jade had gone to ground.

The realization pained him. She had left *him*, abandoned him in his moment of need.

But hadn't he told her to do exactly that if threatened? And since she had nearly been killed, not once, but twice, by someone who ostensibly represented the American government, who was she supposed to trust? The local police? The embassy staff? Tam?

He swallowed his hurt and tried to focus on what she would do next, where she would go.

She had already told him her plan. Get the relics, take

them out of play. She didn't need him for that because she already knew where the temple was, or thought she did.

What had she said?

It's so obvious. France. The Freemasons. Libertas. It was right there in that poem.

He stacked these clues together like building blocks, trying to figure out the connection that had been so apparent to her.

The involvement of Freemasons in Revolutionary France was both a well-established and hopelessly muddled certainty, which wasn't at all surprising considering the internecine struggles among the various revolutionary groups which had ultimately led to the bloodbath of the Terror.

But maybe Jade had been referring to something else. If the Freemasons, or cultists hiding among their ranks, had taken possession of the sacred relics following Napoleon's ouster, then they would have been responsible for establishing the temple to house them.

France. The Freemasons. Libertas. The poem.

The poem?

How did a poem written by an American woman at the very start of the American Revolution, a poem about an American war hero who probably did not even imagine that he would one day become the first President of the United States of America, offer a clue to the location of a temple that would not be built for at least another forty years?

More to the point, how had Jade figured it out on her first hearing?

He ran through the poem in his head, almost completely forgetting Kasey's presence. Yann Pierre had not read the whole poem, but only the first two stanzas:

> *Celestial choir! enthron'd in realms of light,*
> *Columbia's scenes of glorious toils I write.*
> *While freedom's cause her anxious breast alarms,*
> *She flashes dreadful in refulgent arms.*
> *See mother earth her offspring's fate bemoan,*

And nations gaze at scenes before unknown!
See the bright beams of heaven's revolving light
Involved in sorrows and the veil of night!

The Goddess comes, she moves divinely fair,
Olive and laurel binds Her golden hair:
Wherever shines this native of the skies,
Unnumber'd charms and recent graces rise.

And then he had finished with the last verse:

Proceed, great chief, with virtue on thy side,
Thy ev'ry action let the Goddess guide.
A crown, a mansion, and a throne that shine,
With gold unfading, Washington! Be thine.

He repeated the words again in his head, trying to hear them as Jade had, or perhaps visualize....

And then he saw what she had seen, and what Phillis Wheatley had perhaps envisioned: The goddess of liberty, shining her light to guide America's destiny.

He raised his hands to his face, ignoring the faint resistance of an IV line taped to his arm, and tore away the bandages over his eyes. He winced at the brilliance of the light, but blinked through it until the pain subsided a little and some of the blurriness went away. He could see Kasey's form, staring at him in astonishment.

"Pete? Should I get the doctor?"

He reached up to his face, feeling the tube that snaked between his teeth, held in place with multiple strips of sterile tape, and shook his head. He had to fight the urge to simply pull it out—an extremely risky thing to do, especially if he wasn't actually up to the chore of breathing on his own. Instead, he raised a hand and made a scribbling gesture.

"You want to write it?" Kasey said. "Hang on a sec."

A moment later, she thrust a small notepad and a pen into his hands. His eyes refused to bring either object into clear focus, but didn't need to see to write. He scribbled out a short message and held it up for her to read.

"'Know where Jade is going,'" she read aloud. "'Need to get out of here, ASAP.' Okay, where is she going?"

He turned the paper around and wrote his answer in just three letters:

NYC.

TWENTY-THREE

New York

In 435 B.C.E, the ancient Greeks built a temple in the sanctuary of Olympia, to honor Zeus, king of the gods. The centerpiece of that temple was a forty-three-foot tall statue of the god, seated upon a throne and holding in his hand a representation of Nike, the winged goddess of victory. The statue, which stood there for nearly a thousand years, was considered one of the Seven Wonders of the World in its day.

The Colossus of Rhodes, another of the ancient wonders, also honored a god of antiquity—Helios, the Titan god of the sun. The 108-foot-tall statue, erected in 280 B.C.E., stood watch over the harbor for just fifty-four years until an earthquake took it off at the knees.

Two millennia would pass before the worshippers of an ancient deity attempted something similarly grandiose. In 1870 C.E., devotees of the goddess Libertas made the decision to construct a temple in which to place the holy relics of their cult. Inspired by those ancient offerings, they crafted a colossal statue of the goddess. They also borrowed imagery from Phillis Wheatley's poem, adorning the goddess with a diadem radiating seven points of light, rather than the traditional *pileus,* and placed in her hands an illuminated torch, intended to serve as a lighthouse beacon.

There was no question about where the temple should be situated. Although the cult was, at the time, headquartered in Paris, the leaders of the group—which was more of a secular movement dedicated to social and political reform than an actual religion—felt there was only one nation that embodied the ideals the goddess represented: The United States of America. This was particularly true in the aftermath of the Civil War, a war fought to end the institution of slavery, at the cost of nearly a million lives on both sides of the conflict. Although it would take another sixteen years to raise the funds necessary to complete the iconic figure, in 1886 the finished work was dedicated in New York Harbor. Named by its creator *La Liberté éclairant le monde*—Liberty Enlightening the World—in the years that followed, it came to be known by most simply as the Statue of Liberty.

As she gazed up at the towering green figure, now illuminated by floodlights, Jade experienced a pang of doubt. It was not the first.

As she had lain motionless throughout most of the day, concealed in the trees on the northwest side of the island, mentally rehearsing what she would do when the last ferry departed, she had been unable to set aside her misgivings. What had seemed so obvious to her a few days ago in Port au Prince now felt a little *too* obvious.

She wondered what Professor would have made of her theory, but then shook her head, trying to force herself to think about something else.

She hated leaving him there, in a hospital bed, clinging to life, but knew that leaving was exactly what he would have wanted her to do. The doctors had been cautiously optimistic about his chances for a full recovery, but aside from holding his hand and thinking positive thoughts, there wasn't a whole lot she could do for him. The fact that Cesar L'Enfant had so easily tracked them down was proof enough that she would be at risk if she remained in Haiti.

In truth, there were no safe places for her, not with the Cult of Libertas *and* Special Agent Purcell hunting her. The only way to end those threats was to reach the temple.

And the temple was there, at the Statue of Liberty. It had to be. Admittedly, there had not been a great deal of time for in-depth research, but nothing she had read or heard in her subsequent exploration of the history of the statue indicated otherwise. Her gut... No, not just her gut, her instincts as an archaeologist told her she was right about this.

It was a matter of record that the statue *was* a representation of Libertas. Even if Édouard René de

Laboulaye—the French abolitionist who first suggested the idea of a monument to American democracy—or Frédéric Auguste Bartholdi—the sculptor chiefly responsible for its creation—were not devotees of the cult, the simple fact that they intended to erect a colossal statue of the goddess in New York harbor would have been irresistible to the true believers. They would have found a way to utilize it as their temple, and she was pretty sure she knew precisely where they had chosen to conceal the sacred relics.

Getting to that exact location would be a little tricky, not to mention illegal, but her experiences with the Cult of Libertas—the ordeal of the *Mohebbi* and a night spent hiding in the Colosseum—had opened her eyes to a whole new world of possibilities. Escaping the chains of the Servus Trial was more than just a symbolic escape from slavery, it had taught her to think outside the box.

Way outside the box.

After leaving the hospital in Port au Prince, she had made her way to the city's harbor under cover of darkness, and stowed away aboard a cargo vessel bound for Miami, Florida. It had been ridiculously easy to sneak past the token security presence on the dock, and now that she knew what to expect from the crew—more or less—she had no trouble at all staying concealed for the duration of the sea voyage.

Three days later, she was in Miami, a city she had more than a passing acquaintance with owing to her brief romantic involvement with Professor's former-SEAL teammate, Dane Maddock. Maddock, a professional treasure hunter, actually lived in Key West, though he spent most of his time aboard his boat, *Sea Foam*. During their time together, she had grown accustomed to making the three-hour plus trip from Miami International Airport to Maddock's condo overlooking the Gulf.

Going to Maddock for help had not been her first choice. She hadn't made up her mind until the second day of the crossing, when she had been trying to decide what to do next. It wasn't that she still had unresolved feelings for him.

Yes, for a long time after he had dumped her—or

more politely, *broken things off*—she had carried a torch for him, but not anymore. The reason it had taken her so long to decide to ask him for help was that he no longer occupied a place at the forefront of her thoughts. In truth, she was surprised at how long it had been since she'd even thought about him. Her feelings for the man were about as resolved as they were ever going to get.

The idea of crawling back to Dane Maddock and begging him to rescue her held zero appeal, but she had other reservations of a less personal nature. Her past relationship with Maddock wasn't a secret. The cult or Agent Purcell—or both—might be keeping an eye on him, watching to see if she would turn to him for help. Practical considerations had won out though ultimately it had been a moot point. Maddock, not surprisingly, was away on some adventure of his own. Since she knew where he kept his spare key, she let herself into the condo and helped herself to his stash of emergency cash, which he kept in a lock box behind a painting of the Queen Anne's Revenge. She left a note on his refrigerator door—just a hasty IOU scrawled on a Post-It note promising to explain everything—and then grabbed the key to Maddock's '75 Ford Bronco, and hit the road.

The old orange and white Bronco got terrible gas mileage and she had to stop about every 100 miles or so to refuel. After the fourth such stop, she crawled into the back for a fifteen-minute catnap, after which she downed a can of Monster energy drink, and got back on the Interstate. She got as far as Charlotte, North Carolina, a little after two o'clock in the morning, before fatigue finally forced her to stop for a longer rest break, but she was up again at sunrise to resume the journey. Late that evening, she rolled into Jersey City where she parked the Bronco in a 24-hour garage and then curled up in the back for a full night's sleep before embarking on the last phase of her journey to the temple of Libertas.

Everything up to that point had been fairly straightforward if exhausting, but getting to Liberty Island had proven a bit more challenging. In her earlier visits to New York, Jade had not attempted a trip out to Liberty Island as it held little interest for her. The Colosseum at least had an aura of real history about it; the Statue of Liberty was a gaudy relic of the modern world, whereas she was a scholar who delved into the depths of America's ancient history. She dismissed it as a mere tourist attraction, and nearly every New Yorker she met claimed it wasn't worth the effort.

She was not wrong on the former count.

When she arrived at the Liberty State Park ferry terminal she found the line of visitors stretching back several hundred yards along the Riverwalk. It took nearly an hour of waiting to reach the ticketing booth where she received news that, in hindsight, should not have come as a surprise. She could get passage to the island, but her ticket would not include access to the statue's pedestal or crown. Full-access tickets needed to be booked at least three months in advance.

She bought an open-ended ground access ticket and got in the security-check line. Thankfully there was no ID check required, only a walk through the metal detector and a bag check—she had none. She overheard one of tour guides telling his group that there would be another far more intensive screening at the entrance to the pedestal, and for the first time since deciding to embark on the trip, Jade began to worry that maybe she was in over her head.

Once she disembarked and felt the solid ground of Liberty Island underfoot, she felt a little more hopeful. She had all day to figure out how to get around park rules and find her way inside the monument.

She started by wandering around the statue and browsing information kiosks and brochures. Much of the information was trivia she had already picked up over the years. The outer skin of the statue was made of copper, the thickness of two pennies, oxidized to a shade of green called verdigris. The internal steel frame had been designed by Gustave Eiffel, who would later be immortalized with the construction of the steel tower in Paris that bore his name. None of this seemed particularly interesting to Jade, but it gave her something to do as she wandered the island, probing its off-limits areas, noting the location of security cameras, and generally trying to figure out how she was going to get in.

But as the historical walk through moved from away from technical details and became more personal, Jade's interest was piqued. She began to see the statue through the eyes of those who had witnessed its construction, and actively worked to fund the massively expensive project, or who had glimpsed the finished statue from the decks of the ships bringing them to a new life in the Promised Land.

Like most people, she had a passing familiarity with the sonnet, *The New Colossus*, by Emma Lazarus, written in 1883 as part of the effort to raise money for construction of the pedestal, which actually exceeded the cost of the statue itself. The line: "Give me your tired, your poor, your huddled masses yearning to breathe free," was almost universally known—the stuff of quiz show questions—though not universally appreciated, especially in 21st Century America.

Jade herself had always had mixed feelings about the sentiment. She was not an immigrant or the offspring of immigrants, but a native Hawaiian—her Japanese father had never immigrated but returned home and remained absent from her life—and as such had always seen the issue of immigration through a different lens than most. The anti-immigrant sentiment of many Americans was the worst kind of hypocrisy, but they were right to think of immigrants as invaders; after all, they were the offspring of invaders. Immigrants, beginning with the first European colonists, had brought ruin to native populations and societies, including Jade's ancestors in the Kingdom of Hawaii.

But reading the poem again, here in the shadow of the world's most famous and iconic symbol of freedom, she saw it differently:

"Not like the brazen giant of Greek fame,

With conquering limbs astride from land to land;
Here at our sea-washed, sunset gates shall stand
A mighty woman with a torch, whose flame

"Is the imprisoned lightning, and her name
MOTHER OF EXILES. From her beacon-hand
Glows world-wide welcome; her mild eyes command
The air-bridged harbor that twin cities frame.

"'Keep, ancient lands, your storied pomp!' cries she
With silent lips. 'Give me your tired, your poor,
Your huddled masses yearning to breathe free,
The wretched refuse of your teeming shore.

"'Send these, the homeless, tempest-tost to me,
I lift my lamp beside the golden door!'"

It wasn't about who was native and who was a foreigner. Those distinctions didn't even matter anymore. In the new global society, nationalism and cultural pride had become tools, used by the one percent who controlled most of the wealth and all of the power, to manipulate everyone else into working against their own self-interest.

The real spirit of the Statue of Liberty spoke to freedom from oppression of all kinds, and that was something Jade could identify with. Her experience aboard the slave ship had been brief, barely a taste of the harsh reality endured by millions in the United States alone, but she would never forget it.

She felt anger too, at how the Cult of Libertas had perverted the idea of liberty and freedom, turning it into a pretext to enslave others.

As the day wore on, with groups of tourists coming and going, Jade had settled on the idea of finding a place to hide until after dark. The last ferry of the day would depart at 6:45 p.m., but she assumed there would be round the clock surveillance and roving patrols of Park Police, so her best chance of avoiding detection was to wait until nightfall.

Her plan was to make a beeline for the elevated foundation of the statue—an unusual eleven-pointed-star-shape called a hendecagram that, she had overheard a tour guide remarking, possessed no symbolic value at all but was merely the remains of the old army fort that had once occupied the site early in the 19th Century. Once there, she would scale the wall—difficult, but not impossible—to the foot of the pedestal where, hopefully, she would find a way inside. Failing that, she was prepared to make a free ascent of the craggy pedestal up to the statue itself, where another entrance—hopefully unlocked and unguarded—would give her access to the interior of the statue.

Before the last ferry pulled away, the Park Police made a sweep of the grounds, presumably looking for stragglers. Jade's pulse had quickened a little, not because she feared they might discover her, but because it had not occurred to her until that moment that they and the ferry operators would have kept a careful head count of arrivals and departures. Had they noticed that the numbers for the day didn't reconcile? Would they turn the park upside-down looking for her?

Evidently not, for after that single pass through, the ferry pulled away, and Jade was left more or less alone with her doubts and fears.

She waited a full hour after sunset—marking the time on her Omega Ladies' Seamaster, which Professor had returned to her in Italy—before stirring from her hiding place, creeping through the woods to the northwest corner of the foundation. There was about fifty feet of open ground between the trees and the wall, a span where she would be fully exposed to view of at least a couple different security cameras. Since there was no avoiding the crossing, she simply sprinted the distance and then flattened herself against the wall, remaining perfectly still. With a little luck, or maybe divine intervention from Libertas, the attention of the guard monitoring the camera feed would be on something else.

After a few minutes, with no indication that she had

been noticed, she decided it was safe to move again. She eased along the wall, seeking out one of the interior corners of the hendecagram, reasoning that the intersecting walls would give her a better chance of making the near vertical ascent. She was just about to start climbing the rough brick wall when a voice called out from behind.

"Dr. Ihara, is that you?"

She froze, an instinctive reaction that seemed silly under the circumstances. The man's tone was not at all threatening, but the faint trace of a Creole accent turned Jade's blood to ice. Whoever it was, he knew her by name. She was caught, with nowhere to go.

Jade eased away from the wall and turned to find a young black man wearing the blue uniform and peaked cap of a U.S. Park Police officer. The name plate over his right breast pocket read: "Christophe."

Jade tried for her best charming grin. "Hi. So, yeah. This isn't what it looks like."

Officer Christophe smiled. "It's okay. I've been waiting for you. Please, come with me."

Jade didn't move. "You're with the cult, aren't you?"

He nodded. "As you can imagine, this job is like a sacred duty for me."

Jade regarded this with a noncommittal grunt. The park cop, almost certainly a Haitian immigrant, was probably like Yann Pierre—a naïve true believer with no knowledge of the dark side of the Cult of Libertas. "So you knew I was here all along?"

"We thought you might figure out on your own that this is the temple. I was told to keep an eye out for you. When you didn't leave, I decided to come looking for you."

"So this *is* the temple?"

"Did you ever have any doubt?"

"Maybe a little." She looked past him, wondering where the other park police were. "So am I under arrest or something?"

"Not at all. As far as everyone else is concerned, you're a special VIP here for an after-hours tour. We get those more often than you might think. No one will bother you." He smiled again. "If you would just follow me," the officer went on, "I'll take you inside."

Jade hesitated, instinctively wary of another ploy to entrap her, but then realized that if this was a trap, she was already in it, and the only way out was through.

She followed Christophe back down the brick walk to the pedestal entrance, situated at the back side of the statue, and entered. The interior was as quiet and empty as a tomb. They passed through the idle metal detectors, past the entrance to the museum, and arrived at an elevator which the officer summoned using an override key. The doors opened and he gestured for her to enter before stepping inside. A few moments later, the car began rising slowly, ascending Jade knew, to the top of the pedestal, some ninety feet above ground. When the doors opened again, he led her up a stairway and into the interior of the Statue of Liberty.

It was a strange and claustrophobic experience. The steel framework rose above her looking like some kind of rickety makeshift contraption imagined by a child playing with an old school Erector set. Corkscrewing up through the middle of the crisscrossing steel beams was a tightly wound double-helix spiral staircase.

Christophe gestured to the stairs. "This is as far as I am permitted to go," he said, his tone now deeply reverential.

Despite herself, Jade rolled her eyes. "Seriously? Like thousands of people go up that staircase every year."

"Tonight is different. It is not my place to accompany the Chosen on this journey."

Jade shrugged, and then started up the steps. There were one hundred and forty-six in all, rising to a viewing platform situated at the level of the crown, which provided a high-altitude view of the harbor approach, as well as Brooklyn, Staten Island and parts of New Jersey, but Jade knew that what she wanted would require her to go even higher.

Jade was not wrong about U.S. Park Police officer Jameson

Christophe. He was a lot like Yann Pierre in a lot of ways.

Haitian by birth, he had spent his formative years in the quasi-foster home servitude of a *restavek*. For him, the 2010 earthquake had meant a chance to escape that life, and he had joined a group of refugees who had made their way to the United States where they were accorded Temporary Protected Status designation.

Accustomed to hard work, and with no ties to his home country, he had immediately begun making a new life for himself. A representative from Lighthouse Worldwide had met with him and suggested military service as a stepping stone to citizenship. During his three-year stint in the USMC, she had guided him through the naturalization process, and when he received his honorable discharge, had helped him find work with the Park Police. He owed everything to that woman, and the goddess she served.

Now, he was one of several members of the Cult of Libertas who worked on Liberty Island, covertly protecting the secret temple even as they daily stood in the shadow of the goddess.

Christophe felt a swell of pride as he stepped from the elevator, knowing that high above, the Chosen was about to embrace her destiny and usher in a world truly free from slavery and oppression.

"Officer Christophe!"

The suddenness of the shout startled him, even though he knew the voice. It was his immediate superior, the shift commander, Sergeant Glenn. But Glenn rarely employed such formality—it was always, "Hey, Jimmy!" to which he would answer, "Yeah, Sarge."

Sergeant Glenn was standing at the end of the corridor, one hand resting on the butt of his holstered sidearm. He wasn't alone. Three more officers from the shift were with him, all similarly poised to draw their weapons, along with another man in civilian attire whom Christophe did not recognize.

"Sarge, what's—"

"Raise your hands, Officer Christophe," Glenn called

out. "Very slowly."

Christophe knew better than to show even a hint of resistance. He raised his arms. "Sarge, what's going on? I haven't done anything."

"Did you permit an unauthorized visitor to access restricted areas?"

"No. Well, I mean sort of. She's a VIP. You know how it is." After-hours visits for celebrities and politicians was an unwritten and unspoken SOP.

Glenn and his retinue began advancing, their hands never moving from their guns. The other man however strode out ahead of them, dipping a hand into his jacket as he drew close to Christophe. When he withdrew it, he held not a gun but a credentials wallet, which he flipped open to display a gold shield-and-eagle badge, adorned with blue enamel and a government-issued identification card with the man's picture. Christophe couldn't make out the agency, but recognized federal government issued documents when he saw them.

Ah, crap, he thought. *What a time for a surprise inspection.*

"I'm Special Agent Purcell, Homeland Security Investigations," the man said brusquely before snapping the wallet shut and stuffing it back in his jacket as he got within reach of Christophe. He then produced a photograph which he held close to Christophe's face. "Is this the person?"

Christophe made a show of studying the picture even though he recognized the subject immediately. "Yes, but she's not—"

"She's a suspect in an international terror plot," Purcell barked. "And now, I'm afraid, so are you." He took a step back and without looking, called out, "Sergeant, get rid of this piece of trash."

Glenn and the others had already closed in around Christophe, relieving him of his weapon. His arms were bent back and manacled, and then, braced between two of the officers, he was walked toward the exit.

"Hey," Purcell called out. "Is she still up there?"

Christophe considered lying or remaining silent, but

knew it would serve no purpose. He nodded.

"Thought so. Sergeant, I think it best if I go it alone from here."

"Sir, I don't think I'm authorized to allow you to do that."

"I'm authorizing you. This suspect is dangerous; I don't want to give her multiple targets. Besides, it's probably better if you aren't around to witness what's going to happen. If you take my meaning." He paused a beat then added. "Don't worry. I've got your back, and the president's got mine. Personally."

Jade moved slowly, patiently, up the staircase, careful not to wear herself out, concentrating on the steps in front of her to avoid becoming disoriented by the relentless spiral motion. As she neared the top however, she came to a landing, roughly even with the statue's shoulders. The area was blocked off by heavy-duty steel fencing hanging from a gate made of the same material was a sign that read: "Here you can see the torch access point. It has been closed since 1916."

But the gate was open.

Of all the possible locations to hide the sacred relics of Libertas, Jade could think of none more appropriate than the torch. In addition to being the perfect choice from a symbolic standpoint, it was closed off to visitors, and had been since 1916, when German saboteurs had blown up several train cars full of war munitions at the Black Tom peninsula, which was now part of Liberty State Park where Jade had boarded the ferry. Although it had occurred more than half a mile away, the blast had been powerful enough to damage the statue, specifically the right arm that held the torch aloft. Citing safety concerns, visitor access to the torch balcony had been restricted ever since.

That was the official story at least, but Jade didn't buy it. The Statue of Liberty had been engineered to withstand hurricane force winds. Even if the distant explosion had revealed some unknown structural flaw, subsequent repairs and renovations would have resolved any structural safety issues. Even liability concerns arising from the treacherous nature of the ascent—a forty-two-foot ladder rising up the statue's arm—would not have justified complete closure. A far better explanation was that there was something about the torch that the National Park Service—which had obviously been infiltrated by members of the Cult of Libertas—did not want people to see.

Jade moved through the gate and over to a rather inconspicuous metal ladder that rose from the landing at a slight incline and disappeared into the darkness of the hollow tube of Liberty's arm. A few minutes ago, she had been ready to scale the granite blocks of the pedestal with no safety rope, but now, confronted with a stationary ladder in an enclosed space, she balked. It wasn't just the fear of falling, or the more irrational anxiety about the metal skeleton collapsing and dropping to the ground some three hundred feet below. This was the temple of Libertas. There was no telling what sort of nasty surprises might be waiting for her at the top of that ladder.

"The only way out is through," she muttered, repeating the mantra that had kept her going. "Or in this case, up."

She started climbing. The shadows enfolded her, but there was just enough light rising up from below for her to make out the rungs in front of her, and as she climbed, her eyes quickly adjusted to the low-light conditions and she was able to keep going without pause. The ascent took much longer than she had expected, but when it ended, it was with unexpected abruptness. Without any warning, she ran out of ladder.

As she hung there in the darkness wondering what to do next, she realized the ladder was moving, swaying gently. She recalled another bit of trivia from the tour sheets; like all towering structures, the Statue of Liberty had been engineered to sway with the wind, like a tree. In a fifty-mile-per-hour wind, the body of the statue might move as much as three inches, while the torch could move twice that much.

Six inches of back and forth didn't seem like much—

she'd stood on the deck of ships moving considerably more than that—but a hundred yards above ground, it was more than just a little disconcerting. On the ground, she had not even noticed a breeze, but up here, it was constant, producing an ominous rushing sound as it buffeted the torch arm.

She shook her head, trying to stay focused on the task at hand. Maybe this was the part where her unique status as Chosen would come into play. Was she supposed to say something? A ritual incantation? Maybe just "open sesame"? Or perhaps there was a secret door she had to open.

She let go of the ladder with her right hand and reached out, placing her palm against the smooth cool metal, probing the concave surface for some kind of release mechanism. She found it almost immediately but it wasn't anything elaborate. Just a simple lever latch, right next to the ladder. It turned without resistance, and when she gave it a push, a small rectangular door was revealed briefly, illuminated by a light source beyond. Then something pushed the door shut with a jarring bang.

"Just the wind," she muttered, and pushed again, more forcefully.

The door opened wide, revealing a deck just a few feet wide, bordered by an ornate braided railing adorned with that most distinctive of American symbols, ears of maize. Topping the rail at evenly spaced intervals were high-intensity floodlights. Even though they were all pointing up, away from the door, the ambient light was almost blindingly bright after the darkness of the ascent. She squinted and kept her gaze down as she stepped through and onto the deck.

A gust of wind caught the door, slamming it shut. The sudden movement of air sent a wave of primal panic through Jade. Even though she couldn't see past the lights, she knew where she was, and knew that just past that barely waist-high railing was a whole lot of nothing. She lurched backward, turning away from the rail to face the now closed access door, and threw her arms around the upraised column from which she had just emerged. As she did, she beheld a vision of shining gold—Liberty's flame, its twenty-four karat gold surface blazing with reflected light.

Jade wondered if that was what Phillis Wheatley had in mind when she used the word "refulgent" in her poem. She couldn't think of a better resting place for the sacred relics of the goddess of Liberty.

Then she saw something else, or more precisely someone else. A figure about the same height as Jade, wearing a black trench coat stepped out from behind the flame, just to her left and spoke, almost shouting to be heard over the rush of wind.

"Well you certainly took your sweet time, darlin'."

TWENTY-FOUR

"Sorry about that," Jade retorted sarcastically. "Oh, wait. No, I'm not."

Diane Lindsey laughed. "I honestly wasn't sure you'd come at all, but then I kept asking myself, 'why did she go back to Haiti?'"

"Maybe I had a score to settle with Yann."

The other woman wagged her head. "Poor Yann. I heard about what happened. A fire in a nightclub. A shame."

"Not really." Jade gave a dismissive shrug. "I heard your business partner died in the same fire."

Diane ignored the implicit accusation. "You might be the sort to hold a grudge, but I don't think you went back there just to take your pound of flesh. The only thing I could figure is that you wanted Yann to tell you where to find the temple. That told me that you were still looking for it. It was only a matter of time before you figured it out and came here."

Jade spread her hands in a half-sincere gesture of cooperation. "Well, here I am. What do I do now?"

"Now? darlin', you've already done it."

"I don't understand. I didn't do anything."

"You came here. That's all I needed from you."

"I thought I was supposed the get your sacred relics." She rapped her knuckles on the golden exterior of the flame.

Diane smiled, but it was a tight humorless smile. "Sorry. Close but no cigar."

Jade raised an eyebrow in surprise. "This isn't the temple?"

"Oh, it's the temple all right, but that—" She nodded at the flame. "—isn't where the relics are kept."

"So where are they, then?"

Diane started to say something but then closed her mouth and shook her head. "Look at that. Get me talking and I just go on and on like that little rabbit in the battery commercials."

"Why me?" Jade asked. "Why select me as the Chosen?"

"The cult needs to be united. Part of that is giving them a leader, one with a bit of a name and reputation, one who's charismatic, attractive, accomplished. You were a perfect choice. They'll all be so sad when you're gone."

Jade didn't have a clue what Diane was talking about, but before she could ask, the woman reached into the pocket of her trench coat and took out a small object that looked utterly out of place in her hand.

It was a small semi-automatic pistol.

"What—?" Jade started, but then saw the muzzle of the weapon rising toward her and realized that a bullet was the only answer she was going to get.

She spun away, trying to put the sculpted flame between herself and the other woman, but not before she saw the muzzle flash. The pistols report was a dull pop, carried away by the wind.

Jade pressed herself against the sculpture, side-stepping, looking left then right then back again. There was only one way off the torch platform—or at least only one that didn't involve a quick descent and a sudden stop at the end—and chances were good that Diane would simply camp out in front of the access door and wait for her rather than chasing Jade round and round. Still, if the woman really wanted her dead, she might not be content to wait. But from which direction would the attack come?

Jade cupped a hand over her mouth and shouted, "What the hell, Diane?"

"Sorry, darlin'." The answer was faint, and it was impossible to tell if the other woman was moving closer. "The goddess needs a sacrifice."

Jade thought she detected a hint of sarcasm in the retort. "So all that stuff about me being the Chosen and recovering the sacred relics was just bullcrap?"

"You didn't really think I was gonna try to change the world with some old bones, did you?"

The response flummoxed Jade. She understood the

power of symbols and had believed Diane's interest in the relics to be sincere, regardless of the overall plausibility of the plan to initiate a modern-day slave uprising. Was Diane now admitting that had never been the plan at all?

Jade felt the platform rocking a little underfoot. It might have just been the wind, but it also might have been Diane moving, circling toward her.

But where is she?

She took a gamble that Diane would have reversed direction to come up from behind her, and began easing back toward her starting point. She had only taken a couple steps when she saw the gun, seeming to float in the air as it protruded out ahead of the still unseen figure who held it.

Jade froze, but realized that she was still hidden from Diane's view. The would-be killer had committed a classic rookie mistake, giving away her position by exposing her weapon to view without being able to see around the bend.

It was an opportunity Jade didn't dare pass up. She ducked low and then moved toward the weapon, rising into it like a striking snake. She caught Diane's wrist before the other woman could register what was happening, and slammed the hand that held the pistol hard against the sculpted flame.

The impact resounded with a loud gong, and then a much louder report as the weapon discharged, sending another bullet whizzing past Jade's head.

Jade did not let go of Diane's wrist, but instead pushed the gun hand upward in a high arc that kept the muzzle pointing skyward, and then brought it back down on the opposite side, twisting Diane's body away from her in the process. Though it had not been her intent, the platform was so narrow that Diane's hand struck the railing. Jade heard and felt the crack of bone breaking. Diane cried out in pain and, with unexpected strength, wrestled free of Jade's grip, cradling her broken arm close against her torso. The pistol was gone.

Jade put her hands on her hips, squaring her body in a defensive posture and took a menacing step forward. "Are you going to start talking," she snarled, "or should I just toss your ass over the side?"

Diane looked up. Tears were streaming down her face, glistening in the brilliance of the flood lights. She was breathing fast, almost panting either from the effort or the pain of her injury, but her expression remained defiant. "You can try. Maybe I'll just take you with me."

Jade shook her head, perplexity supplanting her anger. She tried for a more conciliatory tone. "I don't get it, Diane. Why? Why go through all this just to get me here and kill me?"

The other woman took several more breaths, hissing each exhalation through clenched teeth. "God, I could use a smoke," she muttered, then met Jade's stare. "Like I told you. A sacrifice."

"Then why not just bring me here and kill me?"

"Because then you wouldn't be the Chosen. A captive doesn't have the blessing of the Goddess. You had to come here as a free woman."

"I don't get you. You don't even believe in Libertas."

"Who are you to tell me what I believe?"

Jade was incredulous. "You're buying and selling human beings. You were working with Cesar, a voodoo witch doctor. He was going to turn me into a zombie; did you know that?" She shook her head. "I'll bet you did. So don't try to tell me that you worship the goddess of freedom."

"Freedom is not a natural state and it's not something that's just handed out to anyone. If people don't earn their freedom, they won't value it. And if they can't earn it, they don't deserve it. That's what the goddess expects of us."

"That's not what Yann Pierre believed." Jade made a sweeping gesture. "And it's not what the men who built this place believed either. The statue symbolizes the end of all kinds of oppression."

Something changed in Diane's eyes. She grimaced but Jade sensed she was trying to smile. "Well, maybe we're gonna have to do something about that."

Jade felt a chill that had nothing to do with the constant wind whipping across the platform.

"Something needs to change. The people who truly believe in equality have lost their way. They're weak and lazy, and they've been cowed by a tiny, elite class. Where we once fought with weapons, they fight with funny memes and clever social media posts." Diane straightened and then nodded toward the harbor. "See that boat down there?"

Jade risked a quick glance, just long enough to see the oblong-shape of a medium-sized motor yacht near the southern tip of the island. In that brief glimpse, she saw no wake, suggesting the boat was resting at anchor.

"So?"

"Look again," Diane prompted. "See how low it's riding? Might have something to do with the three tons of ammonium nitrate fuel explosive she's carrying. Just a skooch more than Timothy McVeigh used to blow up that federal building in Oklahoma City. I reckon it'll strip the skin off this sucker. Like peeling a grapefruit. Blast what's left of it halfway to Manhattan."

"A bomb?" Jade's voice rose a full octave in disbelief. "You're going to blow up the Statue of Liberty?"

"Oh, not me. Why on earth would I do that? I'm the priestess of Libertas." She spat out a laugh. "No, a little group of disenchanted folks called the Sons of the Republic are gonna take the credit. They built the bomb and bought the boat. I just agreed to drive it over here."

Jade had heard of the Sons of the Republic, and from what she understood about them, they were on the opposite side of what Libertas claimed to believe. "You're going to let them blow up the Statue of Liberty?" Jade repeated. "Your temple?"

"To the followers of Libertas, it is a temple. To the Sons of the Republic, it's a symbol of political correctness run amok. A symbol used as an excuse to force Americans to take in the dregs of the Third World. And it's French, which believe you me, galls them to no end." She paused a beat, and then added, "Leastwise that's what the Sons of the

Republic think, which makes them perfect pawns in our little chess match."

"And what do you think? How can you possibly justify destroying your own temple?"

Diane grimaced again. "It's not the first temple; it won't be the last. Like I told you, sacrifices have to be made. It's gonna take more than old bones and mumbo-jumbo about a forgotten Roman goddess to get folks off their asses."

Jade frowned as she pondered this revelation. "You're trying to start a civil war."

Another grimace. "Nailed it, darlin'. When the good folks of America hear that a bunch of right-wing nut jobs blew up the symbol of freedom, whose side do you think they're gonna take? After McVeigh blew up the federal building, the militia movement went dark for nearly a decade. It took a black president to coax 'em out of the woodwork, and now they're back, stronger than ever. I mean to put them down for good."

"That's nuts."

"I don't think so. There are more of us than there are of them. We just need to remember that some things can't be won without bloodshed and sacrifice."

Jade struggled to make sense of what she was hearing. Who was this woman? Self-help huckster? Cult leader? Cynical purveyor of the flesh-trade? Domestic terrorist? Visionary?

She shook her head. "Why drag me into it? And don't tell me I was only supposed to be some kind of a human sacrifice. Even you aren't that sadistic."

Jade frowned. "You abducted me and put me through hell on that container ship so I would be initiated into your religion. You put me on the trail of something that wasn't really even lost, feeding me clues so that I would find it for myself. And then, when I finally found it, you try to kill me." She was thinking aloud, but as she did, she saw how these things were connected. "It had to look real. So all the others—the rest of the cult—wouldn't realize that you were the one who wanted to blow up the statue."

"Not just them. When the authorities try to piece together the sequence of events, they'll assume the Sons of the Republic knew you were the Chosen—I made sure word got out—and followed you here. The Sons of the Republic, those right-wing zealots, killed you to keep you from opening the vault with the sacred relics, and then blew up the Temple of Libertas to make sure no one ever would."

"That's why you led me around by the nose? So there'd be a record of my search for the authorities to puzzle out?"

"That's part of it, but also, you had to discover the temple by your own initiative in order to be a worthy sacrifice."

Jade shrugged. "Sorry to ruin your elaborate plan by surviving."

"Oh, darlin', this is just a little ol' wrinkle. Things are gonna happen just the way I planned. That bomb is gonna go off in... Oh, I'd say about twenty minutes, give or take. And there ain't a thing you or anyone can do to stop it. The only difference is that I won't be around to see how it all shakes out."

As soon as the words were spoken, Diane lurched forward, running headlong toward Jade, arms thrown. Jade pivoted away, or tried to, but the unexpectedness of the charge and the close quarters slowed her reaction time by a critical fraction of a second. Diane's outflung right arm wrapped around her, pulling her in tight and sweeping her off her feet.

The forward momentum ended with a jarring impact against the rail, and even as Jade fought to get free of the other woman's grip, she felt her entire body tilting forward.

Over the rail.

Diane was trying to throw herself off the platform, and wanted to take Jade along for the ride.

Jade fought and thrashed. She got her right arm free and sought the rail, but instead her hand found one of the searing hot floodlights. She yelped, more in surprise than pain, but held on to it tightly, even as Diane heaved her body fully over the rail, twisting to maintain her grip on Jade.

Jade could feel the skin of her palm sizzling against the light fixture like a slab of bacon on a griddle, but she dared not let go. Diane's weight was dragging her down, scraping her across the thin metal rail. She was already half-folded over the railing, and could feel it bending under their combined weight. If she didn't find something better to hold onto and fast, she would be joining the woman on her quick trip to the ground.

Diane shouted in her ear, the words coming out in harsh grunts. "Let. Go. You. Have. To. Die."

Jade felt her burned hand slipping, felt the creaking rail slide past her abdomen, onto her hips. Desperate, she focused all her strength into a sort of inverted hanging ab crunch and brought her knees forward under the rail until they jammed into the decorative border. She let go of the light, curled her fingers into a fist, ignoring the immediate rush of pain in her burned palm, and drew back.

"For the last time, I'm not joining your cult," she shouted, and rammed her fist into Diane's face.

The force of the blow loosened Diane's grip and then just like that, Jade was free. She got her other hand around the rail and pushed herself back, away from the precipice, and collapsed against the column supporting the flame sculpture. She didn't see Diane hit the pedestal base more than two hundred feet below. She didn't hear it either. The only sound was the wind.

Jade knew there wasn't time for even a momentary respite. Diane had said the bomb would detonate in twenty minutes; how long ago had that been?

She didn't know what she was going to do to stop the destruction of the Statue of Liberty, but knew she wasn't going to be able to accomplish anything from where she was.

Her legs felt about as firm as wet spaghetti noodles and she would have sworn her feet were twitching, but she managed to roll over onto all fours and push herself up to a standing position, supporting herself with one hand resting against the golden flame. She took an unsteady step forward, then another, searching the smooth curved surface for the access door.

"Well, that was exciting."

Jade was too wired with adrenaline to react, but the sardonic and all too familiar voice filled her with dread. She turned slowly to face the speaker, knowing who she would find, knowing that he would be pointing his gun at her.

She was right on both counts.

TWENTY-FIVE

"Purcell?" Jade took a half-step backward and raised her hands. After a few seconds passed without him pulling the trigger, she decided to try reasoning with him. "You have to listen to me. There's a bomb on that boat down there."

"So I heard," Purcell replied, a hint of a grin on his brutish face.

"Then you know that we have to get down there and do something about it." When he didn't respond, she went on. "Look, somehow you got the wrong idea about me. I'm not one of the bad guys here."

He said nothing. The gun remained where it was, aimed right at her heart, but his stance did not seem overtly menacing. It looked as if he was weighing his options, still trying to decide whether she needed to die. She realized it no longer mattered to him that she had been the Chosen of the Cult of Libertas; he had tried to murder her twice, and no matter the circumstances that had prompted those actions, he couldn't allow her to live, to accuse him, destroy his career and maybe send him to prison.

But he hadn't pulled the trigger, yet. Maybe he could still be made to see reason. She thought a change of subject might help. "How did you find me, anyway?"

He twitched a little, as if waking up from a daydream. "I didn't. I mean, I didn't know you would be here. That was just a little bonus. I was following her." He waggled the gun toward a spot beyond the railing, presumably where Diane had gone over. "One of the suspects in Rome... You remember that cute chick with the hot little Alfa Romeo?" His grin broadened. "Sure you do. You tried to steal it as I recall. I connected her to that Lighthouse outfit, and then I remembered that annoying bitch that gave me such a hard time in Houston was part of the same group. I finally picked up her trail and followed her here. When I saw her anchor that boat out there and come ashore in a Zodiac, I figured she was getting close to whatever it was she had planned.

Guess I was right."

Jade nodded. "Then you get it, yeah? I'm on your side. What happened before was just a misunderstanding. You thought I was working with them. Now you know I'm not. It happened, now we can move on. Water under the bridge. So, let's do something about that bomb."

Purcell didn't move. The gun didn't move. His eyes flicked up thoughtfully for a second, then came back to her. "No."

Jade thought she must have misheard. "What?"

"No," he repeated. "I don't think I'm going to do that."

Jade was dumbfounded. "But… The Statue…?"

"Yeah, I never much cared for it really. It's ugly." He shook his head. "She was right, you know. This thing is an abomination. Everybody goes on and on about immigration making America strong, the great melting pot, blah, blah, and they point to Lady Liberty as proof that it's always been part of our cultural identity. That's a lot of bullshit. Urban globalist propaganda. Americans didn't put this thing here. We didn't ask for it. You know who put it here? The Freemasons. The Illuminati.

"It's a pagan idol," he continued, speaking faster, his pitch rising as he warmed to the topic. "A symbol of Lucifer, the Light Bringer, put here by the Illuminati to corrupt the minds of good Christian Americans."

"You're not serious," Jade blurted.

But there was not a trace of humor in his voice. He was deadly serious. "It's a false god. Or a goddess really, which is even worse. Another way they've corrupted us. Force-feeding us their feminist anti-family agenda." He shrugged. "The Bible says we should destroy idols and graven images. I say let it burn."

Jade bit her lip, stifling a sarcastic retort that probably would have pushed the crazed federal agent over the brink and into full-on insanity, and tried a different tack. "Diane thought blowing up the Statue would start a civil war. No matter what you think of it, destroying an American icon is going to polarize people. Turn them against… Well, against people like you. Aren't you worried about that?"

"Worried? I say bring it on. Real Americans are fed up with all this liberal PC crap. We're taking our country back. Besides, the sheeple and the snowflakes won't fight. They don't have the stomach for it. Or the heart. They'll cry about how their beautiful symbol of freedom is gone, and then they'll go along with it, just like they always do. But even if some of them do…" He grinned broadly. "We've got more guns."

Jade cocked her head to the side. Purcell was clearly unhinged; maybe he had been all along. She wondered how much time was left? How long had his rant been going on. Two minutes? Three? Was there even enough time left for them to get out of the statue and clear of the blast zone?

"I guess you've got it all figured out," she said slowly.

"Yep. And thanks to you and her, everyone is going to know that it was leftist radicals that did this, not American patriots. I don't know about you, but I call that a win-win. Of course, I'm afraid you'll have to…" He motioned with the gun. "You know. Take the plunge."

She had been expecting something like this, but the casual way in which he pronounced her death sentence was chilling. "You want me to jump?"

"Or I can shoot you. Either way, you're not leaving here alive." He shrugged again. "It's your call. Thought you might appreciate having the choice. But I'm not going to let you throw anything at me this time."

Jade lowered her hands and spread them apart. "Darn. There goes that idea." She glanced to the side, past the ring of blazing floodlights, pretending to contemplate the leap he was forcing her to take. What she was really doing was looking for other options.

If she could keep the flame between them, just as she had with Diane, she might be able to run him in circles, stay alive long enough to turn the tables on him. Of course, Purcell was a federal agent, trained for situations like this. He would not make the same mistakes Diane had.

She took another step back, still looking for a better answer. Through the haze of light, she could just make out a great green blob just below where she now stood. Another step, and she could see long points radiating out from it, the head and crown of the statue. It was at least fifty feet below, but only about twenty feet out. Too far to jump, and even if she could make it, fifty feet was still a long ways to fall, but it gave her an idea.

"So, I jump or you shoot me, is that it?"

Purcell shook the gun at her. "You're stalling."

"Hey, you would, too." But she nevertheless reached back and found the rail with her left hand. Her right palm was still smarting from what was at least a first-degree burn, but she knew she would have to push through the pain if she was going to survive.

She insinuated herself into the gap between two of the lights, and with exaggerated caution, eased back into a sitting position on the thin rail, then brought her left knee up and over the rail, swiveling herself into a straddle.

A wave of primal fear surged through. She wobbled unsteadily on the rail, her hands curling tight around it in a death grip. Her heart was pounding like crazy. Her reptile brain had no idea what her conscious brain intended, and was exercising veto authority on her desperate plan to stay alive.

You can do this, Jade. Don't think about it, just do it!

She forced her eyes away from the yawning drop to her left, and instead fixed her gaze on Purcell.

"You're really going to make me do this?"

His only answer was to shake the gun at her.

"You're a psychopath." She tried to sound defiant rather than pleading, but the quaver in her voice betrayed her. In a way, that was probably better, since Purcell almost certainly would have shot her on the spot if he suspected what she was about to attempt.

You can do this, she told herself again. *Just like jumping off that ship.*

She couldn't quite make herself believe that, but it gave

her the courage to swing her other leg up and over....

She inadvertently looked down.

It was a mistake, but not because doing so triggered a wave of vertigo or a bout of acrophobia. Her glimpse revealed something about the statue she had read about but not actually seen during her long hours of surveillance. In fact, she could not have seen it from anywhere but where she was right now.

Could it be?

She pushed the thought from her mind and forced herself to focus on what she had to do next.

Do it, Jade. Don't stop now!

And then, without stopping to think about it, or all the ways it might go horribly wrong, she scooted forward off the rail, and dropped.

TWENTY-SIX

After spending the better part of the day staring at the Statue of Liberty, Jade would not have had any trouble describing it in excruciating detail. She had counted the windows on the crown—there were twenty-five—and studied the seven points, suggesting rays of light, protruding from the diadem. She had memorized the folds of the sculpted robe, the unique keystone shape of the tablet held in Liberty's left arm, and the way the sole of her sandaled right foot was lifted to give the impression of a forward stride. She had paid special attention to the torch, where she had— erroneously it seemed— believed she would find the sacred relics of Libertas.

The torch was held in Liberty's upraised right hand, her forefinger extended straight. The decorative border actually curled outward at the top, about a foot below the safety rail. Beneath it, the edge of the platform sloped down several inches, and then flattened toward the center, and the whole affair was supported underneath by several evenly spaced half-arches, like the ribs of a brazier, that curled down to meet at the stem of the torch just above Liberty's finger.

Most of these details were hidden from Jade's view as she perched on the rail, but she could see them clearly in her mind's eye. She knew that, directly below her, a distance of only ten feet or so, was the V-shape where Liberty's thumb and forefinger diverged around the torch, and below that, the nearly—but not quite completely—vertical slope of the statue's arm, extending down forty feet or so to her shoulder. And she knew that there were plenty of things to hold onto.

She was only partly right about that last bit.

As she committed to going over the side, Jade twisted around so that she was facing in, toward the torch, and grabbed the decorative border below the rail. Her plan was to use the rail to swing herself under the platform in order to grab the arched struts, but as was often the way with plans, things almost immediately went awry.

The decorative border was just that—decorative—and when her full weight came to bear, the thin copper bent and buckled and ultimately collapsed, dropping her a good thirty-six inches in an instant. It might have broken loose altogether had her feet not made contact with the smooth skin of Liberty's wrist, momentarily arresting her downward plunge.

The slope was too steep for her to stand on and the soles of her hiking boots failed to gain any kind of meaningful purchase, but that didn't keep her from trying. She pedaled her feet against the metal—like a cartoon character trying to outrun a bridge collapse—hoping the friction would compensate for the sharp angle, which it did though not enough to stop the inevitable. The border wasn't going to hold her weight, but even if it did, dangling beneath the torch was hardly a solution to the bigger problem she faced.

So, she let go.

As she dropped straight down onto Liberty's wrist, Jade threw her arms wide, hugging the curved surface, palms pressed flat against it, mentally willing her splayed fingers to stick, gecko-like, to the metal.

It worked.

Sort of.

She started sliding, the friction creating a flare of uncomfortable but not quite unendurable heat as she slipped down the nearly vertical slope of the statue's forearm, like a mouse riding a fire pole. She knew, from her earlier survey of the statue, that at some point, her feet would encounter the wrinkles of Liberty's robe, sculpted to look bunched up around her shoulder as if falling away from the upraised arm. That barrier would either stop her descent cold, or deflect her away, ricocheting her from the statue for an unrestricted freefall, but there was one other obstacle in between her and it.

Two of the spikes radiating from the diadem extended out past the statue's arm, one in front and one behind. The latter was only a couple feet away from the arm; indeed, during the 1986 restoration of the statue, it had been necessary to move Liberty's head two feet to the left because wind sway had caused intermittent contact between the crown point and the arm, which over the decades, had gradually worn a hole in the statue. If Jade hit that point on her way down, it would add a third, extremely unpleasant option to the possible outcomes of her slide. This was also something she had factored into her original plan, and so, even though she knew she was perhaps a fraction of a second away from getting skewered or sliced in two, she also knew the rays of the diadem were actually the key to her survival.

She pulled her arms in close, her still open hands now at shoulder level, and pushed. Hard.

As her body arced away from the statue's arm, she twisted and threw her arms out wide. In that instant, she saw the two rays as dark silhouettes against the brilliance of the floodlights shining up from ground level. The one to her left, the one that nearly touched the statue's arm, was close... So close.

Close enough.

She stretched, arching her body like a platform diver, and caught the protrusion with her left arm.

Had she been in free fall, the impact would probably have torn her arm off. As it was, the sharp angles of the copper ray gouged into her. Nevertheless, she pulled herself into it, swinging underneath the spike as she hugged it close, wrapped her legs around it and hung on for dear life.

The sculpture shook with the impact. An ominous creaking sound vibrated through the metal, and for a frightful moment, Jade thought the whole thing might collapse under her weight. It did not, but this apparent reprieve brought no relief, for in the next instant, something hammered into the metal, sending a numbing vibration through the surface above her. A millisecond later, she heard the report of a pistol.

In hindsight, she realized that it had been overly

optimistic to believe that Purcell would be content merely to watch her slip over the side of the torch platform. Instead of retreating back down the ladder and escaping the doomed statue, the renegade agent had chosen instead to satisfy his morbid curiosity concerning her fate, and had quickly discovered her desperate bid to escape him.

He was probably regretting having given her the option, and it was a mistake he now appeared all too eager to correct. Because she was hanging sloth-like beneath the protruding ray, she was mostly shielded from his view, but he did not need to score a hit to her head or torso to kill her. A single bullet in her arm or leg would probably knock her loose and send her plummeting.

She had to get off the crown.

This too had been part of her desperate plan, albeit without the accompanying gunfire.

A quick glance confirmed that the statue's shoulder was directly beneath her, a drop of about ten feet or so. If she failed what she was about to attempt, the odds were good that she would land there, in the crook between Liberty's arm and face, but then she would be effectively stranded, at least until the bomb detonated and blasted her halfway to Hoboken.

She would only have one chance to get this right.

Two more rounds slammed into the crown point, and she felt something hot—probably a bullet fragment—stinging her right cheek. Evidently, the copper sheeting wasn't thick enough to completely stop a pistol round, a revelation which supplied added incentive for her to take the next risky step.

She relaxed her legs, letting go of the ray, and released her right hand as well, so that the only part of her still in contact with the statue was her left hand, curled over the sharp edge of the sculpted spike. As her body dropped and described a pendulum arc toward the head of the statue, she twisted around, facing in the direction she was traveling, and kicked with her legs for an added boost of forward momentum. As she started to swing back up, she fixed her attention on the ridged crest of Liberty's crown and released her left hand as well, soaring forward like a youthful daredevil launching from a playground swing set. At the top of the resulting parabolic arc, where momentum ran out and gravity took over, she experienced a fleeting sensation of weightlessness, and in that instant, stretched out her arms and grasped hold of the crown.

The dream of flying was replaced by the brutal impact of slamming into something solid and unyielding, but she had anticipated this and held fast. The object she had just collided with was not hard cold metal, but glass—one of the twenty-five observation windows. The inside of the statue's head was illuminated at night, which caused the windows to glow with soft light. The largest windows were positioned in the center, and were big enough for a person to put head and shoulders through, though the design did not typically allow them to open that far. Where Jade was hanging, just to the right of the second crown point, the windows were a little smaller, but still big enough for her to pass through, provided of course, she could get one of them open.

Checking to make sure she had a good grip on the crown, she did a hanging ab crunch, raising her knees until they were almost pressing against her chest and then thrust her feet forward, slamming them into the window.

Her boot soles bounced off the unbroken glass. Worse, the rebound nearly shook her loose from her tenuous handhold.

Crap!

She dropped her legs quickly to counteract the effect and inched her hands forward, one at a time, to regain her earlier position. Yet, she knew she was going to have to keep trying, hammering at the window until either the glass or the frame holding it gave way. She lifted her knees again, preparing for another assault and the unavoidable bounce-back, but before she could strike, she heard a harsh cracking sound to her right, followed by another pistol report.

Purcell was still shooting at her. He had missed, again, but it had been close. Her silhouette, dark against the illuminated windows, would make for an easy target and there wasn't anything she could do to find cover.

Then the significance of what had just happened sank in. She craned her head sideways, peering at the next window over. The pane had not shattered, probably owing to some kind of laminate coating, but there was an ugly hole in it, from which several cracks radiated out in a spider web pattern.

Thank you, Purcell, she thought, and began shimmying sideways, toward the damaged window, even though doing so meant further exposing her position to Purcell. She moved quickly, knowing that at any second a bullet might find her, though strangely she heard no further shooting. In a smooth motion, she brought her legs up again and pistoned her feet out into the glass.

The pane simply collapsed under the assault, peeling out of the surrounding frame. Instead of rebounding, Jade kept going until half her body was inside. She wriggled awkwardly through the opening, the constant threat of a bullet lending an urgency to the graceless entry, and then, just like that, she was inside with a solid floor beneath her.

She dared not pause to savor this accomplishment. The clock was still ticking. She glanced at her watch, rotating the bezel until the arrow was aligned with the minute hand. She didn't know how much time had elapsed since Diane had given her vague estimate of the minutes remaining on the countdown time, but at least now she would have a fixed reference point.

Get going, Jade!

Yet, her body betrayed her. When she tried to stand up, her legs gave out, and she went sprawling face-first on the diamond plate steel decking of the crown observation platform. If her struggle to escape Diane's suicidal clutch had left her feeling wobbly, surviving the traverse from torch to crown had turned her to jelly, and with the adrenaline draining away, it was if the circuits connecting mind to body had overloaded and gone into shutdown mode. It took all her willpower to pull herself to her feet using the handrail.

As she stood there, clutching the rail, she heard a rhythmic sound echoing up from the depths of the statue's interior.

Footsteps. Someone was on the stairs, descending rapidly.

"Purcell," she whispered. Now she knew why he had stopped shooting. Grasping her intent, or more likely recognizing that his window of opportunity for escaping the destruction of the statue would soon close, he had given up trying to kill her, and returned inside to make his escape. "C'mon, Jade. Move it," she said aloud. "Hard part's done."

She scooted one foot forward, then the other, coming to the edge of the platform. Beyond it was the descending spiral staircase, nearly a hundred and fifty steps, and that was just to reach the top of the pedestal. She probably wouldn't be able to use the elevator, which meant even more stairs. A single misstep might send her tumbling down, but she knew she had to keep going, had to overcome the post-stress fatigue and dig deep to find the energy to keep going.

She slid her hand down the rail, and took a tentative step down with her right foot, then brought her left to the same level.

"Gotta do better than that," she said, trying to cajole herself into action. "You just did monkey bars on the Statue of Liberty. You can make it down some damn stairs."

Another step. This time, she resisted the almost overpowering urge to bring her trailing foot to rest beside her lead foot, and instead extended it down to the next step.

"Good," she told herself. "Keep doing that."

She did, and then she did it faster. Her legs were still a bit quivery, but she felt she could trust them not to give out again. She stopped planting her feet solidly on the treads and instead tried to make contact only with her heels to minimize contact and increase her pace.

As with her ascent, she had to keep her gaze focused on the metal steps directly in front of her to keep vertigo at bay. Before she knew it, she had reached the end of the spiral and the spot where she had parted company with the Park Police officer. She wondered what had become of the man. Had Diane warned him to flee the island? Probably not. Christophe had not struck her as the kind of person who would stand by and let the Statue of Liberty—the very image of the goddess he now worshipped—be destroyed simply to advance a political agenda. It was more likely that Diane had intended to sacrifice him to her cause, along with anyone else working the night shift.

She would need to warn him, warn all of them about what was happening.

A short dash brought her to a two-flight staircase down to where she had disembarked the elevator. The sliding door was closed and she had no idea whether the car would come in response to a summons, so she bypassed it and headed to the next set of stairs.

She knew she was only halfway down, with at least another two hundred steps to go. Thankfully, the pedestal stairs were a little more accommodating—a typical zig-zag rather than the dizzying corkscrew up the statue interior—but even though gravity was now on her side, it took time to descend sixteen stories, and time was one thing she did not have a lot of. It had taken her about three minutes to descend from the crown. Assuming Diane's estimate had been correct, and further assuming that the subsequent confrontations had eaten up at least five minutes of time, then she had already used up nearly half of the remaining time. She would need to move a lot faster.

She did, but once she reached ground level, she lost several seconds finding the exit, which nearly offset whatever gains she had made. As she emerged into the open air outside the statue nearly six minutes after starting her descent from the viewing platform, she took a moment to orient herself.

She was on the north side of the statue, behind it, while the boat with the bomb was to the southeast. There was no sign of anyone. No Park Police or rangers, no Purcell, nor was there any sign of Diane's body, though she had probably landed atop the star-shaped base. It seemed impossible that the commotion had gone unnoticed, which made her think that Purcell might have already sounded the alarm, warning the park personnel to get as far from the doomed statue as they could.

Which probably meant that Jade was now stranded and alone.

The safest course of action would probably have been to shelter just inside the pedestal entrance. If the blocky granite and concrete tower couldn't withstand the explosion, nothing could, and while there was a chance that the whole thing might collapse down on her, sealing her in, it seemed preferable to facing the blast wave without any protection whatsoever.

Yet, she hesitated.

Purcell's dismissive rejection of her plea for help in saving the statue had struck a nerve. As much as she wrestled with her own feelings about its message and what it was supposed to symbolize, not to mention its importance to the Cult of Libertas, she didn't want to see it destroyed. Nor did she want to live in the world that would result from that destruction—an already divided nation finally torn apart by radical hate- and fear-driven ideologies.

Which meant she had to save it. Or die trying.

TWENTY-SEVEN

As soon as the thought formed, she was running, as fast as her tired and still slightly wobbly legs would carry her. She hopped the nearest fence—a low metal barrier designed to keep people off the lawn—and circled around the broad base until she was in front of the statue. She could now distinguish the boat which purportedly held the bomb, perhaps a hundred yards off shore, but she could also make out other shapes in the water. A medium-sized ferry boat was departing the main dock, presumably evacuating the staff, and a smaller yellow inflatable boat was jetting away ahead of it. She guessed that would be Purcell, escaping aboard Diane's Zodiac, not because there was no room left on the ferry, but to deny it as a means of escape for Jade.

"Bastard," she muttered.

But escape was no longer Jade's intent. Returning her gaze to the nearer boat, she hopped the fence again and crossed the pavement to the slightly taller safety fence that separated the pedestrian walkway from the harbor. She clambered over the barrier, lowering herself down onto the slick rocks below, then splashed out into the shallows. The water was mildly chilly, a good fifteen degrees colder than the Gulf, but by no means bracing. When it was waist high, she lunged forward in a flat dive and started swimming.

Now she was in her element. Her arms, despite being a little strained and sore, were still relatively fresh. She pulled at the water with powerful strokes, stretching her arms out in a freestyle crawl. She kicked too, digging into her deepest reserves, drawing a measure of strength from the knowledge that, one way or another, she was done running. She put everything she had into it, but even so, it took nearly two minutes for her to reach the floating craft.

The boat looked, to her untrained eyes at least, similar in design and length to Dane Maddock's boat, *Sea Foam*. It was sitting low in the water, almost dangerously so. The swim platform at the stern was submerged by at least eight inches, which made it that much easier for Jade to climb onto it and out of the water. She ascended the stairs up to the stern deck, and immediately found the cause of the problem. Not that there had really been any question in her mind. The 90-foot motor yacht was designed to carry passengers, food, fuel and fresh water, not three tons of ammonium nitrate fuel oil explosive.

The stern deck—or cockpit—was completely filled with 55-gallon drums—fifteen of them in all. There were packets of what Jade guessed were plastic explosives taped atop each one, and all of them were connected by a tangle of colored wires that came together at a black box in the center. Even from the edge of the cockpit, Jade could see that the red LED numbers on the box. It was the countdown timer.

06:22
06:21
06:20

Six minutes and change.

She felt a mixture of dread and relief. She had figured it would be closer to two. Either she had moved a lot faster than she'd thought possible, or Diane's estimate of the time remaining had been overly conservative.

Still, six minutes wasn't exactly all the time in the world, and if she didn't get moving it would be all the time left in hers.

She wondered if defusing it was as simple as finding the off switch. Probably not. It was never that easy in movies, and since there were no do-overs, she decided to leave it alone. Disarming the bomb had never been her primary plan anyway.

She climbed over the tightly clustered barrels to reach another short staircase up to the flying bridge. The boat really was similar in layout to *Sea Foam,* and she was counting on the controls being equally similar.

They were in fact, almost identical.

The monitor screen—which displayed real-time GPS, radar, the depth finder profile—was illuminated, indicating that Diane had not switched off the ship's electrical system before departing. Jade located a pair of rocker switches on the panel marked "1" and "2". She thumbed both of them and was rewarded with a low rumble as the twin diesel engines came alive. Next, she located the windlass controls, and activated it as well. The boat shuddered a little as the winch began pulling the boat forward, toward the anchor embedded in the sea floor.

That process, she knew, would take several seconds, so she hastened to the aft end of the flying bridge and checked the timer's progress.

05:12
05:11
05:10

Dread and anxiety began to boil over within her. It was going to be close.

Too close.

Her hastily conceived plan had been to reach the boat, get it started, point the bow toward open water—a south-southeast heading would keep it in the middle of the harbor. The Black Tom peninsula explosion had damaged the statue's torch from half a mile away, which meant she needed to send it at least that far from Liberty Island, while staying on a heading that would keep it away from any populated areas. If the boat went too far, it would pass close to Brooklyn, putting lives at risk, but given its overloaded state, Jade doubted it would get much further than a mile in the few minutes remaining.

That was only part of the plan though. The other part, the part where she survived, required her to leap off the boat, swim back to Liberty Island, and take cover. If the bomb detonated while she was still in the water, the shock wave might very well pulverize her, or at the very least, knock her senseless to drown. She would need at least a couple minutes to make the swim.

The timer rolled past four minutes. She turned, intending to return to the controls, so that she would be ready to engage the screws as soon as the anchor came off the bottom, but as she did, she spotted something moving across the water. Although it was at least a couple hundred yards out, the intensely bright flashing blue light marked it as a police vessel, but that meant little to her. What did matter was the fact that it seemed to be on a direct course for her position.

She worried that it might be Diane's cronies—either from the Cult of Libertas or the Sons of the Republic—on a suicide mission to ensure that the bomb detonated where it was and right on schedule, or Purcell himself, ready to give his life if necessary to accomplish the same goal. Even if it really was just a regular police boat, perhaps sent to investigate a reported bomb, it wouldn't change what Jade had to do or put any more time on the clock.

She headed back to the console, and when the windlass fell silent, signaling that the anchor was snugged into place at the bow roller, she pushed the throttle forward. The engines roared, the screws began churning up white water, and the bow rose several inches, but the boat barely seemed to move at all.

She backed the throttle off, recognizing too late that the overloaded vessel wasn't going to burst forward like a rocket, and was rewarded with slow but measurable progress. The GPS tracked the boat's ponderous acceleration, which had just ticked past two knots—slightly less than two-and-a-half miles per hour.

Jade could swim faster than that.

"Come on," she urged, as if nagging might somehow overcome the laws of physics. "You can do better than that."

But it was something. The boat was moving. Now she just needed to move it in the right direction. Whether accidentally or by design, Diane had left the craft positioned with its stern facing Liberty Island. Perhaps that was to ensure that the boat itself would not in any way obstruct the explosive force. What it meant for Jade was that she only needed to turn the boat a few degrees to put in on the desired course, threading the gap between Brooklyn and Jersey City.

She wondered how much time was left now? Three minutes? Less? She wasn't about to leave the controls for another check.

The GPS ticked past five knots, and the numbers to the right of the decimal were changing a little faster now. The boat was finally picking up some momentum, putting more distance between itself and the Statue of Liberty, which was both good news and bad. Good for the statue, bad for Jade, since she was going to have to swim a lot further now.

Time to go.

She eased the throttle forward a little more, and then turned and headed aft. She could see the statue, not quite as close as it had been a minute ago, and getting further away with each passing second. A long line of white water trailed out behind the boat as if showing her the way to go.

Suddenly, an enormous yellow shape burst from the wake and rode up and over the stern. The jolt of the impact rocked the boat and staggered Jade, who managed to keep herself from being thrown off the flying bridge by clinging to the stair rail.

She knew what and who it was. Special Agent Purcell, evidently as committed to starting the second American Civil War as she was to preventing it, had noticed the bomb-laden boat changing position, and had turned to pursue.

As she got her feet under her again, she saw the Zodiac falling back into the water to bob on the larger boat's wake. She also saw Purcell, standing at the rear of the cockpit behind three tons of improvised explosives. His eyes were full of fury, and his pistol was once again aimed right at her.

"I should have killed you," he hissed. "Turn us around."

"Are you insane?" It was a rhetorical question, and

probably not the best one to lead with, so she rephrased. "You're going to get us both killed."

"If that's what it takes." He punctuated this by squeezing the trigger. The gun spat a gout of fire and a bullet punched into the wall right beside her.

Jade didn't wait around for him to correct his aim. She scrambled back up the steps to the console and with one arm wrapped around the pilot's seat, shoved the throttle all the way forward.

The bow abruptly rose in front of her like a pop-up target in a shooting gallery. Despite her preparations, it was all she could do to keep from being catapulted over the stern by the sudden lurch forward—hopefully, that was exactly what had happened to Purcell—and she would have certainly tumbled down the now sloped deck into the cockpit had she not been hanging on for dear life.

It was a struggle to pull the throttle back to its original position, but as soon as the deck was level, she peeled away and headed for the stairs again. Purcell's unexpected appearance had probably ruined her chances of making it back to solid ground before the bomb went off, but if she was to have even a chance of surviving, she had to get in the water without any further delay.

But as she stepped onto the lower deck, she saw that Purcell was still there. Her stunt with the throttle had not launched him into the water after all. Instead, the abrupt shift had caused the mass of barrels to slide into him, crushing him against the stern rail.

He was still conscious. His face was a mask of pain, and blood was trickling from his lips, but somehow he had managed to hang onto his pistol. As soon as he saw her, the weapon came up.

But he did not fire. Instead, he changed his aim, pointing the gun at the top of the barrel which had him pinned in place.

Jade's eyes went wide. "No!"

She had no idea if a bullet could trigger the bomb, but Purcell evidently thought it would, and there wasn't a thing she could do to stop him.

But then Purcell went rigid. A halo of red appeared around his head, and in the same instant, Jade heard the noise of a gun shot, but the report had not come from Purcell's pistol, which had already fallen from his nerveless fingers.

For a moment, Jade was too stunned to do anything. She had been certain that Purcell's bullet would detonate the bomb, erasing her from existence. This was something she could not have anticipated. But the incongruity of the development didn't change the fact that the bomb was still ticking down to that same eventuality.

But where did that shot come from?

The answer came to her in a flash of blue light.

In the tunnel vision of her focus on Purcell and the bomb and trying to escape, she had not even noticed the police boat sidling alongside the larger motor yacht. It was now pacing the still sluggishly moving craft, just a couple feet off the starboard side of the stern, close enough for a figure dressed in black tactical gear and holding a small sub-machine pistol to leap across to the cockpit and dispatch Purcell before he could detonate the bomb.

Jade did a double-take when she saw the man's face.

"Professor?" she gasped, but then shook off her incredulity at his unexpected appearance, and pointed to the timer, which showed 01:13... 01:12... "Bomb. We have to get out of here!"

Swimming was out of the question. They would never get far enough away to avoid being smashed to jelly by the shockwave, but the police boat might be able to.

If they could get to it.

Professor followed her pointing finger with his eyes, which Jade noted looked a lot better than the last time she had seen them, although the skin around them was red and scaly. Instead of reaching out to her however, he climbed onto the cluster of barrels for a closer look at the countdown mechanism.

"Professor!"

01:01
01:00
00:59

He ignored her, and with seemingly infinite patience, began tracing the wires with his fingertip.

"Professor!" When he still did not respond, she growled and crawled out to join him. "Pete! It's a bomb. We have to go before—"

Her plea ended with a yelp as he grasped one of the bundles affixed to the top of a barrel and yanked it loose. The packet came away, trailing something that looked sort of like a big firecracker—or a stick of dynamite—which had been inserted in the hole in the barrel's lid.

Some kind of improvised detonator, Jade guessed.

Professor set it aside and repeated the process with another of the barrels. And then another.

00:31
00:30
00:29

Six detonators left. Professor had cleared all the barrels at the center of the cluster, those closest to the timer, and now was scrambling along the outer edge, pulling them out like clumps of hair.

Yank!
Five left.

00:25
00:24

Yank! Four

00:20
00:19

He grabbed a detonator in each hand, wrenching them free simultaneously.

00:10

One left.

Yank!

Without a moment's hesitation, Professor scooped up the tangle of wires and explosives and heaved them over the stern rail. Jade caught one last glimpse of the timer as it left his hands—00:04—and then Professor's arm caught her and pulled her down into the space at the forward end of the cockpit, behind the barrels.

Using three tons of ammonium nitrate as a shield didn't seem like a particularly good idea to Jade, but there was no time to register a complaint. A loud *whump* filled the air, and then the deck beneath her rose, pitching forward as the underwater shock wave rolled under the hull, and then reversed into a crazy see-saw motion that lasted several seconds.

Several seconds in which not much happened except for the rain-like fall of spray thrown into the air by the relatively small trigger detonation. Jade just lay where she was, savoring the cool sensation on her face and all the aches and pains that proved she was still alive.

Finally, she sat up and looked over at Professor. "Pulling out the detonators. Didn't know if I could do that."

Professor just smiled. "It's okay, Jade. You don't have to know everything. That's what I'm here for."

EPILOGUE—GREAT AND TERRIBLE ENDINGS

One week later

"Well obviously it couldn't have been the torch," Professor said, with an almost dismissive air. "Not that one at least."

He jerked a thumb in the direction of Liberty's upthrust right arm. "That torch was installed during the restoration in 1986. The original torch is in the museum." He reversed his hand position to point at the concrete upon which they were standing. "Down there. I could have told you that if you'd just confided in me."

Jade let out a little growl of irritation. "Yeah, well you were in a coma. Oh, you're welcome by the way. For saving your life I mean."

"I believe I already said thank you," he shot back. "I think it was right after I saved your life *and* the Statue of Liberty."

"Uh, wrong. I saved the statue when I moved the boat away. You don't get to count that one."

"That a fact?" Professor placed the 22-foot multi-position aluminum ladder he had been carrying on the narrow observation balcony and began unfolding it. "So basically, what you're saying is that when I disarmed that bomb, I risked my life for nothing."

"Hey. I'm not nothing." She slugged him playfully in the arm, which was the best way she could think of to keep from being overcome with emotion. So much had happened, and even now, a week later, she was still struggling to process it all.

After awakening in the hospital in Port au Prince, Professor had spent another thirty-six hours on the ventilator before the doctors determined that the tetrodotoxin was completely out of his system. As soon as his breathing tube was out, he checked himself out AMA—against medical advice—and over Kasey Kim's objections, and headed for New York.

He had actually arrived in the Big Apple ahead of Jade, and had spent a full day on Liberty Island hoping to run into her. On the second day, he cast a wider net, putting in a call to Dalton Shaw, an old SEAL team swim buddy who had recently joined the NYPD Scuba Team and enlisted the resources of the Harbor Unit to keep an eye out for her. When Jade had boarded the ferry at Liberty State Park, Professor had been on the opposite shore, in Battery Park looking for her. He had in fact visited the island later in the day, but with over ten thousand people coming and going, it was understandable that they had somehow missed each other, especially since Jade had been hiding out in the trees and looking at the statue, not the crowds.

When word of an incident on Liberty Island came over the police radio—something involving a Homeland Security agent in pursuit of an international terrorist—Shaw had immediately contacted Professor and set out for the island aboard a Harbor Unit patrol vessel. They had almost reached the island when the reports escalated into something else—a bomb threat. There had not been a doubt in Professor's mind that Jade was at the center of the storm.

Right place, right time, he had told her afterward, but Jade knew how lucky she was to still be alive.

Unfortunately, their victory had not been without cost.

A small army of Homeland Security agents had been waiting for them upon their return to shore to greet them as heroes. The speed with which the feds had mobilized was highly suspicious, almost as if the team had known something big was about to happen. Jade, Professor and Shaw were all arrested, ostensibly for the murder of a federal officer—Purcell—and suspicion of involvement in the bomb plot, but as they began telling their story, the situation took a dark and unexpected turn.

Although federal agents could claim jurisdiction over crimes committed at a National Park, the bomb had technically been in the harbor, and everything that had happened on the motor yacht, including Purcell's attempt to detonate it, fell within the purview of the NYPD who wasn't about to let DHS run roughshod over one of their own—Shaw—especially since it looked to everyone like the feds were trying to cover up the actions of a rogue agent.

After a lot of angry words and territorial pissing, the Secretary of Homeland Security himself got involved, invoking national security concerns to curtail all investigation into the incident. The official reason given was that the mere fact of an attempt to destroy the Statue of Liberty would have had the same effect on national morale as its actual destruction, pushing the already deeply divided nation over the brink, but Jade suspected the real reason was to conceal the sheer scope of the Dominion's influence in the federal government. Purcell might have been crazy at the end, but he had not been acting on his own.

A gag order was issued and the criminal charges were not merely dropped but utterly erased from memory, yet an ominous unspoken threat remained.

Talk about this, and you won't go to jail. You'll just disappear.

There had been one other terrible consequence.

Professor had tried to soft-pedal the news after receiving the phone call. "You know in Mission: Impossible, where the guy in the recording says: 'The secretary will disavow any knowledge of your actions'?"

"Again with the movie references?"

"I was actually referring to the TV show, but same difference. Anyway, Tam had to cut me loose."

Jade had been livid. "That bitch! After everything we've done for her?"

"We didn't do those things for her, Jade. And this isn't something she wants. It might look like things have calmed down, but Homeland can still come after us, and the Myrmidons, if they can prove that I was working for Tam when I killed Purcell."

"What difference would that make?"

"The Myrmidons are CIA. We... I guess I'll have to start saying *they* now... They can't legally conduct operations on American soil. That's a charge they could prosecute without violating the gag order. The only way to close that barn door and save the Myrmidons is for Tam to disavow me."

"Screw the gag order. We should go public with this."

"It's not that simple, Jade. The Dominion is winning. We can't lose the Myrmidons." He shrugged. "It's okay. I've been unemployed before."

Jade was not quite so indifferent about the news, but she had an answer for that. "You aren't unemployed, silly. You work for me."

"Are you sure you can afford me?" he said, but with a smile.

"I'll pay twice what you're making right now."

"Two times nothing is still nothing."

She put her hands on her hips. "Take it or leave it."

"I'll take it."

Not everyone in the federal government was ungrateful however.

Just a few hours after their release, and only minutes after she and Professor settled into their rooms at the Roosevelt Hotel on 45th Street, the front desk called to let Jade know she had a visitor. It was Jameson Christophe, the Park Police officer who had unwittingly led her to the fateful rendezvous with Diane Lindsey atop Liberty's torch.

He too had been absolved of any wrongdoing and was under the same gag order as everyone else, which meant he was back on duty with the Park Police as if nothing had happened. Exoneration however had not lifted the burden of guilt he felt.

"I am so sorry," he said, hanging his head like a scolded puppy. "I had no idea what she intended."

Jade, wary of any further involvement with the Cult of Libertas, folded her arms over her chest. "We're not supposed to talk about this."

"Yes, of course. That is not actually why I have come. I wish to ask a favor."

"Are you asking for yourself or for the cult?"

"The cult is…" He paused, searching for the right word. "This incident has left us broken. I do not believe we will survive this."

"Good," Jade shot back, not sympathetic in the least. "I don't know how you can worship the goddess of freedom, and still exploit human beings."

"The same way that Christians can fight wars in the name of a God who said, 'thou shalt not kill' and 'turn the other cheek,' I suppose."

"Touché." Jade sighed.

"Lindsey was obviously unhinged."

"That seems to be going around," Jade said, thinking of Purcell. In the end, both cared more about killing her than advancing their own agendas. "So, what's this favor you want?"

"Diane Lindsey did not name a successor, and it is unclear who—if anyone—will take her place."

"Well, don't look at me."

"Some of us agree with you that the cult has lost its way. It no longer serves the will of the goddess. Others however share Diane's cynical philosophy and are already fighting for possession of her human trafficking enterprise. Those of us who believe in freedom and liberty, who believe in what the Statue of Liberty represents, would prefer to keep the sacred relics out of the hands of such unscrupulous apostates."

Jade saw where this was leading. "And you need me to get them for you."

"You are the Chosen."

"Not by my choice." Jade frowned. "If I refuse, then the relics stay where they are, right?"

Christophe shook his head. "Another may be Chosen. Someone less worthy."

"Thanks, I think."

"I trust you, Dr. Ihara. So do the others."

Jade sighed again. "Even if I wanted to help, I have a feeling I'm *persona non grata* at the Statue of Liberty these days."

Christophe smiled. "We all know what you did to save the Statue. I promise, you would be welcomed with open arms."

"Open arms, huh? Think you could get me in for one of those after-hours VIP visits?"

Three hours later, Jade was back on Liberty Island, this time with Professor at her side. The last ferry of the day had already departed, but there were still a couple hours of daylight left. Christophe had assured them of unrestricted access to the site, as long as they didn't cause any more damage. The way he had emphasized the word *more* made Jade duck her head, though all she had really done was bend the decorative border on the torch a little. Purcell had been the one shooting up the place.

Professor leaned the now fully extended ladder against the wall. They were on the observation balcony at the topmost accessible level of the pedestal. The narrowness of the viewing platform made for a very steep tilt, but the top of the ladder extended well above the top of the pedestal and the green copper base of the statue itself. He put a steadying hand on the ladder and then turned to Jade. "Up you go."

"So, FYI, I did know about the new torch," Jade continued as she started her ascent. "It was mentioned in one of the brochures. I just figured they moved the relics over when the upgrade was finished."

"I thought only the Chosen could move the relics."

"That's what Diane said, but who knows if she was telling the truth. From what I can tell, the cult kind of made up the rules as they went along. But anyway, it doesn't matter since they aren't in either torch." She climbed up until she was high enough to step off onto the base of the statue, then turned to hold the top of the ladder for Professor who immediately began his climb.

"What makes you think she was telling the truth about any of it?"

"Gut instinct mostly," Jade admitted. "No matter what

she said, the relics were important to her. I really don't think she wanted to destroy them. In fact, pulling them out of the wreckage would have added to their symbolic importance."

"Makes sense. As powerful as that bomb would have been, I don't think it would have budged the pedestal." He cautiously stepped off the ladder onto the copper surface, and they both moved back a few feet from the precipice. There were no safety rails here.

"Right? Anyway, the old torch was the second place on my list, but then when I was up there, I looked down and saw this, and realized there was another symbol of the goddess. A better one." She gestured to a part of the Statue of Liberty rarely seen by visitors and seldom captured in photographs of the iconic monument.

"The broken chains of oppression," Professor said. "Laboulaye and Bartholdi intended the statue as a monument to the end of slavery in America. In the original design, instead of a tablet, Liberty was holding broken chains in her left hand. That was a very unpopular idea in America, especially during the Reconstruction era, and Bartholdi's plan for chains got nixed. He managed to keep these though, even though he had to put them where no one would ever see them."

He gestured to the series of enormous sculpted chain links extending out from beneath Liberty's robes alongside her sandaled left foot. Half of the last link was missing, as if the chain had been snapped in two. The chains could not be seen from the ground looking up or from the observation balcony on the pedestal, nor were they readily visible from the windows in the crown. Indeed, the only place where a person could stand and see the broken chains was from the torch, and that had been closed to the public for over a century.

"Maybe there was another reason he decided to hide it down here," Jade suggested.

Professor acknowledged the suggestion with a shrug. "Well, we're here. What are you supposed to do now?"

"Not sure really," Jade admitted. She walked over to

the broken link and knelt to inspect it. "Maybe Ol' Bartholdi left a clue—"

As her fingers touched the copper, a faint shudder passed through the metal surface beneath her, followed by a loud scraping sound. A crack appeared in the long transverse seam that ran past the end of Liberty's toes and under the chains. The sandal and the links remained just where they were but the section of the base under them began sinking away.

Jade snatched her hand back. "Wasn't me."

Professor came over and knelt beside her, peering into the revealed hollow. "I think it was."

The section—about eight feet wide and half as long—settled about three feet before grinding to a stop. Most of it was eclipsed from view by the sandal and chains, which now appeared to be floating. To either side of the revealed cavity, Jade could see the same kind of structural steel employed in the statue's interior frame, but the far end of the cavity disappeared into the shadows beneath Liberty herself. Professor took out a small penlight and shone it into the opening, but his light revealed nothing of immediate note.

He handed the light to Jade. "I think you're supposed to go first."

Jade took the light and then hopped down into the hollow. She immediately went to all fours and began crawling across the smooth copper surface.

Her light revealed a small recess extending only another couple feet beyond the end of the lowered section, and in it, a pair of small chests. She scooted over to the closest for a more thorough inspection.

The chest, about eighteen inches high and twice as long, appeared to be carved out of soft stone—chalk, if Jade had to guess—decorated with painted bas relief images, although time had muted the hues. The most prominent symbol on the chest she inspected was of what appeared to be a chalice, surrounded by plump grapes, and carved on the bowl of the cup was an eye, radiating flames.

Professor crawled up next to her. "It's an ossuary," he

observed.

Jade was familiar with the term. An ossuary was a receptacle—or in some cases, a room—which contained the bones of the dead.

He reached out and guided her hand and the flashlight beam to illuminate two rows of precise engraved Latin letters. It took Jade a moment or two to recognize one of the names, by which time Professor had already translated it.

"'Wife of Spartacus,'" he murmured.

Jade found this mildly irritating. "That's it? Wife of Spartacus? Her name doesn't count?"

"History doesn't record her name, or his for that matter. Spartacus was just his stage name. This ossuary might have been carved later, long after her death. The Romans practiced cremation, and weren't in the habit of according any special honor to the remains of slaves." He reached out to the chest but did not touch it. "Plutarch wrote that she was a prophetess and a worshipper of Dionysus. The cup and grapes are his symbols. The eye probably symbolizes her oracular gifts."

He tilted the light onto the second chest which was decorated with a coiled snake motif. "And that must be the man himself."

The light revealed another chest, long and narrow, too small to contain human remains. "That looks like a scroll case," supplied Professor.

"The Sibylline book."

"That's a good bet. We'd have to open it to be sure, but that should probably be done in a laboratory." He paused and then added, "If that's what you want."

"Me?"

"You're the Chosen."

Jade did not respond to this, but shone the light past the scroll case to the last item hidden in the niche. It appeared to be a large vase or jar, decorated with a floral design with elegant handles on either side and a lid.

"Does that look like an urn to you?"

"It does," Professor replied. "And quite a bit newer

than the ossuaries. I'd say no older than late 17ᵗʰ century."

"Who do you suppose it is?"

"Maybe there's an inscription?"

There was. A small brass plate, tarnished with the passage of time, was affixed to the square base of the urn, and engraved upon it in a delicate cursive script were the names and titles—both formal and informal—of the man whose remains it held, and the dates which encompassed the span of his time on earth.

François-Dominique Toussaint Louverture
20 May 1743 – 7 April 1803
Président de la République d'Haïti
Gouverneur Général de Ste Domingue
"Spartacus Noir"

"Black Spartacus," Professor muttered. "Well, he's in excellent company. I can't think of a more appropriate final resting place."

"I can," Jade said, her voice a whisper.

"What do you mean?"

"These relics…" She gestured to the collection. "They don't belong here. Hidden away, I mean. Diane might have been evil and crazy, but she was right about their symbolic power. But the thing about symbols is, they only work if people know about them." She shrugged. "You said it yourself. I'm the Chosen. It's my call, right?"

"What have you got in mind?"

"Simple. We're going to tell everyone what we found. And how they got here. The Cult of Libertas. All of it. No more keeping it secret."

"Are you sure that's a good idea? Diane wanted to use these relics to start another civil war."

"The last one was supposed to end slavery. It didn't work. Slavery—human exploitation or whatever you want to call it—is still happening. People don't even realize it's going on right here in America. I'd like to believe that if they did, they'd do something positive to stop it. I know it's going to take more than just this to change the world, but maybe this is how we start the conversation."

Professor regarded her thoughtfully. "Not everyone will be happy about it. They may even try to suppress it."

"That's why we have to do something about it right now."

"Well, we can't remove the relics. Without proper documentation and conservation, we'd have trouble proving our claims. We'll also have to dance around the gag order."

"I say we call the New York Times."

Professor chuckled. "How about we do that first thing in the morning?"

"We should at least get some pictures before we go."

Professor gave her another thoughtful look. "Did you change your mind about being a crusader?"

Jade shook her head. "I'm not a crusader. I'm just an archaeologist. My job is to discover the truth about the past and history. It's up to everyone else to decide what they're going to do about it."

After photographing the relics *in situ,* they exited the niche and made their way back to the ladder. As soon as Jade's feet left the statue's base, an unseen mechanism came alive and elevated the section back into its original place.

"Still not sure how we're going to explain that," Professor remarked.

Jade just shrugged. "You'll think of something."

Christophe was waiting at the exit, eager to hear what they had discovered. Jade showed him the pictures.

"Louverture is there?" The man's eyes were wide with awe. "You can't imagine what this will mean for my people. The father of Haiti, laid to rest at the feet of Lady Liberty."

"Liberty," Jade mused as they made their way to the ferry dock. "You know, it feels like that word has kind of lost its meaning, don't you think? People seem to care about it only as far as it applied to them. It's all 'personal liberty' and screw the other guy."

"Not much we can do about that. It's in the name after

all. The Statue of Liberty. Liberty Enlightening the World."

"I like the other name better. The one from the poem."

"The New Colossus?"

Jade shook her head. "Mother of Exiles. Goddesses expect to be worshipped. Mothers are different. They give unconditional love."

Professor just nodded and said nothing more until they were on the boat, gazing back up at the monument. "Well, I guess I can cross this place off my list. Can't believe it took me this long to finally come here."

"Any other famous New York landmarks we should hit while we're here? The night is young."

"We could head up Broadway. Maybe get tickets to a show." He stopped and then gave her a sideways look. "Unless that sounds too indoorsy for you?"

"I'll give it a chance." She took his arm. "You know, now that we've had our Roman holiday, I think we should try breakfast at Tiffany's."

"The jewelers? They don't serve food—" He stopped and gave her another look, speechless with astonishment.

Jade just laughed.

End

About the Authors

David Wood is the author of the popular action-adventure series, The Dane Maddock Adventures, and many other works. Under his David Debord pen name he is the author of the Absent Gods fantasy series. When not writing, he co-hosts the Authorcast podcast. David and his family live in Santa Fe, New Mexico. Visit him online at www.davidwoodweb.com.

Sean Ellis has authored and co-authored more than 20 action-adventure novels, including the Nick Kismet adventures, the Jack Sigler/Chess Team series with Jeremy Robinson, and the Jade Ihara adventures with David Wood. He served with the Army National Guard in Afghanistan, and has a Bachelor of Science degree in Natural Resources Policy from Oregon State University. Sean is also a member of the International Thriller Writers organization. He currently resides in Arizona, where he divides his time between writing, adventure sports, and trying to figure out how to save the world. Visit him online at www.seanellisauthor.com.

www.ingramcontent.com/pod-product-compliance
Lightning Source LLC
Chambersburg PA
CBHW031659170626
46808CB00005B/1530